CONSUMED

Also by Greg Buchanan

Sixteen Horses

CONSUMED

GREG BUCHANAN

ORION

First published in Great Britain in 2023 by Orion Fiction,
an imprint of The Orion Publishing Group Ltd.,
Carmelite House, 50 Victoria Embankment
London EC4Y 0DZ

An Hachette UK Company

1 3 5 7 9 10 8 6 4 2

A CIP catalogue record for this book is
available from the British Library.

ISBN (Hardback) 978 1 3987 1271 3
ISBN (Export Trade Paperback) 978 1 3987 1272 0
ISBN (eBook) 978 1 3987 1274 4

Typeset at The Spartan Press Ltd,
Lymington, Hants

Printed and bound in Great Britain by Clays Ltd,
Elcograf S.p.A.

www.orionbooks.co.uk

For my parents, Tricia and Glenn

I was angry with my friend;
I told my wrath, my wrath did end.
I was angry with my foe:
I told it not, my wrath did grow.

And I watered it in fears,
Night and morning with my tears:
And I sunned it with my smiles,
And with soft deceitful wiles.

And it grew both day and night.
Till it bore an apple bright.
And my foe beheld it shine,
And he knew that it was mine.

And into my garden stole,
When the night had veiled the pole;
In the morning glad I see;
My foe outstretched beneath the tree.

A Poison Tree
William Blake (1794)

YOU'RE GOING
TO DIE ONE DAY

Lethwick, 1964

'No one ever thinks about it, but you will. You'll die, and as you do, you'll look back at how you treated me, the things you said to me, and you'll regret them. Before you go, you'll miss me. You'll miss everyone. And you'll be so, so sorry. You will. I read it in a book.'

That's what Sophie's mother had said to her, the morning of her seventeenth birthday.

Now the girl was out here, walking with her gift. Unwashed strawberry-blonde hair curled around her shoulders.

All around, forests that had bloomed for decades were receding like a hairline. Heather grew out of the blasted, scorched, exhausted earth at peculiar angles. These plants squatted like beggars, holding out their hands toward the departing sun.

There were pines and chestnut trees, too, and ... and ...

Oak? Was that an oak?

Sophie wasn't sure.

The trees seemed like they were alive that afternoon – as in, really alive. Sophie imagined them as frozen people caught up in silly shapes – dancers forming screams, shaking wigs upon their heads, posing their bodies skyward...

Red ants swarmed in their mounds, sand shifting in the barren grass.

She walked through this graveyard of trees. She had come out here to take a photograph. She bit her nails, sometimes.

There was this one tree, far along round the bend of the hills.

Sophie had noted this particular tree a few days back. She'd walked out here after an argument, as she had so often done.

The whole day changed whenever Sophie fought with her mother. She would want to leave home. She would also want to say sorry. She wished her feelings could be more consistent.

They had even argued this morning, exchanging a few words after her birthday cake. Every year, both mother and daughter mock-screamed, as if that cake could feel the knife, and they'd smile, and eat what they had cut. Every year Sophie's mum would go to work if there was work to be done, and Sophie would not go to school because the date of her birthday always fell in the summer holidays. Every year, she'd stay at home. She would play with whatever she had been given.

This year, a camera. An Instamatic. It was the most expensive thing Sophie had ever owned. That morning, her mother had kissed her on the forehead after giving the gift to her. Fans whirred around the room, all the shut curtains rippling and bloating in their path. They had to keep out the heat.

'Do you think you'll use it today?'

'Can I take your picture?'

Her mother shook her head.

'I could take one when you don't know I'm taking it.'

'Don't,' her mother said. 'Always ask, OK?'

'The first ever photo of a person was by accident, you know. They just got caught in the corner of the shot...'

'Who told you that?'

Sophie shrugged.

'You could go out with your friends, maybe ... Take your camera with you?'

'I'll probably sleep.'

'What?'

'When you're at work ... I'll sleep.'

Her mother had found the idea of spending a birthday

4

sleeping entirely absurd – insulting, almost. She had questioned her daughter, and had brought up her friends again, and … and …

Then it had started, and escalated.

Things had got dramatic, and Sophie knew she'd said awful things, too … about her mother's friends, old crones, all of them … the men her mother saw … the men her mother had thrown herself at … Her mother, who'd used these same words and phrases against so many others. Her mother, who was losing everyone, little by little, year by year. Who kept a list of books she'd read the past twelve months, as if it were a thing she'd done her whole life. Whose happiness began to grow acquainted only with that list, its length, its breadth. As if words could make up for life. As if it were the quantity of her reading that mattered – the fact of it, more than the substance alone.

So here Sophie was, far from the empty fields, her house now entirely out of view.

'There,' she muttered.

She stared at the strange tree. She'd found it at last.

The main trunk itself was ivy-wrapped almost to the top. Around this tree there were three spheres, each composed of a mass of wood and grass, like nests. One floated from the tree top, one to the left, one to the far right. The distance they hung from the main wood seemed arbitrary, held in each case by a single twig.

Sophie wished she had a tripod. She wished she had her own darkroom, her own expensive film she'd read about in a magazine. She had declared herself an enthusiast, using her school's equipment. She always had these obsessions, always threw herself utterly into the next pursuit or interest. There was something about her that was profoundly ungrateful, she knew. And she knew there should be guilt. She loved the camera, really she did. She loved it because it was hers.

'Steady ...'

After a few moments trying to steady her hands, she took a photo of the spheres.

She stood back, satisfied with the shutter's click. She kept going towards the lake, over a mile from her home, now. The trees began to run thicker. Sometimes there were boats out. Maybe there would be some today. A few leaves rattled across the land. The smell grew fresher, the old oaty musk replaced with the scent of water, though it was still far off.

After a while, Sophie came across a piece of pipe, stuck down in the half-ashen soil.

It was a grey plastic cylinder. It did not appear to have been here for very long, or else it would have been dirtier, scratched up, maybe. Just a few inches wide.

Sophie stared at it for a time, shifting her weight. A fly landed on her calf. It walked along the bare skin below her shorts, above her socks.

She bent down, hesitating before she ran her index finger and nail-bitten thumb along the plastic's edge. Looking down it, there was only black darkness, nothing to be seen, to be heard, to be smelled.

She pulled at the plastic pipe, but it did not shift. It appeared to run deep, wedged tightly into the earth.

She put her eye to the pipe, so close that the plastic almost jabbed her in her socket, almost left its print in her skin like a monocle. She held her ear to it, letting the plastic touch her flesh once more. She thought for a moment she heard sucking, shifting, but then realised, on reflection, it was most likely just the noise her own contact had brought.

She rose to her feet.

She held her camera over the pipe. The silver metal of her device shone in the final hour of sunlight. She took a photograph of the pipe from above, a bird's eye view just as a cloud drifted overhead.

She walked on. She wanted to see the lake before the sky grew dark.

She wanted her mother to worry.

She didn't know what she wanted.

The rest of her walk, Sophie encountered more ants. More plants. More trees.

She saw the ridge of the lake, just sixty feet away.

Near the water sat a pale girl. The pale girl dressed like mothers dressed. She sat with her legs hunched up, long arms bracing her either side, as if, when she lifted them, she might then slide down right beyond the shore and beneath the surface. She looked like she was sick, her skin was so drained of colour. Maybe she'd always been sick, or maybe her skin was misleading, a lie.

There was someone else, further away at first.

A man – a much older man.

His walk was deliberate, mechanical, slow.

He came and said something to the pale girl. She didn't answer or turn her head. He spoke again, or his lips moved anyway.

Sophie tried reading them, whispering under her breath, imagining things her eyes could not possibly see. 'Flowers … passing …'

No one heard her whisper.

The pale girl rose to her feet.

More details became clear now. There was a dirty white sock

on her right foot and nothing else. There was a green leather shoe on her left.

Sophie took a photograph.

There was something pretty about the absence. Neither of the strangers seemed to hear or notice the click. Neither said anything. Neither turned to Sophie, so far away as she was.

She went home.

That night, they ate sausages and chips. Her mother didn't say sorry for the argument in the morning, but it was all right. Sophie loved sausages, bacon, everything.

In the morning, Sophie went into town, walking the forty minutes along the hill paths, then down the main road when she had to. The whole region was Lethwick – the A-road running through to the north, the farms and forests, the hamlets and outer shops, and then what people really meant when they spoke of Lethwick – the cobbled mass, sucking tourists in like gravity. Sophie wasn't allowed out here after sundown. Drivers sometimes cat-called her, they did so whatever the time, but something about night was presented as more dangerous than the day. Such behaviour from others had started back when she was twelve. Or maybe she only started to notice it then, she didn't know. After a certain hour, the world was not to be trusted. But somehow the valley itself was always safe. It was their home. No one came there. No one but those who had hung those spheres in the tree. No one but the pale girl with the missing shoe.

In town, Sophie took her now full roll of film into the pharmacy.

An old woman murmured past the shelves, 'What are you

doing out here?' Sophie couldn't see her face or who she was talking to.

With the rest of her money Sophie bought some penny sweets. Newspapers talked of American wars.

Through the brickwork of the pharmacy, a record played in the distance. It repeated the word 'love' through the walls and through the streets. It repeated it so much that something about the voice horrified her, and—

'Sophia,' Sophie said, when the pharmacist asked her name.

She didn't use this version apart from on official forms, on records. Her grandmother had had the same name as her.

It meant 'wisdom'.

She gave her address.

The pharmacist told her the photographs would be ready within a couple of days. On the way out, an old woman started coughing in the main aisle, expelling an endless, sunken stream of stuttered breaths from wrinkled skin. Something inside wanted to escape. Some of the cough hit Sophie.

Sophie spent the afternoon wandering around the town. She saw few other teenagers around.

A couple smoked marijuana and watched her.

A girl at school had claimed to have had some once, but everyone knew it was just catnip.

People in Ancient Greece used to see things when they breathed in fumes. It was a religious experience. She'd read about it in class. She wondered what that would be like, to think you'd seen the face of a god.

Her mother had used to take her to church. Neither of them had been in years. Neither of them talked about it.

Still, they celebrated the festivals. Christmas. Easter. Midsummer and the grand mysteries.

There was no one else on the main roads. Nothing at all, not even a car.

Just silence the whole way.

She went home.

The night came and went.

The fans kept spinning round so fast you could barely see them, shifting the foxgloves, the campions, the roses, all the flowers her mother had taken and assembled on the mantelpiece and shelves and windowsills, some of them in soil, some of them in water, some of them cut, dying now.

The fans ran as the morning grew hotter. Sophie had never experienced anything like this temperature. She didn't want to go outside.

Her mother stayed off work. In the darkness, the curtains shut, they tried to lose their heat. Sophie had told her about the old cougher in the pharmacy, about how she'd looked, how confused.

'Old women like that...' Her mother paused, her voice quiet. 'They should be in homes. They shouldn't be left to bother people.' She lay on the sofa opposite Sophie, stretched out, her face lightly filmed in sweat.

'Would you want to go into one?'

'That what you're going to do?' Her mother half smiled. 'Put me in a home?'

Sophie shook her head.

Her mother turned away and closed her eyes, trying to get comfortable on the rose-emblemed fabric. 'If I ever lost my mind, I think I'd...'

'You think what?'

'I think I'd rather end it, if I wasn't able to be myself.' This, her mother said.

The television went on and on, sometimes just grey static in the midst of all these hills, but neither mother nor daughter could be bothered to go and change it.

At four minutes past nine Sophie saw people running along the hill path to their west, a small group.

At twelve to one, she began her nap.

All these days off school and nothing to do. It made Sophie wonder about life in general, how everyone wanted time off; how when it came, everything just felt empty. Maybe work was all there was – not her mother's work, not the wage of a task you hate, but something important. Something meaningful. Something that might mean you never needed a break at all.

If you didn't have a passion for your life, what was that life? Sophie had felt clever, thinking this, and had written it down in the margin of a book – a pot boiler, some detective story her mother had finished.

When she woke, her mother was gone.

There was no music, no sound, no light. The fans had all ceased.

Her mother couldn't bear to be in a room without electricity, without motion. All the doors were shut. Sophie wandered through the halls, saw all these things.

There was a creak on the roof. Like all old houses, this place shifted hot and cold. It had scared her, more than once.

She went back to her room to get a magazine. She paused at her bedroom window and looked out.

Her favourite tree of all was close to the house, in the centre of an old fenced-off paddock, lately used for nothing at all but weeds. The apple tree grew in the middle of all that mass.

Her mother's car was gone.

In its place was a yellow Ford Cortina. Two men stood in

front of her home. Neither looked up. They had dark hats and dark suits, one of them sharper pressed than the other.

He was the older of the two, had a grey-black beard. The other, thin-faced, walked around to the lounge window and tugged at the frame. The window was open, it turned out. The older man just stood where he was, right at the door.

It was then that he began to hammer on it.

Two days after her birthday, the men took Sophie out to the woods.

She walked ahead of them in the dying light. It was almost the same hour she'd come out here that last time, an unintended coincidence on the men's part, though it was helpful to their task. The same silly trees swayed, ooh-ed, aah-ed. The same ants swarmed the same sand. The smell of meat and oats and earth filled the hot air.

She walked, and the two strangers followed.

They said they were from the police.

She went with them.

They weren't allowed to speak to her without her mother present.

She went off with them anyway.

It made her feel important. It made her feel scared.

They said they had to know. They said they needed her.

They came to the lakeside. There, the grey-black bearded man nodded, holding a photograph in the air before him. 'Same place,' he said, and Sophie wasn't sure if it was a question. This was where she'd taken the photo of the pale girl by the lake, yes. She just said, 'Yes.'

The other turned on his radio and muttered something.

The two policemen spent a while here, asking questions, watching Sophie's face.

What did you hear?

What did you see?

What direction did they go in?

Where did he come from?

What was his accent?

Did they see you?

Did—

She wanted to go home. It was getting late.

'The pipe,' they said, eventually.

She tried to find it for them like they asked.

She searched through those trees, through the wooden arms that brushed her, the fingers that scraped at her legs. She searched, these men watching her, these silent men.

The older one grew frustrated with her.

'You're doing well,' he said, but this was a lie.

She knew lies. Her family had told so many.

The next day, the officers would discover a shallow pit of loose soil, around it dug a seven-foot by seven-foot pit, almost precisely square. Dirt had been dumped in to fill the hole.

It was not a grave. There was no body. A large container had been removed from the earth, apparently long before the authorities had arrived.

The same place Sophie had seen the pipe in the ground. The same place Sophie had taken one of her photos. The pipe was gone too.

For now, the search ended without success.

They went back home after it was dark.

Her mother was there crying, uniformed officers by her side.

Her mother got up and hugged her.

It was so surprising, so sudden a motion that it felt as if it could not be real. It felt staged, like so many other things her mother staged for the benefit of outsiders.

But the woman's skin was cold, even in all this heat.

Was the concern real? And why? She had been out a thousand times before – there was no curfew, no prohibition on exploring these woods.

The police officers questioned them both for a few hours: who Sophie had seen in those hills, why was she out taking photographs the day before...

'There were things in the trees,' Sophie told them. 'I wanted to ...' She hesitated. 'I wanted to know what they were.'

It all felt small, saying these things out loud.

They found the image in question. The pharmacist had processed her film cartridge. What he had seen within had caused his arms to slow, his lips to quiver. He'd contacted the authorities. So here they were.

'This photograph?' the thin detective asked.

Sophie nodded, staring at the three orbs hanging from the bark.

'It's just mistletoe.' He grinned. 'It's what it looks like in the wild. You kiss people under it.'

The most peculiar photograph, and the police didn't even care.

Only accidents gave Sophie importance.

They took all the prints, the pale girl, the pipe. They asked her not to discuss them.

It took her a while to understand the enormity of what she'd seen.

It was about hope, in part, the older policeman said. It was about not letting others know what they knew, until the time was right.

'Keep it to yourself.'

Sophie nodded.

They left her home.

The older man with the grey-black beard, he'd left his card – and his mother put it on the fridge with a magnet. ROBERT KELLY, it read.

The next day Sophie went to the pharmacy. She was relieved when they confirmed the negatives were still in their possession. After all, why wouldn't they be? A different person was on shift, one who had not dealt with the police. He didn't know he wasn't supposed to give Sophie the pictures. After all, she had ordered them in the first place, hadn't she?

Weeks later, unable to sleep, Sophie held one of these images. It was not the first time she had held it. All around were cut-outs from newspapers, from magazines, from doodles. These past years she'd decorated her wall as best she could, the sedimentary layers of all her phases, all her brief flirtations of interest in different authors and animals and singers, her prototype personality.

She held the photograph under her desk light. It shone above the glossy card, as if it were a sun.

The photograph showed the grey plastic pipe, the soil all around, the camera lens hovering above at a perfect angle.

The pipe was dark within, but for a flicker of light, reflected along the tube.

Sophie had looked at it, again and again.

She looked now.

The public was given only the photograph of the pale girl at first, how she had walked with a man against a grey lake, a setting sun.

A girl who had been missing for three years, frozen in a moment.

The Earlsham family would deem this sighting a miracle. They would want to meet the photographer. They would want to ask her so many questions. Within their lifetimes, their daughter would never be found. Sophie was their last connection to the lost, the same age their pale girl would be, if she still lived. Any previous attempts to accept their daughter's death had forever vanished with that one brief proof of life.

The image of the missing girl would adorn newspapers and magazines in the months to come, an appeal made by the family itself. They wanted their daughter to know they still loved her, that she could still come home, that if she came back to their house, or even just Lethwick once more, they could heal, and she could heal too. They wanted to know if this man had taken her, if he still had her, whoever he was, his face so unclear... They wanted him to know that he was forgiven. They just wanted everything to be as it was.

The second photograph, the pipe, would not be published until October.

One day Sophie's mother had showed it to a broker without her daughter's knowledge. They discussed a price. A deal was made. The proceeds would be invested. They would have got more if they'd given up moral rights, too, but Sophie's mother insisted.

Sophia Bertilak would be listed as the photographer. Sophie would be listed wherever the image was licensed, wherever its rights were paid.

It would be the most famous photograph of her career, the front of book covers, the head of each ensemble collection as the decades rolled on, as she moved on from Lethwick to job after distant job, home after distant home.

In the dying days of the war, Sophie would go across the sea to Vietnam. She would capture horrors. She would see the world as it really was, as it could be, as it should have been. She would show all of these things, mastering light and subject, learning the things you had to do.

She would learn so much, and still that photo – that day in the woods, that birthday beneath the trees – would define her whole life.

It would eclipse all that she was.

She had no pride in it. It had just been an accident. It made her sad to take credit for it.

At the time, she'd held her eye against a pipe in the soil and had seen nothing but darkness.

'You didn't see anything there, did you?'

'It was dark. When I put myself against it, I blocked out more light, and—'

'It was luck?'

She shrugged, the television cameras all around. 'It was light.'

'What made you want to take a photograph of it in the first place?'

'It was—'

'It was intuition, wasn't it? It was your eye—'

She nodded.

It was like a Magic Eye puzzle. At first it was hard to notice, if you didn't know what you were looking for. The soil all around, patterned in swirls of chalk and dust and root and brown, made it hard to distinguish what was within the pipe and what was without. Light caught on it all.

The grey plastic, too, caught light.

All that was left of that moment was this photo, carried throughout the years.

Half an eye, red-rimmed and terrified, stared forever at the sun.

Up at the lens, half a face peered from under the earth, alive. Its skin pallid, chapped, smeared with dust and soil. What hair could be seen, long and wet and dark in the black and white. Hints of fingers in the corner of the plastic, whether to scrape above, whether to attract attention or help, whether to try to touch the girl above, no one knew. Its mouth, silent, afraid, quivering.

A child had sat beneath the world. It all came back to eyes in the end, the window of souls, of worlds, of animals. The first crime, and the last.

The light faded.

Decades passed. Sophie grew older, and had her own children until these children were no longer children, losing some in her womb, losing one in the world, and the others, far away, Lucy and Matthew and Joanna, barely speaking to her or one another, as if they'd never meant a thing to each other, as if their time with her had been a lie.

Sophie grew old, and she'd look at it again, one day.

She'd look at the picture one final time.

Lethwick.

Now.

You had to be careful, the night the power died.

That ancient, gentle town, stained with acid and rain and time, it all melted away in darkness. Even the traffic lights. Even the stars, obscured by dark and invisible clouds, faded from view. The world grew lonely, quiet, still.

Some connection – some cable, some synapse passing through the long hills and long valleys – had been broken, and in its breaking, all light had left a thousand homes. All that remained was night and fog, creeping past the ruins of the old abbey, of scalloped stone buildings, beyond the smear of B&Bs and coffee shops and overpriced pubs; it reached through the jittery, half-fearful, half-joyous minds of those who lived there, those who had visited. There was something fun about the loss of light. There was something terrifying.

The night of the power cut, the swollen banks of the river were deserted, silent but for the trickle of their water, the movement of an occasional hedgehog or badger, these miraculous survivors of roads that criss-crossed the hills like veins. Children, too, had been hit by cars throughout the decades, through blind summits and corners too obscure for sight or warning.

For a time, the local authorities had trialled 20mph roads to improve safety and encourage cycling. The resulting delays in journeys and anger from local residents led to a reversion back to 30-40mph speed limits. Five more people lost their lives every year as a result.

The animals could see in the wake of the power cut, far keener than any human eye.

Far away, coal emerged from the earth. Machines drank oil from the sea. Atoms split. The homes of this place had been emptied out, replaced with richer homes for tourists, holiday lets, rentals.

The gentry had grown like an infection, and grew still. Soon, there would be few left who had been born here, who could still afford to remain.

Tourists hurried to their rooms in the broken dark, worrying about their phones' batteries, about what light the devices might yet cast.

The hotels on the hillsides all around, with their spa-town marble white and false Doric columns, hosted parties in the candlelit black. Drinks and refreshments were handed out to their guests, reassuring them that all this was transient, that all this would pass in this lovely place far from the city, from the coast, from any reminder of an outside world.

Lethwick was closed off from time and progress, rich in history, both sublime and bloody.

That old, almost ironic motto, which had come to gain the texture of a joke in the wake of centuries past – of killings on the old routes, of what forgotten people had done, and what kings had once done to them in turn. If you bothered to pay attention in school. If you could even remember it when you were older. If you could still care.

England's legacy.

Oppidum vetus leneque.

'A town, ancient and gentle.'

Population 12,500.

Lethwick.

Still, everyone knew such murderous times were now past.

What few unnatural deaths there had been here in the twenty-first century were seen as unfortunate cases of domestic abuse for the most part, or drink-driving. Nothing dramatic. Nothing that troubled most, beyond the victims' families, or those who'd had to see their loved ones go to jail. *Oppidum vetus leneque*, so it went.

There were some heart attacks, the night of the power cut. All natural causes. Vulnerable people faded in their beds as they faded everywhere; rich or poor, it did not matter. Nurses moved them to the morgues.

One of the deaths was different, that night.

It was for this person that the power cut would be remembered.

After this woman's death in the growing dark, there would be nothing to bury.

There was no body.

By her lonely house, down in the centre of yet another valley, yet another depression in the squeezing swelling world, there was no human sound, not after the act was committed.

If you'd stood there, if you'd walked there, you'd have heard only the cry of pigs.

The old woman, the victim, the final girl who had grown up here, who had come back here in her final years, she had lived alone but for these young animals, these farmyard pets.

There were two pigs. Their skin was sunburned, pink-white beige. Their paddock was small, located right outside the woman's house, which was itself black and white, built of outlandish angles and shifting extensions. In the windows sat dusty pictures of family members, not seen for years.

There was a great tree in the paddock's centre, an apple tree.

The pigs screamed, trampling against each other, their cries undercut, punctuated by a chorus of grunts.

There were tufts of human hair everywhere. There was blood, not red in that dark, not any colour at all.

The final words that this human would ever say in this place were whispered in the darkness: 'flowers, passing'.

The seed had sprouted.

Seventy years vanished within stomachs. Fingers danced within acid.

The woman's mind was divided across her porcine companions as they ate pieces of skin, of organs, of bone. That was all that became of her life, of all those years, of her death.

That was what became of Sophie Bertilak, over seventy years old that year. Just a mile or two from orbs of mistletoe in the trees, from a lake in the woods, from loose soil where a pipe had once been placed, from where she had taken her photos on her birthday, so many decades ago.

You had to be careful, the night the power died...

Everyone soon found out what had happened to Sophie, once morning came. Everyone knew.

It was no accident.

Something like that didn't just happen by accident. Not to someone like her. Not to someone who'd lived such a life. People knew who she was. People knew about her career, about how it had started.

How could it have been an accident, the old woman's death, when she'd walked with death her whole life? Those burned, scarred arms emerging from her red coat throughout the decades, freezing souls for a moment in ink and paper. That easy – faded – gentle smile. One you could trust. The kind of girl you felt you'd known your whole life, even if you met her for just a few minutes.

How could her demise be less than a murder?

The hours passed, and the sun rose through the grey, cigarette-smoke sky. The light came back. A postman reported finding glasses in the front driveway, the door of poor Sophie Bertilak's house left open, no sound within. The police were there within the hour.

There was a question, then.

What to do with these pigs who yet lived, their mouths bloody with human flesh.

These pigs, who ran around, excited in their little paddock beneath the old apple tree, their bellies full, the summer sun rising overhead.

'Twelve voices were shouting in anger, and they were all alike. No question, now, what had happened to the faces of the pigs. The creatures outside looked from pig to man, and from man to pig, and from pig to man again; but already it was impossible to say which was which.'

Animal Farm
George Orwell (1945)

Search Terms:

SEARCH: cough
SEARCH: persistent cough
SEARCH: cough getting worse
SEARCH: ache pain chest
SEARCH: breathing difficulty
SEARCH: tiredness
SEARCH: weight loss
SEARCH: tickly cough
SEARCH: natural cures for cough
SEARCH: cleanest air UK
SEARCH: exercise for lungs
SEARCH: cough clean air benefit
SEARCH: Lethwick clean air
SEARCH: Lethwick nicest places to stay
SEARCH: Lethwick history
SEARCH: Lethwick photographs

FROM: Rebecca Allen
SUBJECT: RE: Goodbye
DATE: 13 April, 18:20
TO: Gwen Lott

We've had excellent weather the past week – the papers are saying it's too hot and that it's never been this hot, but I don't think that's true, there were plenty of hot days in the seventies. There have been heatwaves as long as I can remember and what is a little heat really?

I hope you enjoy your new adventure. It's been a long time since I've had adventures of my own. Joanna is getting married next year to her partner. I wish you could come, but I suppose you'll still be a world away, won't you?

Thank you so much for your suggestion – I'm not sure I can afford a holiday at the moment, but I do think it would be good for me.

I don't think I should go alone. I've never been able to go places alone. Always had to have someone with me. I've seen people eating in restaurants by themselves. It's so sad. I don't want to be sad.

Maybe I'll just wait for the wedding. Maybe my cough will go by itself. I don't know.

FROM: KING'S HOTEL LETHWICK
SUBJECT: Booking Confirmation
DATE: 02 May, 06:43
TO: Rebecca Allen

Thank you, Rebecca! Your booking for King's Hotel Lethwick has been confirmed.

Check-in: 16th June
Check-out: 19th June
Your room: 3 Rooms, 3 Adults
Location: KING'S HOTEL LETHWICK, Kings Parade, L223 7PJ
Breakfast: Included
Cancellation Policy: All bookings between 01/06-01/09 are non-refundable

FROM: Julia Allen
SUBJECT: Re: Holiday
DATE: 02 May, 08:12
TO: Rebecca Allen

I still don't really understand why you would book two separate rooms for me and Arthur. I don't understand why you wouldn't even ask us if we were free. He can't make it – he's not just saying it, he really can't, he can't get time off his work and even if he could, I really don't like the way you went about this or the lack of respect you continue to show for our lives. That's not my problem, it's yours.

FROM: Julia Allen
SUBJECT: Re: Holiday
DATE: 11 May, 07:51
TO: Rebecca Allen

Yes. I'll go if Cooper goes. But I'm not going to ask her for you.

Search Terms:

SEARCH: headaches
SEARCH: throat anaesthetic
SEARCH: Lethwick history
SEARCH: Lethwick murder
SEARCH: Lethwick history tour
SEARCH: Lethwick pipe photograph
SEARCH: Lethwick Sophie Bertilak
SEARCH: best clothes for countryside
SEARCH: lung conditions
SEARCH: warm weather lungs

SEARCH: Cooper Allen
SEARCH: Cooper Allen vet
SEARCH: Ilmarsh Cooper Allen
SEARCH: Cooper Allen manslaughter
SEARCH: Cooper Allen true crime
SEARCH: Cooper Allen family
SEARCH: Cooper Allen Facebook
SEARCH: Family holiday adults

Photo Search:

SEARCH: Cooper Allen

[Photographs of a woman with shoulder-length dark hair appear. Sometimes the hair is tied up in a pony tail. Sharp, wide eyes and a prominent brow. To Rebecca, it's as if she is looking at images of herself, decades past, but for the settings and contexts. But for the farm clothes, the suits, the crime scenes, the press conferences, the trials, the court steps, for all those flashes of camera light in Cooper's pained, half-defiant face... But for the life her little girl ran away to.

Rebecca never understood the appeal of having your photograph taken like this, of spreading yourself out into the world. She wonders if Cooper likes attention too much. She wonders if she raised her right. She wonders why she has to read her daughter's news on the internet, rather than being told it face to face. She wonders if her headache will ever end, and she stops looking at her computer for a while, gathering the courage to send the email that must be sent.]

FROM: Rebecca Allen
SUBJECT: Family get-together
DATE: 12 May, 23:09
TO: Cooper Allen

[DRAFT – not sent]

Dear Cooper,

I hope this email finds you well. Julia and I were just wondering if you would like to join us in the countryside for a reunion. We were thinking of the town of Lethwick, which is said to be a really beautiful place with really clean air, and probably really good for us. I hope you

[Nothing else is typed. The draft ends mid-sentence]

FROM: Rebecca Allen
SUBJECT: Family get-together
DATE: 15 May, 05:59
TO: Cooper Allen

[DRAFT – not sent]

Hi Cooper,

I've bought us three rooms for a girl's trip to Lethwick! It would be amazing to see you again and catch up on all your news, and I know Julia is really looking forward to spending some time with her big sis! I've forwarded the details of the booking and just let me know if you have any questions! I know it's been a long time since we've seen each other and

[Nothing else is typed. The draft ends mid-sentence]

FROM: Rebecca Allen
SUBJECT: Family get-together
DATE: 23 May, 08:22
TO: Cooper Allen

Dear Cooper,

Please find attached our booking for a trip to the town of Lethwick this summer. Julia and I hope you can join us.

It would be good to talk,
Love Mummy

★★★

'To solve,' the lecture had begun, years ago now.

Cooper Allen had sat down in the back. The third day of her Veterinary Forensics MSc. She had been late three times already.

'From the Latin "solvere", to loosen, to unfasten. The Middle English: to dissolve, to untie. The notion of solving crime contains not only a sense of detangling evidence, suspects, and the facts of a case, but of dissolving them, letting them loose, changing them through mere contact. There is no happy ending when it comes to solving. Both investigator and investigated are freed from all ties that bound them. They are in a sense, consumed.'

Cooper wrote notes. She worked hard. She wondered what the future would bring.

PART 1:

THE BREAK

DR COOPER ALLEN
THE PRESENT DAY

I

'Will you take a photo for us?'

A couple had asked Cooper this earlier in the day. She had not wanted to say 'yes'. She was not accustomed to agreeing, not to strangers. But what she was used to in her ordinary life didn't matter anymore, did it? She was on a holiday. She was no longer living an ordinary life; she was no longer bound by the time of day or the day of the week. She was well practised in self-delusion.

Cooper had been looking out from the edge of the hotel's beer garden, her right foot bent into a tiptoe, leaning against the metal railings, staring at the trees in the valley below, their green canopies blooming and bulging like air bubbles in a stew – churches and houses of God emerging at random intervals in the town, in the ruins of ancient woods.

Cooper had heard this happy, cheery girl's voice. Turning to look at her future subjects, the couple was much older than Cooper would have expected. The man sounded young too, his voice clear and fresh and high as he passed Cooper his phone, giving an explanation of why they were visiting the town: a honeymoon.

'Are you here with your boyfriend?' the fifty-year-old girl asked, hair half grey, but still, a girl she was in her voice. The voice, the face, were all Cooper had to go on: appearances and sounds.

This old girl got ready to pose as Cooper accidentally exited the camera app on the old boy's phone. Fuck. Cooper tried to find it again but none of the app icons were standard. In her panic she somehow ended up going into the girl's personal messages. She—

'Sorry if that was too personal a question,' the girl added. 'I just – it's just such a romantic place...'

'No, yep,' Cooper said, her voice vaguely phlegmatic with disuse, with days of not talking, of wondering, of waiting. 'I'm just here with the old boyf.'

'Boyf?' the man rose an eyebrow.

'Boyfriend...' Cooper pretended to take the photo, handed the phone back, and left to return to the main building, acting as if a fictional romantic partner awaited her inside, and not a weekend with a passive-aggressive sister and a controlling, cruel mother.

Sometime later, Cooper had pork belly for dinner, staring out at the sunset through the vast, clear glass walls.

A stranger talked to another stranger about how they were so drunk last night, about how they couldn't remember anything, about why they kept doing this to themselves, why their idea of a good time was collapse and amnesia and self-obliteration.

Other guests laughed, and gambled, and ate and drank.

The sun set.

Cooper went up to her room and there she sat, still alone.

She looked at her phone.

She'd told herself she wouldn't go on it too much, not during this trip.

She'd told herself she would have a break.

She was on a variety of internet forums and message boards before night fell.

Kathleen Daniels missing 2014 (new update)

Family burn in fire (Littleport) – accidental death or murder?

Abductions across south-western United States

She read cases, cold and new.

She posted in response to the theories of amateurs, adding her own. Looking at the evidence where there was evidence.

She sought the posts with pictures more than any other.

She had difficulty feeling anything, except when there were pictures.

She missed this work.

So she sat, alone.

2

Cooper made a friend.

The night before this family reunion, booked without her agreement or knowledge ... the night before her mother and sister arrived at this distant, quiet place ... the night before the end began, though Cooper didn't know it yet ... yes, it was a good night to meet new people.

She had come here early. She had booked days in the calendar for slots before and after the duration reserved by her mother. If she was going to take time off work, it would be on her own terms, she would have time to settle first, she would have time to recover and decompress. She didn't do this very often – not family stuff, not time off, though she had stayed in plenty of hotels, travelling as her job demanded. It made it hard to meet people.

Everywhere fell to darkness that night, all across town, all across the hills and valleys of Lethwick. Yet even so, Cooper made a new friend in the gloom of the hotel's power cut.

It was by chance.

Prior to their first meeting, Cooper's new friend had locked herself out of her room and, desperately needing to use the toilet – and phone-less, without light – had stumbled her way through the long empty halls of the King's Hotel, searching for signs.

Cooper had also been out in those halls, imagining that as a result of the power cut she might somehow get some free stuff from the hotel lobby. Whether candles, water bottles, refreshments, whatever, Cooper had always liked free things. Indeed, in the days after university, she had developed a little shrine of free gifts she'd sent off for in newsletters and email promotions, receiving such treasures as special toilet rolls or kitchen tongs that had in turn given Cooper a sense of bizarre achievement. A silly feeling worth ten times the market price of the objects themselves. Perhaps there would be more here.

So Cooper had departed into the grey and the black, with only her phone's light for company.

Then she met her new friend. She got something free, after all.

The two women came face to face near a silver door marked FIRE EXIT, right at the edge of a stairwell.

Cooper saw her own reflection superimposed over the stranger in the glass.

The only light they had was from the torch of Cooper's phone.

Cooper's dark, short hair still hung damp from the shower, self-cut just weeks before in a misguided decision she still didn't want to think about. Cooper's eyes and mouth were twisted in an unintentional glare which she soon corrected to something more neutral. Her green coat hung loose over pyjamas.

The stranger was shorter by a head, her skin freckled.

Her hair was light brown or ginger, Cooper couldn't tell, not against the smudge of her own reflection – longer than Cooper's though – no self-cutting disasters there.

Her cheeks were puffy, her make-up slightly messy and stained.

She didn't glare, but she did seem surprised at the sudden

contact with Cooper; a little scared almost, but this resolved itself into apology.

'I'm sorry!' the stranger exclaimed, as if trying to go through the same doorway were some heinous crime.

'It's OK, really— A-OK.' Cooper stood back, holding the door open, and the stranger hesitated before walking past.

The stranger hesitated again, a little way down the hall, her back to Cooper.

'*Are* you OK?' Cooper asked, suddenly.

The stranger turned, face barely visible in the dark.

She shook her head.

So Cooper led the stranger back to her hotel room, unlocked the door, and let her use the en-suite bathroom facilities.

It felt like a small thing, though the logistics were more difficult than Cooper had anticipated. There was no electricity, of course, and the stranger had lost her phone stumbling in those long halls. So Cooper had to shine her own phone light through a gap in the en-suite bathroom's door as the stranger sat down on the toilet. It embarrassed Cooper to do this, though why, she did not really know. Cooper didn't know if the stranger was also embarrassed at this strange intimacy. But she had needed her help, hadn't she? It didn't matter either way, what this woman might have drunk, what she might have done to get herself into this state.

Afterwards, they talked for a while, preferring company, now that company was present.

It was all somehow clearer, sitting on Cooper's bed, her phone's dwindling battery giving them light to see each other.

They traded names. They both had boy's names – or, at the very least, names that people assumed were those of men. They joked about it.

The stranger was called Alex, though Cooper heard a slightly different name when it was first spoken, muffled through tired lips.

'What?'

'Alex,' the woman had said.

Alex had been crying. Of course it was that – the redness, the puffiness, the now dried mascara charting her disturbance in falling lines, like a lie detector test, like the rhythm of an earthquake. She was smiling now, though, albeit in a tired, distant way.

Alex talked about it all, the floodgates breaking open. Quite literally. She talked about the event that had ruined her recent life, the secondary blow after her boyfriend had left her earlier in the year. Her basement flat near the town centre had flooded in a spring storm a few months before. This hotel stay had been funded by her insurer, a place that was meant to be temporary, but which had now lasted months. Then there was this power cut at the end of a long day, of long hours.

'I work at Church Home,' Alex said. They'd taken little bottles of whiskey from the now silent mini-bar fridge. Why they were kept cold, neither knew. She drank anyway. 'A care home, sorry.'

Alex looked after the old. Some were as healthy as they could be. Some abandoned. Some had lost the full use of their minds and bodies.

'What about you?' Alex asked her host. 'What do you do? Sorry, I should have asked ...'

Cooper didn't know how to answer. So she changed the subject for a while. She talked about her family. About how her mother and her sister were meeting her for a woodland, pastoral holiday. She hadn't spent much time with them in recent years.

'Why?' Alex asked, and Cooper hesitated for a while, before lying, drinking more of her drink, and lying again.

'We just drifted apart. Like Tom Hanks and Wilson.'

Alex smiled. 'Are you Tom Hanks or the ball in this scenario?'

'The ball, forever floating out to sea ... Definitely the ball.'

So the night went on.

It took another hour for some truth to come.

'I investigate cases involving animals,' Cooper said, sitting against a throne of pillows and cushions they'd scavenged from around the room and cupboards. Alex rested on her left, like they'd known each other for years. Cooper went on. Cooper told her new friend how she'd trained as a vet, how she'd had this whole life planned out, living with her then boyfriend, her two cats, a rented cottage in the countryside, in a place not unlike this place.

Things had changed, but they changed for everyone, didn't they? That was life.

Now she did this. She used those skills to take photographs of crime scenes for the police, to gather and assess animal-related evidence, whatever the species, whether animals were the alleged aggressors or the main victims of an incident. She travelled the country, working as a consultant.

She really was just in Lethwick for a break, though. To have a rest before her family came. She laughed a broken, tired laugh. 'I thought it would be good for me to come early. Whenever my mother talks, it's just about her health these days ... these years, if I'm being honest. She's been dying of one thing or another her entire life.'

'And your sister? What does she talk about? I wish I had a sister.'

Cooper looked at her drink. 'My sister doesn't talk. Not to me, anyway.'

'You drifted apart?'

'Like a ball in the ocean.'

Cooper told Alex a lot of things, then. Stories she'd hardly told anyone. Images that had haunted her waking moments. Cases solved and unsolved. They talked for hours more, and still, dawn did not come.

And Alex – she was enthralled. She responded as if Cooper had begun some kind of performance.

'I had no idea that was even a real job!'

It turned out that Alex listened to true crime podcasts every night in order to go to sleep. Alex admitted this with the semi-defence of knowing plenty of other women who also did so.

'Don't they get into your dreams, though?' Cooper asked, yawning. 'If you're listening right before bed?'

It didn't matter, Alex claimed. Even if these stories of murder infected dreams, they met some need, some yearning, didn't they?

Alex couldn't sleep without them.

'What about you? Do you listen to them?' Alex asked. 'Or would that be a busman's holiday?'

Cooper laughed. She took out her phone and showed Alex her posts – the countless threads in true crime communities she had joined these two years past, the contributions she'd made as part of her hobby.

As Alex looked, Cooper's smile faded. She wondered if she should have shown Alex this. If she should have let her username be seen.

But what did it matter?

Alex was a stranger. She was not part of her life.

It was OK to let her in.

Half an hour later, their conversation was interrupted by a knock on their door.

Cooper went to it, shining her torch light at the knob, then leant out cautiously to see who had come – only to find a middle-aged man knocking two doors down.

Odd that it had sounded like their own.

Cooper shut and locked it.

By the time Cooper had sat back down, her new friend had already taken another drink from the minibar.

'Anyhow,' Alex shrugged, smiling. 'I ended up dating a pig, after all.'

Alex talked about him for a while, this police officer. 'My ex never did anything as interesting as what you do, though. Lethwick … it's not exactly a dangerous area.'

Alex shared the history of their supposed love.

This police officer, he had been distant for months before their break-up, had never really explained to Alex why they'd had to break it off, beyond vague allusions to getting 'serious about his life'.

Alex still slept with him sometimes. He even had a new girlfriend, and now Alex was just his 'bit on the side'.

'Obviously a terrible idea,' Cooper said, and Alex laughed, then apologised for laughing. She asked Cooper what kind of romantic mistakes she might have made in her time.

Cooper avoided answering.

Cooper started asking difficult questions instead – real important questions such as, if mint toothpaste were to be banned across the United Kingdom, what flavour would Alex replace it with? If Alex had to become a dinosaur, which species would she choose?

Alex was horrified by the concept of any other flavour, but resolved on lemon for the alternative universe toothpaste. 'It's a bit more acidic, right?' and Cooper agreed solemnly. As far as dinosaurs went, Alex chose 'long neck' but couldn't remember the names of any actual species.

They waited in a darkness that never seemed to change, never seemed to hint at a restoration of electricity or sunlight. It just went on, and they drank, sitting on a bed that belonged to neither of them. They talked about many things, getting drunk, losing all sense.

'Two weeks ago. I had a ...' Alex paused. 'I haven't told anyone.' She went on, talking fast. 'I – I haven't told anyone I got rid of it, that it was even an "it" in the first place.'

'It's OK.'

'My family would never talk to me again if they knew,' Alex gulped. 'My ex, he—'

'You said he was a pig. Was he a pig about this?'

'I never told him. I love him and I never told him.' Alex shook her head. 'I just couldn't – I didn't have enough money. I can't look after myself, let alone a ... a ...'

'Piglet?' Cooper asked, and immediately, she knew this was one of the worst things she'd ever said; she felt she should apologise, this half-joke, this remark for the sake of making a remark, but Alex just smiled a sad smile.

And they moved on.

They waited for the light to come back.

Alex asked if Cooper had anything else they could have. Anything that might take the edge off.

'Just what's in the mini-fridge,' Cooper said, but Alex's face, her reply ... She meant something else, Cooper realised. Not a drink. Not something kept in a fridge.

And the answer was no.

She didn't. She never did. She hadn't even smoked a cigarette, not in a while.

Alex tried to smile, and said it was OK. They kept talking, practically leaning on each other.

'I wish I had a life like yours,' Alex said.

47

Cooper played what music she could on her phone for a while, the songs saved, the battery slowly emptying in sound.

Eventually, something else came.

A podcast.

A discussion of an old series of murders.

'Yesss,' Alex said, and leant back. 'Now I can go to sleep.'

The vet and the nurse – the investigator and her new friend – Cooper and Alex, listened to the discussion in the powerless dark.

There were hardly ever any answers in these podcasts.

The more unexplained, the creepier. The less there was a resolution or an explanation, the juicier it felt.

The joy of true crime stories – that they felt like they could not be true at all.

The vet and the nurse listened, on and on, sleeping, waking... 'the maid heard a knocking out in the barn,' sleeping, 'food was found on the counter, suggesting someone had been staying there,' waking, 'never found...'

They became friends, dreaming to a massacre.

If they'd never met, things might have been different.

Transcript from the podcast
'Unexplained Mysteries'

You know those dreams where you honestly believe they're actually happening?

How strange it feels when you wake up.

How confusing.

How, if you're dreaming about the wrong thing, the wrong person, waking from a dream can break your heart.

That's what happened to two parents back in the 1960s. This man and this woman, their daughter vanished not once, but twice, within the space of just a few years – in a mystery still unsolved until this day.

So click like and subscribe, and listen to today's Unexplained Mystery . . .

[Theme music plays, a series of oddly chirpy chiptune beats]

Stephanie Earlsham was born in Sadler's Rise, a small hamlet about ten miles to the south-west of Cambridge, England. Ten miles from where, one day, aged thirteen, she would vanish without a trace.

Stephanie was this bright, happy, normal kid with a normal, happy childhood. She had a lot of friends too – she was a really popular girl – and no one seemed to have a bad word to say about her. The only thing was she was a little precocious, maybe – she looked older than her age. She was really pale so she burned easily. She had an unusual fashion sense, maybe as a result of that – covering up, wearing a lot of layers. She had this massive rush to grow up. Teachers would say Stephanie sometimes talked too much in class, but her grades were better than good, and there were just bigger problems to deal with in terms of the other kids, so Stephanie was mostly just encouraged, you know, and trusted.

But shortly before she turned fourteen, things started to change.

Stephanie started coming home late from school, sometimes late at night, sometimes not at all. She'd say she was at a particular friend's house but when her parents started checking, these claims would often turn out to be lies. And this was just not like her at all – it was a bizarre, totally uncharacteristic personality change – and when her parents tried talking to her about it, she just snapped at them, she was just blowing up at every opportunity.

So her parents are thinking, this isn't like our Stephanie. They were really concerned and just at their wit's end as to how to help their little girl. So they did what a lot of parents now do and they booked their daughter into therapy, not really knowing if it would work, but not knowing what else to do. At the time this was completely revolutionary in their social circle – so few people were encouraged to be open about their feelings in this way, so it was really groundbreaking and cool of her parents to do this.

So Stephanie spent several weeks talking things through. The psychoanalyst's records revealed a likely case of teenage rebellion and estrangement – nothing out of the ordinary or disastrous. And although these records wouldn't be released for quite a while, with Stephanie's permission the therapist spoke directly to the parents and advised them to give her some space.

And they were just delighted with the results. Everything seemed to calm down. Stephanie had lost some friends but now, at least, whatever was eating at her seemed to calm down and fade away.

And Stephanie's parents had been making some big changes in their lives. Stephanie's mother had recently become a full-time, stay-at-home mum after Stephanie's father managed to get a promotion. Once they'd saved enough, they were planning to go and travel the world, maybe buy a boat, live the retirement dream, as soon as Stephanie was off to college.

One day Stephanie's father came home from work, parked his car down the road, and walked to his house.

And right away, he realised something was very wrong.

The hamlet of Sadler's Rise only has sixteen homes. Property developers built them in this long, spaced-out ring around a hill in a way that was meant to look like the spokes of a crown, shortly after Queen Elizabeth II's coronation. And they have grown more and more expensive over the years due to their commutable distance to both Cambridge and London. It also became a scenic point of interest, this weird row of houses on a hill that didn't even look like the actual object they were supposed to represent – their sharp points looked more like something out of *Game of Thrones* than the cushioned fabric of Britain's real crown. The tourism campaigns focused on legacy, natural beauty – this lovely, picturesque place people still try to think of when they think of England.

And so when Stephanie's father comes home, he really doesn't expect what he sees next. It just isn't the kind of place where things like that happened.

He comes up to the front of the hillside house, these literal miles and miles of rolling green fields behind his back, and he sees that something is very wrong.

His front door is wide open.

And inside, he can clearly see the front hallway and the stairs.

There are muddy footprints going upwards. None of them come back down.

If someone has broken into his house, they are still there.

There is a chance it isn't a break-in, of course. There is a chance his daughter has started skipping school again, but she'd never been as careless as this before, and these footprints, he just knows...

They're too big to belong to his daughter.

As for his wife, he talked to her on the phone just a few hours ago – she'd gone to stay with her sister for a few days over in Cardiff, the whole opposite side of the country.

Unless he just really doesn't know his family, or a prank is being played on him, someone has broken into his house and is still inside.

So Stephanie's father, he does what anyone would do. He goes inside and he calls the police. The nearest pay phone was miles away, there weren't any cell phones invented yet, and he just thinks, this is my house, my family could have been here, I need to make sure we're safe and that our stuff is safe. He hasn't seen or heard anyone, but he keeps a lookout as he talks, and just really quickly explains, I could be in danger right now; please, please come if this call cuts out.

What the police find when they arrive leads Stephanie's father to book his family into a hotel for the next two weeks. The officers that came round, they agreed with him – they saw something that made them take this very, very seriously.

The muddy footprints led from the front of the house up the stairs and ended at his daughter's open bedroom door. There was no set of footprints showing where they exited.

[Cue creepy musical sound effects, several advertisements, and another musical intro]

Now Stephanie's father is absolutely freaked out by this – his home was, in his eyes, no longer safe. But the police, they give up quickly, though they are still concerned. The police couldn't find any evidence of forced entry or clues as to who made these footprints, nor how they'd left. And what's more, the shoe sizes don't match anyone who lived in the house. Size 12 men's – Stephanie's father was only a 10. Weird as it was, though, there was nothing else the police could do. The police told him to just make sure he locked up properly, and to call them if anything else changed.

Cut forward a few weeks later and life is back to normal – the parents are both home, they're still a little freaked out by the footprints, but they say, You know what? We'll invest in more home security and we'll just keep an eye out. Nothing had been taken or damaged after all, the police couldn't find any leads, we've been safe the whole time we've been living here at Sadler's Rise so let's just try and live our lives.

And Stephanie, she was continuing to get better from her bad patch a few months back. She just seemed to be turning back into the bright, happy girl she used to be. And her parents, they were so delighted they even agreed to get Stephanie a dog – though she'd have to wait a few more months, she'd have to walk and feed it, and she'd need to get the house puppy-proofed. Things were looking up. Her father even says to his friends, you know what, we've had our problems but things are now really turning around.

A month after the incident with the footprints, Stephanie Earlsham goes into Cambridge to go shopping with some friends. Her father drops her off near this gorgeous field named Parker's Piece – these huge, old Cambridge University buildings all around – and tells her he'll pick her up at 5 p.m.

He goes and spends the day walking around the place – he

was a student here once, many years before, studying natural sciences – and he goes to his old college and he even walks on the grass there, which was something he'd never have been allowed to do back in the day, but he's just so excited to revisit this place he'd never really been back to, despite living so close.

At four o' clock he goes back to the car with a glass bottle of Coca-Cola and he waits for his daughter.

Stephanie never arrives.

The friends she said she'd meet . . . Her father uses a payphone and gets his wife to phone the friends' parents, but his wife is confused. What Cambridge friends? I don't know any Cambridge friends.

Worried his daughter has started lying and has fallen in with a bad crowd again, Stephanie's father goes through the whole of town, enters every college and store he can find looking for his daughter and just, nothing – he finds nothing.

But they're sure she'll turn up. The days pass, the police start looking, and Stephanie's father is certain she's just acting out again, that this is just part of the phase she's going through.

Three years go by.

It's as if walking through those Cambridge fields, Stephanie just vanished from history. The police would look through her friend groups and would find no clue as to whatever had been causing her erratic behaviour. And the police just increasingly feared the worst, but had no idea how to get the parents to accept it – that their daughter had probably been abducted, had run away or might even be dead. Some of the police and the press even wondered if Stephanie's father had something to do with it – he was, after all, the last person to see her alive, and he had no alibi.

And here's where a lot of stories like this end. An open-ended mystery where we have no idea what happened, or a body in the bottom of a ditch. Where the parents have a cloud over their souls all their lives.

But here? Here Stephanie's father was half right.

Stephanie did turn up, once, for one brief afternoon.

Miles away, in the old rural valleys of Lethwick, seventeen-year-old Sophie Bertilak received a camera for her birthday. Now, remember, in the 1960s, the idea of a personal, affordable camera was completely wild – and Sophie was just ecstatic. She went into the woods near her home, it was this gorgeous day, and she took a lot of photos, just really excited to try this thing out. She enjoyed it so much that she'd go on to become a professional photographer and, you know, to do this job for a living.

In the woods that day, Sophie saw a girl walking with a bearded man by a lake. The girl was missing one of her shoes, and the man didn't seem like he particularly wanted to be here, but there was nothing out of the ordinary otherwise – it just looked like a father and a daughter out for a walk.

Sophie was just so excited to be out taking photographs, she was snapping all kinds of things – her house, the trees, orbs of mistletoe, anything that seemed interesting.

So she took a photo of this girl, feeling like it was kind of weird, kind of magical that the girl was wearing just one single shoe. The light was hitting the girl in this strange way and it looked kind of like those old, fake photos Victorians made of fairies in the woods. It just looked kind of cool.

The girl and the man, they didn't seem to notice the photo being taken – Sophie was far enough away.

A few weeks later, that image would be on the front cover of some national newspapers in the United Kingdom. It would launch Sophie's career as a photographer.

It was, of course, Stephanie Earlsham.

Three years older than she'd been at the time of her dis-appearance. Alive.

And the man next to her in the photo – the police were able to estimate his shoe size as 12, exactly the same as those muddy footprints in Stephanie's home three years earlier.

The police began looking for known sex offenders, criminals, possible matches for this guy's photo. And there was this national interest, this big campaign with Stephanie's parents front and centre. Some people had this whole time thought Stephanie's parents might have had something to do with her disappear-ance, but this photo, it not only gave everyone hope Stephanie could be found, it seemed to clear Stephanie's parents of any wrongdoing.

They just desperately wanted this person in the photo to, you know, give them their daughter back, this seventeen-year-old Stephanie who they sorely missed.

And it seemed to everyone they'd finally gotten the lead they needed.

There was only one problem. One shocking, creepy detail that not only complicated the case, it would make some doubt whether Stephanie had even been abducted in the first place.

You see, that photographer in the woods? That girl the same age, who'd so strangely stumbled upon the missing Stephanie Earlsham?

Sophie had taken another image that day, one that would lead to a mystery that was perhaps even greater than this first.

She had really been enjoying that new camera of hers, and just started experimenting with it, taking pictures of things she wouldn't even normally have taken interest in, using the film up.

And among all the photographs of plants and trees, she'd seen this plastic pipe in the forest. Just sticking out of the ground far from any kind of building or house, just really kind of odd-looking.

So, snap, and she got the picture, just a few minutes before taking that image of Stephanie Earlsham and the bearded man.

Little did Sophie know, but when the photo was developed, there was this absolutely shocking additional element caught on camera.

There had been a child in the pipe. Eyes had been looking up at her from the darkness, terrified.

And this buried kid in the darkness? This kid didn't have enough identifying details to ever be linked to a specific missing persons case. When police got there, they found dislodged earth suggesting some kind of underground box had been put in place at some point, but nothing else remained.

And the fact Stephanie was still alive after all this time, that she was in proximity to this, walking free and apparently fine and healthy?

It raised a question. Was she really being held against her will?

Or had Stephanie, at some point, begun helping her captor? Had Stephanie helped that man do something to the child in the pipe?

Stephanie's parents would eventually separate, twenty years after their daughter's disappearance, on what would have been Stephanie's thirty-fourth birthday.

Stephanie's father remarried, having new children with a new woman who he'd eventually leave behind as well, having fallen into alcoholism and a gambling addiction.

Stephanie's mother moved to Lethwick where her daughter had last been sighted, buying a house near the childhood home of that photographer, Sophie Bertilak. By all accounts, they remained in contact, Sophie the closest thing she had left to her little girl.

The mother never stopped looking.

To this day, no more verified sightings of Stephanie Earlsham, the bearded man or the young child in the pipe have occurred.

3

DCI Robert Kelly had heard of farmers collapsing unconscious, of getting tired or hitting their heads, of their animals eating them. He'd seen mob movies where old-fashioned gangsters had fed the bodies of their victims to pigs to cover up evidence. He'd heard of all kinds of strange things on the internet, in hearsay. But seeing them in the flesh was quite different.

Seeing them in a woman you'd known ... a woman you'd spoken to ...

Kelly was almost sixty years old. It was almost time for retirement from Lethwick's police force.

He stood outside Sophie's house. Other officers searched within the building, heading towards the darkroom at the back.

But Kelly – he had a different job to do that morning.

The pigs' skin was stretched over their ribs. Their eyes wandered every so often, half delirious. He watched them.

He moved to the edge of the paddock and leant over with the gun. He'd been a firearms officer once. Still had the licence to use one of these. It was only an animal ... they let him use one again.

One pig – Alfie – approached, ambling over past a green plastic bucket, hardly any water left within.

His black eyes looked up at the officer. He began to sniff the air, pink ears drooping.

A bullet was fired. They had to die. Of course they had to die. They'd killed a human. They were dangerous, now, if not before.

The police had to rescue what could be rescued from within the animals' stomachs. They had to know what had happened here. This was a peaceful, gentle community. People needed to feel safe.

The police officer fired again, avenging his old friend.

He had been twenty when he'd met Sophie. A little over forty years ago, he'd first seen that face...

Alfie fell to his side, all four legs stiff, like an invisible hand had suddenly bound them together. He shook, legs running in the air as if there was still a chance he could escape from his killer.

The other pig – Henry – he paced backward, uncertain, ears bent low, tail curled up. He was terrified. He began to retreat, backing up towards the apple tree.

Then he collapsed at the second bullet, shorter, fatter legs curling, mouth hanging open.

Within the house, other officers kept up their search.

There was evidence Sophie had hosted someone. The blood spatter around the apple tree – a specialist was supposed to have arrived already, but what could they really tell, in all this mud, in all this dirt? The pattern did not seem like that a knife would make, or a stabbing.

The blood spatter was random, clouds and swirls erased by now dead tongues. The police would look at the house, the blood, the body. But already, short of some feud, short of inheritance or greed or hate ... Kelly looked at the corpses of the pigs.

Perhaps the responsible parties had already had their justice. The trial of the pigs was over. They smelled like food.

The sun kept rising, and the clouds kept drawing in. It began to spit rain.

Across town, birds scattered outside a hotel window. They cried out as they moved, flocking towards the trees, towards mistletoe.

4

A phone was ringing.

It wasn't hers.

Cooper could not remember going to sleep. There was no sign of her new friend from the night before, though the empty bottles from the mini-bar seemed evidence enough. Alex's presence had not been a dream.

The power had returned at some point, lighting the television opposite with the same film Cooper had been watching prior to the cut.

The Little Mermaid II. The TV screen was frozen on an image of the bloated, aged, yellow fish Flounder. She couldn't even remember the last time she'd seen this film, what she'd been doing at the time. University, maybe? A period of her life she didn't really want to remember, she supposed.

Flounder stuttered as Cooper tried to switch the screen off.

She wondered if this image had been there when Alex had left, and she groaned, turning over to rest on her side. Best not to think about. In her defence there had been little else to watch in this room, cut off from streaming services, only a small DVD library inherited from other guests.

Outside, the birds cried out.

Within, the phone kept ringing its slow, soft ring.

Cooper looked around. There was a white wall phone near the desk on the other side of the room. A direct line to the hotel's reception. She got up, stretching lazily, the clothes of the previous day clinging unpleasantly to her body.

She took the corded phone from its receiver and answered. 'Hello?'

There came no answer, not at first. Just a breath for a moment, a crackle in the static.

As Cooper was about to speak again, a voice came down the line. A man's: accented, quiet.

The police were waiting downstairs.

There had been an accident. There had been a death. An old woman, out in the valleys. They needed Cooper's help.

'How did you know I was here?' Cooper asked.

They did not know. They had just been told by their senior to ask for her help. They had such little time.

It had the characteristic of a dream, hearing this. Of being found on this morning of all mornings, on holiday, to be called back to work.

'How did you know I was here?'

The police officer on the phone line seemed annoyed. He repeated that he didn't know. That it didn't matter.

There had been a crime.

They needed her. That should be enough.

On her way out of the building, Cooper passed a group in the breakfast dining area, all playing some card game, with champagne, morning cocktails, even a little money.

One of the gamblers looked at her and then went back to his friends.

'Into the muck,' he said.

5

Cooper had dealt with the police on multiple occasions throughout her life.

The first she could remember was not the death of her father; it was a policewoman who had come to her school.

She'd talked to them all about what it was like to do her job — that they were there to make people feel safe.

If people did bad things, the police would catch them and stop them doing any more bad things.

Of course that sounded appealing.

They were like doctors, healing the world by explaining the confusing parts and then cutting them away.

Cooper grew up.

Cooper tried to be a doctor of sorts, helping animals.

This failed.

So she went to do what the policewoman had done, so many years ago.

She went to explain the mystery of the world, and then destroy it.

She'd gone on to help, and to kill.

The morning after Sophie Bertilak's death, Cooper sat in the back of a police car, a dark raincoat and hood about her shoulders.

Cooper's family had never been on a trip to the countryside together, not in thirty-three years of life. How her mother had selected this place, Cooper did not know. A place of natural beauty, history, hiking, walks, sure. A place where pigs ate old women, now, too.

The trap began to close around her, though she could not see it.

Pigs had always eaten people. It was, in a peculiar way, the origin of Cooper's profession – trials for animals held throughout the previous two millennia, church authorities sending lawyers and inquisitors to examine the guilt of beasts.

Whose side would she be on? Cooper wondered. The pigs were already dead, after all, the trial carried out and judgement summarily passed.

Cooper looked down at her boots. One of them bore a fleck of mud from a farm far away.

The police officer driving the car, a DCI Kelly, he hadn't said much, beyond thanking Cooper for her help at such short notice. It was hard to read his face beneath his beard, grey and black.

Cooper tried to make a joke as they drove.

Kelly hadn't liked it. He hadn't laughed. He hadn't said anything. It had faded from existence, as if it had never been spoken. DCI Kelly was not a man for laughing.

6

It began to rain. Tall trees shifted a little in the breeze, the roadside blurry, transient. The hills obscured the rest.

Cooper blinked, the rain falling a little faster beyond the car windows.

'Will I be able to visit the crime scene?' she asked, muted. 'When the post-mortem is complete, I mean.'

There was silence for a little while, before DCI Kelly asked why.

'I normally go to the crime scene,' she said. 'To take photographic evidence, to look for anything else that might add to my findings. I have a process, you see.'

Again, another pause.

Eventually, Kelly told Cooper that he did not want to disrupt her holiday any further than they had already.

'My father,' he added, 'always worked in his holidays – he checked on cases, he kept his nose in. I don't think it's health—' he coughed. 'Healthy, sorry.'

'Your dad was a police officer?'

'Worked in the same department his whole life. I work there now, too.'

'A family business?' Cooper said, and Kelly nodded.

'I suppose it is, yes.'

They passed a sign, nestled by overgrown branches that threatened to swamp all human markers.

Oppidum vetus leneque.

The phrase appeared a few times in Lethwick's text, its signs, its inscriptions, its engravings old and new.

'A town, ancient and gentle.'

Elsewhere, it was called 'the painted town'. It was famous for watercolours and oil paintings by English masters – of the river, of abbeys and hills and monks. Even centuries before, artists had come to this place, the rich and celebrated.

They still had festivals here.

Every year, every midsummer, the mystery plays came through town – processions linked to and funded by local businesses and philanthropic organisations, recounting the Bible through theatrical performances.

Just a few weeks away now. Cooper didn't see the signs.

7

The police car passed lichen and moss across brickwork. The greenery emerged from the buildings, weaving in and out of its mass. Long, vine-covered trees spanned over and around the dirty water of the river beside them. Ducks crowded near old stones.

Then there were benches, plaques marking those who had died to create them. The metal was covered in a little rain from the morning, but the wood would have been dry enough to sit on. No one did.

'Who was she?' Cooper asked.

The police car started to pass strangers. Young people and the middle aged milled around the streets, many of them with cameras – DLSRs, disposables, all kinds of revivals beyond their phones. Or else they sat outside the cafés and the bars, lounging in their sunglasses in the white light.

'She took photos for a living,' Kelly said. 'Or did, once. She was retired.'

The world shimmered as the clouds broke, dancing on the shivering branches of trees as if the light itself were alive, like a jellyfish, like a death rattle.

They turned at some green lights. None of the traffic lights ever seemed to go red.

They moved slower now, the road shifting from tarmac to cobbles.

Another bench. Another plaque shining in the sun.

The rain spat again soon enough, though the light did not stop.

They arrived at the laboratory a few minutes later.

'Photos of what?' Cooper asked. Her mind had wandered, strangely, distantly. It seemed to take Kelly a moment to realise what she was asking.

He stopped the car, placing it in 'park'.

'Death,' he said, and opened the door.

8

Seventy years had vanished within stomachs. Fingers had danced within acid.

The woman's life had been divided across her only friends as they had eaten pieces of skin, of organs, of bone. That was all that had become of her life, of all those years, of her death.

That was what had become of Sophie Bertilak.

It was not that consumption never happened – pigs were opportunistic eaters, no matter how much they loved their owners – but if hungry enough, they had been known to devour sleeping or otherwise incapacitated humans in their midst. It was still possible that this was all just some macabre accident, and this was in part what Cooper was here to help prove or disprove.

There were suspicions, nevertheless. Potentially missing items from the dead woman's house. Trinkets, mostly – nothing of any value greater than sentiment. And such material absences could be explained away, of course. We all lost things, the old more than most.

Cooper had been given a laptop while she waited, perched on a stool in the corner of the cold laboratory.

Her dark reflection watched her, gazing from the unpowered screen. She waited for the pathologist to arrive. His presence was required, considering the main purpose of the post-mortem. He was supposed to be here by now.

Cooper switched the laptop on. The police had known of

her past cases. At least, DCI Kelly had. The Knacker Man, the Mortimer abduction, and a dozen more. They had heard of her, as if she were someone worth hearing of. She smiled at this thought, then felt a little silly. She still didn't know how they'd found her at the hotel. DCI Kelly hadn't been told of the circumstances; he didn't seem to find the coincidence important. She was here, wasn't she? She was needed.

They had given her some materials about the case, while she waited. There was video footage of Sophie Bertilak's home.

9

In the video, the ground floor was almost immaculate, despite the dust of the windows themselves. The brown, varnished wood of the dead woman's dining table had two empty wine glasses upon it. The kitchen showed evidence of a meal, prepared the night before, the dishwasher having completed its cycle.

The walls were painted white all around, and the light – a frosted white orb hanging from the ceiling – was only dim. There were no cobwebs in these halls. Mirrors stood in their place, a mass of eight in various shapes, all facing a painting on their opposite.

It was an oil painting, old and worn and unrestored, the frame flaking its tacky dark-gold varnish. It showed horses running through water, surf and spray lifted up into the air before them. There were no riders.

As the video went on, the police in the recording reminded the viewer that they had found no signs of a struggle or forced entry; not in the lounge, nor in the office, in the three bedrooms of the main structure.

One of the rooms they came across was the old woman's own – a few boxes not yet fully unpacked from her move back to this place. The second was a bare guest room. The third was full of a little boy's things, blue bedsheets, a chalkboard with little more than white dust, a map of a world with different boundaries – USSR. Empires. Colonies. All of it was covered in dust, barely touched.

There was a darkroom out back. The pigs' victim had been a photographer once, you see. She'd travelled the world. She'd seen so many things.

Within this room, reality turned blood-red. Images hung from the ceiling, showing the fields outside, the trees all around.

Some of them showed a distant figure, tall and thin, but it was hard to make his face out. Something about his limbs, the motion they implied as he shifted across the images, suggested a spider.

Other photographs were waiting to be developed. The shelves were littered with bottled liquids.

The video showed there had been a spill near the sink. Plastic bags had been mounted within the ceramic, ice melting within.

For all the half-developed images in this room, there were yet more photo frames in the main house, on the dead woman's dressing table, on her mantelpiece, along the white walls.

Most of them were empty, recently disturbed.

Someone had taken the photographs – and what did people hang in their homes but the images of those things and people they most loved?

What had likely been taken from the dead woman, then, but the memory of love itself?

So went the theory.

RESULTS:

RESTRICTED (when complete)

Results of MG21 request:
— Blood samples identified as belonging to Sophia Bertilak (found in outer paddock, trace amounts in main hallway, kitchen, back hallway, darkroom)

— Blood samples belonging to unknown human male (trace amounts in main hallway, kitchen)
— Remnants of cleaning chemicals
— Saliva from wine glass, identified as belonging to Sophia Bertilak
— Saliva from wine glass, identified as belonging to unknown human white male

'I'll be ready to begin, soon.'

Cooper shut the laptop. She picked up her instruments, the pig bodies disappearing into air, into smells, into themselves, into nothing at all.

The pathologist had arrived and had left just as quickly, heading into the recesses of the lab for coffee and biscuits. 'Come get me when you need me,' he said. As if Cooper were an assistant.

She turned with a grimace, with an odd sense of excitement.

Cooper pulled on gloves and climbed into the mystery, into the dead.

IO

Most animals were the devil's creatures.

The old trials of the pigs, the inquisitions and papal courts, had sometimes claimed as much. Jesus, driving the demon Legion into a horde of swine, had revealed the nature of the beasts.

But as Cooper looked at the bodies, they did not look so scary.

They did not look innocent, either.

The truth was, their scent coloured everything.

The truth was, few other animals smelled so much like food. Even though the fridge had slowed down decomposition, the two pigs could not help but smell of pork, laid out as they were on the cold steel tables. Blood had trickled down their heads from where the police had shot them.

Cooper unpacked her instruments, thinking about the human victim. After a terse start to their drive, DCI Kelly had opened up a little – he had told Cooper about Sophie Bertilak's career as a photographer, her employment abroad, the protests, the activist work that followed, the long years in and out of the establishment. He had told Cooper about the pictures that had started it all – he had mused about them, the missing girl, the stranger ...

His father had been involved in that matter too, back when he'd been a detective. His father had knocked on a teenage

74

Sophie's door, and had taken her out into the woods for the start of a great mystery.

Decades ago, now, when he'd been only a child himself. He had his father's names – both of them. Robert Kelly.

A toxicology screening of the pigs had already been ordered.

If Sophie had taken any substances, illegal or otherwise, this might show it.

A substantial portion of Lethwick's crime – friendly as it was – involved drugs and intoxication, you see.

Sophie would not have been the first person to collapse, if her blood proved it so. If any blood yet survived in these bodies…

Cooper's phone vibrated. JULIA: C – where are you?

Cooper began her examination of the pigs, starting by confirming their identity. She held their ear tags, put on them long ago by some farmer when they were just babies. She looked for parcel labels, finding police evidence numbers on the pig's legs. She copied it all down into her notes. It was not an issue of how the animals had died – their own killers had, of course, paid Cooper for this post-mortem – but one of exhumation, of evidence.

Whatever cells of Sophie, whatever belongings might still linger within her pets, might all be rescued for a graveyard burial, or else burned for ashes in an urn. Most importantly – most unlikely – they might provide evidence about Sophie's death. They might provide an approximate indication of when the old woman had been consumed; perhaps, if they were supremely lucky, they might provide clues as to Sophie's state before consumption. In the entrails they might find missing pieces.

According to the pigs' medical notes at their last check-up

six months ago, they had been reasonably healthy, well cared for, with just a few minor, managed conditions. On paper at least.

But the animals in front of her now – the larger named Alfie, the smaller Henry – were not well. Some scratches were deeper than others, big red lines across their necks, like the scribblings of a child. Some were recent, some older, but the vast majority had been doubtless created only hours before death, the brothers gnawing each other, fighting each other in a frenzy to win their food.

There was more. By the time they'd eaten their owner, the pigs had been hungry, perhaps unfed for days. In a live animal, a vet would give a body condition score – one for too thin, five for too fat. But there was no such score for a corpse.

Cooper could only note the presence or absence of fat. The prominence of the skeleton below.

In animals so large and round, the concept of thinness seemed like a paradox, an impossibility but for tell-tale signs. They had not been well fed, either gradually deprived over the last few months, or experiencing a more rapid withdrawal of food recently. The freshness of many of the cuts, combined with the sediment of earlier battles, suggested some combination of the two theories, a frustration and competition for food that had resurfaced over time but come to its final boiling point that night before.

The pigs' skin had been burned by sunlight for weeks. Red scaled areas ran along their backs, their snouts, their ears. The tips of Alfie's ears were almost black, necrotic tissue that – with time – might have rotted off.

The smaller pig, Henry, was a runt compared to his brother. He was missing his tail. Cooper would return to him later. She'd tear apart the bigger one first.

The flesh was hard, heavy on the table, rigor mortis having

set in hours before. The eyes were vacant, dry. His legs were hard to prise apart, even upside down as Cooper twisted them. Alfie's right fetlock joint was full of fluid. The dead had been on their way to being animals instead of pets. The dead had been on their way to dying.

The impact of the bullet had likely rendered the pig's brain putty. Each elaborate neuron, each behaviour, each memory and feeling of an intelligent animal had melted into a sea of flesh, the shockwave of the gun collapsing all.

Cooper touched the pig's head gently with her right gloved hand. She stood there for a moment, on the cusp of stroking it, but she caught herself, she blinked. She took her scalpel and began to cut along his abdomen.

This was still going to be a holiday, wasn't it?

When this was over, she'd go back to the hotel and she'd see her mother again and everything would be better.

II

When Cooper was a little girl, she'd saved a rabbit from drowning in a pond in her family's back garden. She hadn't even known what she was looking at – had just noticed splashing in the corner of the net – had inadvertently alerted her father, who then rescued it. The little animal – a neighbour's – survived. The owners bought Cooper fizzy drinks, chocolate, sweets to say thank you. Seeing splashing in the corner of her eye, murmuring out loud about how strange that sight was – these coincidences were rewritten as heroism, as if her words had been meant to raise an alarm, as if she'd tried to do anything, anything at all to save its life. Her father had been proud of her, not knowing any of this. It was one of the only clear memories she had of the man.

During veterinary school, Cooper killed eight animals. Two stray cats, a dangerous dog, a calf, two sheep with toxic mastitis, a deer savaged by dogs, and a puppy with cruciate disease, which would have recovered from surgery with eight weeks of rest had the owner agreed to go forward with the procedure.

The less hypothetical her training became, the more detritus Cooper would find. Foxes from exterminations, homeless slaughtered dogs and cats donated by shelters – all these creatures who'd have died anyway – the corpses were delivered for people to learn.

In a cold room, hidden in the bowels of the university for use in practicals and training, species had been piled high, much the same as human doctors had access to medical cadavers. There was rather less ceremony in how they had kept practice corpses there, however. Through the plastic curtains, it had smelled wet. Tubs had contained legs and limbs, all clustered like the spare parts of toys. One day Cooper had gone in there to help prepare for a practical and there'd been a donkey hanging from the ceiling, head-first, its legs splayed in place by metal chains. There had been a red sack over its head, a hood that completely covered its neck and its face, there to catch any stomach contents that might fall out after death. It had looked alive, though she knew it was not.

'Bute it or shoot it,' the joke went, and so many of the students felt like they knew nothing, that they would never be good enough in the face of illness, disease, accidents, cruelty, in the wake of all the world's chaos and confusion.

The students had just wanted to help animals. They'd wanted to do their best.

They'd get a job somewhere, somehow – most drifting into small animal work dealing with dogs and cats and hamsters; a few into exotics and conservation work; and the rest into large animal practice – farm animals, horses – which often had their own equine specialists. The old James Herriot mould of a country practice tackling all species great and small had been dying out for years, now.

There was love in what they did. There was happiness, friendship, accomplishment, goodness. But like all light, it cast shadows.

Cooper had found a job at a mixed practice, for a time, working with both small animals and large.

Those people she had met and trained with were scattered across the country and across the world, often far from those they knew. And all of it, all they'd worked towards their whole lives, would start to end.

They'd find themselves throwing away dreams, which were only dreams so long as they still slept; they'd wake to whispers, memories of the grand, strange reality they'd hoped their lives might be. Each happy moment would delay the inevitable, and having them made it sadder, somehow.

They'd try to do their best. They'd try to save living things. And sometimes they would. Sometimes they would live good lives, in part.

They ended suffering, these people who wanted to help.

Some remained. Some were lost, or became lost, leaving the profession, leaving life as the slow days passed, as they made war against death and cruelty.

Cooper found pigs fairly easy to skin. Most of the flesh peeled off in one go. She worked on the larger pig first, splitting the front legs from the thorax by cutting against the pits with her blade. She then peeled the legs back. They flopped away from the life they had once supported, the pig's corpse splayed like an upturned woodlouse.

She then split the abdominal muscles, starting at his sternum, cutting down to the pubis. She pulled his body open on one side, and, using gentle pressure, shifted the cold intestines out of the way so she could have more space to work.

She stabbed the diaphragm to check for negative pressure, listening for air to enter, which it did – of course, the pigs had been capable of breathing when they'd died. But still she checked. Just in case. She had to use a knife to break through the muscles towards Alfie's ribs, then crunching the bones with bone cutters, the sensation like tree branches.

Now, with the one-year-old's guts, respiratory system and heart all exposed, Cooper prepared to cut his throat.

She ran her knife under the pig's jaw, brought her incision

forward to the mandibular symphysis, pulled the tongue a little out from the body, then cut across the soft palate and hyoid bones, before at last peeling it and all that followed right down to the thoracic inlet – rough, cold, firm, the knife loosening the flesh all around.

Her sister typed a message a few miles away.

JULIA: I know you're reading these.
(JULIA is typing)

Julia typed and typed, and her sister did not see.

A final message was sent as Cooper removed the tongue, trachea, heart and lungs from the body, the unit holding together in a heavy pluck. She lifted it to a different table and returned, almost sweating.

She tied off those loose areas of stomach and intestines that might leak. Already, it seemed like little remained of the old woman within, her meat burned up in the animal's final day. They would have to find what they could.

Cooper heard noises down the hall. The pathologist was laughing with someone. Something in that moment made Cooper look down at the scalpel on the table, at the remnant of blood upon it. She stared at it, almost shaking, but managed to stay still, caught on camera as she was. They sometimes watched these tapes. She kept going, trying to compose herself. It was just a scalpel, no matter what memories might enter her mind.

Cooper pulled away the liver, stomach, spleen, and intestines from the body itself, their combined weight heavier than the other unit. She focused on what she had left. She brought it all to a new table.

In this line of work, all the animals Cooper looked at were victims of humans, whether they'd apparently done something to deserve the harm they received, whether they had caused pain, whether they had been killed in cold blood. Even these pigs, who had just been hungry.

Many of these species would not even exist in their current forms but for the ongoing intervention of the human race; their bodies, their hearts, their minds all bred for a world of factories and farms, for production.

And Cooper now, at the end of that centuries-long process, catalogued their corpses and turned their rebellion into data and forms.

She milked the contents of the stomach into a jug.

She expected, somehow, that she'd see teeth, bone fragments. That there would be pieces of limbs, even facial features, perhaps – that something, anything, would have survived teeth and digestion.

There was hair. Strands of it, tufts, recognisable as Sophie's in their strawberry blonde colour, in consistency.

All else was pink-brown salmon paste, shifting in the miasmic, putrid acid. Not even bone had survived the pigs' stomachs. Unless there were root sheaths with the hair, there would be no DNA, no markers of Sophie's life, no clues as to what had happened to her that final day.

Cooper weighed the stomach contents, trying not to gag.

The first time she had ever seen a human corpse, she'd wanted to vomit at the stench. She'd wanted to run and cower, she'd wanted to numb herself, the dead man's hands hidden behind his back, his skull – robbed of an eyeball – having begun to rot in a flame of bacteria and juices, his stomach continuing on without him. But she had not run. She'd remained, focusing only on the evidence, believing she'd rid herself of all feeling.

As if the silence of her mind had meant she was fine.

She wasn't then. She wasn't now. There was silence and there was silence. No thoughts, but a growing tap, sometimes, deep within her brain, physical, tangible. Almost pain, but not quite. Just a knocking.

The worst thing – the most secret of secrets – was that Cooper could not live life without seeing sights such as these. Without pain, without disgust, without mystery.

That life was not so simple as being fine or not fine.

She tried not to gag. That was all.

She put a jug of Sophie down upon the table.

Cooper would return a while later to look for signs of lesions in the mucosa within the stomachs; she would determine the pigs had likely eaten Sophie Bertilak during the final hours of the night before; she would suggest that the consumption had been opportunistic, the pigs feeding upon a woman who was unwilling or unable to move or defend herself.

Even if DNA analysis was not possible, Sophie's blood had been found in vast quantities around the pig pen, the spatter pattern consistent with the pigs ripping her apart. The human contents, the two jugs containing the old woman's remnants – these were for the pathologist, not Cooper.

'What do they expect me to do? Drink it?'

The pathologist would let out a hollow laugh, then.

It made Cooper blink, a movement that would not stop until she was alone.

12

There were only a few persons of interest.

Whoever had dined with Sophie before her death.

Her adult children, who stood to inherit her estate.

Her estranged partner Thomas – her children's father, whom Sophie had never married.

Whoever had stood in those weird photos – long-limbed in the darkroom light, far away across the fields.

And Sophie herself, who might have harmed herself, whether on purpose or through self-decay of her own mind, her age, her exhaustion catching her at last, collapsing in the presence of those vast beasts.

The murder we face, if we escape all others.

The failure of a person to go on.

After leaving the laboratory room, Cooper walked through a few different hallways in the dark. The lights had all been automatic so far, yet here they did not turn on.

Here, they had only the glow of the street lamps outside.

The thin rain falling against the windows.

How does a person ever know they're being watched?

How does someone know to turn around, to see distant eyes on them, prying, demanding?

Cooper knew to turn her head, to see the EXIT sign at a crossroads.

And there was a man there.

13

He was somehow hobbled in his standing, his face unclear without much light. He was no older than forty, he seemed healthy, but there was something diminished about him, something indefinably wrong, even at first sight.

Everything about his height, his appearance, even his face – it was so humanly, abnormally average it could have been a placeholder body, a stand-in for a billion others.

But for his almost lifeless grey eyes.

Whether this man looked at her or at something else, Cooper could not tell, not until she got closer. She found her own shoes screaming like polystyrene against a floor that was either far too clean or far too sticky. He could not have failed to notice her approach.

By the time she was near him – near enough to see those slow eyes, the ill-fitting fabric of a crisp grey suit – still he had not shifted.

'Is this the way out?' Cooper asked.

He did not speak. He just nodded.

She moved forward towards the door handle, and he did not move out of her way.

She pulled at it, trying to keep her distance from the man, but the door did not open. It was locked, but where the keyhole was, where any electronic control might be – such means were invisible.

'You need a keycard,' the man said, and his voice was much

like his suit, his eyes. There was something unfocused about his pitch, something shambling, the voice not quite sure if it wanted to belong to sounds of highness or the deep. There was something trochaic about his stresses, the first syllable of each beat of his tongue stressed, the second trailing off, so unlike the way other people talked, so unlike what the words themselves encouraged.

'I don't have a card,' Cooper said. 'Obviously.'

'What are you doing in here, then? Who let you in?'

'I'm here for an illegal rave.'

His face did not change. Did not show a response at all, not a smile, not disdain. Just nothing.

She hesitated. 'I was doing the necropsy, obviously.' She paused. 'Sorry, who are you?'

'I asked a question. You haven't answered it.'

'I told you, I was doing a necropsy. I was looking over the bodies of the pigs from Sophie Bertilak's home.'

'The ones that ate her.' He nodded to himself. 'I suppose they were hungry.'

'Do you have a keycard I can use?' Cooper asked. 'It's late, and I'm—'

'You're what? What are you?'

'I'm supposed to meet my mum.'

'I thought you were here to do a necropsy.' He smiled.

Cooper didn't know what to say.

There was something repellent about him – not just the way he spoke, but his very presence, the sum of his manifestation in that hallway. All the details her conscious and unconscious mind sent her were in agreement: leave. Get away. Go.

And so Cooper left, not bothering to turn back around, not bothering to engage with him anymore.

The man watched her as she walked away.

14

Lapis — never 'Detective Sergeant' Lapis, never honoured with his title by his peers but for brief moments in official documentation — was a man who knew he would not be remembered, not much past the death of those who had met him. Already he expected he vanished from people's minds within a few hours of his leaving. There were no invitations to the pub for Lapis. Like his rank, he was forgotten.

And then there was no Lapis. There was no one at all. He was paid by the force, he was talked to, he was given his tasks and duties and he performed them, but even if people used his name, they did not really speak to him, they did not really take notice. He rose through the ranks through the brutality of basic competence, through the tyranny of non-objection. He swam towards power as if the world were a thing to be endured, to be passed through by sheer persistence and movement, a question of when rather than why.

Lapis had no family or friends. Not that people knew of — not, of course, that anyone tried to know him.

If a closer inspection was ever performed, the one inspecting would have learned some details. Lapis been raised by parents who had fed him each day and had let him live in their home, but this was not the same thing as having had a family. And these details stood in a vast sea of more details, of facts and statements and figures with no emotion or inflection, no comment or implication. Lapis had lived and survived until the age of thirty-five. That much was true.

Lapis had one of those faces – hard to remember, hard to note down. He was not a small man, but neither did anyone ever mark him as tall. His hair shifted to become whatever style others had, not of choice, but out of request to the barbers – he didn't know what he wanted to look like, but he didn't want to look out of place.

Lapis was a member of online forums that shared discussions of loneliness.

Lapis had watched live streams of lonely people going into churches, into clubs, into communities. Lapis was pale, pallid, blueish in the dim light of his phone as he lay in bed at night.

Lapis had watched bodies fall before those cameras, throned within the light of his little phone. He had read the manifestos that accompanied such deaths, published on blogs and forums so that others might understand the pain of those who killed.

Lapis had long since realised he would cease to exist one day, that the machinery that operated his body would fail, and by extension so would his mind, and all reality with it.

Lapis realised, sometime later, that he could never die, not really. That some people, even if forgotten, would always live on, because they had never lived.

Lapis was a series of ideas, accumulated across the internet and defined in negative space by his body, by the air and stone in which he walked, descending from other realities in which he might have lived into this one – a virus of anonymous, blurring, shifting hatreds that had no real prejudice or enemy because belief was not the point, conviction was never the engine, but the fight itself, the struggle, the wish to find one's self superior to another, the logic of existential might makes right, the sword's logic, the dream of victory and winning and the renewal of all games, poured into words in sentences, pages in a never-ending book.

Lapis was a series of ideas given shifting flesh to cushion their fall.

They fell with joy, nothing if not playful, elated at their own manifestation in a body that had power. He was a man. He should be proud of that fact, he knew. He laughed. He had been accustomed to such laughter all his life, seeing it in people's faces, even when their lips did not move, even without a single sound.

No one knew his pride. No one saw his smile. No one saw him as more than quiet, functional, compliant.

No one knew he was no longer a human being.

No one knew what staggered within their halls and streets, what sang within his brain, what things he still dreamt of becoming before becoming came to its final end.

The evening after two pigs were shot by a fellow police officer, Lapis stood at the end of the long hallway, and a woman walked away from him.

He watched her. He was smiling, though no one knew it. Though his lips did not change their position, though they did not curl, though his eyes were still the same grey abyss, no crow's feet, no crease, not there … still, he was smiling, in that place he should have had feelings, that quiet place.

There was no sign there of what had once been – if it had ever been – if time and circumstance had stamped out such potential, or if he had been born that way, immune to the minds of others.

In his quiet place, he just smiled in the darkness of that hallway. He could have opened the door if he'd wanted to.

He could have opened it, but what was power without the possibility of punishment?

15

There were markers for various rooms that meant nothing to Cooper. But there was no sign for an exit. The rodent part of her brain screamed at the lack of direction, the curious sense of this place. Something about the building induced a kind of culture shock, the more she walked within its halls. If she could have opened a window and climbed out, she would have, but for that English imperative: to pretend everything was fine, even when you knew it was not. Even when the hairs stood up on the back of your neck, you had to carry on.

She tried to head downward towards the car park, but there were only dead ends. She started having to make educated turns, going round corners blind, intuiting a path where the building's creators had never envisaged such a thing.

She considered going back, retracing her steps towards the pathology lab itself. She heard the footsteps following her, the shuffling staggering gait, pauses in response to her own movements.

She kept going, hurrying her pace until she heard those footsteps no more. She turned corner after corner and finally, no longer choosing a direction at all, her surrender to the space led to the logic of the exit, the lobby, its plant life, its own ecology and ranks and rules, and...

And the man from the hallway – the man who'd refused to help her, who'd questioned her so rudely – he now stood at the exit itself, waiting for her like a groom in a church.

'Why are you still wandering around without ID?' he asked, his words falling like sweat. 'Who are you, really?'

She moved to go past the man – she'd had enough, she wanted to go back to her holiday, she wanted to return to that hotel, she even welcomed the thought of family for a few brief moments, but he moved to block her way once more as she did so.

When she twisted to go around him, he grabbed her arm by the bicep, holding it as she tried to shake loose, and when she tried staggering away, when she tried shoving at him with all her bodyweight, through all this she did not cry out or try to talk to him. She did not feel she should have to justify leaving work. She should not have to justify who she was, not to a man like this.

He showed her his police identification, wordlessly, the photo a stand-in for all the ideas that now swarmed within his mind. He still held her by her upper arm, loosely now, but inescapably.

He made no movement to let her go. He just stared, as a cat stares at a bird, as a bird freezes, not sure when or whether to take flight.

'I'm your colleague,' Cooper spat. 'If you just let me—'

'If you were working for me,' he said, 'I imagine you'd have been more respectful.'

'I'm not working for you, you prick – I'm working for—'

'What's going on here, Lapis?'

Both detective and vet turned their head at the sound of the small voice. It was the pathologist, his gloves and hands still wet with blood. The commotion had brought him out of his studies.

So Cooper learned her captor's name.

The pathologist went on: 'What did she do?'

Lapis considered this. 'You know her?'

'Vaguely. She did the necropsy on the pigs. What did she do?'

His question was gentler this time. Cooper's whole body shook, all she could feel was her anger. She didn't know how she must look. She didn't know what this man was seeing.

Lapis paused, and smiled, and looked at the pathologist's gloves in a very deliberate manner. Still, he did not release his grip.

'Caught red-handed.' The pathologist did not seem to understand these words, so Lapis went on, pointing at the man's gloves. 'The blood.'

Cooper tried to break free once more. His grip withdrew at the same moment.

'Are you OK?' the pathologist asked her, frowning, much in the way someone would ask this question of a drunkard or a beggar.

'Your mum is waiting,' Lapis added. 'Isn't she? You can go.'

She did not answer. She did not look back at them. She stammered through the front doors, and left into what rain still fell.

Lapis held his hand loosely where he had gripped Cooper. He did not close the hand, keeping it in the rough conformation of his hold, feeling it as one would feel a phantom limb.

16

Cooper could still feel the fingers on her upper arm. It was like the sensation of a fly touching the skin, or a wasp or a spider, noticed with an excessive chill before being flicked away.

She left. He did not appear to be following her.

She hurried across a footbridge into town, the wind and rain having calmed a little. The river ran fast through Lethwick, sandbags piled against the entryways of every shop and home nearby, the old grey brick buildings with their old grey chimneys. Plastic bags and bottles were caught against rocks below, against cold blue flowers. They all shook, as if dancing.

There was a poster for the midsummer festival.

THE MYSTERY OF LIFE AND DEATH.

Cooper's visit would miss it by a matter of days.

What a shame.

The forecast had grown steadily grimmer throughout the week, knocking out power and flooding already stricken cities and towns. Lethwick itself had already been hit just months before. Even London might drown.

Her phone was on 25 per cent battery. Drained by the weight of incessant messages.

JULIA: You know what, C? Fuck you. You really can't even stop this petty bullshit and make just a single weekend not about you. If you want to act like a baby and leave me on 'seen' go right ahead. When you're ready to grow up and actually have a conversation like an adult then I'll talk to you.

JULIA: I mean, Jesus Christ – we came here for you. This was all for you.

'Cooper? Are you OK?'

She heard a familiar voice.

How long had she been standing there? Cooper felt like she'd lost time, like she'd skipped a beat.

She looked up from the phone, almost at the end of the bridge.

The sky seemed different. Darker.

A few feet away stood the woman from last night, her hotel friend – freckled, light chestnut hair – now wearing a blue nurse's uniform, a nametag pinned to her front. Alex, who'd put up with Cooper's silly, drunken questions, who Cooper in turn had tried to be kind to.

Alex held a polka dot umbrella over her head. Heavier rain had returned, somehow, though Cooper couldn't remember when. The last few moments felt foggy, faint. Cooper remembered looking at her phone, but that was it.

'Are you OK?' Alex repeated.

Cooper laughed nervously. 'Why wouldn't I be OK? I'm A-OK…'

'I'm sorry. I didn't mean anything. You just look—' Alex began, and Cooper interrupted.

'Look what?' Cooper asked.

Alex tried to smile, shaking her head.

Cooper's face was wet, her coat starting to let water through.

Even with her hood up, her short dark hair had clumped, her fringe like a drowned rat.

'Nothing,' Alex said, and Cooper didn't know what the woman was saying 'nothing' to, she didn't know if she'd missed some conversation. Her head still felt light, a little dizzy. 'Want to grab a cup of tea?' Alex asked.

It rained and rained.

They left together, heading to a bar instead.

It was called Carcosa.

Carcosa was high-ceilinged, almost vaulted, its black, marble tables raised enough that stools were required for sitting. Red velvet curtains hung in each window. Around the dark blue walls, decorated in mirrors and black fractal patterns, there were occasional lights, all dimmed.

Beyond this, the yellow-trimmed bar was empty. No bar-tender. No staff. No one. Not even empty plates upon the empty tables.

'The door – it was open, wasn't it?' Cooper asked.

'How else would we have gotten inside?' Alex shrugged. 'Here's something you'll like ...'

'What?'

'This place was a famous person's favourite bar.'

'Whose?'

'You'll see,' she winked. 'Just ask the waiters. Whenever they show up. See, I pick the best places.'

Cooper followed her to the table.

They sat down, waiting for someone to come back. They looked at menus, lists of extravagant cocktails. They had the awkwardness of two fragile and tentative people, with only the seeds of a bond made the night before. They didn't feel ready to talk until the order was made, until their presence here was formalised.

'I'll be back in a minute,' Cooper said, heading to the bathroom, trying to waste some time, supposing she might be able to pee.

It, too, was a grand room like the main hall, its walls marbled.

Cooper went to a cubicle and pulled up her dating app.

On Cooper's profile, she'd already had a few hits. A few local men, a few holidaymakers, messaging her out of the blue.

Her profile photo, though ... It looked nothing like Cooper.

It looked nothing like her because it wasn't her.

This account, it wasn't even in her name.

She put her phone back in her pocket and flushed the toilet.

There were high-quality thick paper towels in a silver box by the mirror, and a variety of ointments and skin care products all around. Cooper's hands were red and dry after the day's repeated washing, trying to get the stink of pig and stomach that seeped through even her surgical gloves off her skin. She used some Rosemary Leaf and Cedar handcream on them after washing once more. It stung for a moment, then soothed. She rubbed it in, looking in the mirror as she did so. Her hair was still wet. She grabbed at some towels and tried to wring out what she could.

When she returned to her table, there was still no sign of any staff member or any soul but Alex.

But there were now two wine glasses there, nonetheless, and a bottle beside them. Someone had apparently come out, served Alex, then returned to the recesses of the yellow-trimmed bar.

'That's trusting,' Cooper said, but Alex seemed puzzled. 'I mean, we could just serve ourselves, leave without paying...'

Alex scoffed. 'I wouldn't do that,' she said.

'I'm not saying we'd actually do it, I'm just saying we could...'

Alex shrugged. 'I wouldn't do that,' she repeated. 'Do you think I'm the kind of person who would?'

Cooper rolled her eyes and picked up her wine glass.

They both drank.

'I used to shoplift,' Cooper said suddenly. Impulsively. 'Just a few times. When I was a teenager. Stopped before I went to university. Mostly books. And stuff.'

They kept drinking. The rain kept falling outside.

No one else joined them. It was as if it had been made for them, for this moment, this building, these drinks within. Cooper felt she couldn't leave, even if she'd wanted to. She put her glass down.

'I didn't think my book theft would be so shocking…'

She tried to look past Alex through the glass, in case someone was watching them. But if they were, Cooper couldn't see.

'This isn't fair,' Alex said suddenly, her face pale. 'I need you to know.'

It was then that Alex admitted it all.

It was then that she told the truth.

17

It was Alex. She was the reason why Cooper had been called in to help with the post-mortem, how the police had known she was here.

'I saw my ex. He told me about the case … I told him about you …'

Alex looked down at her wine. Still, they were alone in vaulted Carcosa, the red curtains in the windows shifting gently from some hidden draught. Outside, the rain went on and on, inaudible past the glass.

'I'm sorry,' Alex went on. 'I should have asked you first.' Cooper tried to smile, though it was just to put Alex at ease.

'Your ex – is he older?'

Alex nodded.

'He's not …' Cooper grimaced. 'It's not Kelly, is it?'

Alex laughed, surprised. 'What? Ew. No, no – my ex is just a sergeant. Not so old, either.'

'And he's not Lapis?'

Alex shook her head. She'd never heard of a DS Lapis.

'Are we OK?' Alex went on, and Cooper had to decide. She had to decide whether to pretend, whether to let it go, whether to challenge or trust or mistrust.

There was something sweet about Alex's nerves. Something that made Cooper feel lighter, the more she saw the flickers in the nurse's eyes, the twitch of her expression.

'It's fine, really,' Cooper decided. 'I'm glad I could help. A-OK, really ...'

Alex asked for a crime story.

Cooper told her. She found herself doing as she was told more and more these days. There was a kind of comfort in being led. In giving up.

Cooper told Alex about the pigs, about their poor state.

Cooper told her things she shouldn't have.

Their personal lives came up, every now and then.

'Charlemagne and Cookie,' Cooper said.

Alex snorted, her face lighting up. 'WHAT?'

Cooper grinned. 'Don't ask. They were just—'

'They're the best cat names I've ever heard.' Then, anxious: 'I'm sorry, I didn't mean to laugh at them.'

Cooper couldn't be bothered to fight against it, not today. This incessant need to apologise for anything and everything ...

Outside, the rain now fell so thickly it was hard to see. The sun had almost set.

'Why did your ex get to keep the cats?' Alex asked.

'I was the one who left. Why shouldn't he keep them? I wasn't going to leave him on his own. I travelled for work, anyway, or I was going to. How could I even look after them? They were jellicle boys ...' Cooper smiled, shook her head, and turned to the bar. 'I want a cocktail, I think. Where did the guy go?'

'It was a woman. She'll be back, I guess.' She got her card out. 'I'll pay. Don't worry.'

'It's my turn ...'

'It's on me,' Alex insisted.

'I thought you were short?'

'I'm doing fine. I'm not short. Just let me – let me treat you. It's my turn to treat you. Don't worry.'

Alex left her card out.

'Cookie loved treats,' Cooper said, feeling that strange friction it was often simply best to ignore. 'He was pretty food motivated… How about you, anyway? You have any pets?'

'No,' Alex said. 'But I had plants.'

'Had?'

'They all died,' Alex said, her lip twisting. 'Could have been a case for you, right there.' She hesitated. 'I'm sorry if I snapped at you before. It's my treat, like I said.'

They talked a little more before it grew dark outside. About their mothers and fathers.

The sky crackled. 'Share a cab?' Alex asked, starting to get up.

'What? Where?'

'The hotel,' she said, and it took Cooper a few moments to remember they were staying at the same place.

'Sure.' Cooper paused. 'You said this place was a famous person's favourite bar. Who did you mean?'

Alex tilted her head. 'Sophia Bertilak. She used to come here.'

A few minutes later, as they stood outside under Alex's umbrella, Cooper changed her mind. 'I think I left something at the lab…'

She lied. She said goodbye and walked in that direction, but she'd lied nonetheless.

The thought of going back – the thought of what waited for her this weekend – Cooper wasn't ready, not yet. And the more she'd related the story of the old woman, of the pigs, the more it felt unfinished.

Everything in her analysis of the old woman's death suggested a lack of foul play. Starving pigs kept by someone who couldn't take care of herself, who then collapsed in their presence.

But then, photos had been taken from their frames in Sophie's house. It was not a great stretch to imagine they'd been of loved ones.

Had Sophie done that herself? Had she decided to rid her home of reminders of her own flesh and blood? Perhaps it was just more evidence for the theory of a collapsing mental state, of a ruined personality on the edge of self-destruction.

Perhaps.

Cooper should have gone to the scene already, she knew. She should have gone and seen it for herself as the essential context it was. Fuck what Kelly had said. Fuck being called in for brief help, when Cooper knew she could do so much more.

She thought of how Lapis had gripped her arm. How he'd said she should be respectful. She thought of the smell of his lactic breath.

She shuddered, thinking of it, thinking of him.

Then she tried to make herself stop moving. She stopped moving. She stopped her shiver.

Then she called for a taxi.

She read as she waited – about the case, about Scotland Yard...

18

Scotland Yard, the FBI, and a legion of true crime enthusiasts had all attempted to find the face in Sophie Bertilak's infamous photograph of the pipe all those decades before. Captured accidentally by a seventeen-year-old girl on her birthday, it was one of those mysteries that had caught the popular imagination, a ghost, a cryptid with no name, no history. The appeal had been less in justice and more in a kind of horrific, tantalising unsolvability. In a feeling it invoked.

Cooper saw it again and again, on all these sites ...

Up at the lens, half a face peered from under the earth, alive. Its skin pallid, chapped, smeared with dust and soil. What hair could be seen, long and wet and dark in the black and white. Hints of fingers in the corner of the plastic, whether to scrape above, whether to attract attention for help, whether to try to touch the girl above, no one knew. Its mouth, silent, afraid, quivering.

A child had sat beneath the world.

Decades had passed.

There had been parallels in other cases, before and since.

People had been buried alive as long as there had been people.

The first murder we know about: 430,000 years ago.

A victim, hit twice on the head.

Thrown into a cave beneath the soil.

Twenty-six other victims followed. It was like a chain letter. It went on and on, added to by different faces, different hands.

★

In the latter half of the twentieth century, there seemed to have been an innovation in kidnapping. Victims began to be captured under the earth, pipes and pumps carefully set up to provide air to try and keep them alive. Often those doing the burial dressed as police officers. Almost always, they demanded money from the relatives of the missing. Geometrical shapes were arranged to contain living flesh and screams, and sometimes reading material and food. The wooden crates lay beneath the soil.

One occurred in 1968, a few years after Sophie had taken her first photos. The burial happened in America. A college student – Barbara Mackle – was abducted by a fake police officer and his girlfriend. Barbara was placed within a tomb made of fibreglass. She was drugged with water that was not water. What air she had was pumped from the world above. Her kidnappers tried to claim half a million dollars for her safe return. She was there for three days, screaming, dreaming of the Christmas soon to come. One of her abductors – the woman – would be deported after a short prison sentence. The other – the man – would, after a little incarceration, eventually be given a pardon to attend medical school, before eventually being arrested again with a boatful of cocaine.

In 1976, twenty-six children were taken from a bus, led down a ladder into a box, a truck trailer buried within a quarry in California, ventilated with fans. After hours in the ground, dust falling from above, the children piled their mattresses up and escaped through a manhole cover.

In 1981, a ten-year-old girl in West Germany was kidnapped while on her bicycle in another attempted ransom. Ursula Hermann died shortly after being put in her box, a failure of the ventilation. A man would admit to concocting the whole scheme, although he took back this claim soon after, and he died before he could be arrested.

In 1982, a twenty-year-old was placed beneath tyres in an old oil field, given bread and a bottle. He was only found after his kidnapper convinced himself he'd face a murder charge instead of abduction. The box had begun to give way around Michael Baucom. Nails and ants had begun to rip into his skin. He had seen other things, astonishing things that had not been there.

In 1987, a forty-year-old businessman in Illinois was buried with a million-dollar ransom demand. He had been taken by another false police officer. The pipe had been too long for much air to reach Stephen Small. Decades later, the governor of Illinois would commute all death row sentences, including that of the man who had killed Stephen. The governor of Illinois had been Stephen's neighbour.

In 1993, a clothing manufacturer was buried in a pit, covered with a giant lid, given scraps of food as his family gradually paid for his release. After one of the money pick-ups, the kidnapper was trailed, and eventually led the police to the burial. The victim – a man named Harvey Weinstein, completely unrelated to the infamous film producer – cried upon his release, asking the police for a cigarette.

For the burial in Sophie's woods, there was no name, no known victim, no sex or age or identifying feature at all beyond that emotion in their face, that terror. There was no blackmail, no ransom, no story of men being forgiven for their violence, no elaborate machine.

There had never been anything but a picture.

It was called taphophobia – a fear of being buried alive. People were so afraid of it, a new invention came into the world – 'A device for indicating life in buried persons', created in 1882, complete with a pipe to breathe through and a bell to ring if you found yourself in purgatory. In 1885, the pipe was improved to feature a clockwork fan to drag air down beneath the soil. No one was ever known to have been saved in this way, as if to die was just to make a mistake, to have been the victim of some mechanical misunderstanding. The coffin's design, built from fear, became an engine of torture.

Internet pages about the Lethwick Pipe Mystery often connected these other cases and precedents. The police officers who had investigated it were sometimes mentioned, but mostly as incidental to the event itself. It was not as if they'd discovered anything. Of the two detectives who attended the crime scene, the original Kelly was still alive – likely the father Cooper's own Kelly had mentioned, his predecessor in this police force. Small towns were full of hereditary coincidences of this nature, but how small was this place, really, with all its tourists? With all its money?

The other police officer who'd come to young Sophie's home – a thin-faced, lanky sort of man named Reggie Barker – had died a few months later.

His obituary noted he had not been on active duty at the time of his death. Suspended with pay, pending the outcome of some investigation.

He'd drowned in the river, near a Bridge of Sighs named after its twins in Venice and Cambridge.

He'd had a lifelong struggle with alcohol.

It was not that uncommon in his profession, after all.

Of all the true crime posts Cooper saw about this case, she was surprised this element was not discussed more. An investigator dying shortly after a case seemed bait enough for a post or two looking into it, surely?

But no.
She couldn't post it herself.
It wouldn't be professional.

19

Cooper read on her phone as she waited in the rain for her cab. She continued on as they drove in the dark, in the thick rain and wind, the radio droning on.

'—urged to stay indoors, securing loose—'

She found some posts that were critical of Sophie herself.

She grimaced at one in particular, tapping 'report' above the message. Some anonymous neck beard, some man who hated women...

> Sophie Bertilak was a whore who fucked her way to money, didn't give a shit about the bastards she raised, she just spread her legs and used her face instead of talent.

Eventually they passed up to a blind summit.

The cab driver talked about his life, how it had been falling apart in recent days. He'd been finding it harder to make a living, now that everyone in his trade had been replaced by phone apps. His children no longer spoke to him. They used to come and stay with him for midsummer. Once, he was even in one of the Lethwick summer mystery plays – he played Joseph, leading a donkey. He played the cuckold stepfather of Christ.

They headed towards the valley. Cooper shut her eyes eventually. The house was twenty minutes' drive, or had been in daylight, at least.

'I can't live without them,' the cab driver said, his voice faint, distant. It was like paralysis, listening to him speak about his divorce. 'I can't…'

'Elizabeth downgraded to a category one,' the radio said.

'Someone once tried to tip me so I wouldn't talk to them,' the driver went on. 'It was a four-hour journey.'

Cooper didn't open her eyes.

'I'm talking to you. At least you could have the decency to listen. I'm a person.'

The driver continued.

'It's forgotten.' He never finished the sentiment – it wasn't clear what exactly was forgotten. His passenger drifted off into unconsciousness.

He talked about how he hadn't seen any animals, not down there, not as he'd driven past. How everyone was talking about it, the woman and her pigs.

There had been no animals, not that he could see.

But he supposed people were animals too.

The world grew black.

APPLE LANE SURGERY

Patient First Name: Sophie
Patient Last Name: Bertilak
DOB: 18/06/1947
Sex: Female

<u>Allergies</u>
Cats

<u>Current Medication</u>
Repeat prescriptions:

Aspirin
Methotrexate
Sertraline
Quetiapine

<u>Long-term conditions</u>
Rheumatoid arthritis
Tinnitus
Depression

<u>Notes:</u>
Pharmacy notes prescriptions not picked up for last two months.
Refer to mental health crisis team for welfare check.

20

In the darkroom, in the red light, images of a distant man with long limbs turned across the field.

The driver woke Cooper from her sleep. His voice was gentler. She gasped, pulled her coat on, and stumbled out of the cab towards the crime scene. It was now night. She pushed the slurred, half-dreamed memories of the police video from her mind. She was going to see the real thing in just a few moments. She was going to Sophie's house.

She wondered if anyone would smell alcohol on her breath.

No police officers were there to meet her outside Sophie Bertilak's home, their single remaining, lightless patrol car discarded a little along the mud.

The cab driver hesitated, looking around.

There were only the distant fires of lodges, the nearer lights of the dead photographer's blue-doored home.

The storm had arrived. The dark was here. What possible purpose could this woman still have? That was what the driver must have wondered.

She told the driver he could leave her.

'But you're alone.' He kept the engine running.

'I am.'

He hesitated a moment longer.

'It's fine, really. I've got work to do.' She paused. 'I'm sorry I didn't talk to you. I was just...'

He cut her off, wishing her goodnight. He departed.

The wind and rain took whatever words remained.

Cooper stepped toward the paddock, the blue-white police tape dancing in its ecstasy, cut loose and uplifted by the storm. The scene was no longer protected. The official analysis was over. She'd come too late to catch any sequel.

She could already sense the way this would go, having read through the case notes so far.

There was the matter of Sophie Bertilak's uncollected prescriptions, versus the number of pills found in her home – she hadn't taken her anti-depressants in weeks. And quetiapine – sometimes used for sleeping, sometimes an anti-psychotic ... Why had she been prescribed it? Why was so much found in her home?

What evidence of malice was there here?

Was it this simple? Had the door been left open carelessly?

Was it the collapse of an old, unwell woman?

Was it a case of suicide?

The mental health team had never phoned Sophie after concerns had been raised.

Cooper didn't know why. Or indeed, who had raised the concerns ...

The brown soil was dark, wet. Smoke drifted from the chimney of the main house. There were lights on within, though the place was surrounded by police tape. When she knocked, no one answered.

There was a slight crunching of gravel, somewhere beyond. The rain was beginning to come down faster.

Around the field were holiday lodges, some with their lights on. Cooper had read about them in a now half-broken website

– someone, presumably Sophie Bertilak's mother, had rented them out in years prior.

But for these lights, she was alone.

21

Cooper examined the length of the fence around the apple tree, her torch in her plastic-gloved left hand. The exterior wood was white, the posts were black – immaculately so. They had been painted very recently – weeks ago, perhaps.

There were no signs of chipping on the outside, or of struggle. The fences were lined with metal sheeting within – it had to be so, considering the size and power of the animals that had once lived here.

The wind howled around Cooper's head, the branches of the apple tree shaking, their eighty years almost at an end.

She opened the gate.

Maybe things could have been different.

Cooper's boots immediately sank in the dark mud, the soil having been thoroughly picked clean by the pigs, no doubt searching for grubs, insects and truffles. Turning back, she looked at the fence from within.

There were dents everywhere in the metal. The pigs had thrown themselves against it, again and again.

Rain thundered through her phone's torch beam. She kept sinking in the sludge, each step more difficult than the last.

That fruit still hung from the apple tree's branches was a miracle. Around its base, some bark had been removed by pig mouths, but not much. The wind screamed at Cooper's ears.

The world grew blacker closer to the tree, though Cooper's

phone light still shone. Her foot caught on a root and she slipped, her phone falling into the slurry; her raincoat, her trousers, her face splattered as she hit the surface.

She turned, gasping, and only the light of the lodges reached her now, like distant stars.

The house itself, lit up when Cooper had arrived, had gone dark.

Another power cut, maybe? Or else someone was inside after all, and had switched them off. She imagined it – a spider-like figure, as with Sophie's photos, stalking the halls...

Cooper pulled herself up, her hood fallen back, the rain hitting her head like tapping fingers, her hands repeatedly dragged beneath the sludge by force of gravity.

Her face twisting, she grabbed out at where her phone had fallen. By some miracle, through the mud and the rain, she found it.

She took images. She could barely see what she photographed. She aimed it at the fences, at the tree, at the ground all around.

She checked the images on the little screen, white light blaring at each captured object.

The dented metal.

Etchings? No, initials on the tree... S-T...

A couple of plastic bags pointing out of puddles.

The house itself, lightless in the storm.

The grass beyond.

A figure standing around twenty feet away from the paddock, turned right towards her by the back door of the home.

Dressed in black clothing – barely distinguishable from the night itself.

It caught in the light. It turned towards her.

Cooper spun around in its direction, her body tensing. She shone the light, but there was nothing.

She took more photos, hoping they might show her more.
But nothing.
Nothing else showed that silhouette.
Nothing proved anyone had ever been there at all.
All around, all alone.

22

Cooper imagined another universe, where she had turned up to her family gathering like this, covered in the mud of a crime scene. Dripping it all over the carpets of her mother's hotel room.

After Cooper's dad had died, they'd moved around a lot, and after the daughters left, the moving continued, accelerated even. This would have been their first meeting in years. *Would*, Cooper thought, as she walked. *Would* – why had she used that word, even in her own mind? The reunion had not been cancelled. It was just de-facto delayed, courtesy of this night-time expedition.

No – it will be their first meeting in years. She was going to go back to them. She'd have a great time.

Cooper went to the back of Sophie's house, right up to the spot where she thought she'd seen a man. There was nothing but broken police tape, curling round a half-open, rattling door. Her torch showed where it led. Steps, leading down beneath the structure. A basement with no connection to the main hallways.

Was it a shelter? A basement extension? A way to hide from war and Nazis, or maybe it was for atomic bombs? Cooper's mother had traumatised her with *Where The Wind Blows* when she was younger, a seeming children's cartoon film with a similar aesthetic to *The Snowman*. It was about an old couple trying to follow absurdly inadequate instructions in the face of nuclear annihilation.

Cooper went down into the tunnel, walking along two sets of stairs until she reached the pit.

It was cold down there.

It was full of eyes.

23

Her torch light reflected in their whites – fourteen eyeballs, their irises at various heights, bearing various colours.

Their arms, up in the air, reaching.

None of them moved.

Cooper's hand shook as she examined one of them more closely.

Her first impulse had been to run.

Her second, to know.

She was glad she had not fled.

These eyes, these arms – they did not belong to the living. They had never belonged to the living.

Her torch light shone upon the first of the men.

A sculpted, wire model of a man with long limbs, placed as if posing for a photograph.

Other wire models, some without clothes, danced all around, frozen in half a dozen poses in the dark. Reaching, glinting, swarming.

Cooper knew, looking at these artificial people.

The developing prints in Sophie's darkroom … the man with long limbs, staring across a field, the enemy who had already infected Cooper's dreams.

It was just a model.

It was just made up.

24

Cooper returned to the open night sky. She wiped the rain from her forehead, her cheeks, her nose, but it was only temporary – it all grew wet again as soon as she was back outside.

She had a brief sensation of being watched, but again, her phone's light showed nothing.

What was happening to her?

She walked on, numb, remembering.

The wind shook the long grass of the long fields, Cooper's boots still clotted with mud. The rain was helping to clean her, even so. It kept throwing back her hood, kept spitting on her face, kept trying to get behind her eyes.

People were still awake.

If those buildings in the night were indeed holiday homes, then perhaps police officers might be there. Perhaps they were talking to the residents. Perhaps she could talk to them, too.

She thought of what she'd say as she grew closer, as she approached the glass and its rain.

Have you seen any police officers?

One lodge was too full, or it seemed that way from the illuminated window. Luggage was spread out within, barely unpacked, toiletries and a few items of clothing spilling out across the chairs. Cooper could see no one inside.

Did the police speak to you? Can I use your phone?

What else might she ask?

A voice called out to Cooper in the night.

'Who are you?'

Cooper turned.

A woman sat beneath the porch of the third lodge, a grey hoodie emerging from beneath her black leather jacket and closing round her face. She held a cigarette and a lighter in her hand, competing with the wind.

Cooper threw the same question back.

'Are you here to see the police?' the stranger asked, her voice rich, cool.

Cooper nodded. She took a few steps closer. She had no idea if the stranger could see her well enough in all this dark and rain to know she'd nodded.

'You'll have to wait your turn.' The stranger hesitated. 'Want one?'

'What?'

'A cigarette. You want one.'

The woman's hair had been dyed blue, the colour of eyes, of imagined lakes and distant seas.

In the porch light, the expression on the woman's face was stale, almost devoid of feeling. Cooper kept catching these moments of half-death in strangers, which vanished almost as soon as they were noticed. After all, Cooper smiled just as quickly, though it was brief.

The blue-haired woman seemed a few years younger than Cooper, but by how much, it was hard to say. Mid-twenties, maybe. Her voice was rich, a little deeper than Cooper would have imagined. Words like crackling, even sultry, might have applied, if there had been some other context for their meeting. But here, in this dark, in this rain, in this lonely valley of the dead, the woman's words just seemed broken.

This woman – she held out a cigarette.

Cooper sat down next to her. She took it and leant for the flame in the stranger's hand.

'Are you a detective?'

'I – I just came from the vet lab. I'm here to talk to the inspector, if he's here.'

The other woman let out a puff of smoke, pursing her lips as if trying to create some kind of ring in the air, but failing. 'Can you believe I've been here for hours now?'

Cooper didn't say anything, and the woman smiled again, as if Cooper had made some joke.

'I was thinking of exploring. Did you know I used to be afraid of it? Those trees. That forest,' she gestured to the woods. 'Silly to think, now.' She paused, the smile fading. 'The man you're looking for – he's inside. He's talking to my brother.'

The main house was invisible. It might as well have been a million miles away, the field was so dark. The rain seemed to slow.

The stranger didn't speak again for a long time. When she did, her voice was slightly softer, harder to hear in the downpour.

Her name was Lucy.

25

'She had two daughters. She had me,' Matthew told the police officers. The photographer's son sat in the lodge, a thick black jacket still on. College cufflinks poked up from the sleeves of his white shirt below. His hair – dark blond, greying at the temples. He looked quite unlike his siblings. 'No other relatives,' he added. 'Her move here, it was not perspicacious.'

'I don't see why she moved back out there.' Joanna paused. She had talked to the police on the phone, hours before. She was still based in San Francisco. 'Why she came back to live in that house, I don't know. She'd seen the world. We had money. This wasn't – this wasn't a happy place for her, she didn't need to ...'

'Did you know my mother had two sons?' Lucy asked, still sitting next to Cooper outside. Both of their cigarettes had faded. The wind was quieter now. They wondered if it had begun to pass. 'One died before I was even born.'

Lucy wiped her eye clean of sleep.

'A road accident. Matthew was twelve at the time. Joanna ten.'

She explained that they'd come back to this place – their grandmother's home, now their mother's final dwelling – to talk with the police and to arrange the funeral. They couldn't stay in the main building itself until the investigation allowed them. The lodges, though, they were free. They were just lying here, holiday homes without holidays – places converted years ago by their grandmother for hiring out after Sophie's photographic windfall. She laughed when Cooper asked about tourists, and her laugh was like her voice – rich, dark, like fire.

'Did you have anyone die, when you were young?'

Cooper did not answer, but for a shake of a head, but for a lie. Lucy went on.

The lodge business had died with their grandmother, of course. And as for all the lights in the main house and other lodges – it was her brother's fault. Matthew had arrived first, getting the train in from Cambridge. He must have wandered around, must have forgotten to switch them off, or else it was just the police before him, she didn't know. Lucy would sort it before they slept. And she kind of liked how it looked anyway, all that electricity, even if it was a waste.

The siblings intended to be here for a few days, and then they'd go back home, not seeing each other until the next birthday, the next death. Lucy hesitated for a moment, looking up as the rain began to slow.

'There isn't anything to bury, is there?'

Cooper said nothing.

Eventually, Lucy let out a breath, as if making some decision, or perhaps it was just a letting go of tension. It felt tired, that sound.

She pulled back her hood and scratched her neck, letting her blue hair fall.

It began to catch rain drops.

They waited, almost leaning against each other, separated only by inches.

26

DCI Kelly emerged from the lodge, Lucy's brother Matthew beside him.

DCI Kelly was looking forward to going home. He was looking forward to the warmth of his car, his house, his dog. He was looking forward to the end of a long day.

He looked forward – and saw Cooper, her short dark hair soaked, her clothes dripping in the storm.

'What...' Kelly scowled. 'What are you doing here?'

'Thought I'd go for a country walk...'

'Inside,' he said.

And he led the vet inside, leaving the Bertilak siblings out in the rain.

He led her inside, where DS Lapis was helping him with his notes...

Cooper assaulted Kelly with facts and usefulness, hoping he'd let the issue go. Hoping he wouldn't say anything about the wine on her breath. Hoping he wouldn't push too much more on that most obvious of questions: why was she here, when she was supposed to be on holiday? Why was she here, when she'd only been hired for a post-mortem of pigs?

All the while Cooper wondered if Lapis would say something, anything; she wondered briefly why he was here, as if the vet lab had been another universe rather than a place she'd left hours before, a location only twenty minutes from this one.

The officer just kept writing his notes as if he'd never met her, as if she meant nothing to him.

She couldn't bring it up – she wouldn't – his bizarre questioning of her at the lab. He'd excuse it all as a misunderstanding, the police would close ranks around one another, and Kelly would have one more reason to doubt her presence. No – Lapis was being quiet, he was being well behaved. Cooper half started to believe she'd imagined the whole affair, that once more she'd taken things too seriously. She tried not to look at him. She tried to stick to her expertise.

'The animals were emaciated – badly kept, without much of a shelter from the sun,' Cooper said. 'In the absence of any other information, either Ms Bertilak wasn't able to keep her animals anymore, or didn't want to.'

'Which means?' Kelly asked.

'If she were alive, there'd have been grounds to seize these animals from her, possibly for a criminal prosecution.'

He sighed, shaking his head. The lodge was dusty, its furniture rusty, decades old. On the table between them sat a laptop and a tape recorder. In the corner, on a stool, Lapis went through his documents, silent but for the flicker of paper. It was as if he wasn't even there.

'Sophie Bertilak was alone towards the end of her life,' Kelly said. 'She ...'

He hesitated, seemingly distracted. He scratched at a blinking eye, and it stopped blinking.

There was a sadness to him, but it was gone as soon as it had arrived.

'There's some evidence we're still going to look into,' he went on. 'Some items missing in the house, the presence of a few sets of fingerprints and blood—'

'Blood?'

'Old, though,' he said. 'Not recent.'

They talked for a while longer, moving on to more mundane details. Cooper suggested that if she could help in any other way, Kelly should not hesitate to let her know.

But he made his expectations clear.

This was a human investigation. Cooper's role was over.

It was the victim's daughter who brought their conversation to its final end, knocking on the lodge's door.

Lucy stood there, the rain now falling faster behind her. She was beautiful in the light, Cooper thought. Sharp cheekbones, an old scar on her lip long-healed, not noticeable before. A childhood accident, maybe. It curled with the rest of Lucy's lip as she smiled, though hers was a grim, mechanical motion. It was politeness.

Lucy wanted to know what was going on.

When it became clear Kelly wasn't going to share anything, Lucy asked if they could call it a night.

'Of course,' Kelly said. 'We were just finishing anyway.' He lingered for a little while as Lapis collected their things. 'How are you getting back?'

At this, Lapis finally spoke.

'I don't mind driving her.'

27

'We go way back. Met at the pathology lab,' Lapis confirmed, and Cooper said nothing. 'I'll drive her.'

She didn't move to go.

She didn't know what to say or do. She'd decided to keep quiet about his behaviour after all, hadn't she? She felt as if a trap had closed around her. If she raised it now, she knew she would become a 'problem', someone to be kept even further out of the loop, and Lapis would win, whatever winning meant for a man like that.

Lucy stepped forward. 'We'll drive her back.' Her voice was pleasant but firm.

'I assure you,' Kelly said. 'She'll be perfectly safe with a police officer.'

'I know,' Lucy continued, 'but it's just she's agreed to stay for dinner.'

The police officers left a short time later.

Cooper could tell Kelly disapproved. She couldn't determine anything about Lapis's response. He'd just shrugged, and had left into the darkness.

'I don't like him,' Lucy said when they were gone. 'I don't like either of them.'

Cooper laughed with relief, then stopped almost immediately, her face growing red. 'I'm sorry, it's not appropriate for me to—'

'No, no,' Lucy said. 'It's fine. I agree. It's laughable. The whole

institution of the police ... A corrupt, festering institution drain-
ing money better spent on actual public services. Compassion
instead of brutality. All very laughable.'

Cooper said nothing.

'Don't you agree? I saw the way you looked at that one.
Something happened, didn't it?'

Cooper still did not answer. She felt awkward. She felt awkward at this woman and the way she looked at her, the way she
asked these questions.

Lucy considered her for a moment.

'You really should stay for dinner,' Lucy went on. 'I'm cooking. We can talk.'

28

'She's a fine chef,' Matthew said. 'None of that vegan crap...
well, not that there's anything wrong with being vegan, but,
well... she makes the most delectable beef bourguignon...'

Cooper, a long-lapsed, guilty vegan, did not look up at him.

'Really,' he went on. 'You're in for a treat. It's delectable.'

Cooper had wanted to say no.

Having said yes, they now sat at the wooden table of Lucy's
lodge, Cooper's unease rising.

She'd already seen it in Kelly's eyes, surprise, even judgement,
at the mere fact of her arrival. But it was like he said – her
involvement in the case was over, wasn't it? She could visit these
people if she liked. She could have dinner. And the weather...
how was she supposed to travel back in this storm?

There was professional curiosity, also. The siblings were so
welcoming – she might as well use the opportunity to learn
more about their mother.

She tried not to think about the other possibility, pushing it
deeper into the back of her mind. That she now sat, alone, in
the dark, far from help on the night of a storm, with potential
suspects.

'Vegan crap' – Cooper hadn't liked that. It kind of made
Matthew seem monstrous, though possibly unfairly so. It was
hard to imagine he didn't go into deep critiques about political
correctness and cancel culture in his spare time. And there was
something strangely familiar about the man – something that

made her think they had met before, though she could not place it.

Cooper smiled at some joke, and kept looking around the room.

This new lodge was almost bare, sterile but for the used-up antibacterial wipes sitting like ornaments along the windowsills and shelves. Lucy had powered on the unplugged fridge upon arrival. She'd brought a bottle of wine, some lardons, beef, carrots, onions, mushrooms, tomato, and more. She now cooked at the little electric stove beneath the red-tinged light while rain battered the windows and her brother sat opposite their guest, silent on his phone. She'd taken off her leather jacket, the material dripping now from the back of one of the chairs. It looked like real leather in this light.

Lucy kept asking Cooper questions, how her journey here had been ('It was so warm all week'), how her parents had given her such an unusual name as Cooper ('It's normally a surname, isn't it?'), if she didn't need more towels ('I have no idea why we aren't all sneezing.') For the most part, Lucy ignored any mention of animals or death.

Somehow, it was stranger this way. The evening had the texture of a dream, of something born to be an anecdote.

Cooper felt like their hostage at times. Maybe just Lucy's hostage. But Matthew had insisted too, hadn't he?

Were they this uncomfortable in each other's presence?

And then, with that thought, she knew why she'd stayed, post necessity.

In some fantastical, almost familial kind of way – in some essential, inherited part of her mind and soul—

She was like them.

★

Apart from his comments about Lucy's cooking, Matthew had barely said anything, had barely looked at Cooper since their first meeting out in the rain.

He left for a little while to use his own bathroom, right on the cusp of dinner being ready. His sister warned him of time and proximity, but Matthew said nothing, just kept walking out into the rain until he was gone.

'He's always doing this.' Lucy blinked. She spoke quietly, as if he could somehow hear them through the walls, across the storm. 'Right when food's up, he chooses then to go ... It's not personal. He does it anywhere, restaurants, halls ...'

'It looks lovely,' Cooper said, her wine now gone. Lucy topped it up when she brought the plates over. They were white ceramic, ringed with blue circles, heraldic birds flying around the lines.

'He's barely said anything to me, either. It's not personal. I just don't ...'

Cooper drank more of her wine.

'It's just rude,' Lucy shook her head. 'He must have made a terrible impression, hasn't he?'

Cooper wanted to be alone. She didn't want to be alone.

The two halves of Cooper sat there with their food for a couple of minutes.

Near the kitchen counter, there were shelves, some board games, some old books for guests.

The victim's name lay in black upon one of the spines, written with an -ia instead of an -ie.

Sophia Bertilak, 1962–1972. A large hardback collection of photography.

Cooper did not ask about it, not then. It did not seem right to mention the reason they were all here.

She complained of a headache.

'I can give you something?' Lucy asked, deeply concerned. 'They're out of date but I'm sure it would be fine –'

Cooper laughed. 'Anything is fine.'

Soon Matthew returned, his hair and face wet again. He sat and ate without speaking much, beyond vague updates about his life and career, mainly aimed at his sister's questions. He thought he might be taken on to a permanent position at the university, soon.

The edited collection of essays he was being asked to assemble...

The lecture series...

Years in his job, in his place, even a flat in a centuries-old late Gothic building, but no job security, not yet, that was the way it worked, contributing to human knowledge, to the study of literature, and—

'Any girls?' Lucy asked suddenly, looking more at Cooper than her brother. She brushed something out of her eye.

Matthew was quieter when he answered. 'Women, you mean.'

Lucy scoffed, rolling her eyes.

'He's a real feminist, my brother. Has written all about us. Academically, I mean. Haven't you, Matthew?'

'Us?' Cooper tensed, but Matthew corrected – women, Lucy meant, he's written about women, their place in fiction, in made-up stories. Gothic romances across the fog, amidst the old ruins.

His most recent paper: 'Women as Food in Nineteenth-Century Literature'.

'What food would we be?' Lucy asked.

Outside, the rain kept falling.

'She's a guest,' Matthew said. 'It's not appropriate. I can't—'

'You can't what?' Cooper asked.

'Turn you into a meal,' he said.

'And me?' Lucy asked. 'There's no problem saying what food I'd be—'

'Easy with that ridiculous hair,' he said, and his smile was fond. 'A blueberry macaron.'

They ate, and drank, and finished their meal.

Lucy poured Cooper a final drink.

They all drank again.

'What's in this?' Matthew smiled. He raised an eyebrow.

29

In the vet lab, the pig bodies sat in cold storage. Their skin just sleeves, now, all other components bagged up and catalogued. The remnants of Sophie sat next to them in plastic: tufts of her hair, the rest of it unrecognisable flesh and acid.

The three companions sat alone in the storm.

The weakened Hurricane Elizabeth would lead to flooding across Ireland, Wales, southern England, soon swirling further north to Scotland. All these towns, lacking long-promised defences, were drowned again and again, homes and businesses and streets held beneath the surface, fragile structures collapsing into distant streams, pavements cracking under the force of the slow waves. When all was said and done, more people would have to find new places to live.

In Lethwick, the sandbags did what they could. Most of those living near the sewage-filled river just suffered water on their ground floors, electric wiring spluttering into the liquid, furniture and devices floating out in joy. The true damage would be revealed within a month, the scars opening as more rain arrived, a third, greater storm to engulf the remnants of this second.

In the old hotel, floors down from Cooper's uninhabited bedroom, the gamblers kept playing.

In that night, few walked among the hills. Few walked the roads.

In the valley, water swelled from a lake.

Another apple fell from a tree.

In Sophie's old home, in the basement, wire models, some without clothes, danced all around, frozen in half a dozen poses in the dark.

Cooper didn't mention them to her hosts. What else was to be said? Sophie Bertilak had been unwell, unsound. Sophie Bertilak had been old and maybe they knew this.

The world died, every time someone went to sleep.

A doctor made a bed for a doctor.

30

Matthew laid out fresh sheets in Cooper's lodge. She had a lodge now. Being offered a bed for the night was a fait accompli, really – the idea of going back to her hotel all those miles away, it felt absurd, this dark, this late.

She'd had two bottles of wine.

'No one's stayed in here for years, you know.' Matthew's voice was curt, thick, affected He barely looked at her. He had avoided eye contact almost the entire night, dark blond hair sometimes falling across his brow. 'We should have sold the whole place after my grandmother's death, but...' He shook his head.

The lights flickered.

For a few moments they were in the darkness of another power cut, Cooper's back stiffening as she stood a foot from the door.

There was silence for a little while in the absence of light, even as they shifted. The power returned.

Matthew was now sitting upon the bed, Cooper now leaning against the wall, her hand near the door handle.

The storm must be causing more problems with the grid, she thought. It must have been why the lights had gone off in the main house.

'I'm sorry,' Matthew said, his voice grown tired.

'A power cut really isn't your fault.'

'Hah.' It was the first time he'd laughed. It wasn't really a laugh. 'I meant I'm sorry about all of, this. You—' The light came back on. 'You should have been left alone to do your job. Lucy – she doesn't know what's appropriate. And when she's upset, it's worse. It's like the question about girls,' he shook his head. 'It wasn't just academic. I broke up with my girlfriend a few weeks ago. She knows that. I've not told her about the break-up obviously – I hadn't even told her about my girl-friend's existence, but she's online, she sees things, she knows, she … well. She can be vituperative …'

'I'm sorry,' Cooper said. She had no idea what vituperative meant, but it didn't matter. It didn't even matter that she wasn't sorry about anything in particular.

He smiled suddenly, wiping at his wet fringe, then seemed to feel guilty at the smile. He hesitated.

'I had a question for you,' he said. His brown eyes were empty.

'As long as it's not about the kind of food I am.'

He didn't smile.

'Shoot,' she said.

'How much was left of her?' he asked. 'How much was left of my mum?'

He shook his head before an answer could be given, then moved towards the door, hesitating again as Cooper stepped aside.

'They told me one of the pigs was called Alfie,' he said. 'That was my brother's name, you know. She loved us … I don't want you to think she didn't love us, but she wasn't always there for us, and … after what happened, she never brought him up. Had to be forced into talking about it. Me and my sisters, we had to talk to each other, to our dad if we wanted to remember …' He hesitated, cold, quiet. 'But her pet … that animal …'

He twisted his lips, trying to find words that eluded him.

137

In the end, only a few came.
'She gave away his name.'
He wished Cooper goodnight.
He left her by herself.
She waited a little while, and then yes, she remembered.
She had recognised him; she had seen him before.
He'd messaged her, hadn't he?
On the dating app ...
He'd messaged her, though he hadn't known it.

31

Cooper had been pretending to be someone else.

She'd encountered this peculiar phenomenon in another case a few years back – a person using a puppet account online, a catfish, to lure a man to his death.

After everything that happened in that strange, distant place, Cooper had looked into the messages, the history of the false account.

It had originally been invented by their suspect as a way to cope. To pretend they were someone else. To act as if they had a different personality, without the weight of their history, without the restrictions of who they really were. Free of all of that had been done to them, and what they had done to others in turn.

In a dark lonely moment, Cooper had gone online and had tried this herself – to see if the pretence would help her cope with her own troubles.

She had never told anyone. Not her whole life.

She hadn't stopped since.

Even sitting in the dark of Lethwick, she opened her phone, lonely once more.

The most recent name Cooper had used on her dating app was Emma. She'd stolen some random woman's photos a few months ago, as all such liars had to do, changing up her false online personas each time. She never actually met any of the men or women she talked to. She never wanted anything from them, not really, just the pretence of being someone else, the thrill of not being caught out in the pretending.

The app showed a few messages since Cooper had last opened it. All of them were from Lethwick, a few digital nomad app developers who spent their days travelling the earth. A solicitor (who was in the process of a divorce). A few of indeterminate jobs (one of them obviously a university student). A self-proclaimed artist (almost certainly a misogynist). A butcher.

And Matthew Bertilak.

His photo was almost unrecognisable, despite Cooper having seen him just minutes before.

Here, he was smiling, he was in daylight, he wore expensive sunglasses and his hair was not quite so prematurely grey as it had seemed in person.

His profile talked about his favourites in various cultural categories – *The Secret History* by Donna Tartt, the music of King Crimson, hiking, wild swimming, wines, history.

There were questions he'd answered for potential matches: he did not smoke, he wanted kids some day, he didn't support the death penalty, he self-identified as left-wing politically speaking.

He said he was a doctor at a university.

Hey! he had said.

Just that. A few hours ago. And then, now ...

Three dots showing him working on some other message. Men often sent short, uninspired openings like this.

Cooper paused for a long time.

She was half sure she didn't find him attractive. But then, she felt that way about most people lately – unsure, middling.

Hi, Cooper typed. She went on when there was no response. **Your profile said you work at a university – there aren't any near here?**

Cambridge, he typed. I work on eighteenth-century literature. Well – mostly. Recently I started broadening out into critical theory.

It was funny that he'd found her profile – that this coincidence could come into being. But the world was like that, wasn't it?

Critical theory? she asked.

An umbrella term for a field of enquiry that seeks to analyse the nature of modern culture – gender, race, sex, class, everything.

He sent another response when no message came:

You have a beautiful smile.

Another message:

What do you do for work, Emma? Your profile doesn't say.

She wondered what Kelly would make of this, if he found out that she was chatting to a member of the victim's family in this way.

She could use the old defence: fuck Kelly, fuck being prevented from doing all she could do...

But then, she wondered what absolutely any other human being would make of this aspect of her behaviour, the stolen photos, the fake name, the false hopes. The playing with people.

She put the thought of judgement aside.

She thought for a long time before deciding on her character's job. Before making up a story.

I'm a photographer, she wrote.

He didn't answer.

32

Cooper had a cold, upsetting shower.

Now Cooper lay in bed. Hours passed as she tried to get comfortable. She thought about Lucy, about the cigarette, her first in years.

Matthew had been right about his sister's cooking, regardless of whatever sarcasm might have been intended. It had been a lovely meal. Cooper thought about the siblings' smiles, so similar, and wondered if their mother had smiled like that too.

She thought about the contents of the pigs' stomachs. She thought about their faces. She thought about their names.

The ceiling began to drip. The sound of the storm itself had become the most soothing, normal element in the habitat.

Maybe their smiles had all come from their father instead.

In place of love, there were photographs in the books of Sophie's life. They rested along the shelves of this lodge.

Images of Vietnam, of the Gulf, of Africa, of America, of life and death and atrocity.

She took one of the books and turned to the first pages of the collection.

To the photo everyone knew.

There were references to a 'Quentin Medina' here and there. Cooper didn't recognise the name. The curator of her exhibitions. Her finances. He had long limbs in his own image, taken decades ago. So much like that wire model in the basement.

Cooper thought back to her reading in the taxi. All those

pipe cases over the years, all those eyes looking up through the dark ...

She thought of that loose thread: the police officer who had died shortly after Sophie's photo was taken, an officer who had investigated alongside Kelly's own father. There was no post about him on any of her true crime sites, no thread pursuing more information on it. It was like gold dust, finding a route of investigation no one else in your community had pursued.

She logged in to one of them.

Her username was different on each site to avoid any traceability or link with her real-life career.

POSTED BY U/MOTHMANIA89 – *JUST NOW*

SERGEANT REGINALD BARKER – KILLED 50 YEARS AGO IN LETHWICK

So a possible unsolved case – Sgt Reginald Barker – from what I can tell he was one of the investigators on the original Lethwick pipe case [see: [link] – two missing children were accidentally photographed by a teenage girl on her birthday in 1964, one of them in a pipe in the earth].

What I can find:
– References in these documentaries [link], [link], [link], and this book [link]
– They indicate between them that Barker was suspended with pay pending the outcome of an investigation but no mention of *what* that investigation involved.
– He'd had a lifelong struggle with alcohol [no actual sources given for this but unsurprising maybe, if a little stereotypical].
– Drowned in the River Leth, near a bridge named the Bridge of Sighs [renamed in 1930s for tourism, originally had no name].

GREG BUCHANAN

– Cause of death thought to be accidental drowning.

Hoping someone knows of other sources?

[POST REMOVED BY MODERATOR: REASON – 'possible unsolved
case' – no justification given for considering it unsolved]

REPOST WITH ADDITIONAL TEXT:

Reason for thinking it's unsolved:
a) He died shortly after investigating the case of two presumed
kidnappings, one of which involved a pipe box, which historically
suggests ransom. Multiple victims suggests trafficking, possible
organised crime link? Therefore not a stretch to consider Barker
might have learned too much etc.
b) A lot of the posts on this board are stretches tbh, none of you are
solving anything. Put my post up

[POST REMOVED BY MODERATIOR: REASON being rude]

REPOST WITH ALTERED TEXT:

b) I'm an investigator working on the pipe case right now, and I
need help.

[MESSAGE FROM MODERATOR: provide proof]

[MESSAGE POSTED]

At 3 a.m., Cooper saw a hint of light in her window.

She had locked her door as soon as Matthew had left.

She thought about all her mistakes. The post-mortem had gone well. It was the only thing that had gone well. She was tired.

She shouldn't have said yes. Not to the case, not to dinner, not to her mad impulse to come out to this valley, not to helping a stranger in a hallway, not to giving up her holiday, not to cutting open those animals, not to – well, not to all this. She should have gone back to see her own family, her own mum, her own sister.

She shouldn't have answered Matthew's message.

When she went to her window, she looked at the main house so far away.

Its lights were on again.

She went back to her bed, thinking about pigs.

33

Cooper opened her eyes. She couldn't move.

It was almost dawn. The light that came through the windows had changed, it had seeds of sunshine. The storm had stopped. There was no rain. There was silence. The world couldn't move, either.

There was a heavy feeling on Cooper's chest, as if something was pushing down upon her. She could only shift her eyes a little. She couldn't even shut them anymore. She couldn't move her head.

There was a figure in the corner of her room, at the edge of sight.

Cooper tried to breathe, but she couldn't.

The figure was still at first, and Cooper wondered if she was dreaming. She wasn't dreaming. The figure might have been motionless for a while.

It was like a shadow through her blurred eyes. She didn't know what she saw, she—

It began to move closer.

Cooper tried to move, but nothing happened, nothing but the opening and closing of her lids – she had that back now. She could hide her vision if she wanted. She could pretend she was alone. She—

It was next to her bed. If it was saying something, she couldn't hear. The curtains moved. It took Cooper a while to realise it was just a breeze, that they hadn't just shifted of their own accord. She watched the curtains rippling.

She closed her eyes.

She opened them, and the world had changed.

The door hung open for a while. Eventually it shut.

She thought she could hear barking, briefly. It faded.

Cooper tried to move.

She lay there for minutes, unable to speak, unable to shift a muscle, reduced only to her eyelids.

She lay there, alone.

The darkness drops again; but now I know
That twenty centuries of stony sleep
Were vexed to nightmare by a rocking cradle,
And what rough beast, its hour come round at last,
Slouches towards Bethlehem to be born?

The Second Coming
William Butler Yeats (1920)

PART 2:

THE GIRL BY THE LAKE

SOPHIE BERTILAK
THE PAST

Lethwick, 1965

One year after the photographs

How would she die?

Sophie sometimes wondered this when she heard about other people.

Getting shot in a distant country.

Getting stabbed walking down a street.

Dying in your sleep – your body breaking down, your heart failing at long last.

She'd always assumed she would be buried. Most people were buried, weren't they, their bodies rotting in coffins? But the more she'd become aware of mortality, the more she'd become aware of other methods.

Some people were burned, rendered dust.

That night, the Bertilak house smelled of such dust. Smoke and peat drifted through the damp, fading moonlight. A spider – the sole survivor of a grand purge of cobwebs – lingered in a corner of the ceiling. It was one of a long line of spawning and breeding spiders in that valley. No one could ever really grow crops here. What settlements developed and fell over thousands of years of human habitation inevitably crumbled in isolation, in the need to leave. Glaciers had formed this place.

Now Sophie Bertilak sat with her mother and two half-grieving parents on tatty old sofas, eating their dinner with plates awkwardly perched on their laps. The spider watched them, waiting.

All the animals waited for their meal.

Sophie had met with Stephanie Earlsham's parents a few times. Always surrounded by police, the smell of aftershave and the flash of cameras, at appeals for this missing girl – for someone Sophie had not even known, but to whose fate she was now inextricably bound. The father always thanked her, always asked how she was doing. He was tall, broad-shouldered, handsome. He worked in the meat industry. Sophie had thought he was a butcher at first. It turned out the truth wasn't so interesting. He helped manage accounts. His wife had been a teacher. Now Mrs Earlsham didn't work. Not for a few years now. She didn't say much, or talk to Sophie much. She didn't do much of anything. She just sat there, breathing, blinking, eating.

That night, having dinner in the Bertilak house so close to where their daughter had been photographed, the wife spoke more.

A fire burned in the fireplace, wood smouldering in the coal and flame, reflected on the eyes of the insects that hid in the room's corners, of all those forms of life no human could see.

'So what do you think?' Sophie's mother asked.

'What do I think?' The father looked up.

'About vegetarians. About that lifestyle.'

'Why would I have an opinion about it?' He looked back down at his food and continued eating.

'You said you worked in the meat industry.'

'I don't actually kill the animals myself,' he said, without smiling. He looked at Sophie, as if they shared some secret opinion of the woman. Which, they probably did…

'Would you?' Sophie's mother asked.

'Would I what?' He gave another quick look to Sophie.

'Kill an animal.'

'Why?' He seemed almost annoyed.

'To eat it.'

'I don't need to,' he said. 'That's what the supply chain is for.'

'To hide where food comes from?'

'To make life easier,' he said.

There was silence for a time, but for their chewing.

'Well,' Sophie's mother went on, 'I would. I think everyone who eats meat should be willing to kill it themselves.'

No one answered her.

Outside, the moon was almost visible in the window, huge, earthbound.

'I used to go shooting, you know,' Sophie's mother added. 'On shoots.'

'With your husband?' the father asked.

'I was quite good at shooting,' she went on. 'You really should go on a hunt, sometime.'

'You don't—' Sophie began, and then hesitated.

Everyone looked at her.

'I don't what?' her mother asked.

'You don't go on hunts.'

No one said anything.

Sophie's mother looked at the guests; her face, her shoulders, suddenly dropped, as fragile as glass. She looked at their plates.

Mrs Earlsham hadn't eaten much.

'Are you not going to finish? Is something wrong?' Sophie's mother asked.

'My wife is just a bit full,' Mr Earlsham said. 'She never eats much.'

'What hobbies do you have?' Sophie's mother went on.

'I don't have time for them,' he said.

'I meant your wife. What hobbies do you have? I read, mostly. I love books. Do you read?'

'I sketch.' Sketch was said with a kind of crack in Mrs Earlsham's voice, as if the 's' was too much effort to push through her throat. Her expression rarely changed: a faint smile on a beautiful face, the kind of face you'd see in old black and white movies.

Mrs Earlsham didn't look like she was really there with them in that room.

'What do you sketch?' Sophie asked, getting up to take their plates.

'Buildings,' Mrs Earlsham said. 'Old houses.'

Sophie's mother laughed. 'Nothing living, then?'

Mrs Earlsham did not answer.

Sophie took all the dinner plates and scraped the leftovers into the kitchen bin.

When she came back, the atmosphere had changed. Everyone – even Sophie's mother – was quiet, still. Only Mrs Earlsham remained as she had been, that strange, faint, otherworldly smile on her face.

It was only later that Sophie found out what the woman had said.

'She joins me, when I go places,' Mrs Earlsham had continued. 'Stephanie draws, beautifully ... You should see them ... We have a process.'

They walked through town the next day. Spires of worship pierced the sun in triangles. The detritus of centuries lay in pitted stone and brick all around, porous, lightly wet from the morning's now ended rainfall.

A masked busker in the main square strummed at an instrument but no sound came out. Sophie did not know if he was just practising or if this was part of the performance.

'I know him,' Sophie's mother said. 'Where do I know him from?'

But she wasn't talking about the busker.

Sophie followed her mother's gaze, and saw a man leaning against the edge of a bridge.

It was one of the detectives who had walked her through the woods, all those months ago.

Detective Barker.

He wasn't wearing his suit; he wasn't wearing a uniform.

He seemed sad, the way he looked out at the water.

They didn't talk to him. Why would they? They didn't know him.

They went to the pub for lunch. Mr Earlsham asked more questions about where Sophie's father was.

Sophie's mother just shook them away, but gave a story, a while later, as they finished their chips.

'He ate a block of butter at my friend's wedding. We couldn't understand what he was doing. He kept asking what that delicious cheese was – he said it reminded him of his childhood. I think he'd eaten blocks of butter before.'

Mr Earlsham laughed.

'You never told me that story,' Sophie said quietly.

She'd not been told, when she'd been told so much else about her parents' marriage. More than a daughter should know.

'Never marry a man who eats blocks of butter, Sophie,' her mother said, laughing. 'I was told your father wasn't good enough ... I didn't understand what those words meant. Not until it was too late. You have something in your eye.'

Her fingers lurched forward to Sophie's skull, and scraped out a bit of sleep in the corner of her eye socket, even as Sophie recoiled.

Mrs Earlsham went to get them more drinks from the bar.

Sophie was allowed to have another glass of wine, which she was excited about. She was eighteen now. She had been so for a few months.

Still, she asked permission, surprised at the offer. They all had wine, but for the husband.

When Mrs Earlsham came back, she accidentally spilled one of the glasses on Sophie's mother's lap.

Everyone acted like it was a mistake.

Through much of the trip, the Earlshams went out into the woods by themselves. They never asked Sophie to come. Sophie never offered. It felt private, inviolable, what they were going through and processing.

In the night, Sophie found Mrs Earlsham reading a book in the lounge. It was 3 a.m.

Sophie sat down, and asked about it.

'It's about a man who gets killed on a train, and there's this famous detective on board who investigates all the suspects,' the woman explained.

'What are you doing up?'

'I'm not tired,' Mrs Earlsham said, that faint smile rising on her face. 'That's why I'm still up.' She paused. 'I could ask the same of you, you know. Sit up straight...'

'I haven't been...' Sophie began. 'I haven't slept well. Not for a while.'

Mrs Earlsham's smile faded.

'Isn't that...' Sophie began, and then stopped.

'Go on. Ask.'

'Isn't that too much of a coincidence? In your book. That a famous detective happens to be on board the train the same day there's a murder.'

Mrs Earlsham smiled, and it was so different from before, from anything Sophie had seen on her face. Genuine warmth. 'That's the fun of the genre. It's a popular thing, to have detectives on holidays.' She paused. 'And besides, it doesn't even matter that he's there, in the end. He doesn't even achieve justice. He just lies when he finds out the truth.'

Sophie wondered. 'Why do all these stories involve holidays?'

Mrs Earlsham stared at her for a moment, watching her eyes, as if she recognised the girl from some other time, some other life.

'Because no matter how hard we try,' Mrs Earlsham said, 'we can't escape ourselves. We can't escape our jobs. We can't escape who we are, and what we are, but what we're paid to do? What we accept from the world?' She picked up her teacup and drank a little, not answering her own questions, just letting the thought trail off.

'And the lie?' Sophie asked.

'I'm not going to spoil it for you,' Mrs Earlsham said quietly.

'Why does the detective lie?'

'You look so much like her.'

The words were so sudden, Sophie did not know what to say, and seeing this, Mrs Earlsham grew vaguer, distant, that faint and lifeless smile returning to her face.

Sophie went back to her room a short time later. She hardly slept, the image of the masked busker from the square going round her head, how no sound had come from his instrument.

Her mother had said something to her, months ago now.

'You could have died,' she'd say. About that day. About the photographs of the missing, the entombed...

But how could Sophie have died?

No one had threatened her.

She had not even known there was danger.

159

And if she hadn't known then, how would she know in future?

If a monster lurked out there, its teeth ready to gobble her up, how would Sophie know, if it just looked like a man?

The next day, Mrs Earlsham was gone.

Her husband didn't even look for her anymore. He admitted to having no idea where she was, but he couldn't look. He just remained on the sofa in the house, listening to the radio in all that dust.

Sophie's mother complained, privately, about the complete lack of planning and notice. 'It's rude, is what it is, Sophie – I have no idea what we're doing today, I have no idea if they're staying or going...'

But the father spoke to Sophie, briefly, as the teenager walked through the lounge. He'd come back from a journey into the woods, to the old sights, in case his wife might be there.

'I can't look for anyone,' he said quietly. 'Not ever again.'

Sophie had no idea what to say. She didn't say anything.

Near dusk, Sophie went out to the woods herself. It felt like checking for her keys in a place she'd already looked. Like an itch.

Bogwood dried in the remains of the day. There was a fungal smell, water dripping from what branches it could penetrate, the sound of those drops and her own footsteps all Sophie could hear, but for the low rattle of the leaves and the trees, the ebb and flow of their shivers.

Her shoes dug into the soil, as if the ground were trying to take them from her, gently, delicately.

By the time she reached the lake, the dark moon stood above it, the sky almost empty of stars once more.

Mrs Earlsham stood there, right where her daughter had once stood.

She was taking her clothes off.

Sophie stepped on a twig, and the snap caused Mrs Earlsham's face to turn a little, but not by much.

She was beautiful.

Sophie stepped closer.

'Why were you out in the woods?' Mrs Earlsham asked, her voice soft, relaxed. She took off her shoes and stepped into the cold water, tensing but not shaking as the liquid hit her.

'I was looking for you.'

'No. Not now. Then. When you saw Stephanie.'

'To take photographs. That – that was all. I got a camera for my birthday, and—'

'Why take photographs?' Mrs Earlsham interrupted.

'I don't know.'

'Yes,' Mrs Earlsham said. 'You do.' She wasn't even facing Sophie now, but neither did she step forward into the water.

'I wanted to use my gift ... I wanted to have fun, like I said before. That was all.'

'Why did you ask your mother for a camera?'

'I used a camera at school ...' Sophie paused. 'I'd never owned anything like it. I wanted one for myself. I deserved it.'

'Deserved?'

'Yes. I'd been to every session of the club so far. I'd started reading the journals they get in, and – and I planned to take it seriously.'

'And then you saw my daughter.'

Sophie hesitated. She was not sure what to say.

Mrs Earlsham said nothing for a time either, and neither of them moved. 'Have you ever swum out here?' she said at last.

Sophie shook her head.

'It's OK,' Mrs Earlsham said. 'Just have some fun.'

Sophie found herself, a time later, in that same water, her clothes mostly left by the side of the lake.

Flies kept landing on them, sometimes, in that dark.

Biting flies, they took her blood, cells of her skin.

Mrs Earlsham asked if Sophie was OK, the way she swatted at her neck, how she splashed, sometimes.

Sophie smiled gently, and just explained it was nothing.

The flies, they were eating her, that was all.

When they were almost finished swimming, by some silent, invisible agreement between them both, Mrs Earlsham told Sophie that she was never going to stop looking for her daughter.

'I know that now,' she said. 'I know it.'

And Sophie, she promised. She promised to never stop helping Mrs Earlsham in her search.

And that moment, that remarkable night in the lake – the dark moon, the trivial, quickly given promise ... Sophie kept coming back to it, again and again.

She would come back to it, a few years later, unable to sleep.

Sitting by a fire across the world, watching a dog eat a piece of meat encrusted with bloodied cloth. Sophie had gone to Vietnam. She had gone to take more photographs. She had gone to follow her dream.

The air was stagnant in the night. Bodily fluids, oil, the crackling of a stream somewhere, the noise of the dog licking flesh in the heat.

Its eyes in the red light, the smoke.

The soldiers who slept all around, with Sophie in their midst, three weeks before she'd suffer burns across her arm and portions of her torso. Injuries and scars she'd bear her entire life, treated in a hospital in Saigon.

But for now, Sophie sat, and thought of the lake and the promise as the dog ate that piece of meat — that strange, clothed piece of meat.

It looked like a segment of an arm. Of another army's uniform.

She'd taken photos of it throughout the last few days, this dog they'd found. The soldiers didn't send the animal away. How could they? It was the most human thing in their lives.

They took it with them, tying it somewhere during fire fights, and somehow it had not died or barked. It was a quiet animal.

It sniffed at their hands and slept at their sides.

It watched Sophie as it ate meat.

Sophie watched it back.

In the morning, the animal was found dead in the woods, a little way away from their camp.

It had been shot in the head. No one remembered hearing anything.

Sophie thought of the promise, how beautiful Mrs Earlsham had seemed in that water, how Sophie had wanted to make her feel better, how she'd wanted to do anything for this grieving, dissolving woman. The coincidence of taking that photo, of a birthday present transformed into an entire life...

She would do anything, anything to find the missing daughter. Anything to find the truth.

No matter how long it took.

They talked about dreams one day, these soldiers.

Whether the people they imagined at night could think, could feel.

The horror of waking, these shards of selves dissolving, the slow invasion of the light.

FILE: SOPHIE BERTILAK (DECEASED)
EVIDENCE: VET RECORDS

LETHWICK VETERINARY PRACTICE
O = Owner

JULY 1ST

O has bought 2 piglets, 8 weeks old and wanted them checked
over. Both in good condition. Pig A is slightly larger than his sibling
Pig B. Both piglets were castrated at the original farm. Advised O
to change feed as was giving them kitchen scraps and dog food.

SEPTEMBER 18TH

Pig names given as Henry and Alfie. Visit to farm as O found Henry
caught in barbed wire, LH superficially lacerated below the level
of the hock. Doesn't appear that joint capsule has been infiltrated.
Cleaned wounds, given LA ABX, and tet antitox. Asked O about
intentions for the pigs – says they're for Christmas slaughter.

NOVEMBER 25TH

Alamycin spray
Metacam 100mls
Discussed with O plans for Christmas slaughter of both pigs. O has
elected not to proceed and will instead keep them as pets. Advised
that adult pigs are difficult to handle and can be dangerous; O
has stated she has researched this and is comfortable with her
decision.

DECEMBER 12TH

O says Alfie has stopped responding to name and seems
withdrawn. Alfie is still 2/3 lame on LH, PEX otherwise NAD and
no swelling around hock. Advised O to continue Metacam for
pain relief, offered X-rays or referral but O declined. Will manage
conservatively.

DECEMBER 15TH
[telephone call]

O has tried CBD oil on Alfie and says he has partially improved.
Asked about Henry, O says he is well in himself and is mostly
housetrained.

DECEMBER 16TH
[telephone call]

O asked if other clients ever found it hard to put animals to
slaughter. Has changed her mind about slaughtering them, wants
to proceed before Christmas. Reassured O and discussed what to
expect.

[NOTE: No contact received from O after December 16th. Vets
assumed pigs have been slaughtered, had no knowledge that they
were alive for another six months. No further treatment sought.]

'It's like saying I work in an abattoir;
it's like being called a criminal.'

Don McCullin, on the term 'war photographer'

PART 3:

THE REUNION

DR COOPER ALLEN
THE PRESENT DAY

I just said goodbye to Julia – Cooper's definitely checked into the hotel, but the front desk won't tell me anything else. She was always doing things like this growing up – she once disappeared for three days when she was seventeen, just went out for shopping and didn't come back for three whole days, claimed she was at a friend's house, but she didn't have many friends. I didn't have many friends when I was that age – not real ones – it's weird, isn't it, how it's easier to get on with people in writing than in person? I always found that. I always liked letters. And the Lincoln Ladies – it's been so nice getting to know you all. So I suppose even if you've gone, maybe we'll be even better friends now, now that we're just writing.

I don't know if the air is already working but my lungs have felt better than they've felt in ages. I can breathe and I'm not coughing and it reminds me of how it felt to breathe when I was younger – when there wasn't all this pollution in the air. How is the air where you are? I hope you're keeping well.

Julia thinks Cooper is testing us or playing games with us by not answering our messages but I do worry. You know the kind of work she does.

It made Cooper kill someone once.

I think I told you about it before, but I don't know who I've told what things, lately. I wonder if that's a symptom of what's wrong with me. As if I need to add to my health worries. Maybe I already added it and can't remember, how odd and like me that would be!

It was self-defence. It didn't even go to a trial – the crown prosecution service decided it wasn't in the public interest. The person she killed – they'd poisoned people, they'd driven people to suicide, they'd hurt and maimed and murdered at least three people and god knows how many animals. In the papers it said that she was attacked and this person, this person hit their head. That it was an accident.

It can't have been an accident, though, that's what I know. Because if someone did something to me like that, if someone had tried to hurt me, I think of course you'd have to defend yourself. And if that's in me, it's in her – she is me, isn't she? Half of her. Not just my blood, but half of everything she's been in her life came from how I raised her, didn't it?

It all started after she left Arthur. I know she started the course before then, she'd already given up being a normal vet after all the ways I'd supported her, but the start of the rot – it was when she left him, I think. He kept her normal. She didn't even have an explanation for him or us. I thought maybe she'd cheated, maybe that would make sense, but no.

In love one moment, out of it the next.

We felt so sorry for him. Of course we all did. And when he met Julia, it was years later, it was through his work – I think Cooper blames her, somehow; I think Cooper thinks if she doesn't want a man then no one else should have him – but what does Cooper know of the things love does?

Julia and Arthur fell in love as different people. Julia even asked Cooper! She asked if she was all right with them seeing each other, that she would stop if Cooper wanted her to stop, and it had been years since Cooper had seen him, so what was the problem? I don't understand the problem. Cooper said yes, it was fine. And whatever my problems with the man, I still felt sorry for him. And Julia wasn't one to fall in love, really – I'd always worried about where she'd end up. That maybe she might go with the wrong man, just to get the whole game over with.

It's a game, isn't it, being in love? Testing limits. Testing affection. Testing the whole of another's personality until one of you breaks and runs. I've loved with kindness in my time. I've loved the worst of people, too. How many times have you been in love, Gwen? I hope you find it again where you've gone.

I hope this weekend is civil. Julia's going to be marrying him soon. That's the thing. She's marrying Arthur. She told me tonight when she should have told me a long time ago, and she wants to tell Cooper. She needs to tell her.

I've asked her to wait until I say so. Julia was always good. She'll do what I say.

Anyway, tell me your news! I want to hear everything!
Love,
Rebecca

FROM: Gwen Lott
SUBJECT: RE: Goodbye
DATE: 14 June, 10:11
TO: Rebecca Allen

Wow! A lot to read. I'll get back soon. I believe in you.

34

'The photographer, notoriously reclusive in her final years, maintained a friendship with the parents of missing teenager Stephanie Earlsham. The subject of her earliest photographs, the case remains unsolved to this day...'

The television crackled in the hotel entrance.

No one seemed to watch it, not even when an image of a famous photograph appeared. An eye, terrified, looked out through the screen, through all these years.

It saw Cooper and her sister Julia and her mother Rebecca, as they all left for their day out. Her mother didn't want to hear about this case, didn't want to hear about Cooper's experiences the night before, didn't want to hear about the dead photographer — in fact, the very mention of pigs, of this Bertilak woman, it all made Rebecca's skin crawl.

She didn't like any stories about abductions or runaways. She thought them unsavoury, and the fact that Cooper had allowed herself to be dragged into another tale of death on their weekend, on their chance for a reunion, upset Rebecca beyond measure.

'Leave the past in the past,' Rebecca said.

Cooper's work had always upset her. The sight of the police filled her with dread. The sight of a police officer revealed the fundamental sickness at the heart of the world. Their presence meant a cure was needed.

When the drama of a crime ended, when the heartache

stopped, there was just a vast emptiness, complete, without meaning or future. It was what no one ever told you when you were a child – that most of the time you're alive, you're just living to get through the day.

And that second secret, that so few ever learned: there was nothing you could not get over. Nothing you could not hide in the back of your mind. Nothing you could not forgive, of yourself or others.

Human beings were so changeable, if they just let themselves change.

Rebecca hoped this weekend would change things.

Lethwick, it was a special place. It was a place of healing. That is what the internet had promised.

35

They went to an abbey for a while. Cooper's mother and sister walked ahead of her, where they had to look at every single plaque, every sign, every artefact of that ruined place. These ancient stones had sheltered fugitives throughout the centuries.

Red-brown flowers shifted along the green grass, flicking back and forth like eyelids. The occasional leaf fell from old trees, though it was not yet autumn. The sun was never blocked, never fell through branches or rose-carved architraves, but just hit Cooper from the sky itself, endlessly, uneclipsed. The only darkness was second-hand.

She missed working as a vet sometimes. The thought suddenly struck her there, sitting on a bench while the others talked.

She missed watching her patients get better.

Before they left the abbey, Cooper's mother made a complaint to the front desk.

'The way your tour guide spoke to me—'

The front desk protested that there was no tour guide.

'He was so rude – and I have these headaches, it just made them—'

The poor girl repeated that they didn't have—

'Are you calling me a liar?'

They went for a walk. Their mother complained about the long paths, the cobbles of the town, the way they sought to trip her up. She complained about the temperature, the inaccuracies of the day's weather forecast. She complained the closer they got to the woods, too – suggesting other routes, other possibilities.

'If I'd known, I would have brought wellingtons, I would have brought better footwear.'

'What did you imagine?' Cooper asked. 'We met up for a countryside getaway ...'

'I don't want to go walking in there. I don't want to go off the path.'

The old woman – she was almost shaking. The town, the temperature, nature itself – none of it was what she had hoped it might be.

In the quieter moments of the day, Cooper would open her phone wallet, a clasped, blue false-leather thing decorated with faded stickers of fat cats in various poses – grumpy, sleeping, hungry, all three moods a person might have.

She checked her true crime communities, but there were no more updates on the Detective Barker thread, and she already felt a little guilty for having posted about it in the first place. She was normally so good at maintaining that line between her personal and professional lives, anyway.

Yep ...

As the day went on, Cooper also talked to Matthew Bertilak on her dating app, still under the false identity of 'Emma'.

After his initial silence, Matthew didn't seem to be put off by her claim that she was a photographer. On the contrary, this second day of their electronic relationship, he asked a great number of questions that Cooper had to do research to try and answer. The whole point of the game was to remain undetected in the deception.

She deflected a request for a meet-up by claiming – as Emma – that she was out of town for the week.

When I'm back, maybe.

If I'm still here, he said.

Depends on how much you want to see me, really.

He seemed to like that style of talk.

When they talked about past relationships, 'Emma' insinuated there was a failed marriage lasting six months, among other lies.

Matthew mentioned a student.

A student?

She wasn't much younger than me – she was doing a Master's, and I was helping advise her on her dissertation.

Why'd you break up?

She wanted us to be more. But I figured out the kind of person she really was.

What kind is that?

She was a liar.

'I hope you're not like this when you're working,' Cooper's mother said.

Cooper put her phone away.

'Like what?'

The woman stared at her as they queued for the restaurant, and shook her head.

'I suppose you've had a lot of time to be on your phone, though. What with being off sick.'

Cooper didn't answer.

'I was here when I was young,' the mother went on. 'I came here in love ...'

'You came here with Dad?'

'Not your dad, no,' the mother said. 'I had a whole other life before I took his name, if you can believe it.'

She smiled, and her daughters smiled at her smiling.

Still they waited.

Cooper went back on the app.

'Emma' asked Matthew to describe his ideal woman.

And don't describe me, she wrote.

So, second most ideal woman then . . .

He typed for a while.

I think someone artistic . . . someone creative, for sure, like an artist or something.

Looks? Cooper asked.

I don't know. I always liked coloured hair. Bright, vibrant looks.

'Cooper?'

She put her phone back in her pocket.

A few minutes later, their table was ready, and the three women went in to eat their dinner, Cooper thinking about Matthew's description of his ideal partner.

How much like Lucy it sounded.

But there wasn't time to process it.

'Do all vets have career breaks like that? I don't know how you'd hack it if you had a different job.'

Cooper tried to eat. The restaurant was full of plant pots, a mess of branches and leaves. 'I'm not a vet anymore . . .'

'You stumble around with animal corpses. What's the difference?' Her mother swallowed a mouthful. 'You didn't work for a year. Isn't that right?'

'Yes.'

'Must have been a nice holiday. All right for some. How did you support yourself?'

'I sold pictures of my feet.'

This got a surprise laugh out of Julia, who quickly pretended it was a cough.

Their mother just scowled.

'Savings, Mum,' Cooper went on. 'Credit cards. Loans. That's how I survived.'

'If you'd asked. If you'd talked to me, I could have helped,' her mother said.

'So why come back here?' Cooper asked. 'Where'd the idea come from?'

Her mother shrugged. 'I was talking to my friend, and she recommended it. With my headaches the way they are, it might help, being here. For the festival. For midsummer.'

Her mother had said she was into this time of year, its energy...

Whatever that meant.

'You booked the wrong days, then,' Cooper said, but her mother shook her head.

'The festival isn't on the right days. I mean midsummer itself.'

'What friend?' Julia asked. 'You don't have friends.'

'I've got you,' her mother said.

They kept eating. Occasionally, her mother complained of stiffness in her arms, the skin so pale you could see the blood vessels. She complained about getting old.

'This food... it's delicious,' she said. 'Is yours delicious?'

She went to the bathroom.

There was blood in her urine.

Rebecca did not tell anyone.

There was blood, she was sure of it. The urine was slightly darker than normal. And the blood, it must have mixed in to make it so dark.

She spent a while at the mirror. The unisex cubicles each had basins and mirrors to themselves. She wanted to check her face. She just wanted to check she still looked nice. She had spent a lot of time that morning trying to make sure she'd look less pale, hiding the veins on her hands. It had washed off since then. She hadn't replaced it... she concentrated on her face, more than anything.

She walked back out into the restaurant. The lighting by the bar was weak, and the reflections of those bulbs, those glittering bottles on all those glass shelves... the almost blue light compared to the orange of the bathroom... of all things, this place reminded her of her wedding reception.

'Allen', a dead man's surname, attached to her forever. She did not marry again after the girls' father had died. She'd had options, but still.

She had given everything to this new life. What was the alternative?

She hesitated as she passed a row of plants in pots. The place was heaving with waiters, with other diners hiding from the rain. She was near their table now – she could hear her daughters. She could see them through the leaves.

She heard them talk – her flesh and blood.

'Woe is you,' Cooper said to her sister.

'It's only one more day. God...' Julia avoided her sister's eyes. The briefest of contacts, then a look away... 'You know she's not been well.'

'She's always had something wrong with her. Why have a personality when you can have Munchausen's? Why—'

'What exactly the problem is, it doesn't really matter – it's still illness.'

'You can never just let yourself see the worst in people,' Cooper glared. 'You can never just agree, you can never—'

Her mother stepped forward, and as she returned to her seat, both daughters stopped talking.

A waiter arrived and took an order for some more wine.

★

'Your hair is shorter,' her mother said, after a few more conversations about films, most of which Cooper had never seen.

'It is,' Cooper agreed.

'I remember all your phases,' she drank from her glass.
'Generally speaking, men don't like short hair. If men are still
your target audience. Or maybe you're becoming one of *them*.'
The corner of her mouth turned in a slight smile. 'Given the
look you're going for, you'll be pleased to know ... the toilets
are unisex here. Gender free.'

'So?' Cooper asked.

'It's not safe,' her mother said. 'Is it?'

'How exactly is it not safe?'

Julia coughed. 'Cooper, could you pass the—'

Her mother went on. 'You should keep growing your hair
out. It'll look nicer by the wedding ...' Her mother grabbed a
passing waiter's attention. 'Another bottle of red, please.'

The sisters remained silent.

Her mother looked curiously at Cooper. 'Did he ever ask
you? Arthur, I mean ...'

At this, Julia stiffened. 'God, Mum, that's—'

'Did Arthur ask me what?'

'Before you left him. Did Arthur ever talk about the future?
I imagine you'd have run away quicker, if he had. It's the same
with everything you do. Abandoning things. Dropping people.
I only say these things because I know you could be so much
more than you are, if you just – if you just had the right attitude.'

Her mother shook her head again, trembling.

'You never talk to me. You never phone or message, not
like you used to. Not since Arthur. It's like we don't even exist
anymore. What happened to us? I think your father would want
us to be friends, at least. I think he'd want—'

Cooper and Julia's father – dead when Julia was a baby, when

Cooper was in the single digits of her life – was only ever brought up in mythical, argument-ending circumstances.

Their mother talked for a while about him, about how she wanted things to be from now on. 'You'll miss me when I'm dead,' she said. 'You'll miss me, or you'll be glad, I suppose. I don't know which one. I don't know when.'

Their dessert arrived. They ate it.

She made references to her potential death a few more times during the meal.

They finished their dinner. Her mother tried to get money off their bill, complaining about the food.

When Cooper got up to go, she saw Lapis, sitting in earshot, food on the table.

His grey eyes followed the women as they left, the food on his plate uneaten, long since turned cold.

36

When Cooper got back to her hotel and parted ways with her family, she went to Alex's room unannounced. She didn't want to be alone.

It was oddly fascinating as an experience for Cooper. Within Alex's room, the sterile hotel hallways transformed into something more akin to a messy flat. There were clothes everywhere in laundry bags, boxes stacked around the hotel desk.

A small stack of flyers for one of the midsummer festival plays.

THE HARROWING OF HELL.

Alex saw Cooper's eye on them.

'My friend is playing Jesus,' she said, rolling her eyes. 'I'm just helping spread the good word.'

Alex led her through to the balcony.

There were a few metal chairs out there, all surrounding a glass table as if Alex had been holding some meeting, glasses there, a partially full bottle of wine, cushions. The glasses and the bottle were old, uncleaned and unthrown away. They stood as a jealousy-inducing monument, a living reminder that Alex had a social life with other people who were not Cooper.

There was a strange smell too, despite the crisp air.

'It's me,' Alex frowned, putting her cup of tea down on the glass table. 'It's where I work. It rubs off on you.'

'What rubs off on you?'

'Antiseptic.' Alex grimaced. 'Sorry. Well, not really sorry – I didn't expect company tonight.'

'You don't have to be sorry. You don't really smell, and even if you did, I'm used to it,' Cooper protested, but Alex just laughed.

They sat, and they drank. In the mornings, apparently, Alex usually took a dozen or so sachets from the cleaner's cart in the hall – coffee, tea bags, milk cartons – and had amassed quite a collection in her time here.

The hotel's terraces and balconies were quiet. Cooper looked around, occasionally.

'They contact you about the case?' Alex asked.

Cooper shook her head. 'I'm finished. If the police need me, they'll tell me. None of my business otherwise.' Cooper hesitated. 'Why? Did you hear anything about it?'

'They're looking for Sophie's ex,' Alex said. 'A man named Thomas something. Her baby daddy, the technical official term. He hasn't even answered his kids' messages, let alone the police.'

Below the balcony, down in the restaurant terraces, some-where within the ivy-draped wooden walls, a piano began to play.

'I didn't know he was a suspect,' Cooper said quietly.

'It's always the husband,' Alex shrugged. 'Though I don't know. I don't think it's a suspect thing. They're still thinking her death was just an accident.' She drank some of her tea. 'Enough about this anyway – you're on holiday. I'm sorry.'

'Allegedly on holiday. And stop apologising.'

The piano played on.

'I'm s–' Alex hesitated. 'I mean … I …' She took a breath, then tensed to smile. 'Is seeing your family going well?'

'As well as it could have gone.'

About two hundred feet away, two friends sat in the dark,

about the same arm's length distance away from each other that Cooper and Alex themselves sat. These two strangers – like a reflection of a mirror in a mirror – they didn't seem to talk much. They just looked up in the half-cloudy sky, out at what stars still shone.

Cooper realised she was still holding her empty cup and put it back down on the table. 'No, actually. It didn't.'

'Arguments?'

'Not really. It was just … just, fine.' She glanced down at the hillside below. No one there moved. 'It had just been a few years since we'd last seen each other. Oh, and we bumped into that creep at the end – that Lapis.'

'It's OK,' Alex said, and it struck Cooper that this was an odd response, that it didn't seem to connect to what she'd just said.

Cooper looked at her, and saw Alex peering into her cup, absorbed, distant. She wasn't listening anymore, not really.

'My sister's getting married,' Cooper said. 'I expect that was the whole purpose of inviting me to this, wanting to see how I'd take the news.'

'Why? Wouldn't you be happy for her?'

'I should be. I have no right not to be.'

Cooper didn't know how to explain. Not any more than that. She thanked her new friend for the tea and company, and lingered in the doorway. 'Are you sure you've never met a DS Lapis?'

'I don't know many of them,' Alex said. 'My ex, he liked to keep me separate from his work colleagues. Sorry …'

'But he still likes you right? You're still …'

'Still what?'

'Still not entirely exes …' Cooper ventured, and Alex nodded, sheepish. 'You said you were sorry for getting me involved in this case. You said you didn't mean to tell your ex about me, not without my permission.'

'I meant it,' Alex said. 'I am sorry.'

'Then could you do me a favour?'

Cooper explained.

Immediately, Alex seemed troubled, protesting that it would likely be impossible, that there was no way her ex would do what Cooper asked.

'Just ask him,' Cooper repeated. 'Find out what he can about DS Lapis. Any complaints, rumours, anything he's ever done wrong. Find out, and let me know.'

'That would be more than a favour.'

'Then I'll still owe you 20 per cent of a favour … I don't know, Alex. Can you do it or—'

'You could just pay me.' Alex didn't smile.

Cooper did. 'What's your price?'

'I'll think on it.'

'You're so …' Cooper shook her head. 'I'm glad I bumped into you.'

'What? You came to my room, you didn't—'

'No, that first night. When you were lost in the dark. I'm glad I found you.'

'That's my price, then,' Alex said. 'The next power cut. You have to find me, bring me back to your room, have drinks on your bed again …' She smiled, and there was no more apology. 'Goodnight, Cooper.'

REPLIES TO MOTHMANIA89'S POST ABOUT THE DEATH OF
REGINALD BARKER:

U/SWITCPOKEBL – *11h*
The police officer's death – it isn't the only drowning death near
that bridge. I checked Google Maps and there are multiple pubs on
the route back to hotel, poor lighting – I don't see it as a problem.

U/SCRABBLELEO – *10h*
It's not true that he had no surviving family – his father outlived
him. The name was just the wrong way round on the birth
certificate – see? [LINK] Middle name first, LEWIS FRANCIS BARKER,
should have been FRANCIS LEWIS BARKER.

U/88HOLDUP – *10h*
Were there any smiley faces near the body?

U/CSMITHGR – *9 hr*
[Photos] [LINK]

U/SWITCPOKEBL – *9 hr*
Need to add a warning tag @CSMITHGR

U/MOTHMANIA89 – *9 hr*
Where did you get those? @CSMITHGR

37

Cooper lay in bed, looking through the photographs CSMITHGR had posted. They showed the corpse of Barker, curled up in the water.

Black and white, the legs were beneath the surface; the feet, fragments of shirt and skin and hair that formed the body were in a kind of foetal pose, as if hugging some invisible friend.

Cooper stared.

Where had this user got these from? Was he someone in the Lethwick police service? Someone who'd investigated the past, just like her? And if so, why?

In any case, she had never seen a drowning victim look like this in their discovery.

Such bodies were typically face down, the forehead and legs pulled beneath the surface, wounds to limbs, to forearms and hands like stigmata as they drag through the soil...

The police could have manipulated the corpse, tampered with the scene through sheer incompetence or perhaps in rushing to see if their old colleague could be saved. But how would Barker's body then have come to rest in this position? Barely decomposed, barely bloated...

What body would there be to test, now? What evidence would remain? Only ashes. Only a photograph – only an image, only memories that were most likely dead by now, or dying...

And what good was a photograph?

38

Around 5 a.m., Cooper woke up and went to the toilet.

After she was done, she lingered at her window.

She looked out at the rising sun, visible just through the trees on the horizon.

The restaurant and hills below were mostly empty, but for joggers, dog walkers, Alex.

Alex?

Cooper pulled open the patio doors of her balcony and leant against the rails, straining her vision. It looked like Alex was down there, not in her work uniform but her own clothes, walking towards the hotel from far away. Whether she'd not been able to sleep, whether there was some different explanation for her being out this early, Cooper didn't know. She waited until her friend was closer, planning to shout out 'Hello!' or 'Oi, fucker,' or something friendly like that, but got her phone out instead, realising it was indeed 5 a.m. and other people were probably sleeping.

She was about to phone her, until Alex got close enough that Cooper could see the woman's face, her downcast eyes, her still-unwashed hair, her hunched shoulders.

There was a bruise around Alex's right eye.

Cooper hesitated, then tapped on her phone to ring Alex, and Alex looked down at her own phone before putting it back in her pocket, ignoring it.

Alex went inside the hotel.

Cooper tried to go back to sleep.

As the hours passed, as room-cleaning moved down the outer hallway, 'sleeping in' pinned to her own door, Cooper thought about the police officers on these cases, then and now.

How Lapis had likely sat in that restaurant listening to her, her family for so long… the gall of it, the implied malice of his repeated appearances.

And Barker in those photographs, looking like he had gone back to the womb, in that deep, dark water.

Like he hadn't drowned at all.

Her phone vibrated. She must have fallen asleep at some point after all.

It was Alex. 'Meet me at work. Got something for you. Sorry if it's too early. No worries if it is.'

Cooper was due to meet her mother and sister in just a few hours, after a lie-in, a late brunch.

Cooper could afford the time, she knew. They would never miss her. Her mother's conversation at dinner, and Julia's lack thereof. Cooper's alienation had been made fully clear.

She entered the address of Alex's workplace in her phone.

As she did, she noticed some more replies to her true crime thread had arrived in the past hour.

U/88HOLDUP - *4hr*
The photo link doesn't work?

U/SWITCPOKEBL - *4hr*
Looks like they were taken down.

The photographs of Barker's drowned, potentially posed body had been removed.

But they were still open in some tabs on Cooper's phone, from a couple of days before. She saved them to her picture roll.

She'd come back to this.

For now, she had a meeting.

She went back to her map app.

It wasn't so much of a walk. Just fifteen minutes towards the nursing home, towards the house.

FROM: Gwen Lott
SUBJECT: RE: Goodbye
DATE: 18 June, 11:45
TO: Rebecca Allen

So how did it go?

FROM: Gwen Lott
SUBJECT: RE: Goodbye
DATE: 18 June, 14:17
TO: Rebecca Allen

Is everything OK? Hope you're OK – you can always talk to me, about anything.

FROM: Rebecca Allen
SUBJECT: RE: Goodbye
DATE: 18 June, 22:45
TO: Gwen Lott

I said some things I shouldn't have said. I shouldn't have come here. It's not helping me.

Along the shore the cloud waves break,
The twin suns sink behind the lake,
The shadows lengthen
In Carcosa.

The King in Yellow
Robert W. Chambers (1895)

PART 4:

THE HOUSE

SOPHIE BERTILAK
THE PAST

The Creation of the House

In 1388, after the Black Death, after the murder of a girl in Oxford, after the foundation of a university in Cambridge, the new institution gave its namesake to a new law.

The Statute of Cambridge declared that it was now illegal for poor people to go too far from their home towns. If you were found somewhere you didn't belong, you could be placed in the stocks. It wasn't just humiliation; chained in wood, unable to move your head, people could do anything they wanted to you in the dark.

In the mid-1800s, a large building was erected in Lethwick to house the descendants of poor people. Some descendants of the rich joined them, having lost fortunes throughout the centuries. Most remained the same as they had been, their capital tied to blood.

This workhouse was built with rows of brick interrupted by barred windows, external staircases crawling along the structure like veins.

The building smelled of pears and disinfectant at its best, if a modern nose were to sniff it. In the summer, it reeked of piss and shit in the unlit night, in rooms with too many beds, too many breathing mouths caught behind locked doors spreading coughs and silence.

A Bertilak stayed there in 1920. The great-grandfather of a girl who would one day take photographs in the woods.

People were free to go at any time, of course. But if they left the building, if they signed themselves out, if they were found begging or without a place to live, they'd be breaking the law. So they didn't go. The great-grandfather died in there.

The photographer's grandfather married a woman in town. In 1930, the workhouse was abolished.

The photographer's father married when his own time came. His brother-in-law died, far away. The workhouse was turned into an old person's home.

The daughter, Sophie, lived. She walked past the house every so often, seeing the old people walk around the outside, moving, looking as if they were some other species entirely, something that she would never be …

Moving in

There was a new arrival at the home.

People left all the time, one way or another.

Some came to this place because they were old and had nowhere else to go, whether as a result of the choices of their life or society or the unwillingness or inability of their children and loved ones to keep them under their own roofs.

Some came to this place because they were sick, in body or in mind.

Some came here because they were alone.

Mrs Earlsham was all of these things.

Even Sophie Bertilak, middle-aged, a far cry from the teenager she'd been when they'd met, did not really want to look after the older woman, did not really give her enough companionship to quell the heartache of that word – 'alone'. She did not want to ruin the image of Mrs Earlsham as she had once been that night, beautiful in the lake…

The nursing home smelled of soap and food, the kind of smells a school might have. They heard laughing in the halls as Mrs Earlsham walked through with her cane, the sounds of televisions playing.

'It's so warm in here,' Sophie said, but no one seemed to notice.

The nurses just walked with them, leading the old woman and her companion along.

The ceilings were cream white. The carpets were formed of zigzags where once there had been no carpet at all.

The walls were thin, the hallways thinner.

When they finally got to the room where one day, many years from now, Mrs Earlsham would die, she had a kind, twinkling glint in her eye.

'Is my husband here?' she asked, and the nurses said they did not know.

'Did he say he would be?' one asked, younger than the others, confused. This nurse asked Sophie if she knew anything about it – they didn't have a visitor logged.

The older nurses looked embarrassed, or indifferent, and said nothing.

'I don't – I don't know,' Mrs Earlsham said. 'Maybe he's out working. Maybe he's out looking.'

'Looking for what?' the young nurse asked.

Looking for who.

Her years in that place

Sophie sat in Mrs Earlsham's room.

She thought of that night in the lake, years ago.

She thought of how Mrs Earlsham had held her in the water – so beautiful then, so cold, quiet, small now.

'Who are you?' the ancient woman asked, almost ninety years old.

Sophie explained who she was.

'Oh. Oh yes. You took lovely photos, didn't you?'

Mrs Earlsham then added that she was tired, and asked if Sophie was tired.

Sophie nodded.

'Sit up straight...' Mrs Earlsham told her, and blinked, and turned away.

Sophie switched on the television in the corner of the room and remained there for a while. It was a way to make these visits go by quicker, to pretend they were both engaging in some activity together.

The news played.

Wars.

Global warming.

Eyes, buried in the earth.

Horse eyes.

The murders followed the discovery of these animal heads in the soil of a farm near the seaside community of Ilmarsh. Forensic veterinarian Cooper Allen provided the following statement...

Sophie saw a young woman on the screen.

'Stephanie ...' Mrs Earlsham said.

'She'd by my age by now,' Sophie shook her head. 'That isn't her.'

It wasn't her.

Sophie wrote down the name in her pocketbook. Cooper Allen.

There was something about the staging of the crime scene. The way the eyes of those animals looked up at the sky ...

The way they'd been buried.

She thought of her seventeenth birthday. She thought of wandering through the woods, holding a camera, looking at trees ...

The final visit

Shaded lights stood in each corner.

Laminate had replaced many of the carpets. Stains had grown in long fingers on the lower parts of the walls, sweat and smell rising in each hallway as it had a hundred years ago, the building becoming its original self again ...

The poor and the weak were imprisoned, unable to leave.

Urine mingled with tears and screams.

Each window was only able to be opened thirty centimetres, lest residents jump out of them. Some didn't open at all.

A voice in their minds told them it might be possible to fly.

In this place that was now emptier than ever before, of staff who had fled, of the elderly taken in bags.

Sophie Bertilak had walked past this building many times in the past few decades. She had come back to live in Lethwick, in the valley, in her childhood home. But in these last years of solitude, in this year of raising her pigs ... she'd not come to see Mrs Earlsham. She couldn't bear to, not yet.

Today, so close to her own death, Sophie finally had something to say.

'I know.' Sophie stared at Mrs Earlsham. 'I know where your daughter is. I know the man who took her, I—'

Mrs Earlsham did not stare back. She did not look at anything at all – her body now shrunken, her mind feeble, joyless.

'I did it,' Sophie said. 'I kept my promise.'

I live,
But live to die; and, living, see no thing
To make death hateful, save an innate clinging,
A loathsome, and yet all invincible
Instinct of life, which I abhor, as I
Despise myself, yet cannot overcome—
And so I live. Would I had never lived!

Cain
Lord Byron (1821)

PART 5:

BURIED

DR COOPER ALLEN
THE PRESENT DAY

FROM: RSPCA
SUBJECT: PORT-MORTEM, SURREY [URGENT]
DATE: 15 June, 16:23
TO: COOPER ALLEN

Dr Allen,
Are you available for a post-mortem in Sutton, Surrey, tomorrow afternoon?

O claims cat hit its head on counter but we suspect blunt force trauma: potential abuse of over fifteen other cats at property. Local vets back O assessment of criminals but attending officer concerned. PM worth it? If you can't attend, would you be able to phone us to discuss concerns?

Thank you,
Vem Symington

FROM: ANONYMOUS SENDER
SUBJECT: Open for a surprise
DATE: 17 June, 23:46
TO: COOPER ALLEN

[Photograph of a dead body]
Murderer cunt.

FROM: Criminology Dept, University of Manchester
SUBJECT: Keynote Speaker Confirmation
DATE: 18 June, 11:32
TO: COOPER ALLEN

Dear Dr Allen,
We are delighted to confirm your attendance at our September
conference as Sunday's keynote speaker. Please can you send
through a recent photograph for use in our publicity.

Cooper looked up from her phone. There were no emails about
the Bertilak case, no answer from Kelly, nothing promoting
further involvement at all.

She'd rescued Sophie's remains from the pig stomachs. She
had given the family something to bury.

She wondered what it would have been like to have taken
those photographs – the pipe in the ground, the abducted girl
and the man who had likely taken her...

Had Sophie really gone her whole life without finding out
more?

Could she really have died of confusion, of old age?

The police were set on their path.

And one of their number was following Cooper, intimidating
her – watching her, even at dinner with her mother...

What were they so afraid of?

39

Cooper was signed in by Alex as a guest of the nursing home.

'I can't give you Lapis,' Alex said. 'But there's someone else you might want to speak to, if you can keep things quiet – I don't want to get in trouble. I can't afford it...'

The hallways through which she led Cooper were sweltering, overpowering in their heat.

An old woman, toothless, wearing a nightgown, begged her for help.

'I'm sure – I'm sure this nurse will—' but as Cooper spoke, the old woman broke off, and kept going, and Alex didn't even turn her head.

'No, I'm sorry. She doesn't need help,' Alex said. 'She doesn't need anything. She's a liar.'

A group of residents struggled in another room, trying to collect the documents of their amateur crime club. They seemed to have been looking into the case of an old shop robbery. 'I've left my phone somewhere,' one complained, while another talked about the risk of burning to death.

A man cried – long, tall, almost like the spidery figure in Sophie Bertilak's final photos, found developing, hanging in her darkroom after her death. This pale imitation, this crying man – he had long grey hair, and sat in a wheelchair.

Further into the building, there were quiet, almost motionless men and women sitting in their squalid, flaking rooms.

They found Mrs Earlsham back here.

Alex didn't even normally work in this part of the building.

But in the hum of the aftermath, in the boiling over of Sophie Bertilak's death – people had been talking. Rumours had been spreading. And anyone connected with the dead woman began to occupy greater spaces of the world again, even if they'd forgotten that world, even if they wouldn't understand the nature of the death that had just occurred.

People like Mrs Earlsham.

Alex had read the visitor logs – Sophie Bertilak had been to see the mother of the missing girl multiple times over the years.

And giving her to Cooper – it was something to say sorry. Something to make up for involving Cooper in their mystery – an eyewitness to events themselves.

And Mrs Earlsham, seeing this stranger come into her room – she smiled, and realised it wasn't a stranger at all.

'Stephanie...'

40

'You've come back,' Mrs Earlsham said. Alex left them to it.

One day, your flesh will lose its supportive structures and wrinkle. One day, your mind, your arms, your legs will not be what they once were. One day, you will die before you die – the final years of your life taking memories and personality.

Cooper was scared of the old.

'She lied,' Mrs Earlsham went on, and she was almost crying now.

Cooper still stood a few feet from the bed. She had not said a word. Alex had left them – she had to get back to work.

All around were pictures of this woman's life – including the real Stephanie. Including, to Cooper's horror, the photograph taken by Sophie Bertilak of Stephanie's final sighting by the lake and her presumed abductor, the man with size 12 feet... It stood directly opposite the old woman's bed, in her line of sight always. Who had put that there? Who had done this to her?

'She said you were dead. She said—'

'It's OK,' Cooper said, and Mrs Earlsham shook her head.

'She said your mouth was full of apples,' the old woman added. 'Like a little boy.'

'What little boy?' Cooper asked, and then repeated herself more loudly, the old woman clearly straining to hear her.

'The one under the tree. It was a story, wasn't it?'

'It was,' Cooper nodded.

So they went on.

★

Cooper had never had a grandparent.

They'd all died before she was born.

She had grown up without ever visiting people like this. Without ever being loved by them.

Looking at the crumpled, confused face of Mrs. Earlsham in bed, Cooper wondered if she would ever live to look like that. To have her mind become like that mind.

'I'm not Stephanie,' Cooper said gently.

The old woman tittered, as if she'd told a joke.

'You said "she" lied – do you mean Sophie?'

'She looked so much like you,' the old woman nodded. 'But... she grew up...'

'What did she tell you, when she visited? She visited you a few days ago, didn't she?'

On the lawn outside, an old man in his pyjamas walked in white towards the trees. No one stopped him.

No one saw him.

'What did she say?' Cooper repeated.

'Your father... he's gone, you know. He's gone.'

Cooper watched as the old woman's eyes welled up.

'He's been gone so long and I waited, thinking it might make a difference but you never... you never came back.' The old woman trembled, hugging herself, sitting up. 'I dreamt so many times...'

Cooper approached her, and hugged her, and the woman cried.

'I told the – I told the police. Just in case Sophie was telling the truth. I had to know.'

'Which police officer?' Cooper asked.

'He's here. I'll—' The old woman began to get up with some difficulty. 'I'll show you. He'll want to talk to you.'

41

Mrs Earlsham walked ahead of Cooper, taking an age to move the span of four doors down.

She stopped.

Two men had once stood in front of the Bertilak house. They'd had dark hats and dark suits, one of them sharper pressed than the other.

He had been the older of the two, had a grey-black beard. The other, thin-faced, had walked around to the lounge window and tugged at the frame. It had been open. The older man had just stood where he was, right at the door.

Then he had hammered on it...

All these years, all these decades later, and the same man sat in his armchair, taken from his home when his son had moved him here.

His nose was attached to tubes to help him breathe.

He said nothing, showed no sign of understanding Cooper or Mrs Earlsham's presence.

The lead investigator on the pipe case and on Stephanie's sighting in the woods of Lethwick sat, almost catatonic, staring into nothing.

Robert Kelly Sr sat, breathing, and nothing more.

'I told him,' Mrs Earlsham said, 'But he didn't do anything. He didn't listen, not about the apples, not about—'

Cooper found herself stepping backwards, turning towards the doorway.

She hesitated.

She stared at the ancient man, and said a name.

'Detective Barker. You and Detective Barker investigated this case, didn't you?'

Kelly Sr cocked his head.

'He was your partner. What happened to him?' Cooper asked. 'Why was he suspended? You fell out, didn't you? Why?'

Kelly Sr grimaced and began to dribble shortly afterwards.

'He was missing for days before his death – did you know where he was?' Cooper asked, and Mrs Earlsham seemed to tear up also. 'Did you know?'

What was she doing?

She needed to get out of here. This wasn't right. She shouldn't be here – he wasn't in his right frame of mind, and to try and interview him in this state, without a responsible adult present to safeguard his needs ...

'Do you know a man named Lapis?' she went on, unable to stop.

'Stephanie,' Mrs Earlsham whispered, looking at Cooper's face. The old woman lent forward and stroked her, and Cooper flinched at its wrinkled warmth, and turned, and fled back to reception.

Alex was not around. Cooper waited outside for half an hour for her friend to come back, texting her to say her visit was done, but there was no answer.

Cooper went back to her hotel. She went back to her holiday.

42

There was a flash. That's how it started.

Cooper's mother looked up from her phone and saw a family coming towards her. One of them was taking pictures of the hotel, of the trees outside its lily-white veranda, of all the people who happened to be out there. They looked like they had just arrived, two teenagers and two parents.

Her husband had not lived to see Cooper and Julia as teens. He had saved her, he had given her children, then he had gone, leaving it all up to her. And what had she done with those gifts?

She didn't want to be in these photographs.

She didn't want to be in any photograph.

It was almost a phobia.

She left the lobby, picking up her handbag, putting her phone away.

She was going to say sorry.

She had to say sorry. The things she'd said to Cooper in the restaurant... she couldn't let them sit. She had wanted to hurt her daughter, time and time again. Something she'd never imagined she'd ever want to do. And the realisation that she was capable of this – it could make her feel differently about her own mother, if she let herself think in that direction... She'd sworn to herself she would never see her parents again, it had been one of the defining features of her entire life, and to go back on that, that would be a sin, wouldn't it? To betray all she'd ever been.

She went up to Cooper's room.

It was open. The door was hanging open.

She looked in. Her heart caught in her chest, a murmur on her lips...

'Hello?'

A face turned, and smiled, but it wasn't smiling – it wasn't—

The face, it was terrified – it was like it was looking up at her, even though it was just on the other side of the room, even though it was going through her daughter's things – it was waiting for her... it...

Seconds later, Cooper's mother fled outside, into the warm air, into the light of the sky.

43

Cooper returned to her hotel to find her mother almost hiding outside, out in the trees.

'Someone is in your room,' her mother said, holding her head in her hands, her pale face already red from sunburn. She began to cough and then, when Cooper didn't show any concern, the cough seemed to magically clear. 'Someone was watching me,' her mother went on, 'and I ran but... but I didn't know how far...'

Cooper and her mother walked back to the hotel, up the path, up the veranda, up through the lobby and escalator. Her mother seemed to treat Cooper as a protector. There were no words of apology, no reference to the night before.

'I think it's best,' her mother said. 'We can catch up again in London? I don't think this air agrees with me at all...'

The trip was being cut short.

Cooper agreed it was best. Of course it was best. They'd all go. Cooper would remain for a little while longer and then follow.

'And you'll see me again? You'll come visit me?' her mother asked, standing at the threshold of those revolving glass doors, a television echoing through the room, guests queuing up to check in nearby.

'I hope you feel better soon.'

'I want to – I want to have a proper relationship with you,' her mother went on, taking a step forwards, almost aggressively so. 'Just …' She paused, eyes flicking to her daughter's eyes, to their squint, moist redness, the trails of blood and stress beneath the white. 'I want things to be how they used to be.'

'I have to go check on my room. If someone's in there, I—'

'You had a happy childhood. Happier than mine. I made sure of it.'

'I have to go to my room—'

'I'll see you soon,' her mother said. The revolving doors behind her were empty now. They were ready. 'We can have lunch – the three of us – I know a place, and we—'

Cooper stepped back, half twisting, caught on the edge of going.

'Bring someone with you, bring a man,' her mother said. 'It's not safe. I told you, there's someone up there.'

'I can handle myself.'

'You can't,' her mother said. 'You think you can but—'

'I'm still here, aren't I?' Cooper blinked. 'Everything that's happened … I'm still here.'

Cooper went back to her hotel room. Her mother had always been paranoid, about illness, about bills, about anything. Never signed up for 'databases', for any collections of personal information at all. Seemed to believe conspiracies about vaccines, about autism, about anything the internet wanted her to think. The woman had become worse since she'd learned to use her smartphone. She'd changed to become more of herself, those negative qualities intensified, reinforced, made normal.

Cooper went back to her room and found cleaning staff finishing up.

Her bed was made. They'd committed the crime of replacing her towels and left new soap. Someone call the police!

Cooper rolled her eyes and sat down, thanking the workers as they left.

It was almost half an hour until Cooper found it, not looking, not left out, just catching her eye as she pulled her laptop from its case ...

It was almost half an hour until she found the envelope.

DON'T TRUST THEM, scrawled in black ink on top, in handwriting she had never seen before, scratchy, each capital's corners like the prong of a fork. The letter had been hidden in her suitcase.

Cooper opened it with a knife and tweezers.

Within, a piece of paper with a postal address ... a house on the other side of town ...

SHE NEVER STOPPED WATCHING YOU.

44

Her mother and sister left from the train station, claiming it had been good to see her. Cooper claimed the same.

Cooper took out her phone. She'd taken a photo of the address – she might need the paper itself for evidence down the line. She hadn't told her family about the envelope. Of course she hadn't. She'd just told her mother that the people in her room had been cleaners, and her mother had taken that as a greater sign of her own illness, so that she was now panicking, now coughing, her head hurting more than ever... Her mother had to get away, she shouldn't have come to this place, it hadn't healed her at all...

'We're getting married,' those sheepish words, 'we'd love you to come, if you want to...'

These words her sister had said at the station.

Cooper tried not to think about them.

She tried to focus on the letter. DON'T TRUST THEM. SHE NEVER STOPPED WATCHING YOU. That was what was real. That was important. The mystery.

Not the relationships of her past.

Not Arthur.

Not Julia.

Not her mother.

She kept going. 'Don't trust them'. What else could this be about but the case of Sophie Bertilak?

Who could 'THEM' refer to? The Bertilak children or the

police? What other groups had she interacted with since her arrival? What other groups existed in the plural that might be watching her? She couldn't tell the police about the letter, not yet. She couldn't trust them, not after Lapis had started following her.

Who was 'SHE'?

She thought of a memory, of a case a long time ago. Of a police officer who had put his finger into a bullet hole in the side of a sheep, then proclaimed it was not a bullet hole, that it was a bird, that no poaching had occurred at all. All the while, the accused standing near him, smiling.

Even better men and women than that... even they let her down, in the end. Everyone let her down, one way or the other.

She felt better as she went towards the mysterious address, and then grew troubled for feeling better. Like a person who slows their car at the thrill, at the sight of a car crash. Like someone who takes a photo.

The town of Lethwick smelled like cut grass as the day went on, the humidity and heat rising as the summer sky soared to an ocean blue.

It was like the town didn't know there was rain on the way.

There was always some storm or another, following from the best of weather. Some chlorinated odour behind the peaceful, near-motionless streets. Some threat of being washed away.

Cooper felt the warm breeze on her cheeks, on her bare neck.

She passed some cars parked near a boutique supermarket. She was halfway towards the address, stopping periodically to check her phone for directions.

There was a baby in one of the cars. It looked almost like a doll at first, a thing of plastic, it was so motionless.

Cooper hesitated. The windows were all shut. She tried tapping and then knocking, but still the baby did not move.

She looked around, feverish, trying to find something to smash the window with to free the baby from that heat.

As Cooper did this, a woman came up to the car, keys and shopping bags in hand.

She looked at Cooper like Cooper was someone to be afraid of.

When she opened her car door, the baby woke up.

They drove off.

Cooper remained there for a moment, letting her heartbeat slow to the pace of the breeze that was barely there, the shimmer of hot air on the road.

In a pub nearby, a group of men crowded round some slot machines, trying to double whatever money they had.

They all felt pleasure as they won, as they lost.

Cooper kept going.

The address took her to a suburban street up an incline from the river. No risk of flooding here, the winding streets and elevation acting as a buffer from any storm that might come.

It was a detached home, a two-floor property that stood alone, maybe seventy feet from the nearest building. There was no sign of who lived there, but it had been immaculately and anonymously kept. The blue paintwork was perfect, so lacking any stain or weed or dissolution from weather and time that it seemed unnatural in its way, quite wrong.

She didn't know whether to knock on the door. All the other houses around were grey, beige, or the original brown brick. Trees and hedges hid most.

She waited and saw no light, saw no movement or smoke within. She walked around the length of its outdoor fence, wooden with plant life crawling through. Nothing. No sign of anyone.

So she went round into the back garden to have a better look – the fence latch easily manipulated through the wooden panels. There were bins out there, there were weeds in the flowerbeds, trimmed to make them look like they had some shape, like they were desired plants, rather than random growths in the soil. There was no garden furniture, no sign anyone had ever spent time in the garden at all but for the trimming of those plants, the presence of those bins.

The kitchen seemed to jut out the back of the house, an extension beyond its original form. On the floor above, several windows were cracked open.

Because someone was home? Because someone had forgotten to shut them, or had maybe left them open to stop the accumulation of heat?

Cooper went round the front and knocked on the door.

There was no answer, no answer at all for what felt like an eternity.

She went round the side, rapping on different windows. Again, nothing. No movement. No answer.

DON'T TRUST THEM. SHE NEVER STOPPED WATCHING YOU.

Cooper climbed up the side of the kitchen annex, onto the little tar roof, her hands scraping against that blue paint.

She pried upon the window further, but already she could tell it was a bedroom.

She took a pause, looking around. No one was watching her. No one seemed to even be outside, not in this heat.

She hoisted herself through the window, and then she was in.

45

The bed did not look like it had ever been slept in.

There were no decorations of any kind in the room. The walls were all white. The bed was white.

Cooper walked into the hallway, wincing at the creak of a floorboard beneath her feet, but no one came, no one seemed to be there.

She kept on.

The hallways were much the same. Sterile. Divorced of any human stain.

The bathroom had a single toothbrush, shampoo that seemed to be branded for a man. That was something. 'She' was referenced on the envelope left in her room... Did 'she' live here, or did that word apply to someone else?

There were aftercare instructions for jaw-filler. A non-surgical cosmetic treatment to make one's jaw look more defined. Cooper had watched enough trashy reality TV to know her stuff.

She walked through the rest of the top floor, finding another, equally unlived-in bedroom, and a storage room full of boxes. She would go back to that.

She went downstairs, and saw no photographs, no frames on the wall. It gave the impression of absolute newness, of surgical freshness.

The kitchen held a dishwasher that had finished its cycle, its display flashing. A stack of ready meals in the fridge with various cans of cola, a bottle of milk. Nothing else.

In the lounge, there was a games console, a PlayStation. The remote control and the PlayStation controller were lined up on the coffee table, as if it waiting to be inspected.

The back room had a tower computer, a desk, a keyboard, a mouse, and runes – that was all she could think they were – painted all across the far wall.

The computer was password-protected, but she could see the username.

RFER109.

There had been no other sign of habitation, but for boxes, a games console, microwaveable ready meals, and this.

Cooper backed away and took out her phone, opening the camera, beginning to sweat as if her body had only just remembered the heat, as if the sterility of the rest of the house had been the same as refrigeration.

She took a photograph of the computer, of the runes, of the room from a distance, then further again. Three at intervals, just like she did with a crime scene. The username could be useful. The symbols – who knew what they meant?

She turned, and went back up the stairs to the box room. She looked through them. Most were just storage for old board games, tools, cables.

All of the games she saw – electronic and physical – were generic. Like those someone would buy from a list of bestsellers, rather than expressing any individual taste.

There was something else in those boxes, too.

Some had oddly personal possessions, both from men and women.

One, a box of driving licences. Cooper took as many photos as she could, her sweat beginning to drip onto the carpet now.

She opened her phone, looking for the meaning of those symbols.

Image search solved the problem.

They were Icelandic. Typically used by Neo-Nazi movements.

A shiver passed down her skin, one of disgust, of fear, were she to be found.

She looked at his computer screen, at his username. Maybe she could guess the password.

Maybe the name could tell her more about him – because it was a him, she knew. All of this – it was a man's home, in the worst ways it could be.

She searched on her phone.

RFER109.

Posts came up, sent to a variety of message boards. She flicked through them rapidly, homing in on a few.

RESULT 1:

RFER109 – 1yr

I stopped taking my tricyclics. The SSRIs already failed. Might as well be sugar pills.

I keep thinking about Limitless. I loved that film. I took everything I could find – got prescribed medication for ADHD after talking to a few doctors, tried caffeine mixed with L-theanine, even experimented with a few homebrew neurotropics. I don't think any of them maxxed my thinking. And I don't know if it's the fact I can't maxx it but what else could have followed if I was smarter and my stupid cunt mother hadn't drank and whored while she carried me? What if she'd raised me with the right food and vitamins? She's stolen who I could have been. Doctors deny there's anything wrong with me but that's the problem, it's 'me', the person I am now, not the one who could have been, *this* face, this ugly fucking face, ugly fucking suit, ugly fucking genes, ugly fucking mind, I was given nothing. How can there be something wrong with nothing when it's never been something?

Rick and Morty – Marvel – Everything Everywhere All At Once – all these dramas about infinite worlds, and they all show they mean absolutely nothing. If anything can happen then nothing can happen. Every story now is about how there is no meaning, as if that's not obvious. But don't worry, if you have friends or family who love you then that's not true, is it, Morty and Captain America and a daughter all make it worth it because we make our own meaning! If you don't have anyone at all you should just die because what's the point, really? Tell me seriously, what's the point if you're alone?

RESULT 23:

RFER109 – 178d

I'm tired and I'm scared that I'm not scared.

Who am I supposed to talk to? I would lose my job. I can only talk to all of you. You're my people. You're my people and I've never even seen your faces. I've talked so many of you out of dying and I'm a hypocrite. I have some rope too. I don't know if I'll ever use it but I have it in one of my boxes. I bought this house like I was supposed to and I've not even put up a single decoration outside of this room. This is where I talk to you. I don't talk anywhere else because they wouldn't understand if they saw it. I don't want to hurt any of you.

I thought joining the police would give me a community. It never did. It's like they can smell the difference in me. They have an old boy's club that doesn't share anything and it's like they smell how weak I am. None of them know what it's like. All of these chads and wannabe chads have wives and girlfriends and the female officers, they don't even look at me, but they don't even look like women either. And they're too busy taking money to have babies and fucking parasitise. I wouldn't even give them a baby if I could, no baby deserves my genes. If it were a boy he'd laugh at me and if it were a girl she'd run. It doesn't matter how much I looksmax, I'm so plain it's like my face is a mask. And it's my mum's fault. Who else's would it be? How else do you think babies are made?

Being a police officer doesn't get you much. I know this sounds blackpill but it's not careermaxxing, it doesn't get you anyone. All it means is people have to show you respect and you're allowed to make them do it. The rules aren't some made-up vague thing but something you can actually demand, and which sometimes you don't have to demand, people just do it, even females. And it's not the same as what it should be but it's sometimes enough, if I'm not feeling low. It's sometimes enough that I feel like I think a chad must feel.

RESULT 58:

RFER109 – 2d

There are so many pictures of her and so many videos. She was stalked once by some Elliot Rodger type. He followed her and another police officer and tried to go ER on everyone. Does she like police officers? She stayed in a hotel with this one. In the same bedroom. That's what the case notes said. Did she fuck him? The chad cop in the small town. And this ER guy who manages to follow her and take a video of her just inches away from her face, tossing and turning. I can't get that close.

RESULT 109:

RFER109 – 1d

Sophie Bertilak was a whore who fucked her way to money, didn't give a shit about the bastards she raised, she just spread her legs and used her face instead of talent.

46

A car was pulling into the drive.

It was like something out of a film.

She put her phone back in her pocket and ran to the back bedroom, those words running through her mind.

There are so many pictures of her and so many videos. She was stalked once by some Elliot Rodger type. He followed her and another police officer and tried to go ER on everyone. Does she like police officers? She stayed in a hotel with this one. In the same bedroom. That's what the case notes said. Did she fuck him? The chad cop in the small town. And this ER guy who manages to follow her and take a video of her just inches away from her face, tossing and turning. I can't get that close.

Years ago, in a case in a faraway town by the sea. Someone had filmed her secretly. Had left the tape as a threat.

She'd only seen the footage once.

What was an ER?

She'd had therapy to deal with it all; she'd tried not to think about it or him or the police officer for so long and … and …

She pushed the window open and dropped down onto the roof of the kitchen annex, tripping, hitting her knee as she did so, falling onto the soil below.

She got up.

She went round the back, heading out the gate, hurrying to the street beyond.

And there he stood.

There DS Lapis stood in his grey suit, staring at the woman who had just broken into his house.

47

'You broke into my house,' he said.

His hate shone through everything. The speck of each vowel infecting each leaf, each flower, each speck in the still air around them.

Lapis's presence, it made the sunlight seem dreary all around.

No one came outside to witness. They were alone in the midst of all those homes.

'The door was open,' Cooper said, trying to stand broad, trying not to look afraid. 'I thought I heard someone in distress. I didn't break into anything.'

His mouth looked like it was being forced shut, as if to open it for anything other than speech was to summon a laugh, or perhaps a lie. 'You came in through my first-floor window and came out the same way. You look like a little thief.' Still his voice had that same collapsing quality, that same trochaic, falling rhythm forced upon its words.

'Prove it,' Cooper said.

Prove it.

That was what their jobs both involved, wasn't it? Proof.

'Why did you come to my house?' he asked, and she did not answer, so he went on, his forced-shut mouth twisting into a slight curve. 'Easier ways to get someone's attention.'

The malice of his joy, of his mock-coyness in the dog day light... Everything about the way he stood was not to resist laughter at all – but to mock the very idea of holding it back.

'I saw your computer,' Cooper said, stiffening. Lapis was in her way. There was no exiting this alley without going past him. Still, no stranger came to witness their exchange. No one looked from any window. 'I saw your posts on the internet. About your good job looksmaxxing… about me… about Sophie…'

He stared at her for a moment. Was that vulnerability? Was that embarrassment? Was that any hint of his online persona, the grief at being the man that he was?

If there was, Cooper did not see it.

There was only a stare.

'Driving licences, there must have been a hundred of them—' she went on, but he interrupted this.

'Confiscated in the course of my duties. Awaiting return to the DVLA.'

'Held in a box in your house?' she scoffed. 'I can't see your senior being pleased with that, or—'

'I can't see my senior – or the superintendent – or a judge, perhaps… I can't see any of them, or anyone who really matters, being pleased with your breaking into my property.'

'Who will listen to you, when you get suspended?'

He shifted his weight, as if to move closer.

'I have photographs of everything,' Cooper added, stiff, now. 'Uploaded to the cloud. Even if you delete those posts. The one about Sophie – calling the woman whose death you're investigating a "whore". I don't think—'

'Good for you,' Lapis interrupted. 'I have footage of your entire break-in. It's in the clouds too.'

There were cameras.

How could there have been cameras? She hadn't seen anything…

He took out his phone, and he showed her the footage. It

was Cooper, climbing his fence, climbing his roof, then internal clips, showing her walking through his home ...

'Tell me again how my door was open,' he said, quite calm. 'Prove it.'

She didn't know what to say.

'Another video of you,' he said, smiling. 'Another one to collect.'

48

The question of what it meant to talk to another human being – Cooper had heard variations of it, everyone had.

What were stories, other than attempts at telepathy?

What was a conversation, other than an attempt to be closer to another mind?

Cooper had struggled. Everyone had.

In Lapis, the struggle found form, a silhouette in the blinding sunlight, a void where feeling should have been.

Lapis stood there for a few moments, like a stain.

No one came. It was as if this part of Lethwick had been frozen. Even the trees failed to move, the breeze failed to come, the spiteful sun failed to descend in the sky. The world's clockwork broke. But in all this, Lapis seemed paler, somehow.

'If you tell anyone what you saw in my office, I'll show everyone that you broke into my home. You'll never be allowed to work with another police force again.'

He told her that he didn't hate her.

He strangled through his words.

'Go home,' he said. 'I don't know why you're still here. I don't know how you found this address. I don't know why you're so obsessed with me.'

He grinned to himself, and the smile was without warmth, without amusement.

'It's like you're following me,' he said, and walked past her into his home.

49

Cooper's mother sat in the train carriage, watching her other daughter sleep in front of her. Julia had taken up God a few years before, then had let Him go. She wondered if Julia still dreamed of Him, why she'd felt the need to adopt Him in the first place. Was it guilt for what she'd done to her sister? Did Julia sense the stain of her mother's soul? It was what she felt like, inside her skin. Like damp and mould found beneath wallpaper, once all else is peeled away – like the illusion of a face found in all those swirling patterns, pareidolia...

Cooper's mother never really felt like a person with a name. She was 'Mummy' as much as she'd ever been Rebecca.

And what about all the other Rebeccas in the world? What about the Rebecca Allens, the hundreds of them, the thousands on Facebook and everywhere else – what good was a name when there were so many strangers, summoned at the click of a button? What good was a name when your husband replaced your own, when your own was from your own father, nothing unique to you at all?

Her own father, who she would never see again...

Her own father, who had...

No, Rebecca didn't want to think about him. She didn't want anything to do with him, in life or in death.

There had been someone in Cooper's hotel room when Rebecca had gone up the stairs, when she'd opened the door...

Not a cleaner, not like Cooper had said afterwards, not paranoia, none of that.

It had been a short, mousey face ... freckled cheeks ... the look of someone who should not be there.

The woman had been putting something in her daughter's bag.

The woman had turned, and had acted like it was her own room. Had asked Rebecca who she was.

Rebecca had not challenged her. Rebecca had fled.

Rebecca had fled the hotel, she'd fled Lethwick, she'd fled even their assigned seats on the train. She wanted to get away. Going to that town, trying to cure herself, trying to purge herself of her headaches, her coughs, her symptoms, her regrets ... it had all been a mistake.

Her other daughter slept on the train.

Rebecca opened her phone. No messages from Cooper.

Of course there were no messages.

She searched for an article.

She'd read it before.

She read it again.

*[Published two years before the
death of Sophie Bertilak]*

DISCORDIA MAGAZINE
February Issue

PROFILE

HOW SOPHIA BERTILAK RETIRED

*The war photographer – mother – activist – gives up all
her roles in search of a fundamental truth*

By John Stevenson

The Bertilak name has long been associated with death. From
the fictional, duelling, headless lord of *Sir Gawain and the Green
Knight* to politicians, soldiers, provocateurs, and even slave traders,
the family has a legacy befitting their moniker: 'Bertilak' translates
as 'contentious'. Of no daughter is this more true than Sophia
Bertilak, the Lethwick-born photographer, sometime activist, and
chronicler of an oeuvre that can best be described as extinction in
all its forms.

Born in the late 1940s, Sophia was raised by a single mother in
a valley home in central England – the same home in which she
received her first camera, the same valley where she took her first
macabre, shocking images.

Bertilak's representatives have already told me that any discussion of the infamous Lethwick pipe case is off the table, but it's

impossible to tell Sophia's story without repeating its inciting incident. As legend has it, Sophia was walking the woods near her home when she took photographs of random objects that caught her eye – a strange pipe in the ground, mistletoe, trees, and a girl by a lake. Two of these random acts would lead to an eventual true crime sensation, with a series currently rumoured to be in early development at Netflix; once the photographs were developed, it was revealed that the girl by the lake was missing teenager Stephanie Earlsham, and that within the pipe, a still-unknown abducted child had sat.

Philanthropist, gallerist and noted financier Quentin Medina invested in Bertilak's career after seeing these images in the press, not only buying the rights and original prints, but acting as Bertilak's patron in her further endeavours.

With this investment, Bertilak then did what any self-respecting photographer of her generation aimed to do: she went to war.

When Bertilak talks of this and other experiences, she speaks with a polite punctuality that suggests a detachment to the experiences that have shaped her. 'All you needed was a letter of recommendation to verify you worked for some magazine, and you needed a camera. My mum had bought me the first. Quentin helped with the former, though really – they gave them out to anyone who wanted one.'

Of those who set out with Bertilak on her flight to Vietnam, many were young photographers. In her award-winning documentary *Seat 19A* a middle-aged Bertilak tried to track them down, struggling not only with her memory of events decades later but the trail of evidence regarding the loosely regulated war photographers of the time. The majority had died or gone home within months. Although many of the photographers were embedded within US army units, their actions had frequently placed them in harm's way without the requisite training or equipment to survive. One of the photographers had developed a lifelong problem with alcohol and abusive relationships; near the end of the documentary, Sophie sits with the woman on her porch, talking about her own life in a rare moment of on-camera frailty.

As a patron of STOP THE WAR, Amnesty International, and numerous other anti-war and anti-censorship organisations, Bertilak has—

Rebecca Allen began to cough, putting down her phone; the magazine article, a photograph of Sophia Bertilak by the Houses of Parliament, still visible.

Julia did not wake, even as Rebecca found herself unable to breathe.

A concerned passenger across the way – a mother, she looked like a mother – brought water over and asked Rebecca if she needed help.

Rebecca drank it, and nodded, calming down.

'Are you OK?' the woman asked.

And Rebecca said no. No, she was not OK.

Yes, she needed help. She had gone on holiday to feel better. She'd thought the air would make her feel better. But there were still these headaches, still these symptoms ... She felt like her body, 'Mother', 'Mummy', 'Rebecca', 'you' ... she wondered at how it fell apart, how it fragmented. How the stain, long hidden beneath her wallpaper, beneath her skin, began to seep through; the dark, dread damp – the face there, the shape, all of it visible at long last ...

50

At the same time Cooper's mother began to cough on the train home, Cooper walked back through the town of Lethwick.

It was Sophie's funeral today. She hadn't been invited – why would she be? Sophie had never even heard of her. Still, Cooper wanted to catch a glimpse of it.

The old among them staggered down the street, slowed in this great heat. How that coffin was held up high – a joke, surely, a trick, they all surely knew only paste remained? Did it smell in this heat, or had they put a lid upon the jug of flesh?

The streets seemed as if they were made for an event like this. The slow procession of the pallbearers, Matthew Bertilak not among them, lingering further back with his sister...

People stood and stared as the wooden box passed above cobbles. The procession took so long that it felt like they'd always been here, nuclear shadows against the shopfronts, the cafés, the water beneath the bridge...

Cooper could barely remember her father's funeral. She could barely remember the man himself.

But with all that was about to happen to her, she'd never forget this sight: the procession of Sophie Bertilak's remains, the way Matthew and Lucy paused at the corner.

He had his right hand around Lucy's arm. Lucy moved as if to get away, not making a scene but clearly gripped by her brother.

His face was hollow, his eyes wide and almost empty, his lips hanging loosely, almost sad.

Lucy's lips were broadened in a bitter grin, but the rest of her expression had not followed suit.

Her eyes were wild, terrified.

It was something to be expelled – all their mother had meant to them.

All she still was, inside their minds.

And then the moment was gone. They were swept up by the other mourners, and within a minute it was like it had never happened, a rogue frame in the film of their lives, the march going on and on.

Cooper would never forget these sights.

You always remember the end, even if you forget the beginning.

51

Her mother lost consciousness on the floor of her train carriage. Cooper lay down on her hotel bed, miles back. If you could have seen them side by side ... the two women's faces were versions of each other, parallel, one far more worn than the other, but the resemblance there, in their expression as much as anything else ...

Cooper rolled to her side and clicked the aircon on via the wall panel, dazed, light-headed from the walk and the heat. She thought of the baby she'd tried to get out of the car. She thought of Lapis himself, his threat, his talk of mutually assured destruction. If she outed him, he'd out her.

Was it a bluff?

She thought of Lucy, her wild fear at her brother Matthew, the way he had gripped her arm ...

DON'T TRUST THEM. SHE NEVER STOPPED WATCHING YOU.

Who did these words refer to? Who had written them? She'd asked Alex for information on Lapis – who had she told? Who had then given Cooper Lapis's address?

Cooper ordered a bottle of wine on room service. White, cold, it arrived in a big metal tumbler full of ice.

'Thank you,' she said, waiting for the man to leave. He left.

She drank, cooled down, and napped for a while.

When she woke, it was evening, but still light.

She went to her desk and copied the photographs she'd taken in Lapis's home onto her laptop.

The sterility of all those walls.

The Neo-Nazi runes.

The desktop.

The driving licences from his spare room.

The envelope still lay on her desk, wrapped in the plastic not of an evidence bag, but of shopping.

What had its sender meant to happen, giving her Lapis's address?

Had Cooper found what she was meant to find? Why didn't they speak to her openly, why weren't they clearer in their suggestions?

From the photos she had taken of the driving licences, Cooper looked up their names on social media.

There was no racial or religious preference in whose licences had been taken.

There were tourists, residents, people dead and living.

Cooper made a dummy account to ask whether they had lost their licences or whether they had been confiscated, sending private messages to a selection of people on the list. She didn't expect to get any answers, at least not soon – the messages would likely end up in their spam folder. She wasn't their friend.

The accounts were mostly active, mostly real. Few appeared dead or missing – and even those who might be dead or missing, there was no real sign of the possibility beyond a lack of updates for a few weeks. She did not think anything had happened to them.

She saw their jobs, their photos. Car mechanics, checkout workers, commuters, credit controllers . . . no one common element, no profile of victims.

The sky had grown thick with cloud when Cooper arrived

near the end of her search. The day was breaking from heat to thunder.

Outside, through the open window, the rain began.

The driving licence image in front of her, fifth from the end – it belonged to a veterinary surgeon.

Cooper recognised the name.

52

Cooper left the hotel, the world still light, even at 7 p.m. She left her laptop switched on, its camera recording – if anyone came into her room to leave any other messages, she'd catch them.

There were sandbags outside a lot of the properties in town, flood warning signs, though the sky was still blue. It was happening again. There was no rest, no cessation, no peace.

The town wanted to be watched, again and again.

She went to the veterinary surgery.

She had a missed call from her mother on the way.

CALL ME, a text read. PLEASE CALL ME.

She ignored it. She wasn't giving in. It was a matter of certainty, without doubt – a boundary had to be established and set.

In the abbey ruins where Cooper had walked with her mother and sister the day prior, crows cried in the trees.

There was a kind of edible smell in the air, like the baking of bread.

The only other noises were thin and muted – the footsteps of tourists gazing at the remnants of the centuries' dead, talking about them as if they were at a funeral service. The stonework – if they had touched it – would have been cold, completely resistant to the heat all around.

There was even some discussion of the Dark Ages, referred to on various plaques.

Of a witch said to have lived here, who gave a choice to a knight of King Arthur's Court. The man had – so legend went – raped a woman. The task he was given in punishment was to discover the answer to what women truly desire deep in their hearts. On finding the witch of Lethwick, she offered to give the knight this answer and to save his life in the process, so long as he agreed to marry her. She was an old ugly crone, but she offered him a choice as to her eventual state of being. She could remain old and faithful and full of the sorrow of long years, or she could be beautiful, young, alive, faithless, lonely.

The knight said the choice was up to her. She should be whatever made her happy.

So she was both beautiful and loyal as a reward, synthesised between the two possible lives she might have lived. She saved her new husband's life by telling him that mastery over men was what women wanted.

So the old legend went, through Chaucer, through others.

So it had happened here, in the woods of this quiet and gentle place, the image on the plaque showing that witch in both her forms, both wearing red cloaks.

The heat began to break, raindrops spitting onto the heads of all these tourists, all these semi-silent parishioners.

Some of them held open their mouths to the sky as if screaming, letting the water fall directly into their throats.

53

'I shouldn't have let them be shot,' the vet said, a man named Jason, with thin yet muscled arms and a polite, oiled lumberjack beard that somehow remained static with every movement. He wore purple scrubs, even in the spitting rain. He was preparing for a flood. 'I know I shouldn't have ...' He paused. 'You did the post-mortem, didn't you? On the pigs.'

Cooper nodded. The surgery had been built in a pit, land sloping up either side, as if squeezed by the surrounding world. The parking spaces were all empty apart from a single 4x4, big, laminated animal cartoons in the window of the building itself, a foyer with open double doors.

Soon, the inhabitants of this practice – few as they were in number – would be evacuated to another surgery. Sheep and cows would be swept away in the flood, some of them, at least – the young, the old, as it always was. The sky, the town, white, trembling, like tissue paper. And still the sun shone low, the spitting rain like a mist where just hours earlier the heat had been unbearable.

'I've put down animals before,' Jason went on, dropping another bag at the side of the building. 'Of course I have. They asked me to do it – when I refused, an officer took over. It just ...'

'It didn't feel like mercy,' Cooper said. She had offered to help him with these preparations, had explained who she was. He'd been glad of the help.

And now, at the truth, he let out a 'heh', almost a shudder in the form of a noise. 'When does it ever? So much for dreams of hanging out with puppies and kittens.'

'I wasn't in practice for very long,' Cooper added. 'Not before I started, well ... all this.'

'I'd have liked to learn some forensics. Would have been useful.' He paused, the rain slowing around them. The practice was almost surrounded with bags now. Cooper was empty-handed, and so was he. 'Plenty of animals come in, and, you know, you wonder ...'

'Wonder what?'

'How they've been treated ... when a fall is just a fall, a bruise just a bruise. Separating accidents, and, you know.'

'Conspiracies?'

'Feels like a grand word for it, you know,' he said. Still, he nodded.

'Just because it's a grand word, doesn't mean it can't be true ... "you know",' Cooper smiled, almost sheepish, mocking Jason's speech habits.

He turned away.

Inside, there were animals that needed help, preparations that had to be made. He told her that if she had to talk to him, then she could keep making herself useful.

As they worked, they discussed accidents and evil. Cooper didn't think they were necessarily different things. On the topic of mistakes, unintended consequences, coincidence ... most bad things in Cooper's own life had, one way or the other, emerged from events no one had meant to come into being.

There were three cats and two dogs still in their cages.

One of the cats was long-haired, almost sorrel brown, like a squirrel. She meowed at Cooper through the bars, and Cooper reached forward to let her sniff her hand.

'I once had a cat like this,' she said.

Jason was switching off computers, moving equipment to bags, to cupboards.

'My boyfriend and I... we had two cats,' Cooper went on. 'One like this, a Somali breed, and another a tabby. They adored each other. We were close when they were kittens, but I was away at work, wasn't I, and I don't think they understood why I left every day... how could they understand? They just withdrew a bit, into each other, into their dad.'

'You're one of those,' Jason said.

'One of what?'

'Someone who thinks cats are children.'

'Every animal is a child at some point,' Cooper said, trying not to scowl.

'Ask what you came to ask, then you can go back to your kids.' This wasn't said with malice. It was almost gentle, accepting.

'I don't have cats anymore.'

Outside, cars passed in the rain, more and more as the minutes went on.

'I left them with him, when I left him,' Cooper said. 'But even before... even when things were good, I just... the more animals I put down at work, the more I kept thinking about how they'd die. It's fucked up, I know, but... I didn't even have them very long, they were just babies, and all I could think of was their death, the grief I'd feel, everything way more...'

Cooper paused.

Jason looked at her. She hadn't spoken in a moment. Her movements had slowed in her work. 'Are you OK?' he asked.

She wondered what would happen if she never told anyone anything again – if all her thoughts and memories and mistakes just died with her.

She wondered. She helped.

And he avoided eye contact, as if her silence was a demand, a condemning. 'They rushed me, I think. The police rushed me in my work. They wanted me to sort this quickly, even when I—'

The dogs began to whine as the vets came closer, reading the labels on their carriers.

'I wanted to anesthetise the pigs more humanely, but they said it was too dangerous, that I had a gun, didn't I? That I should use it. That the animals were dangerous. And after . . . when they took my statement, that didn't even give me time to get it right. They wouldn't even let me correct it, I—'

Cooper stiffened. 'Correct it? Why would you need to correct it?'

Jason didn't let the dogs sniff him before picking them up, didn't try to calm them down or say hello. He just opened the cages of the dying, the feeble, the scared and confused, and lifted them into plastic and metal, the animals whining as they went, and in some cases nothing, giving no noise but faint breath.

'I told the officers that Mrs Bertilak had last contacted us at Christmas. I said that there had been no contact for six months afterwards. That's not true. A month ago, she called and asked a question.' He paused. 'It just wasn't in her file, and I didn't know, and Reception didn't know I needed to know – didn't even mention it, until they found out I'd given a statement, and—'

'What did Sophie say in this call?'

He sighed. 'The police weren't interested. I don't know if—'

'Anything could help,' Cooper added.

'Aren't you just in forensics?' He asked. 'I'm surprised this is all relevant to your work.'

'It is,' she lied.

'Mrs Bertilak called up to ask about leaving the pigs on their own for a few days, if she needed anyone to check on them, or if she could leave a pile of food.' He opened the final cage. 'Reception asked her to phone back after lunch so she could consult with me directly, but she never did. And I just ... it sticks in my throat. The call, it doesn't make much sense with what we know happened later. I can't see how someone who'd apparently cared so little about their animals as to underfeed them would show such concern about leaving them by themselves.'

Cooper hesitated. She didn't want to push too far. 'The police refused to include this information in the case?'

He scoffed. 'They told me that due to Sophie's obvious mental instability, it wasn't worth, you know, looking into it ...' He scratched his neck. 'I'm not sure they're wrong. It doesn't change the facts of what happened, it just ...'

'It's messy,' Cooper said, and the vet nodded.

'One of the worst things you can do to a person is suggest they don't like animals,' he said. 'There's something about it that makes you seem less human. And Mrs Bertilak ... I don't know what she was like in the end, but it ... it doesn't feel like she was like that, you know? She seemed like she cared.'

They kept going in their preparations for the flood until all the animals were ready to be taken in their arks, until equipment, paper, everything was all up high.

'It makes me a bad person, doesn't it? That I'm more cut up about the pigs' death than the woman. The way they looked at me. What I ... what I helped do.'

Cooper let him talk.

'I got into the profession to save things. All I do is kill.'

'All anything does is die,' Cooper said.

'Did your cats die in the end?'

'What?'

'You said you were always scared about them dying. After you left them ... are they still alive?'

Cooper shook her head. 'Other people in my life thought they were dying too. They keep thinking they're dying. And everyone's just fine all the time. The world is never on fire for them, but there's always smoke…'

He laughed, raising an eyebrow. 'You sound almost disappointed.'

'My cats are fine, anyway. I know they're fine.'

'How do you know?' the vet asked.

'My ex.' Cooper held her fingers through the bars of a cage, and a little tabby cat nuzzled them. 'He started dating my sister, a few years after we broke up. They met each other and they did the proper things, they asked for my blessing, they took it slow, and I just… I just kept saying yes. My cats are her cats now. So I suppose that would make me their aunt.'

Cooper withdrew her hand, causing the tabby cat in front of her to meow in a pained, hurt way.

'I'll let you know if I have any more questions.' She paused, looking around. 'You should make a complaint. You should make a complaint about the police. About them not taking your statement. You should complain.'

'What good would that do?'

'It's corruption. It doesn't matter if it's born from negligence or malice, but it's still not right,' Cooper said.

'Maybe I will. Once all this is done,' he said, looking around at all the sandbags, all their defences. 'Maybe all this will have been for nothing. I can hope.'

She scratched her neck. 'But it's England, isn't it? Of course the river will burst.' She paused. 'Out of interest – which officer did you deal with?'

'What do you mean?'

'On the Bertilak case. Who got you involved?'

Cooper tried to raise this as casually as possible. If the vet noticed anything different about her face or voice, he did not show it.

He did not show much emotion at all, not at first.

'DS Lapis,' he said.

'Is there any reason Lapis would have your driver's licence?'

'You're saying he found it?'

'It's in his house,' Cooper said. 'In a box.'

The vet hesitated, then laughed. It was a forced laugh. 'I wished I hadn't ordered a replacement, then. Thank you for letting me know.'

He didn't seem to want to talk more. The storm was coming.

But as they finished up, he grew more nervous.

'Why were you in his house?' he asked.

She made up some lie about the case, but it did not calm him.

FROM: COOPER ALLEN
SUBJECT: QUICK HELLO
DATE: 20 June, 12:02
TO: ADA SOLARIN

I need that favour. Police officer from 1960s. Was suspended –
need to know why. And any other info you can give.
C.

FROM: ADA SOLARIN
SUBJECT: RE: QUICK HELLO
DATE: 20 June, 13:08
TO: COOPER ALLEN

Name?

FROM: COOPER ALLEN
SUBJECT: RE: QUICK HELLO
DATE: 20 June, 13:12
TO: ADA SOLARIN

Reginald Barker. Died 1965. Apparently drowned in the River Leth
shortly after suspension.

FROM: ADA SOLARIN
SUBJECT: RE: QUICK HELLO
DATE: 20 June, 13:27
TO: COOPER ALLEN

The records won't be computerised from back then. Unlikely there
will be any info in an NCA-linked database. Why the concern?

FROM: COOPER ALLEN
SUBJECT: RE: QUICK HELLO
DATE: 20 June, 13:34
TO: ADA SOLARIN

Possible corruption relating to a historic case. Don't know yet. A feeling. Died a few months after the case.

FROM: ADA SOLARIN
SUBJECT: RE: QUICK HELLO
DATE: 20 June, 13:42
TO: COOPER ALLEN

I can shoot it over to Professional Standards. You won't be kept in the loop, obvs, but it'll get looked into. Got anything more than a feeling I can base it on?

FROM: ADA SOLARIN
SUBJECT: RE: QUICK HELLO
DATE: 20 June, 16:11
TO: COOPER ALLEN

[5 DOCUMENTS, 3 PHOTOGRAPHS ATTACHED]

FROM: ADA SOLARIN
SUBJECT: RE: QUICK HELLO
DATE: 20 June, 16:15
TO: COOPER ALLEN

OK. Favour redeemed, we're even now. Sent it on. Might be a while before you hear back, though.

FROM: COOPER ALLEN
SUBJECT: RE: QUICK HELLO
DATE: 20 June, 16:29
TO: ADA SOLARIN

If you do hear anything back, let me know – it would be helpful.

FROM: ADA SOLARIN
SUBJECT: RE: QUICK HELLO
DATE: 20 June, 19:01
TO: COOPER ALLEN

What do you think 'we're even now' meant? I won't be sending you anything.

Good luck with your case.

54

Three days after her visit to Lapis's home, three days after Sophie's funeral and her visit to the vet, another envelope was placed within Cooper's room.

WHATEVER HAPPENED TO STEPHANIE EARLSHAM?

Cooper had left a 'do not disturb' sign on her door when she went out. The minibar fridge kept being refilled, in spite of the message. She left the air conditioning on every day. At least no one switched it off.

She spent her time listening to podcasts, reading articles, forum posts – the whole gamut of true crime fandom.

She liked listening to them, it was true.

Some of the videos and podcasts Cooper saw were about her, or must have been about her, given their titles. They must have mentioned her at least, surely? She must be part of the discussion – she was an important investigator...

Very few of them did.

'Police.'

That was the catch-all term for their work in solving things. Only when Cooper had become part of the events themselves, hunted or hurt by the perpetrators of crimes, did her name appear.

And it was baffling, invasive, what these people said about her, when the rare topic arose. They attributed thoughts and feelings to her as if such things could be known by strangers, as if implication were the same thing as reality.

'Now, Cooper Allen was absolutely terrified as she went into the woods – she just had no idea what she—'

This podcast – how did it know she had been scared?

The funniest thing was that in her listening, she did what she was expected to do. She heard these scraps of information and began imagining this character, a version of herself, going through these exact experiences. A second, phantom Cooper walking into the darkness of a cold night, heading towards the scene of multiple murders long ago ...

She listened to the podcasts about the disappearance of Stephanie Earlsham. It was better when these clips had nothing to do with her. When these characters could be enjoyed as others enjoyed them – at a safe distance, at a remove of time and feeling.

True crime prompted her to want to make a guess. Like all stories, it tried to engineer that guess in advance, shaping it through the structure of its telling. And it was seductive, this logic – that you didn't need permission to develop a theory of guilt and responsibility.

WHATEVER HAPPENED TO STEPHANIE EARLSHAM?

It was the father, wasn't it?

Stephanie's father had been abusing her.

When he talked about someone invading his home, some of the podcasts elided the details but it was clear he'd been staying with Stephanie by himself for vast periods of time while the mother travelled away for work.

Her apparent fall into misbehaviour had coincided with this change and this change alone.

He was dead now. Stephanie's mother was still alive, and some of the podcasts exhorted people to avoid contacting relatives of individuals discussed in the case. A good idea. Cooper had herself received a number of messages on different social media profiles from 'fans' throughout the last few years, changing them and her online name only to be found again and again...

But what kind of insanity would it take to go from reading about events to joining them, without authorisation, without sanction, without expertise?

What kind of monster would disturb the disintegration of Mrs Earlsham, her mind slipping away in that old nursing home?

Cooper had her theories.

And one day, when Cooper came back to her room, there it was – a letter as if a response, as if someone had indeed been watching her, a phantom friend who wanted to know her thoughts.

Cooper had left her laptop camera on in her room multiple days in a row, trying to catch her intruder in the act.

The letter was left out of sight of this camera, down on a side table near the door.

Cooper had left this camera on, knowing it would make its red light, knowing it would be obvious. The real camera was planted down the hallway, pointed at her door, hidden in the midst of a potted plant. It shed no light.

Cooper left her room, took this second from its mount, and went back to her desk and laptop.

She plugged the spy-cam into her laptop, and loaded its recordings for the past day.

She would soon know the truth.

55

Tourists left their rooms for a day of holiday.

Cleaners came and went, and Cooper watched herself leaving, too.

Time passed, and nothing happened.

It got closer and closer to Cooper's return on the video timestamp, so much so that Cooper wondered if she hadn't missed something.

But finally, a figure came down the hall, short, furtive.

The figure came to the door, knocked, waited, and after a while of no response, opened it using a keycard.

Cooper saw the person's face. It was not hard. She saw it again and again, poorly hidden from the camera, poorly hidden from anyone.

What would they have said, had Cooper caught them in the moment?

How would they have tried to explain it?

They were supposed to be friends, after all.

The first friend Cooper had ever made in this place.

Cooper watched the figure go inside her room, and then, a few minutes later, leave.

The night of the power cut. It felt like a century ago.

The stranger was shorter by a head, her skin freckled.

Her hair was light brown or ginger, Cooper couldn't tell,

not against the smudge of her own reflection – longer than Cooper's though – no self-cutting disasters there.

It seemed like she'd been crying, her cheeks puffy, her make-up slightly running.

She didn't glare, but she did seem surprised at the sudden contact with Cooper, a little scared, almost, but this resolved itself into apology.

'I'm sorry!' the stranger exclaimed, as if trying to go through the same doorway were some heinous crime.

'It's OK, really— A-OK.' Cooper stood back, holding the door open, and the stranger hesitated before walking past.

The stranger hesitated again, a little way down the hall, her back to Cooper.

'Are you OK?' Cooper asked suddenly.

The stranger turned, face barely visible in the dark.

She shook her head.

They had sat on Cooper's bed, leaning against each other, telling stories in the dark.

'Alex,' the woman had said her name was.

Alex.

56

Alex had told Cooper a story about work, once.

Cooper walked there now, searching for her 'friend'.

Alex's story:

It's the place itself. The smell — even if you don't get anything on you, it all smells like this. Most of the windows are bolted, or only open a little bit. This one woman — her room smelled different. It was always so tidy and clean — she was well enough to sort it herself, so the assistants used to let her use some of our supplies. It kept her busy and saved us time. She had been a doctor, once, had left the profession in her seventies, had retired with her husband. The old man died just a couple of years later, and so she was alone.

I felt sorry for her. Back then, I still felt sorry for them — for all of them.

She wanted to live somewhere nice. Sometimes she thought she was still there. From what I could gather, her children had sold the house at the first sign of her mind slipping. They used the proceeds to ship her here. She always tried to keep her room tidy. She never seemed to rest from the task, and no one really noticed, not until she started losing weight. By the end, we had to spoon-feed her as she walked down the corridors. If we tried when she was resting, she'd just get right up and keep on going. She didn't sleep by choice. She never sat down, not once, not if she could help it. And she just kept losing weight.

She died when someone left a fire escape door open in the summer. Staff were smoking on it, they were there in case anyone tried to go down the stairs, but she didn't. She just did what she always did. She

*just walked right past them before they realised what was happening;
she only had to clamber up a small bit. She tumbled over the edge of
the metal railing, fell six storeys, cracking open her head.*

*I really liked how her room smelled. Still smelled. She did it really
nicely.*

Cooper was down in the care home's books as a previous visitor
of Mrs Earlsham.

The person at the front desk had asked if Cooper would like
to visit her. Was she a relative?

WHATEVER HAPPENED TO STEPHANIE
EARLSHAM?

Cooper said yes. Of course she said yes. How else would she
get in? How else would she find Alex, when Alex would not
answer her calls?

They walked through the halls, the barred windows, the dirty
floors.

They walked through suffering, quiet and loud.

When they got to Mrs Earlsham's room, all around were
pictures of Stephanie as a girl, just as before.

Stephanie's final sighting by the lake. Her presumed abductor...

Mrs. Earlsham herself wasn't there.

'She'll be out for her walk,' the nurse said. 'If you just wait
here, I'm sure she'll be back soon.'

And with that the nurse left.

Mrs Earlsham did not come back. Cooper walked around
the room, examining her possessions, looking through her old
clothes, her toiletries, her novels – Christie, Greene, and more.

Cooper waited for a long time.

After getting up to go, she hesitated in the hallway. He was looking at her, she knew. He was looking. The person who lived opposite was staring at her, hunched in his wheelchair.

Robert Kelly Sr sat, saying nothing, but his stare said more.

He knew something, didn't he?

It was impossible to imagine that the old police officer was ignorant – that this man who'd worked on this case, who'd somehow ended up opposite the mother of the girl he'd sought to find – it was impossible that these things were not connected... wasn't it?

And so Cooper told him as much.

And so she asked for an answer – she showed him the envelope, Alex's scratchy handwriting upon its white.

WHATEVER HAPPENED TO STEPHANIE EARLSHAM?

Cooper showed him, and she waited.

'What did you find?' she asked, and he did not answer. He just stared at the paper. 'What did you do to your partner? What did you do to Reggie?' She swiped on her phone, finding the photos of the dead officer posed by the river.

She shoved them in the old man's face.

He murmured. His breathing changed from struggle to a sound. Barely audible.

She lent closer, asking what he found.

'Ap—' he began.

Closer.

'Apples,' he said, and spat at her, the spray of phlegm hitting the side of her ear, her face.

57

In the end, the Bertilak house began to crack apart. It had only belonged to them for a few days. Lucy had noticed it first; the way lines had finally started to arrive on the ceilings. Matthew had lived here when he was a child, just for a few weeks, and so his memories of the old place had been much like dreams, half distorted by irrelevancies and unconscious fabrications. It had been their grandmother's house, a place for holidays, until their brother had died.

In the weeks following their brother's death, Lucy had been conceived.

She knew it.

Her mother had told her, just a few months ago. She'd told her the secret of her existence, an accident born in the aftermath of an 'accident'. That was how her mother had described Alfie's falling beneath a car. It was unclear whether she said these things out of spite or if some dam had broken within her, some restraint that held back the old truths crumbling just like the home.

As if defying the inevitable fate of all Bertilaks, their grandmother had gradually allowed the house to rot for a while on the edge of old Lethwick, joining the abandoned abbeys, the waters that could no longer be swum in.

She'd allowed the building to rot, until it called for her, just like it had called to all the others.

She'd allowed it to rot, until she'd died here too.

Their mother – Sophie Bertilak, famed photographer, activist, witness – had moved there in the wake, to do what they now did: to sort through all those things that remained of a life.

In the absence of any body, her adult children began to dispose of all those things that still clung on. They began to dispose of themselves, too, jettisoning parts of their old personalities, their old priorities and guilts. Taking another day off work, more days without their old lives, more days in this strange place, the treeline just a short walk away. They'd think about the end of their family. Three Bertilaks gone over the span of sixty years. Joanna hadn't even flown in for the funeral.

Curved items seemed to slide along the kitchen counter. Were the foundations weak, too? Were there more problems?

'We need to do something about it,' Lucy had said.

Matthew had not refused to discuss the problem, but neither had he engaged with his sister, lost in his mother's affairs, trying to get the creative and intellectual legacy in order, tackling it all in intermittent bursts, their true inheritance. Days would pass between attempts to sort these problems, and it would be called mourning.

They abandoned their lives out here.

The internet talked and talked about Matthew's affair with a student, about his pattern of abusive behaviour.

TWITTER THREAD:

@CamillaMacaulay
16:19 – 12/04
I didn't know whether to post this for a long time. But here we go.

@CamillaMacaulay

16:19 – 12/04

Is it right for a 30-something academic to f***, gaslight, emotionally manipulate, multiple young women in his care? Asking for a friend.

@CamillaMacaulay

16:20 – 12/04

Multiple relationships, some overlapping, each girl told they're special – made to feel like they seduced him rather than the other way around – cut off from their social circles.

@CamillaMacaulay

16:20 – 12/04

Often plied with alcohol and encouraged to submit 'creative-critical' pieces of writing about their own lives, used further in his manipulation.

@CamillaMacaulay

16:20 – 12/04

And those around this man who report his behaviour are typically ignored or swept under the carpet by college officials. Why wouldn't they? They've done it for others for years.

@CamillaMacaulay

16:22 – 12/04

Women are afraid to leave him because if they leave him, if they disagree with him, it could cost them their grades and their whole degrees.

@CamillaMacaulay

16:22 – 12/04

Women who, once discarded, are left broken-hearted and second-guessing their own autonomy, sometimes changing courses.

@CamillaMacaulay
17:52 – 12/04
People are asking me who this is. It's Matthew Bertilak. He's been given every opportunity to change and he's taken none of them, because people like him CAN'T change.

@CamillaMacaulay
17:56 – 12/04
These women can't go back to their studies. Some of them have been diagnosed with PTSD and trust issues. He's wrecked lives. He deserves everything that's coming for him.

The siblings looked at their phones less and less. Matthew still insisted there had only been one, that he had loved her for a time, that all this talk of a pattern of abuse was just a lie.

Lucy tried to comfort her brother, when she could.

They'd lie there on the sofa, her arms creeping around him as they fell asleep in the dark.

The children of Sophie Bertilak had not been raised with rich excess, but their mother had earned a decent living in her life, and the walls of her final resting place showed these marks, extensions where the house had reached out to new purposes, where darkrooms had been erected, supply units, workspaces, and the like. A once-modest three-bedroom detached property had metastasised in the space of two years.

'Building scars,' Matthew called them. 'You can see them on ruins, too. Places where there were once extra features, or where things have been changed. The history of all that's been done to them. Redolent with time ...' He looked at Lucy's blank face, and smiled. 'Redolent – meaning suggestive, fragmentary.' He always tried to teach her. He did not know how she felt about it, but he enjoyed it, discovering she did not know things.

'What did you see in her?' Lucy would ask, and Matthew would not answer. He would not talk about the girl from his university. He would not talk about the scandal.

Lucy saw the way he looked at others sometimes.

One of the officers in the station.

A second cousin at the funeral.

The specialist, who'd stayed with them.

The specialist, who'd left their home without saying goodbye, even after Lucy had hosted her, even after they'd started to befriend her...

Had he looked at the student like this, Lucy wondered?

The siblings had grown lonely, separately, in different ways in their different lives, but it was still loneliness. And so much can go wrong with the world, when such people meet again.

They told lies to each other, to themselves. They acted like these might last forever, these strange, post-mortem days and nights.

Everyone told lies, but not everyone was a liar.

One day Matthew said he needed some time alone.

She checked his search history when he slept, and found he had been reading about the specialist.

Cooper Allen.

And though the hours turned to days, both of them still imagined that that night Sophie Bertilak had lain down by the apple tree a few metres from where they sat...

No one had seen the moment itself.

No one had seen the pigs, as they'd eaten their mother's flesh.

Lucy went for a walk. She went into the woods.

She did not want to be afraid. And Matthew – he did little for her loneliness. Their solitude compounded, like two sums added together.

Was it good for her to remain in the house of her mother's death, of her own birth?

Was it good for her to remain here?

She went out into the light.

She went out into the woods, not telling a soul.

58

Cooper saw her, a while later.

Lucy was wearing a yellow day dress. It looked almost like her hair was white in the sun, the blue emerging in shimmers. Of course, Lucy didn't realise she was being watched, didn't spot Cooper higher up the trail. It was odd seeing Sophie's daughter again, and after the awkwardness of Cooper leaving her a few days earlier without so much as a goodbye, there was no real need for another meeting.

No.

Cooper decided to say nothing. She could still feel the spit of the retired police officer on her face, no matter how many times she had washed it.

She had gone back home (no, to her hotel room – it wasn't home); she'd waited for her friend (Alex wasn't her friend); she'd got changed and gone out for some fresh air, to run, to exercise, because she was on holiday, wasn't she? (Because she was afraid, because she couldn't bear to be inside, because she didn't know what to do ...) And here she saw Lucy Bertilak by chance.

(There's no such thing as chance.)

None of Lucy's clothes suited the trail. She wore sandals, she had no water bottle, no bag. She seemed inattentive to her surroundings, sometimes entering into the hiding places between the trees, sometimes in view.

When they'd first met, Lucy had told Cooper she never went into these woods. That she'd been scared of them.

Good for her.

Good for her, then, that she'd come here and faced it.

It was three days since Lapis's home. Three since the vet. The leads regarding Lapis's driving licences had come to nothing.

When Lucy was gone from view, Cooper ran, finally, wearing her running shoes, brought for an imagined holiday full of running, her purple RVC hoodie, her running trousers.

She wanted to see it.

She wanted – like so many local boys and girls over the long years – to see the site of the pipe, of the photo.

Maybe if she did, she'd have some realisation, some epiphany, and maybe then she could stay, maybe she could be useful...

'Apples,' the old officer had said.

'Apple tree,' Mrs Earlsham had raised, again and again, 'full of apples...'

There was an apple tree outside the Bertilak home. She should go there, she knew, but she didn't – she couldn't face confrontation, not now, not feeling as she did – she just needed to stabilise, she just needed to...

She listened to music on her headphones as she went.

She listened to 'The Court of the Crimson King' and turned left down the hill, keeping an eye out for any police officer who might follow. She always kept an eye out now.

Through the woods, she passed ducks, clouds, the odd rustle in the twigs, other runners, mothers with prams, dogs off leads.

Fewer and fewer living things, the deeper Cooper went.

Cooper walked sometimes instead of jogging, but maintained her progress, even till the sun was low.

She had no music playing in her headphones by the end. Songs had autoplayed on and on, but had just stopped at some point, like they always did – an internal, unknowable mechanic of her phone had decided it must cease.

She wasn't sure if she had found the right place, but the lake seemed familiar enough.

An old stag was there, too.

It ignored her.

It focused on something near the water.

It ate, and it ate.

59

The stag was eating flesh. The red on its snout was blood. Its antlers were bright and mossy.

They were herbivores, of course, but even vegetarians ate meat, sometimes, given certain conditions, certain enticements to go against their natures, their vows. Even sheep could do so. But what those conditions were, exactly, could be debated – if there was even any logic to the affair. Certainly the phenomenon of a carnivorous deer was more commonly witnessed in winter, suggesting hunger could push some species over the edge. Most herbivores often preferred their own kind to the meat of others. Cannibalism started sometimes as affection or mourning for the dead, as a licking of a face, as a kiss, meaning one thing once, now touching cold, empty skin…

The stag ate something, licking at it, occasionally tearing. Cooper's presence seemed to briefly distract the animal, but it did not stop. It stood its ground on the lake's bank, only looking up every once in a while.

It was hard to see the dead thing at first, obscured as it was in the purple, shaking reeds. There were flashes of red and grey, of a mottled surface, covered in scratches, in holes enough to spark a phobia in some, like the pits of a sponge, like a mass of craters.

Cooper came closer, and the stag seemed annoyed at this, rising from its meal to look at her.

'You'll get sick if you keep eating that,' Cooper said.

The stag didn't reply, which was rude.

'What was it to you? What you're eating, I mean. Did—'

There was a rustle in the trees behind her. Both human and stag turned their heads immediately, but even that was not quick enough. There was no motion in the trees, no sight of whatever had made the noise.

A few moments later, the stag ran off, too.

So Cooper was alone, but for the pitted, rotting shape in the reeds. There was little to smell from this distance, and little noise but the water. The light though – the sun that fell upon the scene was like the work of an old master, like an image of Icarus falling from the sky. It cut through the branches of old oaks and sycamores like rainfall, golden, warm. They were the kind of sunbeams cats sought out their entire lives, the kind that made you want to curl up asleep.

Cooper stepped closer to the dead creature.

Two stumps split off at the top left and right, two from the base. All it had left was its grey, pallid bulk, its hairs splitting off all along, spiralled by water and bloating into strange, distinct patterns. Its head had twisted to its side, now lacking a nose, lacking ears, lacking any kind of face.

This thing, this stag's meal.

It had been human once.

The waves of the lake, driven by air and wind, lapped against what remained of the thing's hip, seeping into all those holes pitted along its length. It seemed to expand and contract a little, though Cooper did not know if this was just imagination, or an illusion of sight and sky.

She heard a noise again, out in the trees. A rustle. A snap. This time, there was no stag.

She left, the golden rain fading. There was only a quiet, gentle wind.

60

Cooper phoned the police as soon as she had a signal, five minutes back along the route.

She asked to speak to Kelly Jr, but was put through to someone else.

She explained it all as best she could, the sun low, just a little, but the day still bright. The world even became golden again; it grew warm as Cooper spoke of the corpse, of the stag, of why she'd come out to the woods alone – just for a run, she'd said. Just a run.

As Cooper waited for the officers to arrive, she began to think about it all a little more. She wasn't sweaty. Even in the mild heat, she wasn't sweaty – she didn't know why she wasn't. She began to jog on the spot, trying to build it up a bit. She should look like she'd been running, that this discovery had just been by chance. The person who discovers a human body is always suspected, always interrogated. She needed to take away their doubt, she—

What the fuck was she doing?

STOP IT. STOP IT. STOP—

She gave up running after getting a little sweaty in her armpits. She sat down on a log, and waited.

When they came, she showed the police officers to the site of the corpse. They soon carved the area off with tape. One of the officers retched nearby. The first murder victim he had ever seen and it'd had no face.

The drive back to the station was quiet and cold despite the air outside. The fans in the car hit Cooper's damp t-shirt, her now glistening forehead.

You're never going to leave this place.

She had only been to around twelve or so police stations in her life. Nine of those for cases she'd worked on. Even the other three, she supposed, were most than most people went to.

These police forces, they rarely required in-office meetings. The battering or death of an individual pet was more likely to be investigated by a legion of charity workers, the RSPCA, private prosecutors, hired solicitors, and the like. If the matter actually reached a station desk, an officer might feel obliged to take a statement, to make a record of the complaint, but this did not mean resolution was inevitable, or even likely. And if they did, what would happen other than a few months of suspended sentence; perhaps a soft, barely enforced ban on keeping pets for the miscreant in question?

The police car arrived at its destination. And it became clearer in-person how full, well equipped and disgustingly invested in this place was. The building had a blue lantern hanging above two wooden doors, the stonework all around old and weathered enough to be that of an Oxbridge college. More officers milled in and out of them than Cooper had seen in towns with twice the populations, their gleaming clean patrol vehicles lined up outside.

She even passed a receptionist on the way in, a representative who could be spoken to in person. No sign telling visitors to phone a call centre. No sealed hatch. There was a sense of showmanship, of authority.

Past the sea of desks, beneath a ceiling that looked like shredded paper, Cooper followed through the dim LED white.

Through to the office of a man she'd tried to joke with just days before, sitting in the back of his car.

She sat down to wait.

She saw a priest walking through the corridor, black top, white collar. He was a pale, surprisingly young man with dark hair.

He entered a corner room.

CHAPEL, it said above. And next to it, an amendment: ALL FORMS OF WORSHIP WELCOME.

She watched and waited to see if anyone else went in or out.

The room remained empty but for the priest and whoever had already been in there.

Cooper waited for her interview, thinking about her current situation.

She didn't believe things were going to be OK.

In her interview, Cooper tried to explain everything she'd seen, repeating her phone call, going through the same stupid bureaucracy these people always demanded of her. She went through it all: the stag, the likely level of decomposition, the noises around her; that perhaps she could help consult for them and—

'Consult?' DCI Kelly looked at her, uncomprehending. 'You're a witness now, Ms Allen. You're involved.'

'Doctor,' she said. 'It's Dr Allen.'

'Why did you accept their invitation?'

'What invitation? What are you talking about?'

'Sophie's children – the night you did the post-mortem on the pigs. You came to the crime scene, uninvited, when I expressly told you not to do so. They asked you to stay for dinner and you said yes. Why?'

'Why does it matter why I said yes?'

He just kept looking at her.

'They were mourning. I wasn't going to refuse a friendly invitation.'

'So you claim you did it out of kindness?'

'Claim?'

'Why did you come here, Ms Allen?'

'You asked me to.'

'Why are you in Lethwick at all?'

'I told you the other day – I had a trip with my family.'

'Can we speak with them?'

'They've gone.'

'And you're still here. Why?'

She stared at him and then – hesitating – spoke: 'Is your father the same Kelly who worked on Sophia Bertilak's case?'

This seemed to surprise him. He said nothing for a moment, clearly searching for words, and so she pushed it:

'Isn't that a conflict of interest?' Cooper asked. 'Should you really be involved in this, or—'

Too far.

He grimaced, his face twisting, and he ignored her question.

'Did you know Sophie Bertilak?' he asked, a dangerous edge entering his voice. 'Did you know any of her family? Before all this, I mean. Did you know them?'

'Of course not.' The denial came out quieter than Cooper had intended.

Kelly opened his tablet and swiped to unlock. He had a picture on the screen.

It was a photo of the corpse from the woods, its arms missing, its face consumed.

As he showed it to her, all Cooper could think about was how artless a photo it was, even compared to seventeen-year-old Sophie's image.

'He was her father-in-law,' he said, surprisingly, oddly gently. 'He was in his nineties.'

Cooper had no idea who the officer was talking about. Not for a moment.

She stared at the photo, at the grey, pitted skin; at the stumps where arms had been cut off; at the half-eaten face, so recently torn at by the stag.

'I knew Sophie,' Kelly said, his voice trembling. 'I knew her since I was just a kid. So yes, I'm working on her death. I'm trying to find out what happened to her, to those she loved. I knew her, I admit it, yes. So I'll ask you ...' He swiped to a different image on the screen – the same man as the stag photo, undecayed, alive, just old ... Smiling back at the camera with a distant smile. 'Did you know them? Did you know *him*?'

Cooper did not know what to say.

She did not know how to explain her continued involvement in this case, even to herself. These last few days, they felt like a dream, somehow.

DON'T TRUST THEM, the letter had said – *Alex* had said; she knew it was Alex now ...

DON'T TRUST THEM.

She thought of the letters.

Of Lapis's home, his hate, the officer no doubt walking these very corridors ...

She thought of the Bertilak children, of all she'd seen and heard of Sophie's life, it was like she knew the woman, having seen all those videos, having listened to all those podcasts ...

And she thought of Stephanie, missing so long ago.

She thought of Stephanie's mother.

Apples.

All this, and apples – apples were the words of Mrs Earlsham's delirium, of Kelly's father in his malignant decay ...

Apples.

She said your mouth was full of apples. Like a little boy. The one under the tree. It was a story, wasn't it?

How Mrs Earlsham had thought Cooper was Stephanie.

As if time could bring back that lost girl across the years, ignoring age and entropy.

As if Sophie could still somehow keep her promise.

Cooper thought of all these things as the police officers spoke, as they questioned her. She wondered what she could say to contribute, what she could possibly speak of that might not risk Lapis's promised reprisal, that might not cost her the tatters of her career – to be painted as some hysterical individual, breaking into an officer's home, harassing witnesses who she'd had no right to speak to.

This was supposed to be a holiday. It was supposed to be a break.

'Apples,' Cooper said. She told them about apples.

There was something buried under a tree ...

Near them, on the sand,
Half sunk a shattered visage lies, whose frown,
And wrinkled lip, and sneer of cold command,
Tell that its sculptor well those passions read
Which yet survive, stamped on these lifeless things,
The hand that mocked them, and the heart that fed...

Ozymandias
Percy Bysshe Shelley (1818)

PART 6:

LOVE

SOPHIE BERTILAK
THE PAST

Lethwick, 1968

Four years after the photographs

Call Centre Transcript #1

VOICE 1: I'd like to change my phone number.

VOICE 2: Why?

VOICE 1: Do I need a reason?

VOICE 2: My form needs a reason.

VOICE 1: Harassment.

VOICE 2: Who's harassing you?

VOICE 1: Someone keeps dialling and hanging up.

VOICE 2: Have you reported it to the police?

VOICE 1: Yes.

VOICE 2: OK, I'll make the arrangement.

Call Centre Transcript #2

VOICE 1: I'd like to change my number.

VOICE 3: OK, give me two minutes. Oh. I can see we've already issued you two new phone numbers in the last year.

VOICE 1: Why does that matter?

VOICE 3: We don't normally issue so many new phone numbers—

VOICE 1: They keep finding my number – if you know how to stop it, then fine, but—

VOICE 3: Who keeps finding it?

VOICE 1: They keep just – just breathing at me, and—

VOICE 3: Who? Ma'am, you need to—

VOICE 1: They know my daughter's name – they called me Sophie – but it only started after she left.

VOICE 3: Ma'am, have you reported it to the police?

VOICE 1: [scoffs]

VOICE 3: Ma'am?

VOICE 1: They've done nothing. Nothing to help me. They act like they don't even believe me . . .

Private Recording #28

UNKNOWN: (breathing)

VOICE 1: (breathing)

UNKNOWN: (breathing)

VOICE 1: It's been days since I've spoken to anyone, you know that?

UNKNOWN: (breathing)

VOICE 1: You're the only reliable relationship I have. Isn't that strange?

UNKNOWN: (breathing)

VOICE 1: Both of us, sitting here wondering when Sophie's coming home, where she is . . . what she's doing. I wish . . . sometimes I wish I'd . . . (pause). Are you out there, now? Are you watching me?

[Silence for 22 seconds]

[UNKNOWN hangs up the call]

The Corpse

1944

Twenty Years Before the Lethwick Photographs

He didn't know if he'd killed anyone.

It was the not knowing that bothered him most.

The young man sat at the edge of the ruin, his boots on the cusp of a grey-brown puddle. The sun emitted endless day. One day his body would be discovered by a lake, consumed by an old stag in the golden light of the trees. That day, in 1944, the light hit his then whole body in much the same way.

His letters home had been as happy as he could make them. He had begun to resent it a little, how eloquent he felt on the page; how trembling, stuttering, stupid he felt in person. He told his family a story of dream logic, of what he hoped for, of things far from this time and place. Of having a wife one day. Of having a son, perhaps. He told his mother and his sister that he hoped for the best. He told them to be good.

The night had been cold, sleepless. There had been a smell of blood and flowers in the dark, but it had passed in the day. They journeyed deeper into Europe.

They walked on.

'Look over here,' another man said. 'Look.'

They went.

They found burned bodies in a ruined, blackened home near a river. The skin of the dead dripped from their bones, charred-red coagulate like embers burning in the air. Two of them had been children. They were contorted, their limbs having contracted from the heat.

The whole world was silent but for the sound of the soldiers' boots, of rustling.

It was a question of what murder was. Of perpetrators, weapons, intentions. The man's ability to perceive the world changed in the powdered light, in the slow sounds of war.

He asked one friend, and another, and another, even though people never really liked this kind of talk.

He asked his friends how they'd known they'd killed people, if they could know. If a man falling down across a stream had been because of their bullet or another.

Among his friends, only three confirmed responsibility for actual deaths, and one of them was a fool. Of the rest, several were like him – unsure, confused – though they would pretend they didn't mind.

'I'm walking down the stairs,' one man said, bending his knees, mock-lowering himself past scattered crumbling brickwork as if an invisible staircase would lead him into the soil. It was stupid. People laughed.

Three days later, the stair-soldier lost his heart, blood welling up like an oil spill.

Over time, his letters began to change. Their writer talked about the future, expanding on his vision. He talked about a nice house and a nice girl and a nice job. He'd never had a girlfriend, but he imagined his unknown wife might be beautiful and kind. Whenever he imagined her face, it was just a white sphere of no particular shape, no particular features. He started writing about the faceless woman in some of his drafts, but he threw them away for the most part. Whenever he mentioned possible children, he just saw himself as a child – as a copy, as a perfect replica. These he threw away also.

Then he stopped writing letters altogether.

Four years ago, his family had killed their own dog. The National Air Raid Precautions Animals Committee had published a pamphlet recommending that pets be destroyed if they could not be evacuated, so as to conserve national resources and spare them the terror of war.

His sister had begged their mother to keep the animal alive. They loved him. The pamphlet recommended a captive bolt pistol for humane destruction.

They were not even poor. They could have kept their dog. They didn't have to do this. All these things were said. They had money. There was a way.

But money, it shouldn't make you different to other people.

Everyone had to play their part.

He had used their father's gun. It was the first time he'd ever used one.

'If you cannot place them in the care of neighbours, it really is kindest to have them destroyed.'

They kept using the word destroyed, destruction.

A few weeks later, 750,000 pets no longer existed, beyond the regular consumption of livestock. It had really happened. He had to remind himself of this. It was real. It was history, now.

He looked around at the other men sometimes, and thought they might be missing the enemy on purpose. That they were aiming at nothing, that only the mortars and the tanks took German lives.

He saw these people fire at the air near heads. He saw the shaking arms, the wild eyes, not just in his friends, but in those who opposed them.

★

At the end of the war in Europe, the man came home.

He got married, he had his kids, though they'd looked nothing like him.

He grew his fortune, and he spent it on all manner of things. He became a patron of the arts, investing in a gallery.

He lost more people, as all people do.

He didn't know if he'd killed anyone.

One day, he met a girl.

The Corpse

1965

One year after the Lethwick Photographs

Everything was perfect.

The estate – its cut grass, its hedges, its trees – was arranged in a cultivated, unnatural, tamed grid structure. The path towards the house was formed of ornate brick. You could be seen from the main house if you approached, and it would take you a while to reach its front door. There were too many deer on the estate because the owner refused to have them shot. He refused to have any harm come to any animal. He was a vegetarian, which most of the people he worked with – and who worked for him – felt was odd.

The grass had just been cut. That smell of summer mornings and evenings, when a mower has culled the heads of all those plants, and the smell that enters your nose isn't the vegetation, it's the perspiration of all that bacteria, freed from a stream of green – it's the rotting of the world itself.

The man came out to meet a girl and a mother.

The girl was seventeen. She'd taken a few photos the year before.

He wanted to invest in her career. He wanted to back her. He had a gallery, he had investments in publications, he knew people.

They all talked and laughed outside in that unnatural perfection.

'Can I use your bathroom?' the girl asked, and he said no.

He apologised, it was quite messy inside. He'd had to let go of some of his staff members.

There was a coach house near the gate. She could use that. She thanked him.

Gardeners cut hedges all around.

The sky grew red as the day went on.

He asked her for her plans when she came back.

And the girl, she began to talk about the Associated Press paying for flights and images.

She began to talk about war.

The man, he just listened. He just sat there, grass drifting in the sunset.

The Exhibition

1969

Some photographs were being exhibited in a small gallery in Whitechapel.

The streets outside were full of men, some with flat caps, some with long hair. Streetlights shimmered gold like eyeballs in the rain, the reflections on the tarmac pools of sleep and dust. Neon and ticker boards whispered names of shops, some only half intelligible, most doomed to be forgotten and usurped.

This small Whitechapel gallery – it had been built near the site of a murder.

Almost a century ago a woman had been stabbed thirty-nine times across her torso, through to her throat, her heart, her lungs. The event would eventually be excluded from the canon of Jack the Ripper murders and forgotten by history, her whole life and soul obliterated but for that possible link, that almost-alignment with a famous story.

The decades had transformed the crime scene into an exhibition. The photographs on display showed the suffering of strangers. It smelled of red wine and champagne in this context, a perfumed, almost acetonic scent. Spotlights shone into the darkness from railings overhead – one of them didn't work, though it occasionally pulsed. Below the feet of the visitors lay a zigzag carpet strewn with a mixture of discarded cocktail sticks and small mounds of carelessly, unconsciously fallen cigarette ash. They looked like the remnants of tiny slain vampires.

The walls were mostly white, but for a few red feature panels – red as Halloween blood, as childish paint. Some of the guests were delighted, fewer still upset at the cost to their expensive clothes – the red was not quite dry, it came off to the touch, to the accidental brush. What was initially assumed to be a mistake or ill preparation became the talk of the night, a participatory work where visitors made handprints in the slightly wet paint, their then reddened, maddened palms smearing on glasses, on pamphlets, on each other's clothes, on cheeks, on hands, on skin.

Small Mediterranean trees in red clay pots were dotted around the room, white stones at the base of their grey speckled bark, the branches and thin leaves above engaging in a similar vague greyness. When people accidentally brushed their backs on them, it felt like someone was touching them. These plants grew red in time, too.

Beyond, there was laughter. There were gasps at gossip.

So it began.

American soldiers posed in the ruins of a Vietnamese school. They looked like they were standing for a family portrait.

Throughout the gallery there were records of the time their photographer had spent with them – in the images of their day-to-day activities, their relaxation, their personal effects, and the aftermath of their attacks. The unit had grown more distant throughout the months. Some controversy had been caused by a whole segment of the exhibition devoted to the personal lives of the soldiers, before and after their tour of duty. Some considered it to be intrusive, voyeuristic. Some thought there were some mysteries that did not need solving.

There were very few images of the injured or the dead. Most photos without human subjects focused instead upon displacement or absence. Like the ruined school of the first smiling photograph, there were homes, streets, play areas, gardens, fallen toys. What children had left behind.

The exhibition as a whole, fronted by the smiling portrait of the soldiers, was titled 'Family'.

The woman who had been stabbed in her torso so long ago, through to her throat, her heart, her lungs.

No one in this gallery knew about Martha Tabram.

None of them would ever know – with the exception of one standing in their midst, drinking a glass of cold champagne. It would take almost sixty years for her to truly know about things like this, what someone like that might go through, what someone like that might suffer. It took a lifetime of images, of watching, capturing, abduction into art.

A man watched this woman, even then. Both of them stood close to each other in a corner of the 'Family' exhibition, looking at a display titled 'Pets'.

A few of the pictures were of animals.

A German Shepherd – tired, sullen by the look in his eyes, a great black muzzle round his mouth – cuddled up to a soldier on a boat. This soldier – you couldn't see his face, a helmet hanging low in the dark greyscale light – he held the animal limply, like someone might hold an unwanted child. The boat was full of other American animals, dogs, some people, guns and rifles, assorted weapons they'd been issued by their government, and some they'd brought with them, and some they'd just found and taken along the way.

It had been one of the unit's last operations – to rescue a number of pets from an enemy advance.

The person who had taken all these photos – she had been embedded within the unit in question for five months. One image showed her kneeling with the animals, smiling, stroking a Labrador with her burned, scarred arms.

Some contextualising images from the photographer's child-hood – visible much earlier in the exhibition – showed no such burns. Nowhere was there an explanation of what had happened to her in those two years.

On a second wall, there was a framed image of a stray cat walking along a market-side in Saigon, scooters parked nearby, people smiling, chatting, posed eternally. The cat stretched its front paws out, its back high and its head low, its mouth curved, but whether that meant a smile was unclear.

A third display – mounted on one of the red, wet walls – showed a man and a woman in torn clothing, their faces blurred with blood and dust. A child leans over them, their face looking back at the camera, their eyes closed, their mouth open, consuming, drawing in a silent scream.

There were bite marks on the woman's arms, old, partially healed. They were not created by humans.

'What do you think?'

Two strangers got talking about this last photo, a different man, a different woman. All around them, the guests talked about the stolen fragments of distant horrors. The man asked the woman for her opinion, complete, entire.

'What do you think?' he asked again. She didn't look at him, just kept looking at the art.

'I don't know.'

'You've been staring at this piece for a while,' he went on.

'So you've been watching me, then?'

She turned her head to him, smiling, gripping her empty glass with folded arms. She took a look at the stranger. He was a waiter, that much was clear from his outfit, though he wasn't holding anything. He didn't have anything to offer.

She didn't reply. She just turned back to the image, and her smile began to fade.

'I don't understand how everyone can eat,' he went on, 'Staring at things like this.'

'It's reality,' she said. 'It's vital that we face what really goes on in the world, and—'

'I hate it when bad things happen to animals.' He paused. 'That's terrible to think, isn't it? I should care more about the people, I know. I don't know.' He paused again, still ignoring the complete absence of any non-human animals in the photograph in front of them – the man, the woman, the child... the bite marks on those arms, like footprints. 'At least they saved the dogs,' he went on. 'That's what happened, isn't it? They got them to safety?'

The woman nodded and then glanced sideways. There were no other waiters nearby. 'Aren't you going to get in trouble, talking to me?'

He shrugged. 'Hopefully.'

She looked at him again, at his intense, twinkling eyes underneath a protruding brow.

She walked along to another image, and he followed after a few moments.

They looked up at the dogs, at their muzzled leader: the German Shepherd at the front of the riverboat.

His eyes kept flitting to the woman, who still pretended not to notice. 'It's like a Rorschach test, isn't it?' he asked.

'What do you see, then?'

'It's supposed to be universal, right? Anyone who's ever owned a dog sees their dog.'

'I never had a dog,' she interrupted. 'So what do I see?'

'The dog you wanted, growing up. What kid doesn't want a dog?'

'Kids who get bitten,' she said.

'You got bitten?'

'I'm covered in scars.' None were visible, but then again, she wore long sleeves and a long skirt. She looked serious for a moment, nonetheless. 'I'm fucking with you.'

She put her glass down, resting it on the floor against the display.

'I was wondering...' she began.

'Wondering what?'

'If you'd like to go...'

'Go where?' he asked.

'Get me a drink. It's your job, isn't it?'

This woman in the gallery – she had read Superman comics as a girl. For a while, London had been the closest thing to Metropolis in her mind – it was the main character, the protagonist of England, its grey-white-sometimes-metal starving plant life and hills and trees that belonged by right to kings and queens, the land now gorging on red and blue phone boxes, these hordes of men in suits all around, beautiful people, strangers. The more she travelled, the more the fonts on buildings elsewhere began to seem so strange, the lettering of every country alien to the other, even if English still dominated.

The gallery was an odd place too. Its white walls and hoardings were not all straight, not all level. Its angles stretched out in mockery at the idea of a flat world.

The red walls were covered in handprints, now. One of them – the red paint now sufficiently scraped off – had revealed a final photograph, an image of a box of human ears, apparently found in the possession of this unit, this family.

The commanding officer had claimed it was confiscated from the enemy.

He had told her not to photograph it.

She had already done so, secretly, quickly. No newspaper had wanted to publish it. No magazine had wanted to feature it.

She had heard one of the men talking about it, once.

About cutting them.

About the feeling of tearing.

Towards the end, most of the guests had gone. The woman remained, standing in front of a different display – the photographer's pre-Vietnam work: older pictures of a missing girl, a stranger, and a child trapped in a pipe, staring up from the darkness.

The waiter came back, his shift over.

'I took all these photos,' the woman said.

'I know.' He scratched his neck.

'You already knew I took them. Before you spoke to me, you knew.' She paused. 'It's obvious you knew I was Sophie Bertilak. Why else talk to me?'

He sighed. 'The signs say you're So-phee-a. Not Sophie.'

'I'm Sophie as a person,' she said. 'Call me Sophie.'

'Grab a drink with me sometime?'

She shook her head. 'I don't want to grab a drink. Why would I want to grab a drink?'

★

They grabbed a drink together that Friday, round the corner from the gallery.

Sophie and Thomas – that was his name, it turned out, 'Thomas', not Tom or Tommy, the full thing without shortening or alteration – they drank wine by the Thames, by the South Bank, by the same place people met their future husbands and wives, by a setting, dying sun.

They went back to her flat, they kissed on her sofa, they went to her bedroom and slept together, both a little drunk, both – if they'd been asked – never having done a thing like that before. In the weeks that followed, they kept meeting up. They never went round his place, those early days. Sometimes Sophie would wake up and he wasn't there anymore, but he hadn't gone. He'd be in her kitchen making food, or sometimes reading through her books, looking through her work.

He said she should get a new television – her set was black and white. She had the money – he told her that it wasn't necessary to 'live like this', whatever that meant. They'd drink brandy and listen to old songs, and he'd bring new ones.

One night, as they drifted off to sleep, Thomas lent his hand across the sheets.

Sophie sneezed into the air in front of her, bolting upright, and the sneeze hit his hand, causing him to recoil – 'You sneezed on my hand!' – Sophie immediately denying, sheepishly apologising, Thomas running to the toilet to wash the snot off him. As they tried to go to sleep again, he held her tighter and kept trying to sneeze on her in retaliation. Nothing came but giggling.

They talked about their parents, their families, what it was like at home. Well, Sophie did.

She'd had an uncle; he'd died in France before she was born.

She didn't know how far into Normandy he'd managed to get. She'd spent a lot of time in his room growing up, even though she wasn't supposed to. It was left intact, but it wasn't intact, it was cleaned, it was tidied, it was changed, because nothing can stay the same.

'I sold my first pictures when I was a girl. Or, my mum did.' Sophie stretched out. 'You know she won't even let her own picture be taken? She's properly afraid of it...'

Sophie thought for a while that those woods had been haunted. That perhaps the child in the earth had never even existed. It felt almost like her success since then had been some kind of supernatural bargain, some extraordinary gift or reward for having noticed the unnoticeable, for having captured the light of the missing and the dead.

Thomas told her a few days later.

His father was the owner of the Whitechapel gallery. The one which had bought many of her prints.

Thomas had worked there, just like he worked anywhere, because his dad had wanted him to work. Thomas claimed to have no passions, nothing he wanted to do in life, nothing that made him special, not like her. This Thomas said more than once. And she'd say things like – she had just been at the right place at the right time, that her career was just luck.

'You love it, though,' Thomas would say. 'Your life. What you do. Whatever else it makes you feel, you wouldn't stop.'

She'd say nothing.

Thomas wanted to introduce Sophie to his father. He dismissed their long acquaintance as an irrelevancy; he wanted to introduce Sophie as his girlfriend.

'Is that what I am?'

He told her that she was. And one day he told her something else – that he loved her.

And then he finally got his revenge. He managed to sneeze on her hand.

The Second Visit

1969

Sophie had first visited the old, grand house back in 1965 walking past cut grass down a long path in the red, setting sun.

Now she went for her second visit. There would – in spite of all she'd share with this man, in spite of their work together, the bloodlines they'd mingle, the people they'd know – be only two other times she'd come here in her whole life.

They drank and ate in the coach house, right by the gate. Quentin had long since taken the structure over as his primary residence. The main house was too unwieldy for him now. Things had been brought over here. The head of a stag his own father had killed a long time ago had been mounted on the wall, taxidermied, filled with plastic.

The food that their host served, it was all plants, of course.

He didn't eat meat.

Sometimes, the head of this stag seemed to smile at them all.

'Nothing's wrong,' Quentin would tell them, whenever they asked.

He'd been thinking of how blood had welled from the mouth of one of his friends, back in Germany.

Sometimes flashes still came.

Quentin tried not to think about it.

It wasn't the done thing. It wasn't his fault. It had happened to a lot of soldiers.

He wondered if it had happened to Sophie. She'd been to

war, hadn't she, even if she hadn't actually taken a life? Maybe she had. Maybe she had.

He hoped she didn't have nightmares.

He wondered if she'd marry his son. If they'd be family.

He asked as much, and the young lovers laughed, embarrassed. He didn't know what was funny.

The grass was much longer around the paths. The buzzing of insects seemed to drown everything out beyond.

There were few staff members left. The estate rotted around him, most of his investments sold off.

He didn't need money. He had all the money he could ever want.

He was alone now, increasingly, intentionally.

He hoped they'd get married.

They'd make good parents. That he knew. That he knew, in his head, in his heart.

'Call me Quentin,' he said, as she'd stumble over his surname, over whether he was her patron or a future father-in-law. 'I'm just Quentin.'

The Girl

1972

The first gift Sophie could remember receiving in her life was a pushchair that'd had a fake baby in its seat. Before that, three original toys she couldn't remember receiving, which had just been with her since always – her Moo, her lion, her penguin.

Sophie had tried playing with the fake baby at the same time as these other toys, but she'd been dissuaded. 'You're his mum,' her mother would say, 'It's not safe for him to be out of his chair.' So Sophie had kept the baby in the chair.

When she was in secondary school, when she started seeing boys, her mother had grown terrified of potential pregnancy.

When she'd turned eighteen, when she sent letters back from Saigon, her mother had answered with queries about soldiers, about whether she'd met anyone.

A chorus of others joined in throughout the years. Interviewers would ask if Sophie was married. They wanted to know when she planned to start her family. Would she stop taking photos after she had children?

As she'd approached her twenty-second birthday, even her new friends began to warn her about waning fertility, about the marriage market, about spoilt goods.

One day she stopped using birth control. She didn't even tell Thomas.

She thought about the fake baby from when she'd been a four-year-old. She wondered where it was now – what dust, what materials clung to its plastic skin. Whether it was still in the attic, back in her mother's house, back in Lethwick – or a landfill.

When Sophie missed her period, she went to the library to find books on raising children.

The elderly woman at the counter laughed and told her there was no need.

'You'll know what to do,' she said. 'It's the most natural thing in the world.'

1980

One day, many years after the show at the gallery, Sophie went on an assignment near the Jurassic Coast. She was going to photograph a forensic training facility. It was full of staged crimes, like a grand crossover of a thousand murder mysteries.

There were hairs outside a concrete building, rustling in the long, long grass. Dew dropped from oak trees, plopping into mud, some of it formed by the rain of nights past, some of it invented by the owners of this place. There were car wrecks out in the open fields, in the swamp land too, and dogs barked somewhere in the beyond. It was cold that day, the breathing of these people who worked here like speech bubbles, their eyes held in stasis by the frost.

Sophie wore gloves and boots. She had been told not to touch anything, but walking wasn't exactly without contact, was it? Her companion crossed her arms, frowned, fidgeted, and it was unclear if she did this only when Sophie looked at her, or if – philosophically speaking – a person could still be in a bad mood, even if no one was there to witness it.

As Sophie took her photographs, the other woman asked her questions. How had she got into this line of work? ('The

Associated Press gave me a pass.') What was it like, travelling the world? ('Exhausting. Especially when you're not doing it.') Wouldn't you rather settle down? ('What do you mean?') Find a husband? (' ...')

There was a shape in one of the cars ahead of them. Sophie thought it was just a car seat, but there was a human body there, partially decomposed. There was blood spatter on the window. The people in the distant fields looked like they were watching her.

'I have four children,' Sophie said. 'But no. No husband.' She smiled, faintly, accusatory.

The other woman grew silent for a time.

They kept on.

Eventually, Sophie took her last photo of the day. Bullet casings lying near a tree, splinters of wood carved off several. She asked her companion to go and stand a little in the distance. The woman would be out of focus, but it'd complete the effect, bisected by all these trees, all these cylinders in the semi-darkness.

It was the first corpse farm in the United Kingdom. It would train a generation of forensics experts and scientists in the dissolution of human bodies. All the dead were donated. From what this woman had told her, many of the dying had been delighted for the opportunity, wanting their death to have some meaning. But it was more than that. Some of them could have been organ donors. Some of them had previously wanted cremation. No, it wasn't just being useful. It was an exciting thing, for this to be their afterlife, extras in a play. It was becoming a story.

Sophie told stories, too.

Her companion had overcome her apparent moral objection to Sophie's unmarried status. So Sophie told stories of her past, jumping around through time. It wasn't a justification of who she was – she supposed she didn't know why she chose the stories she did, why she flashed back to this moment or that. Her companion just listened.

'You sneezed on your boyfriend's hand?'

Sophie laughed, putting her equipment back in her bag. 'We broke up a few months later. We got back together again. Probably both unrelated to the sneezing. Probably. I think.'

They went back inside and cleaned up. They had coffee in the cafeteria, the sky now dark outside. They parted ways and never saw each other again.

Sophie went home after the corpse farm and held a birthday party a few days later for her son Matthew. He was seven now. She gave Matthew his own camera, a small, toy-like thing made of blue plastic.

He was happy, as far as she could tell.

And he had this imaginary friend for a while.

A boy who lived in the ground.

Sophie had been worried; it had sounded so unlikely, so specific, that she wondered if someone had been talking to him about her past work.

But no.

It was a thing in stories, wasn't it?

People who lived in holes or caves.

The friends – those that came from beneath the soil.

1981

Once upon a time, Sophie had walked in the woods on her own birthday. She'd received a camera, too. And on that camera, she'd captured three individuals: the missing girl Stephanie Earlsham, an unknown man, and a pair of eyes hiding in the darkness of the earth, cocooned eleven feet down within a plastic pipe...

'He's covered in dirt,' Matthew would say about his imaginary friend.

It became mixed in her brain for a while – these memories and her child's mind.

Sophie would make Matthew show her where he'd seen this friend, and the little boy would say his friend lived under their house.

He lived under the floor.

It was just a game.

She tried to shake the association, but her family's life, her children's imagination, it all bled into her past.

She kept a file of information on it all. All she could gather, all she could work out...

Specialists had estimated the owner of the eyes in the pipe to be between seven and twelve years of age. There was a 92 per cent probability they were indeed a child, based on observable facial features, the size of the box they had been hidden within (the measurement deduced from the amount of displaced soil at the burial site), and the likely psychological profile of the victim, who would have had to agree to keep quiet even upon the unlikely event of seeing another child such as Sophie leaning over him or her with a camera. Either the obscured child could not distinguish between potential rescue and potential threats, or – so a fringe interpretation went – whoever had captured them might have previously played tricks upon their victim to test loyalty.

The coincidence of two abductions, two child-related crimes in such proximity, made it extremely unlikely they weren't in some way connected. Stephanie Earlsham would likely have been in her captor's custody for a long time, based on her previous last sighting three years beforehand; this suggested in turn that the girl had been press-ganged or otherwise manipulated into compliance with her own captivity. The recruitment of the abused to perpetuate more abuse was likewise not unheard of. And this led to the most hushed of all interpretations.

That the missing girl had in some way assisted with the capture of the pipe victim, or otherwise had at least not interfered with the process.

The police never said this out loud because they didn't need to, not to the public, not to the victim's family. Strangers would happily speculate about it whenever they saw a documentary. And the Earlshams still had hope – even now – that their pale girl might somehow come back to them.

Sophie heard as much from one of the officers on the cold case, a man named Kelly.

The assignment had been passed down to new officers, men who'd been in primary school during the time of the original crimes – this one, the son of the officer who'd once come to Sophie's home to take her to the woods. This second Kelly, he had just been a child playing with toys that day. He was a decade younger than Sophie.

He had a nice smile.

She sometimes met him when she came back to her home town.

Sophie's mother had agreed to look after her kids for the week. Thomas was in rehab and so could not help. And Sophie had work, didn't she? She had to travel. So she brought her leads here. She brought them back to Lethwick and her mother's valley, then decided to stop off at the police station before driving on.

She'd wanted to know what they'd found, and what they hadn't.

There were still too many missing children of that approximate age, that set of features, that lightless greyscale, to narrow the pipe victim down to less than two hundred potential souls.

'Listen, I get off at eight,' Kelly said. 'Buy you a drink?'

'I don't—'

'We can talk more about it. You can ask your questions.'

Sophie hesitated. 'I'll buy.'

One imaginary child had grown to encompass these two hundred in her mind, each face merging beneath the dirt, the trees, the light of the wood near her home, balls of mistletoe suspended all around the ancient paths, the forgotten water.

She learned little that night that she did not already know, though Kelly had kissed her on the way to their cars.

His face, so much like his father's.

She didn't say yes or no to the kiss. It just happened.

'I'm not a good person,' Sophie said, and Kelly laughed. 'What's so funny?'

'Few people are good,' he said.

'The police are?' Sophie smiled, vague, uncomfortable.

He snorted.

'What?'

He shrugged. 'If you knew the things I know …'

'So tell me. Tell me those things.'

He smiled. 'Give me another kiss and I'll tell you.'

She did.

But he didn't keep his promise.

He kept all those things in his head, and she left disappointed, empty, the thrill of potential discovery faded into the night.

★

Sophie and Thomas divided their childcare at first, whether or not they were in a relationship. One would stay while the other would go, and this was extended to their single surviving parents: Sophie's mother, and Quentin too.

Thomas would drop the children at that grand, historic, inheritable building, though they would stay in the guesthouse. Sophie had only ever been to the estate twice – that first meeting to be set up with her future source of income, the second to meet a potential father-in-law.

Half the visits down.

Two to go.

They were all invited to spend the week with Quentin one winter.

One of their 'let's get married' phases. They were engaged.

The world was silent and warm in the snow, each footstep a crunch in frost.

No one worked there anymore. No one but Quentin himself, tending to the vast estate alone, like an old emperor making war against the sea.

The children played in the gardens.

One of them went missing one day.

Matthew.

It was only for a few hours.

Sophie's mother had never been overprotective of her daughter, back when she'd been young. Sophie had always had the freedom to play and explore – why not, after all? How else would she make friends?

Things had changed for them, that day Sophie had encountered the missing girl.

The story of their life changed to one where such things were possible.

In Sophie's seventeenth year, she was watched constantly. She wasn't allowed to go out. So of course she went out in secret. She wasn't allowed to have a boyfriend. So she had several. She wasn't allowed to be hurt; she wasn't allowed to leave her mother all alone.

So Sophie went to Vietnam. She had her own children and tried to avoid her mother's mistakes. She tried to lead a life separate to the kids. She tried not to place too many boundaries or expectations.

She didn't dissolve her identity in motherhood.

She didn't become Matthew's mother. She didn't see herself as that word. She was called it sometimes, just like sometimes people called her Sophie. Even her children, sometimes.

When Matthew went missing, she realised she was full of shit. She realised she didn't know anything about herself.

She still cried about it days later, when she was alone.

How part of her had gone missing. How the world had not seemed real when he was gone.

Is this how Mrs. Earlsham had felt? How she still felt?

They found Matthew by himself, but he said he hadn't been alone.

His imaginary friend had come back – the person who lived beneath the soil.

He'd emerged at last.

Hearing this, arriving back from his own search to find the child had returned, Quentin got quite upset.

'You're not Matthew ...' He trembled. 'What have you done with Matthew?!'

He asked them all to leave.

Some of them never went back.

Sophie found herself in the bizarre position of apologising for another man's father, while Thomas himself was raging, 'You don't know what he was like growing up—'

'You're upsetting the kids.'

Thomas turned, still driving, angry, 'I'm upsetting them? My father was the one who—'

'Keep your eyes on the road.'

Thomas turned away.

They drove in silence for a while, four children in the back rows of their little van.

'The man can't cope,' Sophie said. 'You must see that. You saw how he lives – how confused he got about Matthew ... I don't see how we can abandon him there on his own.'

'What? Because he fired all the staff?'

Sophie didn't answer.

'He f—' Thomas hesitated, looking at the kids in the rear-view mirror. 'He fudged one of the cleaners, you know,' he said. 'When I was young ...'

They kept driving.

'She was sent away. She was the first to go. What does that tell you about a man like that? What does that say?'

The sun disappeared.

'I don't want the kids going back there,' he said. 'I don't want to see him.' He paused. 'I wish you hadn't undermined me,' he added.

'Undermined you?'

He didn't explain.

He refused to say anything else about it.

And so things changed.

So the kids just started going to their grandmother's home instead, in old, gentle Lethwick.

It became a regular occurrence. They had a great time in the valley, no longer cooped up in their mother's city house – there were places to run and play and hide, trees to climb, fields and stone ruins to explore.

After one visit to Lethwick, Sophie went to stay with the parents of the missing girl from her youth.

The Earlshams. It was only for a night, one more stop on the way to her job.

They always put her in Stephanie's former room.

Mrs Earlsham, she always hugged Sophie a little too tightly.

When they met, they'd catch up on the case – the progress less and less over the years – and so also did this overt element of catching up dwindle, until the Earlshams seemed to care more about Sophie's life than the flesh and blood they'd known for far less time.

They even had framed pictures of Sophie from her work abroad, copies of articles in newspapers and magazines.

That night in June, Mrs Earlsham gave Sophie a gift. It had become so unseasonably cold that week, and Sophie had so little with her in the way of warm clothing.

Mrs Earlsham gave the photographer a red coat. She told Sophie to keep it.

People could always see you if you wore a coat like that.

No matter how far away you stood.

'So no one will ever lose you.'

1983

'What's wrong?' Thomas asked one evening, as he held Sophie's belly, his knees fitting into the angle of her bent knees, his chest resting against her spine.

'Nothing's wrong.'

They began to fall asleep again.

'I want to go to your new flat,' Cooper said. 'I want to see it.'

Thomas held her, his voice tired, groggy. 'I'm not going to stay there long.'

'Why don't you want me to see it?'

He didn't answer that.

The next night Sophie bit him. He was kissing her neck, and she bit him, almost hard enough to break his skin.

She told him she loved him.

They both fell asleep eventually, and neither remembered their dreams.

They broke up once more before the end of the year, and got back together almost as quickly.

'The final time,' she said.

He nodded.

'Things have to be different now.'

'That sounds like you're blaming me,' he said.

She shook her head.

'You're blaming me,' he said. 'It's like you said. Once someone's bitten by a dog, they don't trust any others, and—'

'You're not a dog. And I never said that.'

'But you did bite me.' They lay in bed again. 'You know … if you bite a human finger with the same force you bite a carrot, you'll go right through.'

'Did you read that somewhere?'

'I just know a lot of things,' he said, grinning. 'You're lucky you're with someone who knows so many things …'

'Are you planning to eat my finger? Is that what you're telling me?'

'Not your fingers.'

'You understand ... When I said things have to be different, I wasn't blaming you.'

He disappeared under the sheets.

'I just want this to work,' she said, sitting up a little. 'I just want – I want this to – oh – oh fuck ...'

'That's ...' came the voice from under the sheets. 'That's a pound in the jar.'

'We're not – we're not still – still doing that ...'

1984

There was a body on the road. Sophie caught a glimpse on her way back to her mother's home. It was impossible to tell the age or gender. The body was twisted, arms lowered and raised at once as if climbing, as if a piece of clockwork had fallen from a tower.

Sophie slowed her car, like anyone would. It looked like the figure was standing, somehow, if you held your head at its side – as if the grey road were the sky behind it, blood drifting from his head all over it, like a thought bubble in a comic book. Like an oil spill. A police car obscured the rest.

There were tyre tracks beyond. There was no sign of a stopped driver, no one but the professionals, which suggested to Sophie that no one had sat with the victim as the victim had died.

It was sad, really.

No one had heard any of the words the victim might have said, or sounds they might have made. The quieting of a face, a jaw dropping slack, eyes losing sight, the only witness the bees, the blue sky all around, the sun, the nicest day for weeks.

There were bodies everywhere. This is what life had taught

Sophie. A secret, universally known, that death was everywhere, that it happened to everyone, that it wasn't really very interesting, least of all to the person who left the world.

She had stopped photographing death, lately. She'd started working for newspapers again, demand for her own exhibitions having somewhat dwindled. She'd resisted asking Thomas's father for any artificial help – their connection should not dictate things, not when it came to her work. She already felt like so much of her career had come from luck rather than talent.

All around, the forest ran past the road, but so too did distant steeples, churches, cemeteries, the ebb and flow of her home town – its two layers, the old grey stone and terraced rows, the new red roofs and crimson structures manifesting from a legacy of halls and manors and Manderleys...

Sophie drove along the road she'd once walked on her birthday, where she'd once brought film to be processed in a pharmacy.

She drove down into the valley.

Rabbits ran in the thin light of the grass.

It had all changed so little since her childhood. Heather still grew at squat angles. Isolated trees still stood way out from the forest proper, as if emissaries to her home. She'd used to think of them as screaming silly dancers, though they did not seem so silly now.

She parked her car near their apple tree, right outside the main house. She switched her engine off. She blinked strangely, as if a nerve were trapped.

She walked to the blue front door, which hung slightly open. No one came to greet her.

Bicycles were strewn outside. She did not count them. She did not notice there were only two.

She called out her children's names – 'Matthew! Joanna!', and then, quieter, 'Alfie?'.

She called for her mother too, as she took off her red coat. She saw herself in the mirrors of the hallway, and for a moment, she saw that girl from the lake, that poor, pale girl.

She went to her uncle's room, took a sleeping pill, and fell asleep, assuming her family would wake her when they got back from the shops.

When she did wake, it was dark.

She crept to the window, and saw no other car.

No phone call came.

She rang Thomas, but he didn't answer either, or perhaps he wasn't home.

An hour later she left the building, counting the bicycles.

Noticing one was missing.

When she phoned the police and waited to speak to them, she just kept thinking about it.

That body on the road, that strange shape.

Before his funeral, Alfie had been filled with plastic.

His body had been painted and put back together so that an open display casket might be possible. They did an excellent job, considering his injuries. Everyone said so.

They used his grandmother's home. He'd been staying there prior to his death in an area that would one day be remodelled into part of a darkroom. Alfie's favourite toys had been a dinosaur and a figure of Batman, which he often combined together in his games. He had not been that close with his siblings. He had not talked until the age of five. He had been hit by a car a year later.

No one knew how he'd got to the road – not his grandmother, a woman who would never be allowed to see the other siblings again. Who would see Sophie only one last, final time many years hence.

Those siblings, who swore the boy had remained in their eyesight in the woods near their grandmother's home. They swore he'd come back to the house with them. They claimed they'd been alone, that they'd just been playing in that long, blue-skied day.

No one would ever know, not with certainty.

The police never found the car or the driver. Of course they didn't. Sophie would plaster a wall of her next exhibition with everything she could find of their failings, the allegations of incompetence, of corruption that were never answered ... How could a town this gentle, this crimeless, be corrupt after all?

How could you be incompetent, with so little crime to solve?

The child was pronounced dead at the scene. It was not a murder. It was registered as an accidental death.

Sophie would argue with Kelly, she would even sleep with him again, grimacing as they finished, hoping that she might learn something, that he might be persuaded.

But there was nothing. Nothing the man, so much like the elder Kelly, would tell her.

There was nothing they had done, or would do.

Her son meant nothing to them.

Her son didn't exist anymore.

They filled him with plastic, as was the American tradition, proposed by his father Thomas who had in turn received the idea from his own father. They rarely embalmed bodies like this in England – no open caskets, let alone when the body had been as horribly broken and mutilated as this. The father and the grandfather, they spent what money they could to fix the little boy.

Sophie – she gave no preference, she barely spoke.

Beforehand, their guests had drunk outside the house, had held glasses of red and white wine. Some of them were people the mother had once known, but too many were strangers, whether for all time or only recently.

They'd all look at Sophie Bertilak as if they were drinking her face.

She'd heard snippets of their conversation as if moving through fog.

She found him—

Can't imagine what—

Why isn't she crying—

Lost my dad last—

Sophie had looked for her children for a while. Some relative must have taken them away. She'd gone back inside the house, had walked to the bathroom, and had then locked the door.

Some time later – the funeral still not started – she'd returned and had lingered on the stairs, watching Thomas in conversation.

He'd talked about a boy who no longer existed.

He'd talked about how he'd helped build a wooden table with him. Father and son.

A boy who'd only just begun to speak, so late that they'd been worried about him ever saying a thing...

On and on Thomas talked about that fucking table.

Sophie had wondered if the man hadn't meant their eldest, Matthew, and had just got confused, or if he really couldn't remember anything about Alfie, and had to clutch at other people's memories to pretend there was some sense of connection.

When Sophie had entered the front room, had seen the body on the casket, she'd almost laughed. It was so comically outlandish, the way he looked. She'd sat down a short while later.

She heard people talk as they waited for the speeches. She heard them talk about matters completely unrelated to Alfie.

Someone said it was so good to see someone else, how they shouldn't let so much time pass again. A total stranger began talking about her new cats, how she was struggling to introduce them without fights.

She heard Thomas turn around and give the stranger sincere advice based on his own childhood experiences of raising cats.

She saw her children eating cake, hours later.

She went upstairs.

Must be awful—

Did you see—

Poor thing—

So sorry—

At some point, there were flashes of light.

Some of the mourners, their hands wet with sauce and finger food, these pigs posed – they tried to find appropriate facial expressions, sometimes smiling, because that was what you did, wasn't it? When someone took your picture, you smiled.

Most assumed the family had hired someone, and it didn't feel that weird at first because funerals were like weddings in their way, weren't they?

Sophie had changed her clothes. She moved quickly now, with purpose.

She caught Thomas smiling at something or someone. He wouldn't know a photograph of that smile existed, not for many weeks.

She asked other mourners to stand behind her son's casket, to change the light quality.

She went outside and walked to the woods.

At some point, she woke up in her house, lying on the sofa.

For a moment, it felt like all of it had been a dream. The detritus, the remains of the grand buffet, were the only clues to reality.

She even thought her boy was with her still – a little curled lump at the side of her sofa – pyjamaed, lightly snoring on the rug. But it was only Joanna.

In the days that followed, Sophie did not stop taking her photographs. She documented the play of her children, the moments their faces fell, tears when they thought they weren't being watched. She documented Thomas's slow return to alcoholism. They hadn't even discussed sharing a room – she slept where the little boys had slept, in the room that would one day become her darkroom. Soon Matthew moved out of that place, preferring to sleep in his father's room, and Sophie said nothing.

Quentin came to visit them one day.

He spent some time with his son. Sophie could see them out of the windows, the old man's long legs, long arms, so much like a spider, like a cartoon in a way – a minister of funny walks.

She took photographs of them too.

He left.

Thomas took the children from her and briefly tried to get sole custody, before tearfully apologising on the phone. He just asked Sophie to stop photographing all of them. To let them grieve. To fucking say something, anything, to act like a mother. She did not respond.

Lucy was conceived the night of that argument. Thomas had Sophie one last time, and Sophie did not respond, did not say anything. What was there to say?

Lucy would discover the secret of her birth years later.

She would wonder how much it had shaped her. If it explained all the bad things she'd had done to her, that she'd done to others in turn.

★

Quentin came back a few days later.

He made Sophie a generous financial offer for all the prints and photos she'd taken of her grieving family, plus a few items to give the exhibition context.

'Thomas doesn't see what you see. He doesn't understand,' the man assured her. 'No one will remember your boy, not unless we do this.'

Sophie couldn't remember what she said next. She couldn't remember if she questioned it – his sense, his sanity in light of his bizarre outburst at his home...

But did it matter if a question was asked, if Sophie said 'yes' in the end?

If the two relatives, bound in the children's blood, worked together one last time...

One day, at a gallery in Whitechapel, an exhibition began. Not just photos of their grief, but births, birthdays, scans in hospital, even what pictures Sophie had of her earliest dates with Thomas.

In the place she had first spoken to him were chalk outlines on a wall, a recreation of the way they'd stood and talked about animals and people.

Even Quentin didn't remember that time after Alfie's death, not really. When he thought of his dead grandchild, yes, all that really came to mind in his later years was the exhibition of grief. How it had felt, to stand by those silhouettes, alone, wondering.

About a dog he'd had to kill long ago, when a letter had come from the government, when a war had come from Europe.

About a man pretending to walk downstairs past the ruin of a burned building, soon to be shot by sniper fire. A soldier named Matthew.

About a boy, wrapped in plastic...

The thing was, Quentin didn't know. He hadn't known as

a boy, a man, as this old form, so much unlike the way he felt inside his mind – so remarkable to see in the mirror, so alien, so repulsive, really.

He still didn't know.

He didn't know if he'd ever killed anyone.

The Envelope

A week after the death of Sophie Bertilak

Alex packed her things. She was ready to leave her hotel room, soon.

She had said goodbye to her police officer ex.

She'd put laxatives in the coffee jar the man shared with his new girlfriend.

Alex been paraded in front of the woman again and again, like some figure out of myth – like Medea, like some wife who did not count, discarded for the new.

She would never see him again. She was finished with him.

She would sell her old home when the insurers paid out on its refurbishment.

She would leave this place, this job, this life of antiseptic, of nights alone regardless of company, of trying to earn enough – as if any sum caring for people could be enough, as if the world ever rewarded hands that met piss and shit, day after day.

She still cared for all the residents. She'd never stopped. Few of them ever stopped.

It was why they couldn't stay.

Caring about those you knew would die, those you knew were broken – it could break you too. If you were too dispassionate to feel that, you shouldn't even be in the job in the first place. The same quality that made them good nurses forced them from the profession – she'd seen it time and again with colleagues.

People did the things they did for money or love.

Her whole life, she'd worked for the latter.

It had grown time to work for the first. To make something of herself.

To make sure she never ended up like them – the old, the lost ...

To make sure she could leave this town.

Oppidum vetus leneque.

'A town, ancient and gentle.'

Population 12,500, though that couldn't be right, could it? No such number could be right, tourists arriving and leaving; people, dying and being born ...

Lethwick.

She would be gone, soon.

She would be gone, her work almost finished.

She had messaged several family members, looking for a place to stay while she looked for her next step.

None had answered.

She hoped one would, soon. Of course they would. She knew they would.

They were her family.

Of course they would help her.

'Look on my Works, ye Mighty, and despair!'
Nothing beside remains. Round the decay
Of that colossal Wreck, boundless and bare
The lone and level sands stretch far away.

Ozymandias
Percy Bysshe Shelley (1818)

PART 7:

THE SIGNS

DR COOPER ALLEN AND
LUCY BERTILAK
THE PRESENT DAY

61

The sun began to fall.

The ancient gentle town, stained with acid and rain and time, dissolved in borrowed light. Traffic signals were barely visible, the heavens were so bright that afternoon. The world was still in motion, in joy.

The soil was broken in the long hills and in the long valleys – first, by the tyre tracks of machinery, of police cars, of diggers. The roots of an old tree were ripped from the world. They were taking the apple tree.

A report had been made. A historic case of suspected murder.

Was there someone buried beneath the roots? Was there a child next to Sophie Bertilak's house, underneath the soil?

The sun fell and fell.

The riverbanks were lower than they should have been.

Cars ignored speed limits, only a bit. Only a tidy 24mph instead of 20.

Tourists continued to dance, to delight.

Apples fell from the tree as it died. The bark snapped like a neck.

Sophie Bertilak's daughter sobbed, begging them to stop what they were doing, that it was theirs, that it was their home. Her brother would be back soon ... please ...

The police kept them back. They'd received a tip-off.

'From who?' Lucy asked, but she knew. She knew.

She knew who was ruining her life. She knew who was coming for her.

Men and women stood in white plastic suits, ready to examine whatever was found.

Lucy Bertilak shook in the mud, a week after the discovery of her grandfather.

Her father still didn't know.

About any of this.

He didn't know, and no one seemed to care.

No one told her a thing.

Search Terms:

SEARCH: Sophie Bertilak
SEARCH: pigs eating people
SEARCH: Matthew Bertilak university abuse

FROM: Lucy Bertilak
SUBJECT: Mum
DATE: 17 June, 21:54
TO: Thomas Medina

Dad, please call me.

FROM: Lucy Bertilak
SUBJECT: Mum
DATE: 18 June, 19:40
TO: Thomas Medina

I've tried phoning you more than a dozen times and I don't know why you aren't responding but I need to talk to you. We need you. Please.

FROM: Lucy Bertilak
SUBJECT: Mum
DATE: 18 June, 21:24
TO: Thomas Medina

Mum's dead.

FROM: Lucy Bertilak
SUBJECT: Mum
DATE: 19 June, 03:24
TO: Thomas Medina

Dad?

Search Terms:

SEARCH: headache cures
SEARCH: drugs to help headaches
SEARCH: PTSD treatments alternative

FROM: Lucy Bertilak
SUBJECT: Mum
DATE: 19 June, 11:34
TO: Thomas Medina

The police said they can't find you either. They told me to get in touch if you called.

FROM: Lucy Bertilak
SUBJECT: Mum
DATE: 20 June, 18:03
TO: Thomas Medina

They called her death a misadventure, an accident, but she wouldn't leave us like this.

Please don't leave us too.

FROM: Lucy Bertilak
SUBJECT: Mum
DATE: 20 June, 23:54
TO: Thomas Medina

I'm scared, Matthew said you never check your messages and that you are travelling but I'm scared so please just answer me please.

FROM: Lucy Bertilak
SUBJECT: Mum
DATE: 23 June, 08:43
TO: Thomas Medina

They found Granddad.

He was by Mum's lake.

I went walking in those woods. I was trying not to be a coward and I was trying to change and the woods are where they found him and they're going to find you, aren't they?

Search Terms:

SEARCH: psilocybin
SEARCH: Matthew Bertilak messages
SEARCH: Quentin Medina obituary

FROM: Lucy Bertilak
SUBJECT: Mum
DATE: 24 June, 22:34
TO: Thomas Medina

She's still here. The woman who found Granddad – she's still here.

I think she's following me. Matthew thinks I'm paranoid.

Matthew never trusted me. None of you ever trusted me.

FROM: Lucy Bertilak
SUBJECT: Mum
DATE: 25 June, 01:34
TO: Thomas Medina

I know what I'll do, if I see her again.

Matthew doesn't understand but I do.

She's dangerous. She's killed people and she's dangerous.

How did she find Granddad? How is she here, the same day
Mum was found?

It's her. It's Cooper.

62

Cooper saw the signs.

There were only a couple of days left until the midsummer festival. Until the whole hidden history of the world would be told on the streets of this place. Already the gallows had arisen. Already Noah's Ark had been wrought within the world, already hell had been prepared, the Romans, the guilty, the flood, the saints, the sinners, the innocent and angels and demons prepared for the most ancient of British plays.

The mysteries.

There had been a few missed calls from Cooper's sister.

Another from her mother.

She's really sick — call me, Julia said.

A story told a thousand times before.

Sickness was a trick, a lie designed to gain attention.

Cooper thought about the discovery of the old man's body, of his flesh in the mouth of a stag. All the creatures of Lethwick seemed to imbibe Sophie and those closest to her. Cooper smiled at the strangeness of the thought, as she sat in the back of yet another taxi, heading toward the old photographer's home — uninvited once more.

Turning near the pit of the valley, there were no more lights in the lodges below. The only fire came from within Sophie Bertilak's home, visible from far away, like a camp, like a temple. The dim moon spread its reflections.

They had found nothing beneath the apple tree. Her 'tip-off' to the police had led only to the destruction of an old plant.

And Alex – she'd not come back to work, she'd checked out of the hotel, she wasn't answering any messages.

Cooper sure as shit didn't trust this police service when people like Lapis and Kelly Sr had worked there. She wasn't going to tell them about the envelopes or Alex's activities.

After all, the woman could still perhaps be an ally to her, she could still be a friend, even if she had lied and acted in secret. Cooper did not know.

Cooper wanted to visit the photographer's home again in any case. She wanted to spend time with Sophie's children.

Two family members had died in quick succession, and the children were still here, they hadn't gone back to their lives or their jobs.

Why didn't they just go home?

Why did they stay?

It wasn't healthy.

And no one could find their father. No one knew where Thomas was.

The Bertilak children claimed they did not know.

Maybe that was true. Maybe it wasn't.

But there was a larger question, wasn't there? Sophie and Quentin had been joined by more than just blood.

They had been tied by art, by money. They had been tied for her entire career. Even in the face of her break-ups with Thomas, she stayed with the old man.

Why?

What made Quentin do it?

What had enabled Sophie's whole life? What made her not an amateur, but an artist, a professional?

Did it kill her?

Did it kill them both?

63

When Cooper approached the front door of Sophie Bertilak's home, she found it slightly ajar.

Within she could hear their voices, the sibling children of the consumed photographer. She went inside, not bothering to knock or announce herself.

The whiteness of the hall, its frosted orb light hanging from the ceiling, its mirrors – a mass of eight in various shapes and sizes spanning the wall to Cooper's right, facing the doorway. All this brightness faced a painting in turn, an oil representation of horses running through water ... it was smothering, breathless, this thin passage. It felt even more so to Cooper, to be alone within the building's throat.

She heard the siblings talk.

She wondered what they'd be like this evening.

If they'd still be caught in the grief of their mother's death, if they now faced a second grief in the form of their grandfather's passing ...

She hesitated near the hall's end, unseen, and watched the poor siblings.

Nothing in Cooper told her to leave, not now.

She watched them like a show.

Matthew sat at an oak dining table, reading a book with a green cover. Lucy read from little cards on the other side. A fire crackled, a real one by its smell, by its light smoke. Lucy read aloud, and Matthew answered.

'The Pilgrimage of Grace was a peaceful process that ended in a massacre – under which English king did this occur?'

'Henry.'

'Which Henry?'

'Eighth.'

'Hm.' Lucy looked for another card. 'What happened to Hypatia of Alexandria?'

'She was stoned.'

Cooper kept watching them, kept listening in the shadows.

'Nope.'

'She was,' he protested, 'I saw it in—'

'She was flayed.'

'Rachel Weisz was stoned. In the film, at least.'

Lucy shrugged. 'It's not what killed her. Hypatia, I mean.'

The hall smelled of fire and garlic, onion, and mince somewhere beyond. The empty picture frames were still hanging on the walls.

'What gets bigger the more you worry about it?'

'Mount Everest,' Matthew said, still looking down at his book, barely paying attention.

'It – the answer was blood pressure,' Lucy laughed. 'What? Mount Everest? Why—'

Cooper laughed too. Both of them turned and saw her.

64

At the moment of their turning, Cooper had already ceased smiling, caught between the darkness and the fire.

Lucy pretended it was all OK. She acted like they hadn't heard the door, and said as much, and welcomed Cooper in, invited her to sit down, to get warm by the fireplace. 'You're back! We didn't know you were coming!'

As if they were the oldest friends in the world. As if Cooper hadn't spied on them. As if any of this were normal.

Lucy invited Cooper to dinner once more, as she had on their first meeting.

Cooper thought of Kelly's words: Why did you accept their invitation?

She had to know.

So she remained.

So they sat, and ate, and talked.

As before, they were disarming, lulling.

She had to keep reminding herself.

They weren't her friends.

She just had to understand. That moment at the funeral... of Matthew's right hand around Lucy's arm, how Lucy had shifted to get away... how terrified she'd looked... how empty his own face.

How time and time again with these adult children, with this family... something was not right.

★

Ingredients littered almost every single surface of the dining room, the Bertilak children's contagion having spread forth from the kitchen area. Bundles of potatoes in sacks, fruit, garlic bulbs hung from hooks, pots of herbs harvested from the hills, even smoking meat, drying near the old fireplace. The meat was from pigs, Cooper knew. She knew that smell.

There were containers, archive boxes, envelopes of photos, evidence that their mother had lived and worked and died in a hundred places and a hundred times, but whatever system had been established to organise it had not yet been finished, or else was not intelligible to Cooper's glances, her strokes as she passed them all by.

Lucy was wearing the same yellow dress she'd been wearing that day Cooper had seen her in the woods, apparently overcoming a lifelong phobia of the dark trees. Over it Lucy now had on a black jacket. Lucy was slightly sweating, obviously too hot, but still, she didn't take the jacket off. Not the whole evening. Not even when Matthew suggested she do so, as he did a few times, met only with his sister's coldness or more mistakes, more accidental burning herself on the stove, more dropping food, more bumping into things, more shaking.

They'd moved through to the dining area. Lucy had to cook.

Soft, dreaming eyes stared at Cooper as they prepared the meal.

Whatever purposes Cooper had come there for, she was still hungry.

Lucy kept touching her own face, kept making excuses, kept apologising for the lateness of it all – she just didn't know they'd have company...

She bombarded Cooper with questions.

What was your childhood like?

You've not mentioned your father – why?

352

Who are you seeing? Are you seeing anyone?

Do you sometimes feel lonely?

Do you ever feel like a brain on a stick?

Have you ever lost anyone?

Do you ever have problems sleeping?

All these questions, Cooper barely answered, smiling, laughing, trying to change the subject to anything else.

Matthew looked over at his sister, hunched as she was over some boiling pot.

'She's been cross with me, you see. The internet's decided I'm a bad person.'

Still, Lucy did not turn around.

'My ex-girlfriend did a big Twitter thread about our break-up. I'm being hounded,' he went on.

'His *student*, like I told you,' Lucy said, turning her head just a little. 'His ex-girlfriend was his *student*. He cheated on her.' She went back to cooking.

And Cooper watched her, as Matthew talked of that girl…

What was that in Lucy's face, in her heart, that seemed so pained by what Matthew did?

Why did the woman care so much?

As the minutes passed, as they drank their drinks and waited, as Matthew watched his sister pour a second glass of wine for him, the fact of Cooper's intrusion seemed to become less important. She couldn't understand why they had let the matter go so easily.

They asked where she was staying. If she had anywhere to stay.

They offered their home once more.

Cooper told them she had a place in town.

'Where?' Lucy asked, taking a sip.

'I've found a nice place.'

'You're staying?' Matthew blinked. 'Why? I thought the case—'

'You shouldn't spend money on a hotel. Stay with us.' Lucy put her glass down.

'I'm just tying up a few loose ends,' Cooper said quietly. 'Have you heard from your father yet?'

There was a brief silence. Had she gone too far?

But no. She hadn't gone too far. These siblings seemed to roll with it as if by invisible decree – that all should be fine. That they should welcome her. That they should comply with whatever she asked, no matter how intrusive.

'He's travelling,' Matthew said.

'He'll be back in touch soon enough,' Lucy added. 'Are you sure you can't stay?' She seemed agitated.

'It's OK,' Cooper repeated, quieter.

'It's just… it's getting late. Are you sure you should be alone?'

'I'll be fine,' Cooper said. 'I'll be leaving soon, anyway. I just had—'

A few more questions.

Eventually the topic of the photos from 1964 came up.

The police had barely looked into a connection between their mother's death and those ancient photographs of the pipe and the missing girl, despite Lucy's questions. Matthew, however, had been on the police's side.

'Whoever hurt those children… they'd be old now, too, if not dead,' he snorted. 'What would one thing possibly have anything to do with the other? And what motive would they have for hurting my grandfather?'

★

354

Cooper copied the kind of thing her mother would say throughout the years – about these migraines without explanation, about the kind of pain that meant you couldn't think, about how she wasn't well. She said these things so that Lucy wouldn't keep asking her to stay.

But the woman still claimed to have a remedy, just as she had at their first meeting. 'It will sort it right out. It's almost proven…'

Cooper laughed and refused.

'I really think you should take it,' Lucy insisted.

Cooper refused again.

'Whatever you think of me, whatever I think of you… it's not words, really. That's what I've begun to think about. We think in chemicals. And pills, they're just bits of soul. And so when my mum didn't take hers, her soul changed. She didn't eat her pills and so the pigs ate her.'

Lucy smiled.

Cooper drank her drink, and it didn't seem so strange, what Lucy was saying. And it felt odd that it was not strange.

When she went to the bathroom, she splashed her tired face with water.

She tried to wake herself up.

They ate a little before midnight, and drank.

'It's raining,' Matthew remarked, looking at the glass.

'It is,' Cooper agreed.

'You should head back soon.'

Cooper hesitated. 'There's something I need to ask you,' she said.

The siblings waited.

'Your grandfather's death…'

Their response at this phrase… their lack of grief… it was

like Quentin had been some distant actor, known from his appearances rather than any real acquaintance, someone whose death brought only an intellectual sadness.

'He invested in your mother's career, didn't he?'

Matthew nodded.

'And when was that?' Cooper asked.

They drank their drinks.

Matthew looked down at his glass.

'From the beginning,' Lucy said. 'He's a very kind man.'

'What do you mean, "the beginning"? How early are we talking?' Cooper asked. 'Before she even got a camera, or—'

'From the pipe photograph,' Matthew explained. 'A broker sold him the rights to it, and from there, he wanted to talk to the photographer.'

'But why?'

Lucy laughed. 'Why would anyone ever invest in any art? If you met him, you'd see he's just this lovely man ...'

'But it wasn't art when he invested, was it?' Cooper paused. 'I don't mean any offence, but was it intended to be anything at all? From all the interviews I read—'

'Interviews ...' Matthew scoffed. 'Feels like you're interviewing us now ...'

'It sounds like it was just a seventeen-year-old having fun with her birthday present in the woods.'

'Her whole life was built on it,' he said.

'And your grandfather hadn't invested in art much before that, had he? At least not photography. So there was obviously something in this that resonated with him.'

'What does it matter?' Matthew asked.

'Because he died in the exact place that photograph was taken. Because—'

'Because you think my mother died because of that case,' Lucy said. 'But you're wrong.' She hesitated. 'Let's have some dessert wine,' she went on cheerfully.

When she went to the toilet, Cooper stole some of Sophie's bank statements from a side table, hoping to find some hint as to the woman's final days. It was not the first time she'd looked through documents and letters in another's home – she'd done it to friends as well as witnesses in other cases. Was it really her fault, when people so carelessly left pieces of their life on display? When they'd agreed to let her into their homes?

Lucy came out to find her, to see if she was OK. Cooper managed to get the documents into her pocket without being discovered.

Cooper decided to leave a short time later.

Matthew did not see Cooper off. He just remained in the dining room, near the unseen fire. He did offer one piece of assistance, though. In the process of going through and archiving his mother's possessions, he'd found the file she'd made on the pipe case, annotated with her own notes throughout the years. Matthew lent it to Cooper, in case it was useful.

Then Cooper left into the corridor and Lucy followed her, even to the entrance.

'I hope you had a good time, Coop!'

'You keep calling me Coop ... I'm not sure what to call you back.'

'There's not much point shortening Lucy.'

Cooper hesitated, then smiled. 'Lu.'

'That's stupid. It—'

'Goodnight, Lu.' Cooper turned to leave.

As she passed near the door, she noticed a wicker shape,

leaning against the window. It looked like the sun, an orb of woven spikes.

'What's wrong?' Lucy asked.

Cooper had seen that shape before, but she didn't know where. She didn't ask.

'Something's wrong,' Lucy repeated.

'There's a question, something I wanted to ask you.'

'Then ask.'

'You were arguing with your brother...' Cooper began, and before she could finish, Lucy interrupted, confused.

'When? I don't argue with anyone. I'm—'

'At your mother's funeral. You argued with Matthew. So I was told, anyway.'

'Why were they paying attention to what we said?' Lucy blinked. 'Why do they care?'

'What were you arguing about, Lu?'

'The girl. The girl Matthew abandoned. His student.'

'His ex?'

Lucy nodded.

'At your mother's funeral, you were arguing about a girl?'

Matthew emerged round the corner, nodding at them both. He was a few metres away. 'Everything OK?'

The women said that it was.

Cooper left into the night, the file on the old pipe case and abduction in her hands, and more in her bag – the bank statements in her pocket...

She was going to phone a cab. It wasn't raining now. The sky had grown peaceful. The night was almost clear.

The pit where the apple tree had previously lain – it was near her, now. As if some asteroid had fallen from the sky and destroyed the pigs, not a police officer's gun.

Cooper waited, and she felt like she was closer to the heart of things.

Her phone vibrated in her pocket, and she felt peculiar, dizzy at the sensation.

She checked it, her vision hazy.

It was her mother again.

Some other false illness. Some other attempt at connection through the threat of dying and disappearance, as if the woman had never learned human emotion at all.

Cooper stood in the dark, and thought about what came next. The Bertilak siblings were not in a healthy state. They were tied to this home, unable to go back to their normal lives, yet did not show the usual signs of grief Cooper had come to expect.

Cooper could feel that same pull upon her. And she did not know why. She did not know why she felt compelled to stay – Kelly said he might need to get in touch regarding her discovery of Quentin's body, but even then, that was more a request than a command. Why stay, then, when her only friend had been watching her, when Lapis had been following her, when no one did what they said or meant what they did?

When all Cooper's days were filled with watching videos, listening to podcasts about these old crimes ... when she felt so close to solving a mystery that had eluded so many others ...

This place to which Cooper's mother had sent her, a holiday recommended by some mythical friend ...

This place in which Cooper's sister had told her of marriage, of a door closing forever with a man she had once loved.

Cooper felt faint, thinking of all of this. She felt like rain would be a blessing at this moment, to cool her scalp, to quiet her thoughts.

But nothing came. Nothing helped.

She stood there, and realised she hadn't even contacted a cab. She realised that realising was difficult. The door opened behind her.

She could hear it, but she couldn't turn round – it felt like too much effort, like something in the world would snap and crumble, like she'd turn to salt...

She could hear their eyes.

She lost consciousness a short time later.

65

Cooper woke up. People were dancing around her. There were half a dozen of them, posed, their long limbs stretched out in the almost-dark.

No—

No, they weren't dancing.

They were frozen still. They were just sculptures, wire frames in a basement. The same basement Cooper had discovered that first night she'd come to Bertilak's home. It took her a moment to recognise it, to pull herself up.

She couldn't feel her legs, her arms. She...

There was more darkness.

More nothing.

66

A voice was talking to her when she woke.

A man's voice.

It was hard to see, let alone think.

This man, he told her she needed to understand.

That she didn't need to tell anyone about this. That the path forward was up to her.

He told her that if she couldn't talk much, it was OK. She could sleep. She could stay here as long as she needed.

He told her this as if he were doing her a favour.

She needed her rest.

The world went dark again.

67

The morning.

Cooper lay on the floor of the Bertilaks' basement.

She could barely move, but was able to turn her head, to see she was still clothed.

To see she was not alone. Not the sculptures – not the man who had spoken before, but someone else – she knew it.

The dark, faceless shape was almost out of view.

It kept breathing against her neck.

It began to whimper.

Cooper shook, the only movement she could make. It did not touch her, but for this breath.

Her eyes welled with tears.

Eventually, she was alone.

Eventually, she could move.

She got up. The space was dim and dusty. It was emptier than when Cooper had last visited – where once many boxes had lined the cellar's edges, now there were only a few. Light shone from a single bulb, hanging down from a wire. It was day above – not that she had her phone to tell, not that she had anything, but it was clear from the hatch, from the corona of light that spread around it.

Cooper rarely remembered her dreams. More than once, though, her ex had told her she talked in her sleep – sometimes brief references to their cats or their friends, sometimes nonsense phrases, sometimes entire apparently half-lucid conversations from which she'd suddenly wake up bewildered or afraid. Once, she'd started trying to inject her ex in her sleep, thumping Arthur's leg with her empty fist.

Soon he was going to be her brother-in-law.

It was thinking about this – this of all things – that brought Cooper back to herself, that lifted the flatness, the delirium of this brief captivity – if brief it had been.

The story Cooper had told herself of Sophie's own relation-ships – of her on-and-off again de-facto marriage to Thomas – had been bathed in the tone, in the essence of her own love. All love stories are, once you have loved. All break-up stories are empowered by the memory of your own. She knew that. Knowing didn't change it.

Cooper looked around the room, searching for something sharp, or something hard. She found a piece of piping, the leg of one of Sophie's sculptures. She hoped Sophie would not mind her taking it. She took all the detritus off it until the pure cylinder remained, and she gripped it in her right fist.

She went up the stairs, slowly so not to creak.

She went to the hatch.

She did not scream to be let out. People always did that in films. Why would it work?

As if whoever had locked you down in a place like this had done so by accident?

As if whoever had put you in a hole in the ground...

Someone walked above.

Someone came to the hatch.

Cooper retreated, trembling, shoving the pipe down the back leg of her jeans...

She retreated, and saw the man's face as he came down from the light, carrying a tray, carrying coffees and breakfast.

She saw the face of Matthew.

'In thee thy mother dies, our household's name,
My death's revenge, thy youth, and England's fame,
All these and more we hazard by thy stay;
All these are saved if thou wilt fly away.'

Henry VI: Part 1
William Shakespeare

PART 8:

MATTHEW

PAST AND PRESENT

The First Home

The first house Matthew could remember living in had a roof through which you could see the stars.

He remembered watching *Blue Peter* in a dark kitchen, sitting on a stool, a wand of stars and glitter resting on the laminate in front of him.

He remembered planting a tree in the garden he'd never see sprout.

He remembered his parents arguing.

He remembered a takeaway thrown across the room.

He remembered the day they moved, the lorries, the car ride with too much stuff.

He remembered arriving. His mother had worked for a man, once. She'd come back to work there again...

The Second Home

The second house Matthew could remember was a grand house. There was another little boy there.

And a woman Matthew grew to be scared of, a woman who stared at him, but he never knew why – nails so long she was on the verge of needing a bag to hold them in, some sack to contain their curling growths...

He remembered climbing out of a window across the rooftop.

He remembered his friend – a friend he knew to be imaginary. A tall man with tall limbs, kind of silly-looking, really. One who put his finger to his lips and revealed his whole life to be a secret – one that Matthew could never share or he'd cease to be around.

There was no roof window you could see the stars through, not here.

The walls trapped heat so much that sometimes none of them could sleep.

One day Matthew's imaginary friend came back.

He had a girl with him – he wanted to take them both far away, to a new home.

Matthew was not sure, but he said yes regardless.

He wanted to go home – to his true home, his first home, the place with the roof where you could see the stars.

So Matthew went, hoping this would bring him closer.

The Third Home

It was not very big. Like a tree house, almost, though you had to go down to get into it.

He had comic books down there ... water bottles ... a pot he didn't quite understand the purpose of.

The comics were about Superman.

His imaginary friend put the lid down on the box, position-ing then a great plastic pipe that would run from the box's roof right up to the air above so that Matthew could breathe.

It was a game.

Matthew had to hide. If anyone came ... he had to hide.

Matthew waited there for a long time, reading about a little boy in a basket, in a space craft, sent out from a doomed world.

Matthew fell asleep.

He heard them talking when he woke up. About their futures. About parents.

Matthew was ready to go home now. He was ready to stop. He began to call out to them. They told him to come up to the pipe … to look up to the light above …

And hot liquid fell upon his face. He began to scream and cry – up above they blotted up the light and the air.

When he'd almost passed out, they uncovered it. They told him again – if he said anything, did anything, they'd hurt him, worse next time.

He read about Superman until his torch stopped working.

He read about a journalist, a photographer, people who tried to do good.

And one day, like a miracle, a photographer appeared in the light above him – flashing him with a second light …

He waited. He waited to be rescued, silent, terrified it was some trick.

A few hours later, his faith seemed rewarded.

The lid came off.

The man cleaned his room while the girl held the gentle, frail, sobbing little boy, telling him it was almost all over. He knew her name because she told him, then.

Stephanie told him that they just needed one more thing. He just had to hold his breath as long as he could.

The man lay down a great sheet of plastic all around the forest floor and asked the boy to lie down. He said he'd send him back home in the post.

The boy held his breath. They covered his mouth, and his nose.

And then he went to sleep.

And then this Matthew was no more.

Cambridge

Four years ago

The Third Matthew

The pub split into an arrow shape as they went in, going down to the riverside terrace below. Every menu announced a tenuous connection with Pink Floyd, Syd having gone to jazz shows here in his youth. Queen's and King's colleges loomed nearby, the river glistened with docked punting boats, birds drifted along the light.

They chose a booth on the furthest wall from the window. It being winter, they went up and closed the door to the water every time some inconsiderate stranger left it opened, the heat seeping out into the void like space.

It had been forty-three weeks since Matthew Bertilak had been to this place, to any pub. It had been thirty-seven weeks since his last drink.

He was here with some fellow staff members and a few students.

There had been a conference on – one about the nineteenth-century poet Lord Byron.

'You wouldn't have mobile phones without incest,' Matthew said.

This was a controversial statement.

He explained it.

'Byron's father left him and his mother when they were little. Like his son, Byron's dad—'

'Mad Jack,' another academic interrupted, giggling with his cider.

'Yes,' Matthew nodded, 'Mad Jack. Like his son, he was prolific when it came to fathering bastards. He had another daughter down the line – Augusta. And when Augusta met her half-brother, both of them were already adults. Rumours started spreading, Byron being Byron. And a baby was born. The authorities started being interested in the weird relationship between the two siblings, so Byron decided to get married to someone else to conceal the truth. The other marriage only lasted a little while, producing his only legitimate child – a little girl who was taught maths and logic from a young age because her mother was terrified she would inherit her father's madness.' He paused. 'Incest created Ada Lovelace, the writer of the world's first app.'

'I'd hardly use the word app…' the cider-drinker said.

Another of the group interrupted, then, telling Matthew his words didn't prove what he thought they proved.

She was nineteen, had hair so dark it looked almost dyed, skin like snow.

He'd tried not to look at her. He'd tried, even as he'd taught her in those small rooms.

'Ada's birth was a reaction against incest,' she said. 'It was a sham marriage, and then the way she was raised, it was just an attempt to be better than her father.'

'Actions have reactions,' Matthew said. 'But it's still cause and effect. It doesn't matter what the intent was, one thing just led to another.'

One thing led to another.

One day she said she loved him.

The Home Inn and Tavern

The sun was gone.

All that was left on the riverbank were thin trees in breezeless air. A few crowds littered the bars and shacks, huddled groups of friends holding glasses, entombed by thick coats.

The Thames spat itself into the sea far away, but neither that nor its movement near them could be divined by anything other than the vague sound of its movement below.

The Bertilak family dined there in honour of their mother's birthday.

They'd never taken their father's name. There were many different explanations for this proffered throughout the years, of feminism sometimes, of the sound of it all afterwards, an aesthetic choice.

The surname was an old name, after all.

It could be traced back to the time of King Arthur, to the tale of the Green Knight.

At a Christmas feast, an emerald-clad figure had entered the court of King Arthur and challenged them to a duel – one hit from his enemy, then he got to return his attack one year later.

The king's relative, Gawain – a knight who, if the Grail Maiden herself were to enter the room, ninety-nine of them would look at the grail, but he would look at the maiden – this Gawain said yes.

He strode over and decapitated the Green Knight. The knight then proceeded to pick up his head, place it back on his body, and give his new enemy the location of the place he would counter-attack in one year's time.

Gawain didn't want to go or face up to this, but everyone made him.

He stayed at the court of a Lord Bertilak while he awaited the knight's challenge. He ended up almost seducing Lord Bertilak's wife, in spite of all the hospitality his host had offered him. He took a kiss.

So when Gawain faced his Green Knight, he discovered that the Green Knight was Bertilak himself... and when he faced the executioner's axe, he was only given a little cut in the neck, to mirror the kiss he had stolen from the lady.

Gawain fled back home, telling the story to the laughter of all he knew, haunted by all he had seen, the tale of chopped-off heads, the hunt of that spectral court in lust and in blood.

And Matthew's family ... they shared his ancient, mythic name.

This challenge of someone who asked for their own head to be chopped off, and then who walked away all the same.

This moral test.

They didn't give up their names for their father's, they didn't call themselves Medina, but for their middle name.

They were Bertilaks.

'I'm sorry if I've annoyed everyone,' Lucy said. She kept tapping her fingers on the table. 'Did I annoy you?' Her hair was blonde this time, a blue sweater, black jeans. She rarely looked at any of them.

Them – Matthew, Lucy, their mother. Joanna was still in America.

They were the only ones around. The ones who never left.

'You haven't,' Matthew said.

'I feel like I have, though... haven't I?'

'You don't need to ask if you've annoyed anyone,' he said, and Lucy did not mention it again for a while.

They talked with their mother about their news, and she

expressed little in the way of comment, just the occasional clarifying question or remark.

Lucy was still trying to be a cook.

She claimed at one point that a television production company had been interested in taking her on.

'They offered me my own show,' she said, and Matthew told her she should take it. She shook her head. 'I don't want the fame,' she explained. 'That's all.'

'You have a big imagination,' their mother said.

They ate their meals.

Lucy did not talk much after that.

'It's nice to hear your stories. To catch up,' their mother said.

'I have a story.' Matthew drank his wine.

'Let's hear it, then.'

'I think I've fallen in love.' He smiled.

His mother corrected him. That wasn't a story. It was only a story if some other element occurred, a twist, a conflict.

Lucy left the table, saying she had to go to the bathroom.

'Who is she?' their mother asked. 'Who is this girl of yours?'

'She's at the university,' Matthew said, watching Lucy as she left upstairs. 'She's—'

'A student?'

'Academic, like me.'

'When do I get to meet her?'

'At Christmas,' he said. 'I'll bring her at Christmas.'

Their mother looked at the stairs. 'Why did Lucy go up?'

'What?'

'The bathroom is behind us.' Their mother paused. 'Is she smoking again?'

'I don't know.'

Some time later, Lucy still not back, their mother got up and went up the stairs to look for her.

And she too went missing.

So Matthew went, too.

He walked past the smells of all that alcohol at other tables, all the dirt and grime of the riverside.

He went out into the dim candlelight, and saw no one, saw nothing he recognised.

He went back inside and remained at his table for another half an hour, all his attempts to phone his family failing.

He went to King's Cross and, waiting for his pre-booked train, kept trying to ring them, to make sure they were OK.

Should he stay?

Should he call the police?

He did not know – but he had a train booking.

He had to go, didn't he? Or it'd be a waste. What would he really be able to do if he stayed?

They'd probably just gone off without him.

He got on the train.

The bright carriages passed a dark world outside, barely visible white homes and small cottages, rusted iron skeletons of abandoned buildings, yellow-and-red silos in a place called Shepreth. Past Foxton. In the depth of night, a bay horse cantered with its rider.

On the outskirts of his workplace, his home, his final stop, glass and concrete rose from dying fields, a new sapling supported in cylindrical grey tubes. Life had to be planned and permitted here.

Men in orange coats climbed along near the track at midnight, cutting tall trees right outside false colleges designed to ensnare the unknowing, or entice those who just wanted that name in their lives, in their history – that history, that final destination announced on the intercom.

Cambridge.

You are now alighting at—

His phone began to ring. He looked at it, in a daze, and saw ten missed calls. How had he missed them?

Why hadn't he heard them, or answered?

They were in the hospital.

Something had been put in Lucy's drink.

'She was raving,' Sophie said to her son. 'She said it was "Matthew" who'd done it—'

'Why?' he protested, rising from his train seat, grabbing his bags. The doors were not yet closed. 'Why would I drug—'

'Don't be ridiculous,' Sophie said. 'I know it wasn't you. She didn't even mean you.'

'What do you mean?'

The Hospital

'There's another one ...' Lucy said, almost in a whisper. 'There's another ...' And so she slept.

The Home for Recovering Adults

Lucy went to rehab a year later.

She had been drugged by another during the family dinner – that much was clear.

But afterwards – she did it to herself.

Something in her changed, or was awakened, perhaps.

While they waited to admit her, Lucy asked the staff if she could cook. They explained that she couldn't, but that there would be other crafts.

It was a place that taught radical empathy. That to feel as others do was the cure for all ills.

She wanted to know if her mother was coming.

'She'll be here,' Matthew said. Matthew promised.

He could still remember the perfume, the smell of the flowers in the vase, even now.

The sound of the fountain in the middle.

The sound of the phone line as it rang, as he tried to get in contact with his mother.

She'd said she'd be here.

She'd said.

And Matthew heard Lucy talking to her father, as their father barely listened. As he spoke on the phone to someone else.

She said that she understood why she'd been drugged, all those weeks ago.

The stranger had known she needed it. He'd known about her headaches.

The stranger had just been trying to help.

Go Home

There was no one incident that caused Matthew's girlfriend to leave him.

No single affair. No single moment, no single piece of evidence or sin.

She'd even seen him kiss someone at a party. She'd kept seeing him after that.

He just woke up one day and found himself blocked on all her accounts.

Messages from friends alerted him to a Twitter thread about his entire romantic life and personality.

How he divided people into groups.

How he played favourites.

How he was an abuser.

His father, once, had told him about how he would have a lot of girlfriends in his life, just like he had.

Just like he had.

Matthew sat and stared at the laptop for a while before closing it.

Ten days later, the Twitter thread still growing, he sat in front of a police officer in a lodge in Lethwick, talking about his mother's death.

Ten days later, his sister first spiked a perfect stranger at dinner, just as she had been spiked so long ago. They'd seen her wandering out in the early morning...

One day Lucy claimed to Matthew that she'd started spying for the police, too, just like Cooper was.

She started claiming she was responsible for all these things that Cooper had achieved, and Matthew did what you always had to do.

He agreed, gently, kindly.

He sat with his sister.

He loved her.

He sat in his home, in the dark, and left the world behind, that awful secret: that he didn't miss his mother.

How could you miss a stranger?

The First Matthew, 1944

'I'm walking down the stairs,' Matthew had said, bending his knees, mock-lowering himself past scattered crumbling brick-work as if an invisible staircase would lead him into the soil. It was stupid. People laughed, Quentin among them.

Three days later, Matthew lost his heart, blood welling up like an oil spill.

The Second Matthew, 1964

Once life had left his little body, Matthew was removed from the plastic. His little finger had then been severed as proof that he had lived.

He was sealed up once more.

His bones were put into a box with a letter, and were buried with love.

The Third Matthew, Now

The third Matthew told a woman in a basement the story of his life, a story that seemed to become more and more about Lucy in the telling.

He did not know of his predecessors.

Most of the people who remembered the first Matthew had died of old age.

Most of the people who remembered the second Matthew had been murdered.

Only the third remained, not yet consumed.

He hoped the stranger would understand what his sister had done. That she'd acted out of fear. That she was not well.

That there was no need to tell anyone.

To please – please – just leave us alone – to let this be …

Cooper

The Sophie he presented was not the one Cooper had seen in the photos, that she'd read about in books and heard about in countless true crime videos. Sophie was a cold figure in Matthew's memory, a distant, almost cruel force in his life who arrived and left without notice, who refused to provide Lucy the support she'd needed in a crisis, who let an embittered Matthew holding all the pieces in the aftermath of the collapse.

Lucy had never been a chef. Not professionally.

Lucy could not hold down a job.

Lucy had drugged her, most likely.

These things Matthew shared with Cooper, down in the half-light of that basement.

'When you mentioned your headaches... I think it must have been her trying to help,' Matthew claimed, feeble. 'I didn't know she'd do it. She was scared of you, Cooper – she thinks you're doing this to us. And you can't blame her for believing something like that.' When Cooper didn't say anything, he then added an instruction, unconvincing, sombre: 'I need your forbearance in this, Cooper.

'Please,' he asked. 'Please don't ruin our lives. You can go – I just – I just wanted to talk to you before you did – when you were better and there wasn't... there wasn't a chance for a misunderstanding...'

He stared at her, and still she said nothing.

'You have to believe me,' Matthew stated.

'Why should I?'

'Because you don't have a choice. Not now. Not anymore.'

It was then that Matthew took out Cooper's phone, unlocked. How was it still unlocked?

Had she been on her phone when she'd fallen to the ground?

Had he grabbed it before it had timed out?

He showed Cooper... he showed Cooper the messages on the screen.

He showed Cooper messages he'd sent to 'Emma'.

'You were pretending to be someone else. You were pretending to date me. You were...'

Cooper did not know what to say.

She did not even register that she had to speak, the sight of those messages was so – so unexpected.

So much like a dream, to see that reality finally colliding with this one.

To see this fiction end.

'I don't think you're well,' Matthew said, angry. 'I don't know why you did these things to me... I don't know why my sister does what she does... Why my mother...' He shook his head. 'I don't know why the world plays tricks like this, I don't understand it, but I don't have to, do I?' He hesitated. 'I took back what you stole. I don't want to see you here – not ever again.'

He held up the bank statements Cooper had taken from the house.

Cooper couldn't speak, her throat caught, her heart racing.

'If you keep Lucy's behaviour a secret...' he went on. 'If you don't tell anyone... I don't see why anyone has to know about you... about us... about "Emma".'

He put his phone back on the table in front of him, sweating, red-faced, shaking.

He was nervous too.

And Cooper knew then, watching him.

It wasn't him. None of this had been him...

He wasn't going to keep Cooper here. He really wasn't.

'Please… don't ruin her life…' he asked quietly. 'She's all I have left. I love her. And I know. Don't forget. I know what you did. I know what you pretended to be.'

68

The midsummer festival was now in full swing. Processions had already told the story of Noah's Ark, of a biblical flood that had washed filth and sin from the world. Parishioners and tourists stood in crowds by the roadsides, jubilant, excited, chatty. Women danced crying round carpenters as they nailed an actor to a stack of wooden blocks.

People took photographs. Men and women and children, they watched the miracle.

The crowd shuddered as Christ stood revealed. What came next would be the Harrowing of Hell – the three days between his death and resurrection where Christ descended into the underworld and fought the Devil for the stolen souls of the human race.

Still, her mother and sister tried to ring her. Still they tried to pull her into the gravity of the false sickness, the threat to be broken, to make the world broken in your wake... Like an infection, they had taken her ex, they had taken Arthur. What else would they take, if she answered them?

The festival was older than the mystery plays.

It was what all midsummer festivals were at their base. An enactment of birth, life, death.

They came for Cooper, all these people.

The teeth of all the places she had been, the breath of all those dead things she had held...

Cooper could feel them close.

So Cooper fled.

69

Cooper paused, crossing a bridge between buildings, a small cutaway across the river. She steadied herself on the black metal railings. She had her bags, she was leaving, she—

Cooper's phone shook in her pocket.

'Will you take a photo for us?'

Cooper turned. She saw a couple staring at her from a few metres away, trees over them all, their green canopy blooming.

The woman held out her phone.

'It's just such a romantic spot...'

Cooper left.

The sun was setting. The streets grew darker and quiet, the drums and laughter of the festival growing more distant the further she went. She was sure this was the way to the station.

Where was home, really? What had been home since the building she'd shared with her boyfriend so many years ago? What had been home but her cats, her children – she smiled whenever she thought of them like that, but what other children did she have, or did she want to have? The life of a woman like Sophie Bertilak, littered with the dead and unwanted and despising and ill? No. Not that.

She had her apartment back in Guildford, but how many days had she really spent living there, that refuge she'd fled to after the break-up, that stopgap, that flat devoid of any personalisation or sentimentality? That place she could pretend she'd decorate, if only she had the time...

The alleys narrowed in Lethwick. She'd never been down these roads before. Reflections of the river danced along the old brick walls, the old stone.

There was a clattering on the cobbles round the corner.

A man ran at her.

Another came, and another, both of them laughing without seeming to make any noise.

Soon the street was full of all these people running along, and then it came, the main procession of the festival, the main play of the day.

Sheep, led along on leashes by farmers.

Cooper hesitated, watching. She walked along and saw a poster listing the timings for each performance.

This play was the Harrowing of Hell.

'A procession of Lethwick's Union of Farmers, driving souls freed from hell by Christ in the three days of his death.'

Had Jesus really been dead if he'd been present somewhere else, regardless of whether that place was heaven or hell?

Was there such a thing as death if an afterlife awaited people?

What about people who had been rendered down into paste, emptied out into jugs?

The sheep passed Cooper by, and they seemed more like lambs the closer they came. Some of them struggled on the leashes, some of them in pain.

Cooper looked for signs for the train station and headed through the growing crowds on a street that had been empty just minutes before.

Oppidum vetus leneque.

The painted town, home of temples and churches, of lichen and moss, of benches and plaques and cafés and trees and light – the sun fell to the edge of the world, and soon there was only dark.

By the time Cooper arrived at the train station, it was completely empty but for red flowers shivering near war memorials, a sea of them moving in the light breeze and street-lamp light...

She walked across lonely platforms. She was served a ticket by a machine. She waited.

Her phone shook again.

She checked it.

All these missed calls and messages. Her sister. Again and again.

Even her ex. Even Arthur. Her breath caught in her throat at seeing his name and number appear,

All telling them to call her. All telling her they had something to tell her.

Pleading with her to talk with them.

'It's Mum—'

She hesitated, and then rang back.

Just in case.

Just one more time.

And they said she was dying. Just like they always said... but this time maybe it was different.

The train would be there in half an hour.

She waited and waited.

A man came walking down the empty platform. She heard his steps before she saw his face, and somehow she knew – she knew who it would be, not even from the sound, but some primal part of her, some hidden depth that watched for the coming of danger.

His hair, his face, his soul calibrated to try to reach acceptance, but failing in every respect, the tragic truth that he was right, he was right about his wrongness, he was right that no one would ever accept him, not because of genes or foolish ideas of how the world worked, but what those ideas had made him into – what formless shape now inhabited that crisp grey suit, that barely suppressed smile, those cold grey eyes.

DS Lapis stood on the platform, watching her.

'Where are you going?' he asked, though it was obvious, wasn't it? There was only one train on the way – a train whose destination filled the display overhead.

She didn't answer him. She had stiffened, holding her bags a little closer.

'You're a witness,' he said. 'You need to stay.'

Cooper took her phone out. She'd had it ready for days.

'Don't ignore me.'

She'd had it ready to go for days.

'You'll look at me,' he said, his voice still falling, descending into its own pit. 'You'll treat me with respect. You are a witness in this case and your actions are . . .'

He hesitated as she stopped and put her phone away. He hesitated as she smiled.

'Everyone will know,' she said. 'Everyone will know what a pathetic maggot of a person you are. How dare you talk about me, how dare you follow me – how dare you even wear that badge.'

'I told you what would happen if you did that,' he said. 'I told you I'd share the video of your break-in. I told you I'd—'

'Share whatever video you like. I should have sent this message days ago. I should never have let you threaten me.'

'Let me?' Lapis stared. 'I heard you. Talking on your phone. Your mother is sick. A woman who can't stand you. I heard your conversation in the restaurant. You are going to see her anyway. You're going to see her. Just like when we first met.'

'The start of our wonderful friendship. A psychopath blocking my way and grabbing my arm.' Cooper stiffened. Why was she talking to him? Why was she bothering? 'She's not sick, anyway, she's … she's …' Still the words came tumbling out.

'She is what?'

'Dying, apparently,' Cooper said, quiet, strangely breathless.

Lapis stood there as the minute count clicked down. Only a few more until the train was here.

'My father died,' Lapis said, his voice still cold, still empty. 'Three years ago he died.'

Cooper stared at him.

'It's how I got my house,' Lapis added.

'And how proud he must have been,' Cooper said. 'How proud, to have a son like you.'

He stared, and didn't speak, and Cooper waited. The train was ten minutes away, now.

He stared, as if her clothes, her skin, her bone, her blood, disappeared into nothingness.

He left the station. He did not turn to look back.

Eight minutes.

Seven.

Six.

'We regret to inform you that the train arriving on PLATFORM A has been cancelled due to unforeseen circumstances. It—'

Cooper did not listen.

The world went grey, just like the police officer's eyes.

She waited for the next train, and it never came.

The internet said there had been reports of a security threat stopping the train on its track …

A replacement would not come for hours.

Had he phoned them?

Had it been him? Had it been Lapis?

70

Cooper found a cab willing to take her back to London. It cost her a fortune.

As they drove, she recognised the cab driver.

'You took me to the valley a few nights ago,' Cooper said. 'You talked about your children.'

There was a pause. 'You pretended to be asleep so you wouldn't have to talk to me,' he said.

They didn't say much more to each other.

It took a while, their journey, and Cooper tried to sleep, closing her eyes in the cloudy sky.

By the time Cooper Allen reached London, by the time she got to the hospital – it was over.

Her mother was already dead.

IT'S NEVER TOO LATE

Three Years Ago

One day, Sophie Bertilak's mother died.

Sophie entered the place in which she'd been born, in which she'd grown up, in which her own youngest son had left the world.

IT'S NEVER TOO LATE, read a poster on the wall. A few things like this were spread throughout the building, badly tacked, representing some spurt of self-improvement in the woman's final years.

As if a phrase, as if the written word itself could motivate anyone to do anything.

Think about the first place you ever lived.

The rooms were like that, these final days of Lethwick.

Red ants swarmed outside the kitchen, outside the apple tree. Dry husks of flowers spread throughout vases, across mantelpieces, the last hurrah of old soon-to-be-discarded sofas. Rotten fruit grew in a graveyard of broken pedestal fans. A frosted orb hung from the ceiling. It was the most beautiful, unexpected thing in this place. Outside, visible through the glass, ruined cottages had now become lodges, bought with the money of Sophie's photographs, of those early royalties, of payments her mother had taken on her behalf.

Her mum was dead.

Sophie had brandy and listened to old songs the first night back.

The next day Joanna came to visit her, one last meeting for now before she went back to the States.

Her eldest daughter – a woman Sophie had not seen for almost a decade – talked with her about their financial destinies.

'Are you going to sell?'

Sophie told her she didn't know. Probably, though.

'Lucy won't like it,' Joanna said.

Sophie looked away.

'How are things between you both?'

Sophie said something about Lucy being her daughter, and that therefore of course things were fine. She wandered up to the bookcase while Joanna kept sitting.

'I'm your daughter,' Joanna said.

'You're a stranger.'

'Sophie ...'

Her mother laughed, taking a camera from the shelf, an old Kodak. 'You're the only one who still calls me that. Say cheese.' She smirked, getting ready to take a photo.

Joanna ignored her. 'You told us to call you that.'

'If I told you to jump off a cliff, would you?' Sophie smiled. 'Lucy never called me Sophie. And you didn't say cheese.'

She looked at Joanna, who had nothing to say.

'Will you come to my funeral?' she asked.

Joanna twisted her face. 'What kind of a question is that?'

Sophie asked if she'd been a good mother.

She asked – if Joanna might sit here one day, going through her possessions just as Sophie now went through those of her own mother – how she'd weigh her life.

'How can I go through your possessions if I'm not here?' Joanna asked.

And then Sophie found herself smiling, then laughing, and so did Joanna.

She wouldn't see Joanna again.

Sophie spent the first few weeks of her stay in Lethwick organising her mother's things.

She spent a lot of time next to her apple tree.

She'd scattered Alfie there.

She took photos.

Her family talked to her less and less.

Sophie's car broke down one day. A farmer helped her. She saw his piglets playing in the field.

'They're so small,' she said.

'They get big. Really big.'

'I heard they ...'

'You heard what?' the man asked.

'That pigs were smart. That they have feelings.'

He remarked that he'd never seen her at church. He asked who she was, and why she didn't go to church.

He helped her fix her car, and she went home, and one day she got two pigs and called one of them Alfie and let him feed on the product of a tree that had grown out of the dust of her son Alfie, who had in turn grown out of the flesh of her own body, which had grown out of her mother whose dust sat on a jar on her mantelpiece.

Sophie went to sleep, drinking brandy, listening to old songs.

IT'S NEVER TOO LATE.

It is impossible to say how first the idea
entered my brain; but once conceived,
it haunted me day and night.

The Tell-Tale Heart
Edgar Allan Poe (1843)

PART 9:

THE WINDOW

DR COOPER ALLEN
THE PRESENT DAY

71

Cooper stood outside the door for a while and listened to her sister talking on the phone. She supposed it was eavesdropping, really, and it had only started out of fear of knocking. She wondered who her sister was talking to – it certainly wasn't their mother, whose voice would have been audible four floors away.

Of course it couldn't be their mother.

She kept remembering the woman's death.

As if something about it hadn't stuck yet.

She'd never felt like this about a death before, untethered, shattered in the sequence of her thoughts, the genres of her days...

She'd never felt like she didn't care, and at the same time known that feeling to be a lie.

Her sister croaked these odd, isolated phrases. Perhaps the person she was talking to on the phone was trying to calm her down. Whether it was about Julia's job, her personal life, their mother's funeral, or some other nightmare scenario, Cooper could only guess. Her sister had these panics all the time, these crumblings of reality, even without a funeral.

Cooper had not wanted anything. She had not wanted any possessions, nor had she wanted to be a part of the planning.

They remained in this hotel as their base for sleeping. Their mother's home only had one bed, and neither daughter wanted to stay in it while they made arrangements.

Something was wrong with her.

She shouldn't be here.

Cooper had told Julia this the night before, and Julia had said OK, quiet, unexpanded.

And now Cooper had checked out. She was going to say goodbye, and her intent felt final.

A week since the woman's death. They still hadn't buried her.

Sentences fell through the door, through the brass numerals 1 6 on its faded paintwork:

God, I wish people would stop saying that to me—

I'm allowed to feel upset—

I shouldn't really have to apologise—

Everybody's crunching at the moment. Everybody—

It's not fair for me to ignore it – Christ . . .

I had to turn down holiday requests—

She doesn't need me—

I'm sorry, I—

I will. I love you too—

It was Arthur on the phone, wasn't it?

'I love you.'

Something they had all said to each other.

Cooper didn't knock. She just left down the hallway towards the lift. She then paused and walked back towards Room 16, her heart beating faster. Fuck. Fuck fuck fuck. She then walked away again.

She pressed the button for the lift.

The door opened behind her, a few rooms down.

'There's no family,' came Julia's voice. 'No one else I can find. No one at all apart from us.'

Cooper did not turn.

'She had no one left, and you – you left her. You're going to leave her again now.' Julia's voice deepened, an edge creeping

406

in. She sounded like she'd moved closer. 'Like you left—' But the sentence remained unfinished.

Cooper turned. 'Say it.'

'You're leaving me to do all this on my own.' Julia was blinking, her eyes wet. 'You're my … you're … I need you …'

'You were going to say "like I left Arthur".'

Julia grimaced. Then nodded, colder.

'There's some …' Julia looked away, scratching at her eyes. 'Some stuff with the banks and her insurance – some irregularity about the birth certificate we sent and, I need you – I can't do all this. I shouldn't have to do all this alone, I …' Julia hesitated. 'You're my big sister. Please stay.'

'Ask Arthur to help.'

And with that, Cooper left.

And she paused the elevator a floor below, her eyes welling up, and she went up again, and the hallway was empty now – of course it was empty, and Cooper returned to the elevator, she punched the controls and cried out in pain at the punching.

She descended.

72

In the months that followed her return from Lethwick, Cooper went to therapist after therapist, counsellor after counsellor. Where once she had despised them, now she messaged them all the time, the more sessions, the more rapid their conversations, the better.

A life coach told her she needed to replace the negative voice inside her mind with a new one, a positive one. She needed to set goals. She needed to draw circles showing what areas of life gave her contentment and which were in need of further improvement.

She was told by a counsellor that she had not learned the life skills required to display an appropriate level of anger in the right manner. Cooper either directed her anger inwards or expressed it in unconsciously passive-aggressive actions, even sometimes in acts of seeming love or closeness with those she hated, as if a form of self-harm.

She was asked if she was allowed to be angry when she was a child, or if such behaviour was a cause for correction, for telling off, for punishment by her parents.

She was analysed by a specialist and told she suffered from extreme anxiety. She protested that she often visited a number of people and places for a living. She protested that she had no problem talking to people. She protested.

'What do you imagine your future to be, Dr Allen? What do you imagine any future to be?'

She answered. She didn't. There was no future but the immediate.

'Imagine yourself in five years ... where are you? What are you doing?'

She thought about her mother. 'Please, just answer me' – the woman had messaged her, time and time again.

'Cooper?' the specialist asked.

She left. She went to someone else.

A grief counsellor wanted to connect her experience of loss throughout her life to this moment: pets, her father, colleagues, the dead she'd seen in cases, the dead she'd brought about herself, and ...

And how could she do that?

How could she possibly hold all that non-existence within her heart?

Life was a question.

What had she lost, when all these others had died, but answers to that question?

What grew in that soil but guilt?

All the good she had not done. All the bad she'd ...

She left.

She began to watch videos of crimes online. People being punched or shot or stabbed, often on foreign battlefields.

Another, and another doctor ...

One wanted to know about her love life. One asked her when she'd last had sex or been in a relationship – any kind of relationship at all. He wanted to know about her love life.

He asked all these things after she told him about her sister and her ex, about the break-up, about the cats.

'Do you still have feelings for this man?' he asked.

She had feelings for the cats.

The rest ...

He asked more and more questions to the point it began to feel prurient, like he wanted to fuck her.

He tried to act all offended.

'The way you described your friendships, going from town to town, brief attachments... It's not dissimilar to how some people describe and use the ease of one-night stands as defence mechanisms against needing to form any kind of connection, when you feel that urge rise within yourself—'

Cooper scoffed at the use of the word 'urge'.

'To love,' the doctor said. 'To be connected. The hedgehog's dilemma – how to be with other people when you're afraid you'll cause them harm.'

'I swore an oath,' she said, 'I promised to do no harm. Just like you did.'

'An interesting profession for people with that fear.' He paused. 'How was your parents' relationship?'

'What do you mean?'

'What were they like with each other as a couple? In a romantic sense? How did they act around you and your sister?'

Cooper couldn't remember.

She couldn't remember them ever acting in that way.

She could barely even remember the man, and her mother's face... Weeks since she had last seen it alive, it had begun to fade hilariously, absurdly, rapidly, from her mind.

It was like the memory of a film.

Cooper contacted the woman whose photos had been stolen for her final dating profile. She pointed out its existence and said that this woman should tighten her security settings.

The woman was from her old university. The woman had been a few years above her, the leader of a night out Cooper had gone on in her first week of university. They'd drunk at multiple pubs and played on train tracks in the dark.

Cooper had never forgotten her name.

She took down the profiles she had made, hesitating before hitting 'suspend' instead of 'delete'.

She went to see someone new.

The next psychoanalyst wanted to talk about her sense of morality – about her increasing draw towards careers where she would not only act with a sense of justice, but help bring it about in the world; where she would be involved in the judging of others.

'Was there some aspect of your childhood you felt was unfair? Some wrong you think should have been righted? Were you always like this?'

She told a story about scratching a man's car after believing he'd hurt his dog. She told the punchline about thinking she'd got the wrong car. She'd been a teenager. She normally got some half-smile at all this.

The psychoanalyst just stared at her and wrote her notes.

'Do you want to hurt the people you judge, Dr Allen?'

Cooper thought then of a lake ... of a culprit, standing by that lake, bleeding ...

And then she thought of Quentin Medina by a different lake, an old man's ruined torso in the mouth of a stag ...

She didn't know why she thought of him.

She hadn't harmed him, she'd never met the old man ... she didn't—

'Dr Allen?' the psychoanalyst asked, concerned. 'Are you all right?'

It was suggested to her that her parents' inconsistency might have made her the way she was – afraid to feel stable, afraid to feel afraid; a world that was worse than hostile because you

could never truly believe it to be bad, there was enough goodness and light...

A world where you never knew whether to feel safe or
unsafe, so could never feel either.

'People who struggle with attachment are often drawn to the
sense of community that law enforcement provides... People
who don't feel safe around other people are often drawn towards work with animals.'

'I don't work with animals,' Cooper said quietly. 'They're
already dead, whenever I arrive. There's nothing there anymore.
Nothing.'

Months passed of these conversations, of gin in the evening,
of quiet nights.

Some of them suggested she was having a breakdown.

Her sister was getting married soon.

Cooper researched the drugs Lucy had given her before her
basement captivity – at least, those Matthew had known about.

She managed to obtain some of the same.

She tried ketamine for the first time in her life, thinking
about life, about questions, about answers.

She kept trying to start drawing again, or watching films, or
any number of her old hobbies, but each time she moved her
body, her hands, her eyes, she couldn't lose herself in anything.

She couldn't do any of it, whatever she thought she wanted.

After the tranquilliser, Cooper had a better night's sleep than
she'd had in a long time. Lucy was right. Lucy was an angel
who'd visited her life and had left her better off.

The police had tried contacting her – from Lethwick. Emails
and phone calls asking her to call them back.

When she ignored them, nothing happened, which struck
her as strange.

It didn't seem like she was a witness anymore.

Which was even stranger, considering she'd found the body of Quentin Medina.

Were they not investigating that, either?

Something was wrong with those police officers, and she found herself smiling.

It did not matter anymore. Lethwick drifted away.

All the pain left her for a while.

The police got through. A different force ... Professional Standards. They were talking to people about their dealings with Lethwick's officers – they wanted to speak to Cooper, to interview her ... Someone had made a complaint.

She avoided fixing a date, a time.

What did it matter anymore?

The figure in her dreams ... the man without a face, the dark figure ... he no longer stood over her, most nights. But some nights he even crept into the sheets next to her paralysed body, and sat facing her, watching her immobilised head, waiting for her to wake up so he could fade from existence, so his unreality could cease.

It took hours sometimes.

Sometimes when it spoke, it was like narration, like someone describing the events of her life in the third person, judging her, parsing her very being through a collection of a hundred thousand words.

One day an invitation came through Cooper's door.

The envelope was blue. A faded barcode, hard to make out ...

The message within: an embossed invitation for a photography exhibition in London, to be held in the memory of Sophia Bertilak.

It was called A TRIAL FOR PIGS.

73

Some photographs were being exhibited in a small gallery in Whitechapel.

The streets outside were full of men and women who had come to see the exhibition, the trial.

Streetlights shimmered gold like eyeballs in the rain, the reflections on the tarmac pools of sleep and dust. A lot of the shops around here had been shut a long time ago.

This small Whitechapel gallery had been built near the site of multiple murders over the years. A Jack the Ripper case. Police killing suffragettes, riding them down on their horses, force-feeding them in dark cells. The Blitz. Gangland executions. The running down of people from far away. An IRA bombing. A car that drove into a crowd of protesters. A police officer who beat a boy to death.

Everywhere you can ever go, someone will die. Someone is failed. Someone has been lied to. Someone died where you sit.

Every piece of art that is ever consumed, is consumed in this.

Dr Cooper Allen, former veterinary student, former veterinarian, former forensics expert, former daughter, formerly sober, approached a world of glass, of an exhibit that showed the entirety of an old woman's death, of the grief of those she left behind, of the strange days that followed.

A TRIAL FOR PIGS, it read.

The photographs on display inside this building showed the suffering of people familiar to Cooper, though that familiarity already felt like a dream, like the memory of some old film or TV series. The room smelled of red wine and champagne in this context, a perfumed, almost acetonic scent. Spotlights shone into the darkness from railings overhead. Below the feet of the visitors lay a zigzag carpet.

A few of the pictures were of animals.

Cooper drifted through the crowds, taking a glass of Prosecco from a waiter.

She looked, and she drank, reading captions as she went.

74

The exhibition opened with a video of pigs. Sophie's pigs, Alfie and Henry, were just babies in the film, barely a few weeks old. Sophie sat with them in the mud, the old apple tree looming behind them all as the little animals ran and played and tried to nuzzle their adoptive mother, climbing around the human's lap, kissing her, causing the old photographer to cringe and scrunch her face and laugh. It was so unlike anything Cooper had seen of the woman – a playful, easy-going lightness – and a smile that seemed like everything you'd ever want out of a friend.

A receipt lay within glass nearby, scrawled with the details of the pig's sale as if it were some momentous historical event – their identification, their registration documents with the authorities. A number of photographs were displayed around, showing the two living beings who cared for Sophie the most in their first and only year of life. Sophie's final year.

The next room, accessible through a dark hallway full of audio, of pig grunts, their shuffling, showed the death of Alfie and Henry.

It showed videos Sophie had recorded hours before her own death, the silent paddock at night. It jumped to images of the house, the trees, of blood, of police tape. It showed the corpses of the pigs, ripped apart in the aftermath of their post-mortem.

Cooper stared at it, not quite knowing if what she was seeing was real. Not knowing how the exhibitors could possibly have access to such images, whether it was legal, whether it was allowed. She felt tempted to ask someone, anyone, what they saw on these walls.

She shouldn't have come.

She shouldn't be here.

She went through to the next area.

Photographs taken with permission from the 1969 exhibition entitled 'FAMILY'.

Sophie Bertilak with the soldiers she'd been embedded with in Vietnam on their day-to-day activities, followed by the aftermath of their attacks.

New photographs, too, not included in the first collection.

Every death the unit had lied about. Sophie's notes plastered the walls. A dreamy confession of having shot a dog after it had consumed the corpse of an enemy soldier. A confession of having stood by as horrors occurred all around her, just wanting to look at this world, not change it. A confession of infidelities, of running from her kids after Alfie's death, of running from Thomas who she loved so much, who she still loved.

Of her affair with a man named Kelly, son of another Kelly ...

Cooper stared, then blinked.

She wondered if he knew this was here. If the police force had suspended him yet. If the case would be passed to other hands.

If Kelly had had something to do with Sophie's death.

Perhaps that was why Professional Standards were now involved, after all.

Cooper read more of the displays.

There were notes, gifts to Sophie from Mrs Earlsham, beautiful pictures of them both together.

Notes that read like love letters.

Promises to never give up looking for Earlsham's daughter, Stephanie.

Promises that the mystery would be solved.

That Sophie would bring the girl back.

So the exhibition went on. Who made this place? Who was responsible for curating the displays, their choices, their claims?

There were photographs of other bodies, too – how could this be legal? How could this be allowed?

There were images of other confessions, other sins...

The body Cooper had found by the lake – the torso of Quentin Medina, No cause of death yet released.

The human Alfie's seven-year-old body on the concrete all those decades ago, blood dribbling from his head like a thought bubble.

A woman, running through the woods...

The hair was short and dark and the hoodie looked like Cooper's, but it couldn't be her, could it?

The bodies of donations, decaying at a corpse farm Sophie had visited...

And...

Them.

It's them.

A person, a ghost from another case.

A person who had killed horses.

A person Cooper had killed.

Cooper rushed through the rest of the exhibition in a haze, searching for the face of someone, anyone responsible for this. She saw Sophie and Thomas fall in love in a dozen photos. She saw Matthew Bertilak's fall from grace retold in a wall of tweets projected around the room, Lucy Bertilak's hospital stays and drug issues, evidence of her lies, her claims to be a chef and a thousand other things, their dating profiles, the messages they'd sent others in the aftermath of their mother's death, how they'd eaten with Cooper in their house, images of her smiling in their midst, befriending them, watching them, even that day Cooper had seen Lucy in the woods, exploring with her yellow dress … There was a corresponding image of Cooper watching above, spying on the woman …

There were photos of Cooper's life and career, towards the end.

Hit and runs, dogs ripped from other animals, dogs who'd eaten parts of their owners and children, animals who had bleeding eyes, who were starving, who'd died of cold or heat or electricity or drowning or guns or poison or snares or being in the wrong place with the wrong soul, 'sudden deaths' of kittens who had turned out to be murdered by some boyfriend, abandonment in bags in rivers, cracked ribs, stabbings claimed in self-defence, farms for puppies and cats to be bred across the world, sexual abuse, people who took their horse and animals and were killed by them or killed them, who did not care or cared too much or cared in the wrong way, committing horrors, engaging in these acts of malice that were then passed on to Cooper, passed on to a young woman who'd had to see the aftermath, who'd had to 'solve them', whatever solving meant, whatever justice meant when convictions and bans were measured in days and months for crimes that had obliterated creatures from this world, and Cooper had consumed them all, hadn't she, all this evil, day after day, these cases that stared at her now from these walls, suspended in tiny Polaroid prints like the web of some great conspiracy, and − and—

They weren't enough, were they?

Not after that first body. Not after the man in the chair. His photo looked at her from the next display.

A dead man sitting in a room, his hands tied behind his back, his right eye missing, a photo of the cat whose hairs were found on the man's leg, who provided the key to the person who did the tying, who had taken that eye, who had ripped a human life from the world.

After that...

She'd never seen anything like it. She'd never felt that feeling...

All the true crime she'd ever watched and read. The scab that had been there since her first lonely weeks at university, pulled at last...

It had been in search of this, hadn't it?

Crime stories... tales that gave life and death answers they could never have if those lives had been normal, if those deaths had been mundane. Mysteries gave her existence solutions.

In that way, they were the closest thing Cooper had ever found to a god, to a religion, to something greater than herself.

Standing, seeing that first dead man, tied to the chair...

It had been a turning point for Cooper.

She had already begun her break-up at the time, her first, her last great relationship.

She had already begun to abandon a man she loved, and those cats of hers along with him...

Exchanging one set of cat hairs for another.

After what she'd seen in that chair, how could she turn back?

How could she be anything else, ever again, but this?

Cooper approached the end.

A video projector stood, flickering in the dark.

It showed someone breaking into Cooper's hotel room a few years before. It showed someone watching her as she'd slept.

She'd seen this tape before.

She'd forgotten.

How had she forgotten a thing like this?

How had she forgotten, waking every night, haunted by nightmares, by figures who were not there?

How had she not thought of this?

All of these strangers watched her all around, compounding the violation of all those years, all those moments.

So you consume.

So the TRIAL FOR PIGS ended in five photographs.

Sophie Bertilak.

Quentin Medina, the grandfather of her children.

Stephanie Earlsham, lost.

A child staring up from a pipe beneath the world. Unknown.

And a police officer, thin, gaunt. A Detective Barker, long since deceased.

It was the question the wall didn't ask. The lack of captions, beyond the names or absence of names...

What was the connection, after all these years, all these months?

Was the collapse and death of an old, troubled woman connected to a chance encounter over half a century beforehand?

If God was connection, if God was a crime, giving the universe sequence and answers and plot...

What was this world, if there was no grand explanation?

What had Cooper done with her life if she ended up like Sophie, unable to solve this first mystery, unable to let go, unable to find peace or justice or understanding?

Cooper stared at the photograph of Barker.

What had he known?

What had Quentin?

What had Sophie?

Why had so many bodies littered that distant, gentle place when the missing themselves had never come to light?

Who had made this exhibition? Who had invited Cooper, after all this?

Who had featured her, wall after wall, with no fear of challenge or repercussion?

Who knew Cooper so well that they'd known she would do what no one else would do – that she would do what no one else would suspect of her, the unthinkable, the unforgivable?

Who knew Cooper so well that in the face of the theft of her life, the display of so many private and personal images, of being stalked, of being documented...

That Cooper would do nothing?

It didn't matter.

It was just another mystery to be solved.

Cooper looked up, tears in her eyes, and saw she was being watched even now.

She looked across the room, and saw Lucy Bertilak sitting on the step of an open fire exit, smoking in the rain.

With that smile, in that light, she looked just like her mother.

75

Her voice called out to Cooper in the night.

'You came. I didn't know if you would. I didn't know if you'd be invited...'

Lucy sat beneath the FIRE EXIT sign, a grey hoodie emerging from beneath her black leather jacket and closing round her face. She held a cigarette and a lighter in her hand, competing with the wind.

She looked like she had when Cooper had first met her.

She'd dressed as she'd dressed the night she'd learned of her mother's death.

'What do you think of it all?' Lucy asked, her voice rich, cool.

'You took my life,' Cooper said quietly, restrained. 'You took my life and you used it for... for...' She struggled to find the word, but Lucy had it ready.

'For art,' she said. 'And it wasn't me who took it. It wasn't me who took any of this.'

'Your brother, then,' Cooper went on, almost shaking.

'You've been crying. Haven't you?'

'Where is he? Where is—'

'It wasn't us,' Lucy said. 'Unless my brother was running around setting up cameras, unless he kept secrets from me... it wasn't us.'

'You drugged me.'

Lucy's hair had once been dyed blue, the colour of eyes, of imagined lakes and rivers. Now it had begun to fade, damaged, green in the face of all those washes, all that time. Things weren't the same, after all.

'I tried to help you,' Lucy said.

'I didn't ask you to. I didn't ask—' Cooper began, but Lucy shook her head.

'You did. The first time you met me, you said you'd do anything to get rid of your pain. You were scaring me. And besides... the pills were already in the house, weren't they.'

'What?'

'Maybe mum needed help going to sleep. Maybe it was done to her...'

Cooper immediately resolved these words as more lies. The police would have found these *pills* if they'd been in the house at the time after the old woman's death. Cooper would have detected some trace of narcotics in the pigs, had Sophie indeed been drugged.

It was all just a lie.

All just a game.

Cooper hated Lucy in that moment. Hated her for the lies after lies, even after there was no point...

'If this exhibition isn't your work, then whose?'

The blue-haired woman let out a puff of smoke, pursing her lips as if trying to create some kind of ring in the air... and she succeeded, smiling with such genuine warmth that in that moment, in that moment alone, Cooper smiled too, briefly, just a flicker.

'I can teach you how to do it,' Lucy said.

Cooper didn't say anything, and Lucy smiled.

'This happened to my family before I was born,' Lucy went on, looking back at the exhibits. 'One of us died, and the whole world got to watch. Murders are like that, aren't they? No one cares if they can't watch... My mother always said it helped people be remembered, if they were turned into stories. So I think at least some parts of us will be remembered, I suppose?'

Cooper blinked. 'Your rehab records are part of this,' she said. 'Your career history, your – your issues, they're … How can you be OK? How is this OK?'

'It's nothing but the truth, isn't it?' Lucy shrugged.

'They have no right to it – they don't have any right to know what – what—'

'I didn't know you were there,' Lucy went on. 'That day I walked through the woods again. But, you know, it … it felt different when I did, Coop. I felt safer than I'd ever felt there, and I guess … I guess it's because someone was watching out for me. So … thank you. Thank you for doing that. Thank you for helping me.'

Lucy's voice grew softer as she went on, harder to hear in all these crowds.

'Where's Matthew?' Cooper asked.

Lucy shrugged, smiling faintly. 'He hasn't talked to me in weeks. He hasn't talked to anyone, as far as I know.'

'Why did he grab you at the funeral? What was there be-tween you?'

Lucy said she had no idea what Cooper meant.

'What did Matthew do to you, Lucy?'

'He didn't do anything,' the false chef, the addict, the spiked, the spiker, the daughter, the sister, the girl with the blue hair said.

She tried to make another smoke ring, the detritus of her life on display all around.

'No one did anything to me.'

'I once asked your brother to describe his perfect woman,' Cooper said. 'He described you – the way you look – the way you act. It was you.'

Lucy blinked.

Her cheeks grew red, and she looked down at her cigarette. 'I was born after my brother's death. Because of it. We just... we just care about each other. He knows we need to look after each other. That's all.'

'That's all? You drugged me – you drugged yourself – you say that's all—'

'You took our mother's tree,' Lucy interrupted, tears rising in her eyes too. 'You dug up the apple tree – you broke into our home! And why? What did you find? Why are you even here?'

'I—'

'My mother told me I was born from my brother's death. That she hadn't even wanted my father that night. That he'd just climbed on top of her... that he'd just wanted her one last time. Can you imagine what that's like, to hear a thing like that? Can you imagine what it's like, to know you're so broken, the very origin of you, the very root? Can you imagine what it's like to be expected to grieve for a woman who tells you that?'

Lucy dropped her cigarette out the door and stubbed it with her foot.

'Matthew... he never liked you,' Lucy said, her eyes red, wandering. 'You know that, don't you? He never liked you. He never liked any of you.'

Cooper staggered away, looking through the guests' faces for someone she might recognise, some person who might explain the horror of these stolen lives...

But there was nothing.

There was no one.

Cooper finished the evening next to the display of Quentin Medina.

She looked up at the man who'd paid for all those works,

who'd enabled Sophie's life and death with his money, his wishes, even his progeny...

She looked up at the final photo, and saw the apple tree in his garden.

She saw the apple tree, so much like Sophie's own...

Nearby, on the wall, a famous quote of the dead photographer, speaking in an interview a number of years ago – on the rationale for her career, for the sharing of pain, for the spread of tragic stories.

It's evidence of all we've done as a species. What we're capable of. What we can become, captured in light.

It's a testament. It's a map...

Cooper saw the apple tree.

RUN, the voice told her in her head, though no one watched her, no one stood near her. RUN, it said, and Cooper left, eyes drying... not to home, not to sleep, but to the station.

Cooper ran, heading back towards her old car...

Cooper ran, heading to the home of the late Quentin Medina... heading towards the tree...

Following that map.

And it grew both day and night,
Till it bore an apple bright;
And my foe beheld it shine,
And he knew that it was mine,

And into my garden stole
When the night had veiled the pole:
In the morning glad I see
My foe outstretched beneath the tree.

A Poison Tree
William Blake (1794)

PART 10:

SAFE

SOPHIE BERTILAK
THE RECENT PAST

A month before the death
of Sophia Bertilak

'It was when I was first on television, I think. Decades ago ...
When I first saw myself there ... a video clip of me walking
past trees, holding my photographs. In that clip I looked at the
camera through the leaves, because that's what they told me
to do. They wanted me to look so mysterious, to look vaguely
threatening – they wanted me to look the part of someone
who would bring a story like this to the world. I was told it
would lead to more work, maybe a job. All these people around
me back then, they told me all these grand things about the
life to come, they made all these promises, they shared all these
compliments about my skills and my artistic abilities ... And you
know what happened, each time I followed up? Each time I
asked about these possibilities that kept being dangled in front
of me, however gentle, however polite, they would act like it
was somehow presumptuous, that I should dare think I could
ever lay claim to more than what I had.

'And it was so lonely, it made me think I had done something
wrong to hope and get carried away when all people were
doing was picking me up, trying to hold me high ... I mean, I
was on television, wasn't I? And the people on the show, they
flattered me a bit – they said such nice things, but they ... I
mean, how can anyone know what it's like, for a million people
to see you criticised? A million people to hear you're not quite
good enough, when the world expects the very first things you

433

produce to be perfect for every consumer in every way ... when it throws you away if they're not?

'And I sat there with my mum and we had this Prosecco bottle and she kept trying to get me to drink from it, she kept trying to tell me that what I was seeing, what I'd seen, the way people had treated my career, was something I should be happy about, that I should be ecstatic about, that it was something we all wanted, wasn't it, to be seen? To be able to do what we love. For the whole wide world to know about it. And the more people saw it, the more they talked about me, the more it hurt to hear, the good and the bad alike, it didn't matter ... And if I'd ever dreamed of doing this job, if this had ever been something I'd hoped for, it became a trap, didn't it? I had to find and spread more pain, now. I couldn't take pictures of anything else because they'd decided, all these people – they'd decided it was what I was good for.

'Based on the coincidence of the first thing I'd ever done, on the coincidence of an accident. They'd decided that pain was all I'd ever spread, all I'd ever make works of. And the more I did, the more money they gave me, the less they spoke to me. The more I did, the more alone I felt. That first year was one of the worst of my life.'

They sat in the field outside Quentin Medina's home. They sat outside a building Sophie had never been allowed to, not when she'd been a teenager, not even now that she was an old woman, and the man before her was even older.

Quentin Medina, grandfather to her children, a man she sometimes called her father-in-law, though she'd never married his son, though she hadn't even seen Thomas in over a year.

'But how could I say how I felt?' Sophie shook her head. 'That my worst problem in my world was that I'd managed to get the career of my dreams? That people knew who I was.

How could I tell people that, in the face of all the sadness I saw? What right did I have to feel so lost?'

They sat in chairs beneath a cloth parasol, which itself gently shook in the spring wind. The sky was grey-blue. It would be over soon.

The day was almost at an end.

Quentin – he had a surprise for his guest.

He did not talk about Sophie's life. He did not talk about her problems. He did not acknowledge much of what she'd said at all.

He smiled, clearly excited.

He had a surprise.

'The house... I'm ready,' he said, almost trembling, though his voice was as rich, as resonant as it had ever been.

That night. Dinner time.

'I sent letters,' the old man said, cutting into his steak. 'Back during the war. To my mother and my sister. Family meant more back then, I think.'

The room was one of the loveliest rooms Sophie had ever entered.

The table stretched on, foot upon foot, like something out of a fairy tale. On the wall were artworks, photographs by a dozen of the greatest luminaries of the twentieth century, each mounted upon the darkest rosewood.

The lights that shone were all from fires, pale, flickering in the old chamber.

What had this great house been like, before Quentin had cleaned his clutter?

What had it been like, all these long years?

He went on.

'The government was worried about food shortages. They suggested we kill any pets we had. I had to do it for my family, you see. Can you imagine what that was like? I think it taught me the value of things. The true value, not just the financial.'

He paused.

'What do you think?'

She asked, 'Of what?'

'This. Where the love of your life grew up.'

'It's easy to forget.'

Quentin laughed, and nodded. 'Hard to imagine, isn't it, the way we both act? That this is where we came to be.'

They spent a few more hours awake, drinking together, talking about the past – or, perhaps, more accurately, pasts.

They remembered so much so differently.

'Why did you invest in me?' Sophie asked, a little after

436

midnight. She'd never asked this before. The enormity of the question stuck in her throat, but — but she still had to. In that moment, nothing else seemed important. 'I understand why you wanted the prints for the pipe photo, but—'

'But what?' he asked, his voice gentle, tired.

'That was all just a coincidence. You knew that.'

The old man shook his head, and said he didn't believe in coincidences.

Not if there was such a thing as God, or even just plain cause and effect.

Everything that happened, happened because of something else.

And that picture had led him to her, and she had led him to his son's greatest happiness, and his grandchildren, and after everything, a life worth living.

She asked him to be serious.

Why had he invested so much in her career, when she'd only been a teenager?

'What I paid you, I could have paid a thousand times over,' he said. 'It was an investment, like any other. And if it didn't succeed, it wouldn't have broken me. You should see all the artists who failed...'

They talked for a time longer.

When it was late, Quentin led her through the grand hall-ways, past all those carpets, and if it were not for the studies, and the odd room she saw full of boxes and papers, she'd never have believed the house to be uninhabitable.

She'd never have believed his reasons for keeping her out, as lovely as the place clearly was.

He had her photos up, too.

Those first two had precedence above all, joined by a third others rarely bothered with.

Not just Stephanie Earlsham, sitting by a lake, one shoe off as a man stood by, watching...

Not just a child, staring up from a pipe beneath the world, terrified...

But orbs of mistletoe, hanging in the trees.

The only thing Sophie had even thought of as a mystery at the time.

The only thing at which she'd felt a sense of wonder.

She'd told Quentin as much in their earliest conversations. That he'd held the mistletoe photo in the same esteem as the others; it was silly, but it meant a lot.

She found her guest bedroom.

Quentin said goodnight, kissing her on the cheek. He went off to his own room, somewhere far above.

She tried to go to sleep.

3 a.m.

Sophie Bertilak woke up on the edge of her bed, looking up, sitting up. She found herself staring at the mantelpiece opposite her door.

She could not remember sitting up. Consciousness just returned to her in its slow way, until she grew aware of what she was doing: staring at the turning, ticking clock upon the wood. It was 3 a.m. exactly.

She turned her head.

Her door was open. Just a little bit, but it was open.

She got up and threw on a blouse.

She went out towards her doorway, and her legs felt lighter than they had in years, not clicking, not cracking, the movement not causing any of the small pains she'd become accustomed to.

There were no lights on, though some fell through uncurtained windows from the dark moon.

She went out on that old carpet, her bare feet crossing against its worn cloth.

She looked out and saw the trees in the distance, the apple tree closer.

She heard a noise, somewhere behind her.

Sophie turned and saw her door creak a little. She passed back in front of the wood and tested it with a little push. After a few moments, it creaked backwards again.

It must not have been shut properly, before.

It had fallen open, merely at the request of gravity, just like it had fallen open now.

A brief, preposterous idea had entered her mind: that someone had come into her room.

But she would have known, wouldn't she?

She looked back at her bed and sighed. She was too awake,

now. She knew it would take her a while to rest again. And she'd had enough sleepless nights in her life to know that trying right now would be pointless, counter-productive, even. She'd need to wake up fully then try again.

Sophie took her phone and switched on its torch.

She made her way along the long hallways, looking for some lounge, some room in which to sit up, taking care not to disturb her host.

She had no idea which room Quentin slept in, so she could not risk opening any.

She just looked in those doors that were already open.

Sophie had lived in Lethwick for approximately twenty-one years of her life; the first seventeen as a child, the rest in scattered, staggered bursts ever since ... But it was as if all that time had counted for nothing, now she was back. That small house in the valley ... it was a stranger's home, really; her mother's home, the greatest stranger of them all. They'd never reconciled after Alfie's death. Her mother had tried talking to her. Her mother had tried all these ways of getting her attention – she'd tried claiming it was Sophie's duty, that she needed her help, that she had all kinds of illnesses.

Her mother had tried talking about some stalker, some cold caller, returning after all these years, asking for Sophie on the phone line.

Her mother had died alone.

They'd found her, cold, her heating bills unpaid, cut off in the depths of winter.

Now, Sophie lived there instead, the heating on full blast.

She heard her mother's voice sometimes.

That's what all inner voices were in the end. Parents, internalised, whatever they had said enough times ringing throughout brains forever.

If you're called lazy enough, you'll forever call yourself lazy.

If you're called stupid, you'll demean your own intelligence to the end of your life.

What voices did her own children have, Sophie wondered?

What part of her would live on in their minds?

Sophie looked from room to room in Quentin's grand home, thinking in the dark. Something about the light made her think the sun was rising, but it wasn't – the moonlight just seemed a little brighter, a fact Sophie couldn't understand, and therefore decided must not be true.

The moon did not rise.

Her phone's torch caught things in its light. Many of the rooms with open doors were piled with crates, sheets, old relics of Quentin's life he had clearly quarantined in certain rooms to save the rest of the house from the oblivion of mess. Judging by the skips outside his home, he'd already managed to jettison an impressive amount.

She began to go inside these rooms. She began to lift those dust sheets; she began to look through the old boxes.

She found all sorts of things.

Plastic boxes that could have been memories, had their lids not been left off; had the papers and journals within not weathered and yellowed over the long years.

There were toys.

There were receipts.

There were so many things: children's clothes, shoes, reports from Thomas's childhood, from Quentin's own.

Thomas was said to talk too much by his teachers.

Thomas was said to need to step back, to let others take the stage.

Thomas ...

You should call him.

You should mend things. Life is too short ...

The old voices whispered in her mind again.

She looked through the largest and deepest of the rooms – a surprising room, for she'd almost walked past it, not noticing the stairs that went down, not noticing the second door within a smaller room.

She opened this one. It was shut, granted, but it was not like the others. It was an extension of the bizarre, grand archive of the man's life.

She wondered if she'd find anything else of Thomas within.

There was more clothing within this deeper room. It was so large and dark, her torch light hardly reached the other end.

It was cold in here.

The clothing belonged to a very young child. Perhaps around three, maybe four years old.

There were toys, too, just like before.

Sophie kept looking at them, touching them gently with her hand.

Touching these fragments of the man she'd loved, and loved still.

There was a safe on the opposite wall. The room was in a process of grand reorganisation, it was clear; judging by the empty bottles of water and half-stagnant cups of coffee, Quentin had been in here recently.

The safe was open, not ajar, just unlocked. Sophie knew because she tested it with her hand, and was surprised to find how the metal swung towards her.

She looked around, wondering if this was OK.

Wondering if she'd get in trouble.

But what was she really doing, other than what she'd done her whole life?

She looked at things.

That was her very purpose. It was what Quentin had backed her to do throughout her career... 'looking at things' – it was what Sophie would be remembered for, if nothing else.

She pulled the safe door and looked inside.

There was a shoebox. A very old shoebox.

She picked it up, taking it from within the safe as if it were a casket.

On the top of the shoebox were written two words: FOR MATTHEW.

For her son?

A gift, perhaps?

Had he started portioning out his estate already? Sophie wanted to see – so she opened it.

She expected to find photographs within, money, ornaments, some heirloom worth protecting enough that you'd seal it away when so much else was just left to the air.

She expected to find anything but shoes.

In the box, there was a pair of them.

Brown, worn with age and use, the smell of old leather, dust... and something almost meat-like, though faint...

These shoes – she knew how large they were. She knew the size without even searching for a label, without a single point of reference to compare it to.

She knew, and her heart ran warm, her breath caught in her throat.

These brown shoes, even in the dark she could see.

They were matted red.

These soles... they had been covered in blood, long ago.

Size 12, she knew.

Sophie Bertilak held the shoes of the man who had taken

Stephanie Earlsham ... who had broken into Stephanie's house ... who had no doubt buried a child within the woods ...

She held those shoes, and she turned, looking suddenly all about her, looking at all those boxes, all those children's toys, all that clothing ...

Sophie took the shoes with her, hurrying through the corridors of that old, ancient house ... She found her room somehow, and she packed everything she could pack, leaving whatever did not fit around the shoebox.

That shoebox ... FOR MATTHEW ...

She shivered, right down to her very soul.

They'd not known what to name their son. Unique of all their children, they hadn't even fixed on one a few days before the birth, even though they'd known the gender, even though they'd known he was coming.

And it had been Quentin who'd made the suggestion. MATTHEW. Biblical. Gentle. Noble.

It had been Quentin who'd named their son.

This box in his home, this thing of shoes and blood ...

What did it mean?

She left the house with the box and without a goodbye, and as she walked across the fields, as the night air bit against her skin, the lights turned on within.

By the time she reached the road, they were dark once more.

...you and I are old;
Old age hath yet his honour and his toil;
Death closes all: but something ere the end,
Some work of noble note, may yet be done,
Not unbecoming men that strove with Gods.
The lights begin to twinkle from the rocks:
The long day wanes: the slow moon climbs: the deep
Moans round with many voices. Come, my friends,
'Tis not too late to seek a newer world.

Ulysses
Alfred, Lord Tennyson (1833)

PART II:

THE PIPE

DR COOPER ALLEN
THE PRESENT DAY

76

Cooper was a mile away from the home of Quentin Medina when she noticed the moon in the sky. It was one of those nights, bright and full of sun, where the moon somehow found its place in all that light.

She drove her car. Hers, not a hire vehicle, not someone else's car – her own mustard-yellow piece of shit, stuttering, in desperate need of repairs or scrapping. The thought of giving it up made Cooper want to cry.

The vehicle didn't break down. Somehow it lasted the whole way there, the whole way back.

She would never drive it again. She would never sell it.

Instead it would lie abandoned, a monument to the life of its owner.

A memory of all Cooper Allen had once been, before it was towed away and crushed, and melted in some anonymous dark.

But not yet.

For now, it was still hers.

She still had something, a tie to who she'd once been.

She drove to the home of Quentin Medina, thinking about the exhibition. Thinking about all the images she'd seen of her own life, thrown back at her. Wondering who would do this, and why.

The exhibitor had been documenting Cooper from the beginning, along with Sophie's children, along with many of the others who orbited the aftermath of the woman's death …

But Cooper wondered, even so.

She wondered why there were so few images of Kelly, given the revelation of the affair. For that matter, considering the presence of Sophie's romantic partners, Thomas was remarkably absent from the exhibition as a whole.

A man she'd never met, when she'd met so many others in Sophie's life.

The main connection between the two victims of the past months.

The father of Sophie's children.

Cooper wondered if she would meet him, before all was said and done.

She drove on, and pulled into the gates of Quentin's home.

She pulled up, finding the padlock on the gates already snapped off, already cut.

77

Cooper did not enter the building. She stopped herself.

It was not because of the ribbons of half-broken police tape, or the smashed windows, or the investigation that had clearly occurred in this place.

It was not any of that.

It was the stag that watched her from across the useless, long overgrown lawn of grass.

Its antlers glistened, just like the antlers of the animal that had eaten Quentin's flesh.

It watched her, caught on the edge of running.

Cooper walked around the old building until she found the apple tree. She had bought a shovel. An axe, too.

She'd once been stronger than she was now.

She'd once had to lift dogs and sheep, she'd once had to go out to farms and grapple with cows and horses and even bulls.

She'd once had muscles.

The years had made her weaker.

She dug into the ground near the tree, mercifully soft from the rain of the past day.

She dug all around, not breaking the tree's main trunk, but seeking beneath it, hacking roots apart only when she had to.

She spent hours doing this; she went on until her fingers felt mottled and bruised, she went until she could stand no more.

She went to her car and slept, locking the door at her side.

If anyone watched her, if anyone kept taking photos of her ... she did not know.

She went to sleep.

She woke up in the morning to find the sun.

It was only 4 a.m., and the sun blazed at her with such heat she felt no more need to rest, though she'd only lain down for a couple of hours.

She went out to the tree, and the stag that had been watching her was now gone. She dug for another hour until she hit metal.

It took another hour to excavate that box.

Hands bleeding, shaking, shivering in the now grey-smogged sky, she almost bent down to open it.

Almost.

She went back to her car, found disinfectant, and almost screamed as it hit her dirty, broken skin.

She found latex gloves in her boot and put them on, eyeing the rest of her tools, her supplies from cases past. It didn't matter if she still worked for the police or not. It had never mattered, not really.

She opened the box, a foot and a half wide.

She opened it, its texture rough and rusted.

She opened it.

Within, lay a few small bones, and dust, and a child's toy. A little boy's toy.

And beneath it all, a letter ...

Two weeks before the death
of Sophia Bertilak

Sophie worked out in the fields, stringing strands of hair around her sculpture, fixing its wire mesh, posing it in each and every position her new series required.

She had not taken her medication for a while.

The problem... more than just the lack of those pills, but the reason for them, the hole in her life... it had predated her visit to Quentin Medina's home. She knew that. She had to be honest about it. She hadn't been doing well. Not for a long time.

Since her mother's death, since the funeral, at least...

She hadn't mended things.

Sophie had never forgiven the woman – not just for being in charge of Alfie the day he'd died, but for everything, for everything she'd done or not done, everything that had become clear those strange days.

Her mother had not just ruined her life.

She had been responsible for bringing it into being.

Sophie missed her, deeply, terribly. She hated her in equal measure.

She'd been struggling. She remembered how they'd cut birthday cakes, how they'd mock-screamed at the cake's imagined pain.

She'd been struggling.

The pigs had suffered for it, of course. Whoever she cared for always suffered for whatever whim of career or mood struck her.

A graph could be formed showing the exact correlation between the psychic damage Sophie had committed upon her children and the ebb and flow of her hobby.

That's what it had been, hadn't it?

The camera had just been a birthday present. She'd just wanted to take photographs of trees on her birthday.

Tears fell down her face as she finished the sculpture, then went back and back, photographing it again and again ... trying to get it looking right ...

She forgot to feed the pigs, sometimes, then would overfeed them when she remembered ...

Sometimes, she didn't feel like herself, but which self was that, exactly?

Which of the thousand people she'd been had she lost, exactly?

Quentin hadn't phoned her after her abrupt departure from his home.

He hadn't written, he hadn't messaged her, he hadn't tried to contact her in any way.

And the longer it went without some explanation, the longer it went without him setting her straight, without context for what she'd found, for what he must know she'd found ...

The more Sophie lost herself.

The more everything in her life seemed to find itself within that room, every memory, lost in a flood of boxes, of safes, of shoeboxes ...

She'd fallen in love with Quentin's son, once upon a time.

Her children had been Quentin's grandchildren.

Her career, her prints, had been funded by him, guided by him ...

And everything ... all those parts of her life that had remained unsolved, that cried out for connection, began to find it.

The voice that had called her mother...

The man in the woods that day ... the man who'd taken that poor girl...

The man who'd buried a child in the earth...

The man she'd caught, all those years ago, and hadn't known the truth of it...

That *he'd* caught *her.* That he'd made her entire life his own, down to her very blood.

What else had he done?

What else would he do?

Had it been Quentin?

Her whole life, caught just like that girl ... just like the child in the pipe...

She knew, suddenly, with utmost certainty.

She knew the name of that child.

Matthew.

He'd named her child after his prey, hadn't he?

How far did this go? Was she safe now? Were her children?

Had they ever been safe?

And Alfie – her boy – out in the road that day, waiting for her when she'd come home, already dead, his blood already forming clouds...

They'd never found the driver...

She sat for a long time in the dark, staring into space.

Eventually, she took out her phone and invited this man – this person she called her 'father-in-law', though she'd never married – and she invited him to dinner at her house. As if nothing had happened.

He sent a message back, accepting. As if nothing had happened.

And then she waited in her room, sleeping, waking, sleeping, waiting for the week to pass, her pigs grunting, shifting, crying in the day and in the night...

78

Cooper placed the box down upon the earth and knelt down, gently removing the letter from beneath the bones.

She held it up in her gloved hands, and she read.

It did not take her long. There were only a few words upon it, scrawled in faded ink.

> YOU ASKED US TO TELL YOU WHAT HE SAID.
> HE SAID HE WAS SORRY. HE SAID HE DIDN'T MEAN
> IT. HE SAID IT WAS ALL JUST AN ACCIDENT.
> HE SAID WHAT ANYONE WOULD SAY.
> WE MADE HIM FEEL IT. DON'T WORRY.
> IT'S DONE. HERE'S PROOF.
> BURN IT WHEN YOU'RE DONE.

Cooper looked around, and still, no one seemed to watch her.

She was alone, but for bones, but for an old house, but for police tape all around.

She picked up her phone and – about to call a different number – hesitated as she saw that VOICEMAIL notification once more.

We'd like to talk with you – please call us back when you can, our number is—

Cooper phoned that number. After checking it, of course.

She took the box and went to her car, locked the door, and went to sleep once more, the world fading from sight.

It was done.

She knew it, deep in her heart.

It was over at last.

YOU'RE GOING
TO DIE ONE DAY

Lethwick, 1964

'No one ever thinks about it, but you will. You'll die, and as you do, you'll look back at how you treated me – the things you said to me – and you'll regret them. Before you go, you'll miss me. You'll miss everyone. And you'll be so, so sorry. You will. I read it in a book.'

That's what Sophie's mother had said to her, the morning of her seventeenth birthday.

Lethwick

1965

'I know him,' Sophie's mother said. 'Where do I know him from?'

But she wasn't talking about the busker.

Sophie followed her mother's gaze, and saw a man leaning against the edge of a bridge.

It was one of the detectives who had walked her through the woods, all those months ago.

Detective Barker.

He wasn't wearing his suit, he wasn't wearing a uniform.

He seemed sad, the way he looked out at the water.

Lethwick

1965

'Please – I won't tell a soul,' Barker spat, and Kelly hit him again, punching his old partner in his ribs, blood welling from Barker's mouth, but the man was still conscious in the twilight. 'I won't tell anyone what you did. I told you that. I told all of you.'

None of his old friends laughed. They just looked at him, predators at prey.

'What can I say?' he asked, and it was genuine, this plea.

It had to be true.

There had to be words that, if spoken at this moment, might stop them from causing further pain.

'Explain to me,' he begged. 'Explain to me why you think you can't trust me – explain to me who you think I blabbed to—'

And they hit him again, and again.

They had drunk before it. They drank now, too, sometimes, as they waited in that old place.

And then it was done.

They made it look like a drowning. They posed the body so the wounds would not show.

They phoned Quentin, and he sorted the rest.

They kept their secret – all of them who remained, they never spoke about it.

They knew what would happen if they spoke.

It was done.

Quentin's Home

1965

Quentin buried his little boy that day, with the same letter that had been sent with what bones could be found.

He didn't know if he'd ever meet someone who understood what it was like to lose a child, to grieve in secret.

He didn't meet that many people, truth be told.

He cried that night, long after the box's burial. A few shoe-boxes in volume, buried in a pit in the garden.

It was done. It was over at last.

Lethwick

A few months ago

There were two pigs. Their skin was sunburned, pink-white beige. Their paddock was small, located right outside the woman's house, which was itself black and white, built of outlandish angles and shifting extensions. In the windows sat dusty pictures of family members, not seen for years now.

There was a great tree in the paddock's centre, an apple tree.

The pigs screamed, trampling against each other, their cries undercut, punctuated by a chorus of grunts.

There were tufts of human hair everywhere. There was blood, not red in that dark, not any colour at all.

The final words that human would ever say in this place were whispered in the darkness: 'flowers, passing'.

The seed had sprouted.

Seventy years vanished within stomachs. Fingers danced within acid.

The woman's mind was divided across her companions as they ate pieces of skin, of organs, of bone. That was all that became of her life, of all those years, of her death.

It was done. It was over at last.

Everything – it was going to be OK.

It was going to be A-OK.

Most arrive at the same awful, unsalubrious truth we arrived at; that same truth Cooper Allen helped expose; the same truth that coincided with her exit from time and history.

We read these cases, we try to solve them, we watch documentary after documentary because those figures we read about, that we enjoyed in book after book — they don't exist.

There is so much unsolved, so much broken, because crime in the real world does not work the way it does in a story, however verisimilitudinous the intent.

The police have failed us, again and again.

The police failed my mother when she was a girl.

They failed her entire life.

They failed, and Cooper revealed that.

She chased leads no one else chased.

In her final days, she found evidence implicating my grandfather Quentin Medina and several officers of Lethwick's police service in the murder of a kidnapper in the mid-1960s, and the subsequent burial of a kidnapped child.

Not just in the box she found beneath a tree on my grandfather's property, the old fingerprints and drops of blood within.

Not just the DNA testing that linked a child's bones with that of Quentin, that of my father Thomas, and my own.

No, not just that.

Professional Standards had been notified months earlier of potential corruption, in an email sent by Cooper herself, which contained photographs of a dead, drowned Detective Reginald Barker, images that — to any modern, trained eye — suggested the beginning of a cover-up. Of guilt. Of complicity. Of a man who could not have drowned. Of a man who had tried to do the right thing.

466

Did Cooper Allen — troubled, sidelined, her own mental health at breaking point in the wake of her mother's death — experience the same end?

Did someone try to silence her, too?

From *A TRIAL FOR PIGS: A POST-MORTEM TO A POST-MORTEM*
by Matthew Bertilak

Published five years after the disappearance of Cooper Allen. Published five years from *now*.

79

Now

Lapis – never 'Detective Sergeant' Lapis, never honoured with his title by his peers but for brief moments in official documentation – he was a man who knew he would not be remembered, not much past the death of those who had met him. Already he expected he vanished from people's minds within a few hours of his leaving. There had been no invitations to the pub for Lapis. Like his rank, he was forgotten.

And then, one day, he was promoted.

Never 'Detective Sergeant', he was made Acting Inspector.

'For your honesty, and your unwavering dedication to the law,' the superintendent said.

He gave them evidence of his colleague's wrongdoing, collected so meticulously – so absurdly thoroughly, containing even irrelevancies, even forms that were incorrectly filled out of laziness – that his hatred gave the impression of competency.

People noticed him, now.

He rose through the ranks through the brutality of basic competence, through the tyranny of non-objection. He swam towards power as if the world were a thing to be endured, to be passed through by sheer persistence and movement, a question of when rather than why.

Lapis had no family or friends, and he never would.

Lapis was a series of ideas, a virus of anonymous, blurring, shifting hatreds that had no real prejudice or enemy because belief was not the point, conviction was never the engine, but the fight itself, the struggle, the wish to find oneself superior to another, the logic of existential might makes right, the sword's logic, the dream of victory and winning and the renewal of all games, poured into words in sentences, pages in a never-ending book.

Lapis was a series of ideas given shifting flesh to cushion their fall.

Lapis was a police officer.

He accepted his new role. A constable received the email from Cooper Allen, a document full of photos of runes and claims of—

'She's raving about driving licences. I don't understand it, sir?'

Another officer interrupted. 'Allen? That cunt who found the old man's body?'

They deleted it as the ravings of a malcontent.

The ideas that formed Lapis's brain and body, they fell with joy, nothing if not playful, elated at their own manifestation. He was a man. He should be proud of that fact, he knew. He laughed. He had been accustomed to such laughter all his life.

Though no one knew his pride. No one saw his smile. No one saw him as more than quiet, functional, compliant.

What was power, after all, without the possibility of punishment?

Lapis went on.

When he thought of Cooper, of the woman who he had followed, whose train he had delayed with the spite of a false call...

When he thought of all he had cost her... when he thought of this woman, it was with fondness.

469

★

He celebrated his new career on Friday.

The whole force descended on a local pub – the town a little emptier, now that midsummer had long since passed, now that winter was almost here.

He sat and drank alone. He waited for officers to join him at his table. Even though they stood all around, no one gave him much more than a passing word.

He stared at the barmaid for a while, then spoke.

'I received a promotion.'

She couldn't make out what he'd said, so he repeated it more loudly, grasping his pint glass of lager as if it somehow protected him.

'That's great!' the barmaid said. Her hair was dark like Cooper's. 'What do you do?'

He explained.

She beamed, and told him the next drink was on the house.

Lapis was pleased.

He went to the toilet and found himself a cubicle. When he had finished using one of his antibacterial wipes on the plastic, when he'd made his toilet paper throne, he urinated for half a minute. He was bursting.

As he came back, he heard two officers.

'...ever have a conversation with him...'

'Trust me ... temporary...'

Laughter.

Lapis sat down nearby. They did not even notice him sitting.

But the barmaid with the dark hair, the big eyes ... she noticed. She gave him his free drink with pity.

'Don't pay them any mind,' she said.

★

The barmaid closed up the pub for the evening.

No one was left. The last police officer had departed hours before.

She set the alarms, locked the front doors, and – out back – walked through the cold night to her car.

She got in. Already the glass steamed, as if she had been breathing here for hours.

She put on the heating, blasted it at the dash. She waited for the evidence of her breath to clear.

She drove off.

Ten minutes down the long winding hills, through the old valleys, the ancient trees of gentle Lethwick, a car began to follow her.

She did not realise it at first.

She turned, and it turned. Its lights were not on. She only saw it in reflections, dark, unremarkable.

The hairs on her arms rose, and she drove a little faster, and—

Red and blue lights danced atop the car. It was a police car. It stopped when she stopped.

She waited, nervous, though she remained seated still, though she knew, she—

A man got out of the police car and moved towards her.

A man who had received a promotion that same day.

'Your licence,' said DS Lapis. 'Let me see your driving licence.'

'To solve,' the lecture had begun, years ago now.

Cooper Allen had sat down in the back. The third day of her Veterinary Forensics MSc. She had been late three times already.

'From the Latin "solvere", to loosen, to unfasten. The Middle English: to dissolve, to untie. The notion of solving crime contains not only a sense of detangling evidence, suspects, and the facts of a case, but of dissolving them, letting them loose, changing them through mere contact. There is no happy ending when it comes to solving. Both investigator and investigated are freed from all ties that bound them. They are in a sense, consumed.'

Cooper wrote notes. She worked hard. She wondered what the future would bring.

80

Before Her Disappearance.

Cooper was not asked to help with the new investigation.

She reflected on this with a faint, sad smile as she sat in the dim light of the pub, drinking her drink, just a few minutes from her flat.

Of course she was not asked.

It did not matter that she'd found the box, that she'd found proof of police corruption.

Cooper would never work for them again.

81

Cooper walked towards her home. She had a few days of food left. After that, she didn't know.

The streets of Guildford glistened in yet more rain. The further into summer they had gone, the closer to winter, the more the midsummer festival of Lethwick seemed like a distant dream; its heat, its fevers...

She passed up the cobbles, beneath banners, past homeless who pleaded for change, and whom she would have given change to if she'd had anything but a card on her.

They're going to die.

The thought came to her unbidden. The homeless would die sooner than everyone else. The probability of it was obvious.

But everyone else would die too, sooner rather than later.

We're all going to die: the cry of panic, the cause of all stories, the centre of every mystery, the most obvious, mundane statement in the world.

Everything has to end.

Cooper went up the long, winding, half-stained stairs of her apartment building.

She got to her door, and found a woman sitting outside, hair wet with rain, almost sleeping against the wall.

She saw the face of someone she knew.

She saw Alex.

And the first words Alex said when Cooper woke her up; the first words when she rose—

'Are you OK?'

Cooper did not answer.

Cooper stared down at the woman, shorter by a head. Gone was all the make-up, the bruises, everything. Just the original skin beneath. Flawless in its imperfections, its light spread of freckles, its red blush in the cold...

'I'm sorry,' Alex said. 'I'm so sorry...'

Alex looked like she wanted to say something else, but no other words were coming, and the emptiness of the term itself – the emptiness the word had always had for them, 'sorry', it hung in the air. And Alex, she just shivered in the cold. She just seemed sad, lonely.

Cooper considered her for a while, then turned her key in the lock.

She went inside, and did not close the door behind her.

82

Cooper had lived in this small studio space since shortly after breaking up with her ex-boyfriend. A long time ago, now.

She had fairy lights around the mantelpiece that she never switched on.

The fridge was almost out of food.

There were boxes, everywhere, full of all her things.

'Are you moving?' Alex asked, as if she had a right to ask anything.

Cooper did not answer.

She sat next to Alex, stiff, not really looking at her, not really looking at anything.

'I just did what I was told,' Alex said, her voice a little weak, a little nervous.

'You just did what you were told...' Cooper repeated, cold, empty.

'I didn't... I didn't want to hurt anyone...'

Cooper turned to her.

Cooper's face was blank – or it felt blank, at the very least. It felt rigid, on the edge of grinding her teeth, on the edge of falling into some void.

'I just did what I was told, like I said,' Alex said.

Cooper stared at her. Cooper began to shake, her heartbeat rising, anger filling every ligament, every tip of her being. Still she stared, and still Alex said nothing – still she had the gall to come here, to try and act like things could be forgiven.

476

'You don't know what it's like,' Alex went on. 'To – to have nothing. I had nothing and they—'

'They?'

'I just needed the money.' Alex shook her head. 'Everything I did, I did so I'd be able to pay my heating, so I'd be able to fix my flat ... so I'd be able to get on with life, so I could move on, so ... so ...' She shook her head again, crying now. She tried to touch Cooper. She tried to place a hand on her hand. Cooper did not move it, to her own surprise, to Alex's seeming surprise, too. So they sat, holding hands.

'The person that hired you – what do they want from me?' Cooper asked, after far too long a silence, far too long a moment. 'What happens now?'

'I didn't mean any of it,' Alex whispered, her eyes still wet.

Cooper's fingers stroked hers.

'I'm so sorry,' Alex said.

'You were looking for me, weren't you?' Cooper asked. 'That night in the halls when we met ... You found me, didn't you? It wasn't an accident ...'

Alex said nothing.

'Why you?' Cooper asked, staring at her. 'Why did they use you?'

'They said ...' Alex whispered, stroking her fingers back. 'They said it was because of my name. Because my name sounded like someone else's ...'

Cooper wasn't going back to work.

She wasn't going to do any of this again.

She just wanted to know. She just wanted to know who had done all this. She wanted to know what had happened, all those years ago ... She wanted to know what had happened, these past few months ...

477

And when she knew, it could all stop.

She wouldn't have to feel lonely anymore.

She wouldn't have to hear that voice in her head, telling her to be afraid of everyone and everything, to keep everyone away...

She'd find an ending she should have found a long time ago.

She didn't want to be alone.

She hated Alex. With every fibre of her being, she hated her, what she had done to her, this temporary friend... this person who'd been supposed to fill a weekend, a short holiday with family, a trip to unwind, to relax, to restore her well-being...

She took her hand from Alex.

Cooper stared at her for a time, and Alex's eyes were still wet, were still so innocent, as if she'd never hurt anyone her whole life. As if nothing could possibly be her fault or the result of her own choices.

'You did it,' Alex said. 'You solved the mystery.' And then, after a moment: 'I... I really did like you.'

'Did?'

'Do. I do like you,' Alex said, quiet. 'I...'

Cooper stared at Alex, and lent forward, and gave her a soft kiss upon her lips.

They went to sleep a while later, and they held hands again, even if neither knew it. Even if dreams had taken all that they were, had changed all they would become.

They woke again at intervals, neither of them comfortable in their unconsciousness yet, but getting there.

Before the world grew black, Cooper asked Alex a question.

She asked where this person was who had done all this to them both... as if they were both victims equally, as if they were truly the friends they'd imagined themselves to be, partners against the evil of some unthinkable crime.

She asked Alex, as if she might answer.

And in the dark, Alex did – from her tone, surprising herself, making herself giddy, freeing herself with the answering.

Alex told Cooper what she knew.

They went to sleep, holding hands once more.

Cooper's Dream:

A memory in two scenes

Enter COOPER (22). Dressed in her purple vet scrubs, she has just come home. She pulls off her shoes, sits on the stairs. Her cats walk around her.

Her first love, ARTHUR (23) approaches with a cup of coffee.

He has no face. COOPER cannot remember his face.

COOPER
More people kill their pets in the run-up to Christmas than at any other time of the year.

ARTHUR
Because they're unwanted gifts?

COOPER
I said the run-up to Christmas. I said before Christmas.

ARTHUR
Why?

COOPER
It's called the Christmas clear-out. I had to kill four dogs today.

ARTHUR
Is it a kind of – is it seasonal sickness, or—

COOPER
I had to kill four dogs and I didn't even get to take my
lunchbreak, so—

ARTHUR
What was wrong with them?

COOPER
The rota was too thin. A few sick vets, not enough locum
cover.

ARTHUR
I meant the dogs. What was wrong with them?

COOPER
Old age for a couple. A skin condition. The final one was just
chewing table legs...
...None of them had to die today.

ARTHUR
Why at Christmas, then?

COOPER
Saves money. Frees up room and mess and time. Guests on
the way for Christmas... new year, new start, et cetera, et
cetera...

ARTHUR
Why do you say yes to these cases? Why do that to yourself?

COOPER
Why do I say yes?

ARTHUR
You can turn the cases down, can't you? It can't be good for
you ...

COOPER
At least they weren't cats.

ARTHUR
Should it make a difference?

COOPER
I was joking.

ARTHUR
(sighing)
It's hard to tell.

COOPER
It's my job. It doesn't matter if it's good for me. What job is
good for anyone?

ARTHUR
Is something bothering you?

COOPER
Is something bothering me?

ARTHUR
I just wondered if anything else had happened today, or—

482

COOPER

You always do this.

ARTHUR

Cooper...

COOPER

You don't take me seriously. It always has to be something
else that's the problem.

ARTHUR

I just worry about you.

COOPER

Which means you don't respect me.

ARTHUR

Which means I love you. That's what people do when they
love each other.

COOPER

Love is worrying, then?

ARTHUR

It can be. You must worry about me. You know you do.

COOPER

I can't say no ... Just because I'd handle a case differently,
doesn't mean I get to say no to the owner. It doesn't give me
a right to take their agency away, not when half of them can't
even afford to—

ARTHUR
I asked you a question.

COOPER
I'm not a bad person for doing my job.

ARTHUR
You're just – you're ignoring me right now.

COOPER
I'm answering your question.

ARTHUR
Which question? You pick and choose and—

COOPER
I don't worry about you. My mind is on my work when I'm
at work … But, it is … It's with you and the cats when—

ARTHUR
Your mind is on dogs when you're killing dogs.

Scene 2.

Their bedroom

COOPER *sits scrolling her phone in bed.*

The cats lie at her feet, on the duvet.

ARTHUR *stares at the ceiling. He turns.*

He has no face, even now. Even in the partial light of his lamp ...

ARTHUR
Did you take your—

COOPER
Let me guess: 'Did I take my antidepressant?

ARTHUR
I didn't ask that.

COOPER
Yes. I did take it.

ARTHUR
I was looking forward to you coming home. The fridge is
stocked and—

COOPER
I wasn't.

ARTHUR
You weren't what?

COOPER
I wasn't looking forward.

ARTHUR
To home?

(silence)

ARTHUR
To me?

COOPER
Of course I was looking forward to seeing you.

(silence)

COOPER
Don't forget. We're going round my mum's tomorrow.

ARTHUR
Dinner, or ...?

COOPER
Lunch. Julia and her boyf will – what?

ARTHUR rolls his eyes.

ARTHUR
I'll do my best.

COOPER
She means well.

ARTHUR
It's hard to believe you're all related.

COOPER
So they tell me.

ARTHUR
I'm sorry.

486

COOPER
What for?

ARTHUR
For fighting.

COOPER
Thank you.

ARTHUR
Are you sorry? Are you sorry too?

COOPER
Let's get some sleep. It's almost 2 a.m.

ARTHUR
I love you.

COOPER
I'm drifting off... Stop waking me...

ARTHUR
What did you call Julia's...?

COOPER
Boyf. I called him her boyf.

ARTHUR
Do you call me boyf?

COOPER
Goodnight, Arthur.

487

The lights go out. Cooper goes to sleep.

Cooper wakes up next to a woman who has betrayed her for money. A woman she'd thought might be a friend.

Cooper gets dressed, and says goodbye to her home.

EXIT COOPER.

83

When Alex woke up, Cooper had gone.

Alex waited for a while, wondering if she would come back. Wondering if Cooper had gone out for breakfast, wondering what they'd talk about – what would happen next.

But Cooper never did come back.

Cooper never set foot in that apartment again, and there was no note, no goodbye, nothing at all.

If there had been some final task for Alex to complete, it was not completed.

If there was some last payment to be sent, it was not sent.

Alex remained alone in the flat, thinking about what she had done. Thinking about meeting Cooper in that hotel, so many weeks ago.

Thinking about all she had done to her.

She didn't mean it.

Alex – she was a good person, she knew.

No matter what she'd done, she was a good person...

The day before the death
of Sophia Bertilak.

A Telephone Call.

SOPHIE: Are you there?

THOMAS: I'm here.

 [Silence]

THOMAS: Are you OK? Is everything—

SOPHIE: I just wanted to ask you a question.

THOMAS: OK. Ask.

SOPHIE: Were we ...

THOMAS: Were we what?

SOPHIE: What we had ... was it ever ... was it ...?

 [silence]

THOMAS: Was it what?

SOPHIE: Did your father tell you to—

THOMAS: To what?

SOPHIE: To love me.

 [Thomas laughs]

SOPHIE: What's so funny?

THOMAS: Where are you, Soph?

SOPHIE: It's a simple question. Was our life together real?

THOMAS: What does that mean? What are you even asking
 me?

SOPHIE: I loved you. I loved you so much. I ...

THOMAS: You're worrying me.

SOPHIE: Then just – just answer my question. Just tell me
    – just—
[There's a sudden burst on the line. A shout, a crash.]
THOMAS: Sophie? Sophie, are you still there?
[Silence. A few moments later, footsteps, and the sound of
the phone being picked back up]
SOPHIE: I'm here.
THOMAS: You're at your mother's, aren't you?
    [Silence]
THOMAS: Joanna told me you'd moved there.
SOPHIE: Joanna talks to you?
THOMAS: It's not good for you to be there. Not with—
SOPHIE: With what happened.
THOMAS: Especially not by yourself.
SOPHIE: I'm not by myself.
    [THOMAS sighs]
SOPHIE: What?
THOMAS: I'm coming over.
SOPHIE: No, you're not. Fuck … just, just talk to me …
THOMAS: You need me. You're clearly not OK, and you
    need me—
SOPHIE: That's the great secret of our lives, right there.
THOMAS: Excuse me?
SOPHIE: I said it's the great secret of our lives.
THOMAS: I heard you. I just don't understand you.
SOPHIE: You've never understood me. Not since the day we
    met. You've never understood me, and—
THOMAS: And what?
SOPHIE: And I don't need you.
    [Silence]
SOPHIE: I don't want to see you again.
THOMAS: And what if I want to see you?

SOPHIE: I don't—

THOMAS: What if I'm sorry?

SOPHIE: Sorry for what?

  [Silence]

SOPHIE: What are you sorry for?

THOMAS: I'm coming round. You're not sounding OK. I'm
    coming round—

PART 12:

CONSUMED

DR COOPER ALLEN AND
SOPHIE BERTILAK
PAST AND PRESENT

84

The detective goes on holiday and finds herself facing a murder.

She goes home, unrested, taught one of three lessons by the world: that the subjects of her work will never stop following her; that she is not allowed to rest, that on some level she does not even want to rest; or ... that this world was a world where awful things happened so frequently that murder was not some aberrant, story-worthy act, but was in fact omnipresent – an essential cog of the Earth, of humanity's machinery. That to find it on holiday was not so surprising, for holidays were times for relaxation, for fun, for entertainment – and what entertainment did the human life love more than a mystery of violence?

Cooper couldn't do this anymore.

Sometimes she thought of the future and saw an endless array of cases before her, of alliances, clashes, affairs, love, hate, death ... of companions she might meet, partners who she'd pretend were friends ... of a now silent phone, no longer ringing with annoyed intrusions, because there was no family left to invade her life. The time for that had ended.

And she knew, to her horror, that even this future sight was pretend, wishful thinking; that what career she had could not lie with the police anymore, with cooperation as it had once been; that even beyond the facts of this case, there were too many people who knew her mind now. Even Cooper knew too much about herself to carry on in the world as that person.

When she had become a vet, she hadn't done it for the

money. She would have cured animals for free, if she'd been allowed. The salary, it was needed of course for rent, but each payment... it was almost a coincidence to the fact of what she'd done, day after day.

It had been the same with all this.

When it was about animals who'd been harmed, really harmed, it had been easier, in a way, to let it go. To feel sympathy, pity, sadness.

When a case revolved around a human, all she could see were the faces of all she'd known, all she'd met...

When she investigated the death of Sophie Bertilak, it was as if she'd stared into a mirror, coincidence after coincidence filling her throat with acid, filling her heart with shivers.

And to see the exhibition, to see that whoever had done all this had known it too...

To see how easily she'd fallen into their traps, how easily she'd been documented, watched, read about...

Cooper did not want to be herself anymore.

She didn't know what that meant, but it was true.

She'd already had a false name – she'd already been 'Emma'.

Perhaps she could have another identity, another history... she didn't know.

She just had to see this out first. No matter the cost. No matter the consequence.

If Cooper could not have love, if she would not have friends, if she would not have trust or be a mother or have children or cats or a job or respect or comfort or happiness or acceptance, she would have her answers.

She would always have her answers.

85

Cooper took a flight across the world.

She left Europe behind.

It was the envelope she'd been sent. The barcode, faded on its surface; scanning it had revealed a return address for A TRIAL FOR PIGS.

She traced it. One address ... another, another, another, country after country, until no more addresses remained.

She took a cab across that distant city, crossing streets that looked so unlike they had in movies, forgetting the filters that made them look more exotic, more outlandish to a casual viewer. Forgetting the tricks of cameras.

Cooper spent the night in a distant hotel and then, leaving many of her possessions behind in her room, crossed into the trees. Down a track at first, and then into the darkness within.

It took her almost a day to find it.

The letter ... the information Alex had given, in a night Cooper already regretted, and beyond it, the case itself. Everything. Everything Quentin had done, everything he'd hidden from those he'd loved. Everything Sophie had photographed, everything she'd strived for, everything she'd regretted and lost and found and sought ...

It all led here, to this place, this clearing by a river, far from Lethwick, far from England, far from any place Cooper had ever been ...

It all led to the house. It all led to the truth.

Cooper saw no one on the approach. She waited for a while to see if there was some hint of the inhabitant, of the man she was about to meet. She waited for an hour, wanting to have her moment, her last conversation, the final truths of her career ... and yet, she was scared, too.

She'd killed someone once, because she hadn't wanted to die.

She didn't want to do it again, and ...

And in spite of everything, she still didn't want to die.

In spite of having nothing else left for her, not even her purpose, not even her name, she wanted to go on, once this was done.

She walked to the house's edge, its log walls, its radio talking away within, the music of an English-language station.

She entered.

Steam rose from a slow-cooker on the countertop of the kitchen.

Two empty wine glasses rested beyond on a black granite counter.

The heat, the hum of the trees and water echoed past Cooper, past every part of her.

The radio sang, on and on.

All around there were photographs of Matthew, of Lucy – of every missing image from poor Sophie's home, every picture taken from every frame ...

More than anything, Cooper wanted to know why the owner of this house had chosen her.

Because they had, hadn't they?

Cooper had gone to Lethwick because her mother had invited her on holiday; had invited her because of a friend's recommendation ...

Cooper had managed to gain access to her mother's accounts

in the aftermath of her death. Managed to trace the posts of friends the woman had never met ... and she saw the recommendation, and had begun to laugh and cry in equal measure.

Cooper had gone to Lethwick because an account named 'Gwen' had befriended her mother and had sent her there.

The account had asked her mother a number of vaguely astrological, new-age questions in the course of their discussions – but one of the final questions was pivotal.

What was the one place her mother didn't want to go, but the one place she should? The one place that would give her peace?

'Lethwick,' Cooper's mother had said.

Gwen had asked why, but her mother hadn't wanted to discuss the town's importance.

So Gwen had extolled the health benefits – had said it was a wonderful idea ... a country getaway ... a gentle place of lovely churches and beautiful valleys ...

For how long had Cooper been watched? For how long had she been groomed for this role, the detective, the adversary, the revealer of all these crimes, all this death?

She moved through the house, and out to the open door on the other side.

She walked out towards the sound of running water, thinking of the boys named Matthew, the children named Alfie ...

Thinking of the video of the pig version's final moments, the bullet, how the second Alfie had fallen to his side, all four legs stiff ... How he shook, legs running in the air as if he could still escape ...

She thought of the stag, its mouth red with human flesh ...

She thought of all those nights on the hotel balcony, thinking she'd made a friend.

She walked to the riverside now, and there she found a tripod set up, a camera pointed right at her.

It was an old-fashioned thing, black, manual, compact.

The logo was emblazoned on its front. 'Instamatic'.

Nearby, the owner of the house sat by the stream, watching as the water drifted past.

Cooper approached, and sat down beside the owner, making no attempt to mask her movements, no attempt to say hello.

Cooper just sat, and watched, and waited.

After a long time, the owner of the house spoke. And the voice that came from that mouth ... it surprised Cooper, though she'd heard it a thousand times before.

It was always different, hearing the real thing. Meeting someone in the flesh ...

'Doctor,' she said, almost in a whisper. 'You're here.'

'I am.'

'Do you know me?' the woman asked, old but not frail. Tired, but not weak ... happy even, sitting in that sunset, looking out on that beautiful water, in that red afternoon ...

'It depends on what you mean by "know".'

At Cooper's words, the old woman smiled, her face creasing. It was a lovely smile, the kind that made you want to trust her, to protect her, to defend her against any claim, any attack.

It was the kind of smile she'd had since she'd been a girl, walking those fields so far away ... walking between trees on her birthday, taking photos of mistletoe ...

'You'll have questions,' said the old woman, and Cooper Allen nodded. 'Sit up straight.'

Cooper scowled, and found herself surprised at her own scowl – at how automatic it was, about how she'd heard those words before from another. It reminded her of what her mother said to her. And it made Cooper sadder than any other moment since her mother's actual death, to hear her voice in another's lips.

Cooper did not sit up straight.

'You've solved more crimes than I did,' Sophie said. 'I suppose you can do what you want.'

'What did you solve?' Cooper asked. 'You didn't solve anything.'

'You know that's not true.'

Cooper looked away. They were still alone. The water still ran alongside them, still made its little noises.

'I can't believe Lucy drugged you,' Sophie said, almost laughing. 'I didn't know she had it in her.'

'Then you didn't know her.'

Sophie's expression didn't change – still the same smile. 'Her father raised her, really. I wasn't around as much. So, you might be right.' She waited for a moment, and Cooper didn't say anything. 'Doctor.'

'Why do you keep calling me that?'

'No one else does, do they? No one else calls you what you are.'

'And what am I?'

'That's why you're here,' Sophie said, her voice growing quieter. 'That's why I sent those emails to your mother. That's why you were in Lethwick.'

Cooper sat up straighter, after all.

'I died,' Sophie said, 'and I needed you. I needed you.'

And Sophie began talking, and kept talking, even as it grew darker...

Cooper rarely asked questions, beyond a few to clarify a particular remark, a particular statement... She just watched the last confession as the sun continued to set, as the world fell to darkness once more.

They grew one day older, one day closer to the end of days, and Sophie Bertilak smiled as she did.

'I made a promise, once,' Sophie said, not just to Cooper, but the air, the world, the sky beyond. 'I found the truth and I ... I made things right. I made things right ...'

I MADE THINGS RIGHT

The Day of the Death

The old man had gone.

Sophie had gone down to the basement, and already, seeing the lock as it was, the door as it was, seeing the marks on the stairs, the marks on the walls beyond... she knew.

He had gone.

She had a bag of supplies in one hand. She'd bought things to help him feel better, to feel more comfortable, to recover. The time for unpleasantness would be over soon.

Quentin would admit what he'd done.

He would admit everything. He was already so close.

He'd told her – he'd told her where the pipe child's body had been buried. And that was a step, wasn't it? It was something the police would consider trading years of a sentence for, when it came to killers in jail... and if the courts considered the resting place of a human being to be such a thing of worth, shouldn't Sophie? Shouldn't it count for something, that he'd admitted this?

He'd told her the boy was under an apple tree.

And then...

And then he'd lied.

The Ransom Note

You could not walk a day in our shoes.

    You asked to hold his hand to hold your boy's hand
when you never held it before we know we saw we saw
and you want to buy him back you want to pay us for
him as if he were a doll as if he is property so here is
a piece of him you can have back here is a free sample
here is a piece of his hand to hold and if you want
the rest you can have it at a discount as we know we
broke him we will give you the whole thing if you give
us some of your possession if you give us enough to
be like you if you give us some of what you didn't even
earn if you give us some of what your father left you
and leave it to us leave it to your son so you have
a son so you have this boy, leave us as much as you
want him back leave us as much as you think is fair
and we will give back what we think is fair and you'll
have your doll you'll have him and you'll be able to hold
that hand if you do what you are told if you do what
we tell you if you want him.

    He's already in his grave, though he can still breathe,
he can still see.

    Burn this.

The Delivery

Quentin didn't know if he'd killed anyone.

It was the not knowing that bothered him most.

He sat at the edge of his estate, his boots on the cusp of a grey-brown puddle. The sun emitted endless day. He held a letter in his shaking hands.

> YOU ASKED US TO TELL YOU WHAT HE SAID.
> HE SAID HE WAS SORRY. HE SAID HE DIDN'T MEAN
> IT. HE SAID IT WAS ALL JUST AN ACCIDENT.
> HE SAID WHAT ANYONE WOULD SAY.
> WE MADE HIM FEEL IT. DON'T WORRY.
> IT'S DONE. HERE'S PROOF.
> BURN IT WHEN YOU'RE DONE.

The officers had given him a box with the man's bloody shoes.

He'd looked at them. Black boots, so much like his own, though made for working.

'You could not walk a day in our shoes.'

They were covered in blood.

Quentin decided to put the man's shoes on, even so.

He walked in them, thinking about Matthew.

Thinking about his son, his little boy.

He hadn't been able to pay the ransom. How could he pay? How could he give them what they wanted, when they had never specified a figure?

The police had said they'd find him ... they'd guaranteed a result ... so it had just been good sense.

And Quentin, he went back to the wife he'd dreamed of being faceless, to the son who bore his name, and he tried to go on as he had. His family had a memory of a maid, and a maid's son, and it didn't have to be more. They never had to know who they'd lost.

He told his family a story of dream logic, of what he hoped for, of things far from this time and place. Of having grand-children one day. Of having a daughter, perhaps. He told his wife and son that he hoped for the best. He told them to be good.

The police had found the man responsible.

They'd hurt him until he'd taken them to the body ... to Matthew's little body wrapped in plastic, rotting in a gully.

And this man ... this killer ... he'd worked for Quentin, once.

That was the thing.

He'd worked on his land. He'd worked with the gardener, once upon a time ... He'd known him, he'd known his child, he'd known all of them ...

The whole world was silent but for the sound of the shoes Quentin wore, the blood squelching ...

'What do you want us to do with him?'

The police officer had waited on the telephone, and Quentin had thought for a while, then he'd answered.

And now he was here, walking across his fields.

He went home. He took off the shoes. He had a bath.

He went to his office, and he looked at the photos ... at everything he had been sent, those weeks past.

Of the man who'd killed his bastard child.

Of the girl who'd helped him.

Of his boy, caught beneath the world.

Of mistletoe, of trees, of light.

He phoned Kelly, and waited till the officer phoned him back.

'I told you ...' the officer explained. 'Your boy was taken by a kid. She was just—'

'What's her name?'

The Day of the Death

The old man had been in Sophie Bertilak's basement for days now: drugged when he'd come for dinner, waking to find himself in the dark ...

'I found your shoes,' Sophie had said. 'But you knew that.'

And she'd done things to him, in that place. She'd marked his body. She'd taken pieces from him eventually, surprising herself in what she was willing to do, how far she'd go for the truth – but then, her whole life had been aimed towards this, hadn't it? Everything Sophie had ever done, anything she'd ever been ... it was for this, this one mystery, this one request.

She tortured her children's grandfather.

And eventually he gave her a piece of useful information.

He had told Sophie where the pipe child's body had been buried.

He'd told her the boy was under an apple tree.

And then ...

And then he'd spoiled it. He'd lied. He'd told her a story about this boy being his child ... about Thomas having had a half-brother, born of some affair ... of how a man in his employ had discovered this, and had kidnapped the child for ransom.

'There was no note,' Sophie said, glaring at him, shaking ... 'There was no announcement in the newspapers, no appeal ...'

'I had my reputation.'

Sophie listened. Quentin explained it: he claimed he'd paid the police to deal with it all quietly. Sophie's photographs that day had given them the lead they needed to find the killer, to torture him to get Quentin's little boy back.

But the boy was already dead by that point. So the police just killed the killer.

'And the girl he was with ... what happened to the girl?'

Quentin seemed confused.

'Stephanie Earlsham. If all this is true, what did you do to her?'

Quentin didn't know. Stephanie had eluded the police ... she'd vanished ... maybe the killer had harmed her, too ... maybe ...

More nights passed. A morning as well.

And now Sophie was back there – and the old man had gone. He had fled.

By the time Sophie found him out by the lake, he was already dead.

She hacked off his limbs and kept them ready.

She tidied her house thoroughly, leaving parts as they'd been, so it wasn't too perfect.

She packed, taking just a few essentials, just her pictures, too.

Then she fed the remaining limbs of Quentin to her pigs.

When it was done, she took her own blood – collected over the past week – and spread it across the paddock floor, as if in pursuit of some ancient ritual. Quentin had tried to run, granted, but Sophie had not been stupid. She'd known there was only one way this could end. She'd known he would have to pay for all he had done ...

The power cut across Lethwick as she went, but it did not matter. She had her light.

She spread her blood, and took her final bags, her final things, and she went to the side of the road.

Thomas would be here soon.

They were going to go away.

They were finally going to make it work, before their time ran out.

THEY WERE GOING
TO BE HAPPY

THE END

Sophie Bertilak finished the story of her death.

She sat there, and so too did Cooper for a time, watching the water, watching the insects skit along its surface, their ripples in the low light...

'What...' Cooper began, and then stopped talking.

'What what?' Sophie smiled, amused by her own silly repetition.

'What if you were wrong? What if Quentin was telling you the truth?'

'Then he decided not to save his son. Then he was the kind of man who valued his reputation more than a little boy's life.'

'And he deserves to die for that?'

'Yes,' Sophie said, and then seemed to lighten up a little. 'But he was lying. I'm quite sure he was lying.'

'How can you be so sure?'

'Because I have faith. I think Thomas will be back soon, if you'd like to stay for—'

'Faith in what?' Cooper interrupted. She expected almost anything other than the word that passed Sophie's lips.

'Myself,' the old photographer said. 'You look so much like her,' she went on. 'Like—'

'Stephanie.'

The old photographer nodded.

'I met Stephanie's mother,' Cooper said. 'She called me that

515

name also. But I've seen her – I don't think she looks much like me at all, beyond—'

'Mrs Earlsham said it right in front of me.' Sophie leant down and picked up her thermos. She drank from it, her voice hoarse in the heat. It seemed to help. 'We saw you on television. It was one of your cases, a town far away. I've spent my whole life looking at Stephanie's photos, meeting her family members and seeing you that day, even seeing you now ... you do look like her, Cooper. You look a great deal like her.'

Sophie smiled, and went on:

'If you hadn't been there ... if we hadn't been in that place, watching at that right time ... I don't think I could ever have done this.'

Cooper looked around at that moment. She didn't know quite why she did so. There was no one else there, no one but the photographer. The river was clear but for insects. The path was clear, too.

The day grew darker as the sun grew lower.

'Why was I part of your exhibition? Why hire Alex? Why – why do any of this?' Cooper asked suddenly, her eyes wide, watering. 'I was trying to help you ... I was trying to solve your death ... Why – why do this to me?'

'Because ... it had to be you,' Sophie said. 'It had to be you that looked into it all. It had to be you that came to Lethwick. It had to be you we captured.'

'Why?'

'For the exhibition,' Sophie said. 'For A TRIAL FOR PIGS. We needed you. And ... and I needed you.'

Cooper brought her hands up to her face, pushing against it, running it through some of her hair, tired, exasperated.

Sophie just watched her before continuing.

'I made a promise,' Sophie said. 'I told Mrs Earlsham I'd

found out what happened to her daughter. I told her I'd find Stephanie.'

'You didn't,' Cooper said, shaking her head. 'I don't care if I look like her – I wasn't even born then … I wasn't—'

Sophie took a sharp breath, and seemed to sit up a little. Something about it made Cooper pause in her protests.

'I'm not talking about you,' she said, and the sun, it almost disappeared past the horizon, now.

'Stephanie is dead,' Cooper insisted. 'She's dead – she died a long time ago – she—'

'She is dead,' Sophie agreed. 'But she didn't die a long time ago. She died in a hospital bed a few months ago, alone, upset, confused. Not knowing what was real, what was not …'

Cooper shook her head.

Sophie went on. The sun set.

'She phoned you before you left Lethwick, didn't she? She just wanted you to listen.'

Sophie went over to her tripod. To her Instamatic.

'We're here together now, aren't we? Just like the first. Just like the beginning. I found your mother – I found Stephanie, and I – I always thought she'd be someone different. Someone more like me. But when I saw you on the television – when I saw what a woman her daughter had become – I knew. I knew I wasn't wrong …'

Sophie set her old gift up, smiling, almost crying.

'Can I take your picture?'

Credits

Greg Buchanan and Orion Fiction would like to thank everyone at Orion and our other teams who worked on the publication of *Consumed*.

Agent
Cathryn Summerhayes

Editorial
Emad Akhtar
Celia Killen
Sarah O'Hara

Proofreader
John Garth

Editorial Management
Jane Hughes
Charlie Panayiotou
Tamara Morriss
Claire Boyle

Audio
Paul Stark
Jake Alderson
Georgina Cutler

Contracts
Anne Goddard
Ellie Bowker

Copy-editor
Clare Wallis

Design
Nick Shah
Tomas Almeida
Joanna Ridley
Helen Ewing

Picture Research
Natalie Dawkins

Finance
Nick Gibson
Jasdip Nandra
Sue Baker
Tom Costello